CW00801514

THE BENEATH

BEHIND THE WALL: BOOK ONE

ROXANNA C REVELL

Original Image by Deposit Photos and design by Rebecacovers

Edited with thanks by Megan Powell
fortheliterature@gmail.com

Join my mailing list at **www.roxannacrevellauthor.com**

Follow me on Instagram
@roxannacrevell

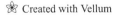 Created with Vellum

PRAISE FOR ROXANNA C REVELL

∽

Take the dystopian edge from The Hunger Games, add in a gritty crime family from a Martina Cole novel, and a dash of high-brow erotica, and you have the breathtaking recipe for The Beneath.

Angela Mack, Author of *I Am Unworthy* and I *Am Unbreakable.*

∽

Where do I even start with this review? Simply put, I am blown away.

Ashlyn Drewek, Author of *The Welles Family Saga*

∽

Roxanna has this way of writing which just really clicks and means you feel like you really know the ins and outs in an effortless way.

Kerrie Goodman - Book Reviewer

~

This is a story that I truly cannot put into words how it makes me feel. It is a story that you have to read to experience. There is no review that will tell you the emotions you are going to feel, and the experiences that Roxanna is going to toss at you.

Alicia Andrews - Book Blogger

~

DEDICATION

~

To the amazing people that have supported me on this journey, most of whom I've never even met in person. The support in the world of Instagram and in particular, within the indie author community has been beyond anything I expected. I've made new friends and bagged myself a few 'fans' and I'm more determined than ever to make this dream come true.

Thank you to everyone who took a chance on this newbie author, you have no idea how you've filled my heart.

~

CONTENT WARNING

∼

This book has been written by a British author and as such, it follows British law with regard to the age of sexual consent — which is 16 years of age. The dystopian world created follows that same law.

∼

This book also contains elements of dark romance with regard to consensual sexual acts. There is reference to suicide and rape, but these acts are not committed. This book is 18+ due to sexual content, violence, and adult language.

∼

WHO IS MY MOTHER?

Who is my mother?
It's the question I ask,
When my heart betrays me.
When loneliness breaks me,
And I simply need to know,
If it hurt to let me go.

So many questions,
Flow through my brain.
It's enough to drive,
An orphan insane.

The answers are something,
I'll never know.
They hide in the dark,
And not knowing,
Breaks my heart.

I have no mother,
Yet I'm not alone,

For she gave me a brother,

To love and to smother.

I have a brother,

He's mine to protect.

To grow and to nurture,

To never neglect.

There's no foe too great,

No wall too high.

Because for my brother,

I'll live.

And I'll die.

Roxanna C Revell

CONTENTS

PROLOGUE

$\mathcal{T}$he world is made up of seven states: Havensmere, Castlepoint, Ryders Field, Deep Crest, Falcon View, High Pier, and The New Order. Each state is separated by a boundary wall, but with a passport, you can access any of them. The history books tell us that these states lived in harmony, with no wars, and no animosity, and yet, ninety-five years ago, for no discernible reason — other than misguided religious beliefs; things changed. Each state built a new wall, splitting themselves in half, creating two sides and two distinct worlds. One side was filled with families, and the other was filled with nuns and babies.

It started in Havensmere, when Baptist became High Minister and immediately put into action his primary policy — to criminalise sexual intercourse outside of marriage. However, unlike most crimes, nobody went to jail. That would have been a blessing, and Baptist wasn't about to give his blessing. The punishment he created was much harsher than that, and although the crime itself was somewhat over-looked; if extramarital fornication led to procreation, then your baby was taken from you. That was your punishment.

The baby that you grew for nine months would be taken from you.

Funny how it seemed to be only the women that paid the price.

It's said that it created mass panic. People were encouraged to report women that they believed to be pregnant. They would then be tested — sometimes by force and if found to be pregnant they were electronically tagged so that they could be monitored. They weren't allowed to leave their state and there was nowhere for them to hide. In extreme cases, the women were kept in a clinic throughout their pregnancy, and naturally, no support was given to them after their babies were gone.

That was their punishment, and that's how the world of the orphans was created.

St Martins church is situated in a dark and abandoned area, of what was once part of their world. That's the spot they chose for the orphanage; an orphanage with a small white fence and a pretty little gate, that stands there still. However, there were times, when the law was first passed, when broken hearted mothers would pound at the doors of the church demanding to have their babies returned. So, they created a boundary line and built the wall. A large wall with a guarded gate, just to make sure that they didn't get in and we didn't get out. Thus, the two sides were created, them and us — and to us, Havensmere became known as The Other Side.

When we speak of St Martins here, we're referring only to the church and orphanage. We call our side of the wall, 'The Beneath', which wrongly gives the impression of a world that is underground. We very much live on the surface. Behind a big wall, but on the surface. We were the ones that renamed it. It seemed fitting, since we're a world full of people who are considered to be beneath their biological parents and whatever siblings we have on The Other Side.

It may have started here, but Baptist's doctrine spread like a disease across the other seven states. A disease, which only one state has managed to eradicate. Only one state built, and then demolished their wall. It was called Farr Point at the time, because it is the furthest from our reach, but once they brought down their wall, they became The New Order. Everyone lives there as equals and it's become a safe haven for orphans that have been lucky enough to break through their wall and find their way there.

For us, however, it is unreachable, because you only leave The Beneath by the will of The Council or in an ambulance.

The Beneath became independent from The Other Side, twenty-five years after the wall was built. For twenty-five years, babies were handed over, and for twenty-five years we took only the scraps that were handed to us. The Beneath was the size of a small town and was only set to grow as people started their own families. That's when five men, who were some of the very first orphans to come here, took it upon themselves to lay the foundations of the future, of our future. They were educated, committed, and The Other Side even funded their plans — thrilled by the idea of St Martins becoming financially independent, and, better still, contributing to the industries and finances of their side.

These five men established the factories, the schools, the banks, the law enforcement, and the entertainment. They became our champions, but also established themselves as our rulers, forming The Council that stands as our judge, jury, and at times... executioner, with Commander Legion, who happens to be one of the most heartless men alive, firmly planted in the centre of it all.

They created new family names to identify them with the

areas that they took charge of. The Manners ran the factories, the Learners established the schools, the Greens set up our banking system, the Legions became our law enforcement, and the Joysons created the entertainment. These men created our self-sufficient, thriving world, and in return, they were named as our 'Founders'.

We all know our biological connections here in The Beneath. Baptist knew better than to allow in-breeding to take place knowing what a medical burden that would be. So, our Founders picked their wives, they had their children, and then they arranged their marriages within their five families, and 'new blood' is brought in, only when it's necessary. Thus, ensuring that the power remains with the few. Nobody questions it, because nobody questions them.

The first set of children born to those families became known as the Founding Family Trueborns, and that's what they remain today. Even in The Beneath, we have a class system; Founding Family Trueborn, Trueborn (born in The Beneath) and Orphan (brought in through the gates). However, we do not abide by the laws of The Other Side, and nobody here would ever separate a baby from their mother.

The Beneath may be an independent town for the most part, but there are certain limitations. Marriage is for life, given that we do not have access to the courts. When things go really wrong, the Church can intervene and grant a separation, but you're still legally married and as such could never marry again.

The nuns at St Martins orphanage are trained as nurses and we have a small infirmary where most injuries or illnesses can be treated. However, if more serious treatment is needed then the patient gets a private escort to the hospital on The Other Side, complete with a private guard — just in case they try to escape into their world.

I guess we should be thankful that they don't just let us die. We; the unwanted, the discarded and the alone. In The Beneath we cherish any blood connection we have, because it's the only true family we have until we create our own. Orphaned cousins are fairly common, and there's even been half-siblings known to occur. However, that's generally only on the paternal side because the mothers learned from their punishment and they didn't repeat their mistake. Well, all except for mine.

I was four when my baby brother arrived at St Martins. It took a few days for the DNA tests to be completed, and at first, they named him Luke. However, when they learned that we shared both mother and father they changed his name to Adam. Adam and Eve. Or Eve and Adam, since I came first. Except, we were full blood siblings, not Biblical lovers, so don't ever let it be said that nuns don't have a sense of humour.

1

TEN YEARS AGO

*L*ife in The Beneath and life as an orphan isn't as oppressive as it may seem. The tall wall that separates us may cast a large shadow over our world but the sun still shines and even here, there is hope for a better future. The Founding Families may be selective about who they marry and procreate with, but they do not see the rest of us as being completely inferior. They remember where they came from and why they're here, and it's the same reason as the rest of us. However, they did create the world that we live in now and we're often reminded to be grateful. That said, they do see us as being worthy of the same opportunities, which is why we are all educated together in the same schools. The Learners established our education system, and it may have evolved, but one thing has always remained true, and that is their original ethos — "Knowledge Knows No Walls".

As such, I found myself in school and being educated alongside Harriet Joyson. We hit it off from the start, and that's how I met her brother, Noah. I was sixteen and he was twenty, and our paths had never crossed before then, but I knew of him; everyone did. Noah is the younger of the three Joyson brothers, with Harriet being the youngest, and only female of the siblings. He's also the most handsome, the most driven, and the most feared. He embraced the entertainment world that his family first created, and as soon as he got the slightest hold of the reins at the age of eighteen, he grew it beyond what was ever envisaged.

The bars and clubs originally intended for our use remain, but Noah expanded them and created a club that catered for The Other Side too. It was no secret that they've always been curious about us and the world behind the wall, and so Noah engineered a way to let them in — for a price. He gave them privacy and secrecy so that they could watch our singers and enjoy fine cuisine in our rather swanky club called The Dome. Or they could take in the slightly darker offerings in The Cell, where women would dance and tease more of their money from them. It's illegal for them to come here, but that was easily overlooked with the guards at the wall receiving their share.

They come in through the large, iron gates that form the only gap in the wall, which separates us from them, and they watch. Only watch, and then they leave again as quietly as they arrived, and Noah is the one that made that possible. There was resistance at first, because nobody wanted to feel like they were part of a circus act, but then their money came in, it was shared, and the objections disappeared.

Noah started that at the age of eighteen, and he's been overseeing and expanding it ever since. It was agreed, when the five families first created the world we now know, that any profits would be shared equally among them, especially as the schools and law enforcement sectors don't make money. They have always lived equally and comfortably, but through Noah they started to enjoy a level of wealth that they never had before, and that gave him power not usually afforded to one so young.

Noah had power and respect, but not freedom. No matter who you are or what your name is, they don't issue passports in The Beneath. There's nowhere else to go and nowhere to hide, and so you do what is expected of you. Noah seemed to struggle with the expectation to conform to his parents' wishes more than most, and that came out in violence, and people quickly learned not to cross him.

Unfortunately, you didn't always need to cross him in order to be on the receiving end of his fist, and that's why he established the fight club. It was underground and technically illegal under our laws, but The Council overlooked it because it was Noah. It was what Noah needed, and as it turned out it was what many others needed too. Who knew being deemed unworthy of your parents' love and dumped behind a wall would give so many people issues? People paid to fight, and they bet on the outcomes, and a percentage of the profits went straight back to the five families.

So, I knew of him, and I knew the stories told by the men and women that claimed to know him, but I had never met him until one Friday after school. A chance meeting that was to set the course of the rest of my life. I'd been held back after class and didn't leave until the gates were almost closing. It was chucking it down with rain, my umbrella blocked my view and I almost crashed into Harriet. She had been waiting for her lift home, had no umbrella, and was soaked. I stayed with her and let her shelter under mine, and it was another ten minutes before a car pulled up.

The passenger door opened, and Noah shouted his apologies to her. I had every intention of walking back to St Martins, but Harriet grabbed hold of me and pulled me into the back of the car with her, insisting that I was driven home too. She reached across me to pull the door shut, so I never heard or saw Noah's reaction, but the car moved forward, so I assumed that he didn't object.

Harriet gave me an accomplished smile and I battled with my dripping umbrella, eventually managing to get it into the footwell. I'd not been in many cars before, but I knew it was expensive, and as it was Noah Joyson's car, I felt the need to apologise for soaking it. I looked up towards the rear-view mirror and made my apologies, and we looked at each other for the first time. Not directly, it was only via the mirror, but our eyes locked for a split second and I was instantly captivated. He simply smiled and assured me not to worry about it, and I quickly looked away, feeling utterly embarrassed and exposed. I'd never really understood the power that intense and instant attraction could have over your body until that moment, and I wanted nothing more than to escape that car and be far away from the man that was making me lose my senses.

I tried not to look at him for the rest of the journey and Harriet and I just sat quietly, but when we passed St Martins, I spoke up to let him know that we had missed it. That's when we locked eyes again and I saw the smile in his, as he told me that he was taking us both for an early dinner to make up for being late, and to thank me for looking after his sister. I wanted to thank him, but I also wanted to tell him that it wasn't necessary, but I was too busy trying to tear my eyes away from his, and I could barely swallow, let alone speak.

It was a pizza place, really simple and we sat at a round table, with Noah in-between us both. Harriet was chatting away about her day and I mainly listened and smiled, but I could feel Noah's gaze piercing me, and every time I dared to look, he was quite openly and unapologetically watching me.

Noah was, and remains, the most handsome man I've ever

seen, with dark blonde hair, shaved short all over, dark brown eyes and the cheekbones and jawline that people on The Other Side probably paid a surgeon a fortune to obtain. You'd hear stories from older girls that had claimed to have slept with him, and they would always say the same thing; that he was cold, distant, great in bed, and much to their disappointment, he rarely went back for seconds. They all wanted to be the one to break through his wall and win his heart, but nobody ever did.

Yet, he didn't seem cold when he smiled at me in the car, but then I guess he was just grateful that I'd helped his little sister. As for him looking at me in the restaurant, well, I had no idea what to make of it. It was like he was studying me, perhaps he thought I wanted to use his sister or something? About a hundred different options ran through my head while I sat at that table. I couldn't figure him out, but he barely took his eyes off me.

I was never really one to be made to feel insecure and was completely at ease with Harriet and the other Founding Family members that I socialised with at school... but Noah was something else. There was something more going on with him, I could see that even then, and I had no idea how to respond to him and felt the need to cower most of the time. Eventually, I plucked up the courage to look right at him and smile. He smiled back, released me from the intensity of his gaze, and my body instantly relaxed. I felt like I could breathe again.

About ten minutes later, he casually reminded Harriet about her dance class and she went into a panic about being late. He gave his sister, who he clearly adored, an amused smile and asked for the bill.

"What time do you need to be back, Eve?" he asked,

speaking directly to me for the first time since we were in the car. "I hope I've not got you into trouble."

The smile on his face suggested otherwise.

Even though I'd been in his company for the best part of an hour, when he looked at me again, smiled at me, and worse still, said my name; I couldn't stop the heat from rising to my face, and I once again had to fight the need to run away. However, I decided to rise to the challenge, swallowed down my nerves, and did my best to come across as charming, mature, and in control of myself.

"It doesn't take much to be in trouble with Sister Theresa," I replied, sounding a little coyer than I had planned to.

Sister Theresa was in charge at St Martins, we all knew that she actually had a big heart, but it was hidden away, very deeply. She ran a tight ship and had high expectations, and there wasn't much room for error.

"As long as I'm back for choir practice at six thirty, I'll escape the worst of it." I felt the blush starting to creep up from my chest and onto my face. I quickly turned to Harriet in order to avoid staring at him like the fool that I felt.

He looked at his watch. "An hour, then. Do you mind if we drop Harriet at her class and then I can drive you back?"

The inviting smile on his face was very tempting, but my scared little heart had other ideas. "I have time to walk," were the words that quickly stumbled out of my mouth. It wasn't far and walking was far less petrifying than the idea of being alone with Noah.

He looked like he was about to object, but Harriet beat him to it.

"Absolutely not!" she said forcefully. "You're here because you saved me when my useless brother was half an hour late to pick me up."

She frowned at him in the way that I often frowned at my

own brother, which had me smiling again. It was clearly going to take more than pizza to appease her. "Noah will drive you, it's the least he can do."

Harriet sat in the passenger seat on the way to her class and I sat in the back, purposely looking out of the window in order to avoid catching Noah's eyes in the mirror. It only took ten minutes to get Harriet to her class and after she'd left, Noah asked me to sit in the passenger seat instead.

"It feels like I'm a chauffeur otherwise," he said, as I sat next to him and closed the door.

I once again forced back my nerves. "I think I could get used to being driven around."

"Where can I take you to then, Ma'am?"

His entire face seemed to light up as he spoke. His smile was so warm, in such a stark contrast with the coldness that I'd been expecting.

"St Martins is perfect, thanks," I beamed back.

It was hard not to smile when Noah was smiling at you, but his started to fade as he looked at his watch, making the car feel colder. "But I thought I had you to myself for another forty-five minutes?"

The butterflies in my stomach went into overdrive and my heart began to pound. "Why would you want me to your-self?" I squeaked out.

"To get to know you better, of course," he added calmly.

"There's really not much to know," I replied seriously.

He looked at me so intensely that I felt almost naked under his gaze.

"I doubt that very much," he finally said, and then he started to drive.

He didn't go to St Martins, instead he drove to the park in the centre of The Beneath. It had rained a lot, so it was quiet, and we just sat in the car for a while and talked. Well, I talked mostly, as Noah seemed determined to learn everything about me.

"All I've heard about you before today is from Harriet, who has said that you are very nice and very pretty," he told me as we parked up. "But I can see that she under-exaggerated."

I laughed a little in response to my utter embarrassment, then I felt the flush in my cheeks, and I had to turn away, but Noah spared me by taking the conversation in a direction that would always put me at ease.

"What's it like having a brother?"

"You know about my brother?" I asked in disbelief. I had no idea that he knew so much about me.

"Everyone knows about the only pair of full blood siblings in the orphanage..." He looked away, as if he was worried that he'd offended me.

"Don't you have two brothers?" I challenged him, and he was at ease once again.

"Yes, but I suspect my relationship with them is somewhat different to yours. What's he like?"

"Adam is a pain in the arse!"

He laughed with me.

"He's also amazing, and funny and I am somewhat fiercely protective of him," I confessed, and he smiled approvingly. "He's twelve, and he has a mouth on him, and I think the problems really started when I was twelve. We have to do Bible studies on a Sunday afternoon..." He shuddered a little. "Yes... it is a bit like that," I beamed back. "I had just started to wear..."

Oh shit.

"What?" He chuckled as he saw my face flush with embarrassment.

"Erm… I had just started to wear a bra..." I glanced at him and he laughed some more.

"I like where this conversation is going," he said, as a dark and very inviting smile started to spread across his face.

His words had me tingling in a way that my body never felt before, but I rolled my eyes at him as I tried to block it out. "Well, Seb – who is my age — was sitting behind me and he just kept flicking at the strap on my back…"

"Seb sounds like a dick."

"He is," I confirmed with a smile. "Anyway, he kept doing it and I kept turning around and glaring at him, because I was trying not to cause a scene. Then all of a sudden, I heard this massive thud, followed by Seb shrieking, because Adam had launched a Bible at his head!" I burst out laughing and so did Noah. "He was this scrawny little eight-year-old, determined to stick up for me, and I don't think Seb has ever lived down the embarrassment."

"I like Adam already," he said, nodding his head approvingly.

"Yes, but that incident pretty much set the tone for how life was going to continue." I shrugged a little. "He's funny and sometimes he can talk his way out of things, but not when it comes to Seb and his friends..." I added, frowning. "And now preventing Adam from getting beaten up is more or less a weekly occurrence."

"He's lucky to have you," he told me genuinely.

"We're lucky to have each other," I clarified, and he nodded in understanding.

"And what about when you finish school?" he asked. "What's next for you?"

Here in The Beneath, you generally only stay at school until you're sixteen, and then you go on to apprentice in your chosen area. Some skills may require staying on until you're eighteen, but we don't have the opportunity to go to university here — none of us. We orphans have a home at St Martins until we're eighteen, and then our employer will help with our accommodation until we earn enough to take care of it ourselves. There's even a budget set aside by The Council to help fund it. There are no homeless in The Beneath. Everyone has a job, and everyone has a roof over their heads.

"Well, the girls that I room share with at the moment are all a year older than me, and I plan to move in with them when I'm eighteen." I smiled at him. "I'm already doing some training at a salon, so when school finishes, I'll be going there, full time."

I liked having my plans and knowing what was coming next.

"You really do like taking care of people, don't you?" He smiled gently as he looked at me intently.

I tried to steer away from his gaze. "Well, at the moment there's always something new to learn, which I like. And actually, yes... I like helping to make people feel good about themselves," I told him honestly. You can't really have too much of that here.

He looked thoughtful for a moment, then he beamed at me and asked, "Are you sure you'll be missed at choir practice?"

I looked at the clock and realised that it was twenty past six, and finally remembered that I had somewhere to be.

"Can you not just pretend that you were there all along and hiding at the back?"

Noah had a hopeful smile on his face, and it felt almost harsh to disappoint him. However, I still wasn't sure why he was so eager to spend time with me and I was still petrified of him. I was extremely attracted to him, but that only added to my fear. I wasn't entirely sure that I could trust myself around

Noah, and yet I found myself trusting *him.*

Noah was known for not going to the Sunday service at St Martins. The rest of the Founding Families were there, always showing their thanks and respect to the institution that raised their ancestors. Yet, Noah never attended, which was made all the more obvious by his question. If he did go, then he would know that with our choir everyone had their place, and there was absolutely no hiding in the background, especially for me.

"That might work were it not for the fact that I'm a soloist."

I gave him an apologetic smile, as if to soften the blow of my rejection, which I knew deep down wouldn't really hurt him.

"Ah, so you're a siren as well as a temptress. That explains it then." He smiled at me gently before starting up the engine.

I clasped my hands together during the journey home, my palms were hot and sweaty, and I felt sick with nerves. What did he mean? Obviously, I knew that Eve was a biblical temptress. People joked about it all the time, especially with my brother being called Adam. I understood the siren reference too, but what did he mean about that 'explaining it'? What did he want? He was four years older than me, experienced, and he definitely wasn't short of options. All I knew for certain was that I both wanted to be near him, and as far away as possible in almost equal measures. I had never felt so torn and so conflicted with myself.

When we pulled up outside St Martins, I turned and thanked him for the lift and for dinner, and once again, he looked at me in a way that I couldn't decipher. Then he looked to the side of me and cringed.

"Is that scary looking nun Sister Theresa?"

I quickly turned, feeling a new wave of dread hit me in the gut, but saw that there was nobody there. I turned back to Noah to question him and nearly head-butted him. He was smiling cheekily, because he had tricked me into looking away, and had used that time to move closer to me. His face was inches from mine, and his smile slowly faded as he moved a strand of my long, dark hair behind my ear. It felt like my skin was on fire where he had touched me, and my mouth went completely dry. I had never really done much with a boy. I'd been kissed, but only by boys as inexperienced as me, but Noah wasn't a boy and Noah wasn't inexperienced.

I started mentally preparing and reminding myself of the techniques that me and my friends had talked about and practised in our room, at night. Then suddenly, he looked to the side of me again.

"Now, she really does look scary," he said, moving back a little.

I laughed at him. "I'm not going to fall for that twice."

Then three loud and abrupt knocks on the passenger window made me jump out of my skin, and I turned to see Sister Theresa with her arms folded, glaring at me with all the might of her glorious fury.

2

*S*ister Theresa rather cruelly made me wait until after choir practice before she began my interrogation. Still, I knew it was coming and I messed up my solo repeatedly because of it, earning me an early morning practice session with Sister Maria, our choir mistress, on Saturday. Sister Theresa had sat on the nearest pew watching me, and as soon as practice was over, she waved for me to follow her to her office. The corridors of the church were always draughty, and the chill radiating from her only added to the prickles scratching their way down my spine.

Sister Theresa sat down in a manner more graceful than her mood ought to allow. I knew the drill because I'd been there before; I was to shut the door and sit patiently until she decided to speak. Sometimes she'd make you wait a while for added discomfort, but she clearly felt that she had waited long enough, as she wasted no time in getting started.

"I assume you know why I've asked you here, Miss Matthews?" Her hands were clasped together on the table, which wasn't the best sign. If she was calm, they would be resting on her lap.

"Yes, I'm very sorry that I missed dinner, Sister."

I'd learned many years ago that being obtuse with Sister Theresa got you nowhere. It was best to sit and take it, and that way it would all be over and done with much quicker.

She honoured my humbleness with her usual bluntness. "No, Eve. You're old enough, and usually sensible enough to be allowed an element of freedom. However, given the company you were in this evening I am now questioning that." She adjusted in her seat, but her hands remained clasped, and she looked me firmly in the eyes, before asking, "What were you doing in Noah Joyson's car?"

"Sister Theresa..." I edged off my seat a little so that I could lean towards her. "I assure you that it was entirely innocent. I helped Harriet after school when Noah was late to collect her, and he took us both for food by way of apology. He drove me back afterwards, that's it," I told her in my most convincing manner.

Her hands moved towards her body as she appeared to relax a little. "It looked like he was about to kiss you."

I laughed and shook my head. "I assure you that's not what was happening, Sister."

Her face made it clear that she didn't believe me. "Eve..." she said, before pausing to think for a moment. "You are a very beautiful and very talented young woman — young orphan to be precise, and Noah Joyson is—"

"A Trueborn," I interrupted her, something that would normally earn her ire.

She let it go. "A Founding Family Trueborn, to be precise, and they have their own rules," she reminded me. "He's also a very handsome young man who is known for having an appetite for beautiful women." Then she softened a little before saying, "Eve, I only have your best interests at heart when I say this, but if he is showing an interest in you then it is only for one thing. I'm sure the attention is very flattering, but I would urge you to keep your feet on the ground."

Her hands rested on her lap. I was free and I had been well and truly put in my place and had to swallow down the sudden urge to cry. "Thank you, Sister. Is that all?"

"Actually, no." She looked stern and her hands were once again clasped firmly together on the table. "There was an incident during dinner. You should probably speak with your brother."

She nodded to the door to let me know that I was free to leave, and I maintained my composure until I left her office, but as soon as I shut her door, I let out a loud growl. What the fuck had he done this time?

I walked to the back of the church towards the newer buildings that form the orphanage. The male and female dorms are separate, but there are a number of communal rooms in the middle where we all mingled together. I walked through the empty food hall and into the TV room where I was immediately greeted by Laura, Sarah, Victoria, Hannah, and Rose — my roommates, my best friends, my sisters in every way except biological.

"Where have you been?" Sarah asked, with an intrigued smile on her face.

I met her smile with a frown, and not just because of Adam. "I'll tell you later. Where is he?"

"Mess room," was their combined reply.

They didn't need to ask who I meant.

The mess room is an in-between space — not quite a TV room, and not quite a games room. There were chairs, tables and music and it often looked like a bomb had gone off in there. I heard him before I entered the room, laughing with his best friends, who were a mixture of those that encouraged his antics and those that tried to prevent them. John saw me and gave a little wave. He was my favourite and worked almost as hard as I did to keep Adam out of trouble.

"Hey, you," I shouted towards my brother, and his whole group turned around and smiled.

"Eve!" Adam called back. "Where were you? I was worried."

"I had dinner with a friend."

He bounced over to me. "Which friend?"

The way Adam bounced always amused me. It was like he had endless energy that just wouldn't quit, and you could never mistake us for anything other than siblings. We had the same thick dark hair, the same chocolate eyes, the same long lashes, and the same full, deep pink lips. Up until a couple of years ago I looked just as gangly as he did, when bouncing around the room, but then my curves came in, along with my breasts, which still seemed to be growing.

He was also nosy and protective, and I had to resist the urge to smile at him, because he was still in trouble. "Harriet, but that's not important. Why does Sister Theresa think I need to speak to you?"

He put his hands in his pocket, rolled his eyes at me, and shrugged. "It was nothing," he replied in his pre-teenage whine.

"John?" I looked over at his friend. John always told me the truth.

"Seb," he replied with a shrug, before giving Adam a look of apology and turning away.

"Adam! He is four years older than you and ten times bigger than you!" I growled. "What happened this time?"

"He was talking shit, so I talked shit back. He tried to hit me but didn't get the chance, end of story," he replied with a look of innocence, which would almost be believable, if I didn't know him so well.

"Why do you even care what he says?"

"Because it was about you!" he said, and I saw the anger flicker in his eyes.

He may be four years younger than me, but Adam has always been just as protective of me as I have been of him. It was ridiculous, though, because Seb was born a twat, and I didn't care what he said.

However, Adam did, and he clenched his fists at the anger that still lingered. "Somebody asked where you were at dinner, and fucking Seb, said that you couldn't eat because your jaw was sore from sucking his cock, and you were full, from swallowing so much of his cum!"

I couldn't stop the snort that escaped me or the need to gag at just the thought of going anywhere near Seb. "That's just gross. What did you say?"

"I told him that you have a shellfish allergy, so you would never go near his tiny, little shrimp dick."

He looked so triumphant that it didn't surprise me that Seb wanted to slap him. However, he was also hilarious. I burst out laughing, as did the rest of the room and I pulled him in for a hug.

"Adam, I love that you want to stick up for me, but you don't need to." I glared at him, hoping the message would finally sink in. "Everybody knows he's full of shit, but he also has it in for you, so could you please just try to ignore him?"

He groaned and rolled his eyes, and I hugged him again before heading off to the games room. I wasn't going to tell Adam where I was going because he would've followed me, but I knew that's where I'd find Seb.

I was right. He was playing pool and was about to take a shot, but I stopped him when I leaned in and picked up the cue ball. "He's twelve, Seb, can't you just drop it?"

He looked up at me and smirked. "He's a little shit."

The arrogant grin that he aimed at his friends made me want to slap him too, but I reminded myself that I was there to make peace. I reminded myself to keep my anger in check, because Seb liked it even more if he knew he was getting to me.

"Agreed. But can you just leave him alone? Everyone knows you could take him, so what the fuck are you trying to prove?"

"I wouldn't normally object to you fondling my balls, Eve…" His pig friends all laughed. "But can I have that one back, please? We're trying to play a game," he said, pointing to the ball in my hand.

I dropped it on the table, gave him a filthy look and turned to walk away. He was never going to back down and I knew it, but I was never going to let him off the hook, and he knew that too.

"Is it true that you were seen getting out of Noah Joyson's car this evening?" he asked, stopping me in my tracks. "Didn't think virgin, orphan pussy was his thing."

His friends erupted with laughter again.

"I'd be careful about what rumours you start, Seb," I said, turning to face him with a challenging glare.

"Why? You going to set little Adam on me?" He was still laughing, and again I had to fight the urge to punch him.

"No. I meant I'd be careful what rumours you start about Noah Joyson. I'm friends with his sister, and girls talk."

The smile quickly faded from his face.

I didn't need to say anything else, and he didn't need to know if it was true. The idea that Noah might hear that Seb had been talking about him was enough to shut him up. He might not be afraid of Adam, but Noah was a different matter entirely.

Satisfied that Seb had been put back in his box for the

night, I turned towards the door, only to find all five of my roommates standing in the doorway. They'd come to see where I was, and the looks on their faces suggested that they'd caught the last part of the conversation. Vic grabbed my hand, and I was whisked back to our room. The door was shut, and I was pushed down so that I was sitting on my bed, and all five of them stood in front of me.

"Tell us everything!" Vic demanded, whilst practically falling over her own feet in her excitement.

3

_I_ didn't tell them everything in the end. I probably would have, had Sister Theresa not reminded me of my inferiority. They would only have become excited and encouraged me to dream the impossible. So, I told them what had happened, minus the looks Noah gave me, minus the things he said to me, minus the time we spent alone together, and minus the fact that I'm pretty certain that he was going to kiss me.

They weren't disappointed though, and the mere fact that I had been with Noah at all had them all in a tizz. They were literally bouncing on their beds, with Hannah going as far as to pick up her pillow and pretend to snog it. The only one immune to their hysteria, was Rose, who was already committed to becoming a nun and was not at all impressed with Noah's reputation, but was instead, relieved to be told that he apparently had no interest in me.

They were still giggling about it when the lights went out at ten o'clock, and my head was still in a spin, and not from the mayhem of the past two hours of excited, feminine chaos.

My time with Noah kept going around my brain on repeat, all the bits that I didn't tell them. The way he looked at me, what he said, and the way my skin was still tingling from his touch. Was he really going to kiss me? It felt like it and Sister Theresa thought so too, and if she hadn't interrupted us then I wouldn't have stopped him.

I had to stop thinking about it though, because Sister Theresa was right; Noah would only ever want one thing from me. I had to keep my head and I had to keep my feet on the ground. Yet, as I closed my eyes and tried to go to sleep, all I could feel was his fingers gently brushing against my cheek as he moved that strand of hair ever so gently and tenderly behind my ear.

I was up before the others to meet Sister Maria to practice my solo, and without the intensity of Sister Theresa's eyes on me, I got through it without messing up, and she didn't keep me for too long. Then I headed to breakfast and got on with my Saturday, which meant a day at the salon. I was in the early stages of my training, so I didn't get to do much more than wash hair, sweep, and practise basic cuts, but the day always flew by. I found it really interesting, which was a good thing, given that I'd be starting my apprenticeship there in a matter of months.

Saturday night was uneventful and pretty standard. I had one final rehearsal with the choir before the Sunday service, Adam managed to not get into any fights, and me and my friends meandered between the games and TV room until lights out. I had friends my own age too; it was only because of logistics that I ended up sharing with girls older than me, and I'd only have one more year with them before they would be moving on, and I'd get new roommates for my final year.

I hated that they would be leaving me. Adam was my

brother by blood, but they were my sisters by choice. I would only be a year behind them though, and the idea of leaving St Martins filled me with excitement and fear. Excitement, because I'd finally be free, as free as anyone is in The Beneath. I'd live in my own place without any rules, without curfew, or lights out, and without the watchful eyes of the Sisters always on me. Yet, that was part of what made it scary too, because as overbearing as the nuns could be at times, they did look out for us.

However, the thing that scared me the most, the thing that kept me awake at night, and the thing that almost broke my heart, was the idea of leaving Adam. I had no doubt that when I left, I'd still see him all the time; but there would be no greeting at breakfast or dinner, there'd be no crossing paths with him at school, and most frighteningly, I wouldn't be there to keep him out of trouble. Still, it would at least be the start of my life. The life that I was choosing for myself, and I really couldn't wait for it to start.

I spent the whole of Sunday service in the choir loft, behind Father Thurleigh. The choir is always the first in, then the rest of the congregation fills the pews from the front, and the inhabitants of St Martins fill the spaces at the back. It's not done as any form of hierarchy. The resident orphans are only seated at the back so that the nuns can keep a closer eye on them. We tend to be a rebellious bunch when we're young, when we're still a bit pissed off at The Other Side for abandoning us, and desperate to rebel from the establishment that keeps us. It tends to be when we venture out on our own that we calm down a bit and just start to get on with life. As such, the young rebels are kept at the back of the church and that way, if there's a disturbance, the guilty parties — usually including my brother — can be quickly whisked away without disturbing everyone else.

I never looked into the congregation. I used to, but the moment they noticed my voice and moved me from the back of the choir, to front and centre as a soloist; I stopped. It was too scary. I enjoyed singing, and I knew that I had a good voice, but looking at people, and seeing their reactions so clearly, was too much. If I ever caught so much of a glimpse of someone's face, I would suddenly freeze and forget my lines, only realising what was happening when I heard the loud slap of Sister Maria's baton against her wooden stand. So, I picked a spot, right at the back of the church. A very insignificant part of the wall really, but I sang to that spot every single Sunday.

Service seemed to go well; Father Thurleigh didn't get too flustered and I didn't hear the familiar shuffle of someone being escorted out too many times. I sang to the wall like I always did, and I smiled graciously at the applause that followed. Sister Maria was clearly still annoyed with me for making her fit in an extra practice session on Saturday morning, and gave me the task of collecting all of the hymn books from the pews alone. It wasn't exactly a difficult task, but it was time consuming and Sunday service was draining. All I wanted to do was crash for a bit.

I stood with the choir and waited for everyone to leave, as we always did and then I was left alone to complete my penance. The church always had such an energy to it, but it was always so changeable. When it was full of people it felt alive, but once emptied, it felt lonely and cold, which is funny, considering that most people found it to be a source of comfort.

I walked along the pews, collecting the books and moving the piles to the storeroom door, then going back to collect more and repeat the process. Then I felt the energy change, becoming stronger and more intensely alive than I'd ever felt before. I turned around to look for an explanation and jumped backwards when I saw Noah, holding a book out to me.

"Oh, my God!" I clasped my hand to my chest as I tried to catch my breath.

"Not quite." He was very amused with his answer, but I was too shaken to laugh.

"You scared the life out of me!"

"Sorry," he said with a cocky smile. "I didn't think it was very polite to just watch you do all of the work."

He held the book out to me, and as I took it from him, my fingers almost set alight at the feel of his brushing against mine. I had no idea if he could feel it too, but it was new to me and it scared me. I had never been so physically, mentally or emotionally affected by anyone like it before, and the lack of control left me struggling to breathe.

Noah looked a little awkward too as he looked around and took in his surroundings. I didn't think it was possible that this was his first time in the church, but he took it all in as if it was completely new. Or perhaps, like me, he needed to find a way to break the overwhelming intensity of the connection building between us.

"Did you find God, all of a sudden?" I asked, smiling at the bravery that seemed to come out of me all on its own.

He laughed in response. "I'm pretty certain I'm a lost cause on that front. I came to hear you sing, and you have an amazing voice. I wasn't actually expecting that, do you fancy a job at The Dome?"

Noah's praise had me smiling like a lovestruck fool, and I had to bite my lip in order to keep it together. "I'm too young to work there," I reminded him. You have to be eighteen to either go to, or work at The Dome.

"Right now, yes." His eyes left my face and slowly trailed

down my body, then they made their way back up, taking me in, before they fixed on my eyes again. "You're not too young for everything though."

There it was. The reminder that I needed. Noah Joyson wanted to have sex with me. That's it. I swallowed hard, trying my best to ignore how naked he had just made me feel, and how aroused I was by it, and I forced myself to stay grounded.

"Did you get into much trouble on Friday?" he asked, giving me an amused smile.

That snapped me out of it — games. I was just a toy to him. A new and temporary amusement, so I put up my guard.

"Not really, no. If anything, I was just given a reminder."

"A reminder about what?" he asked; his face darkening as he sensed my change in tone.

"About who you are, who I am, and the way our world works. Or the way you and your world works, more specifically."

"Don't we live in the same world, Eve?" His eyes penetrated mine, in search of an answer.

"Yes… and no." I shrugged a little, trying to tell myself that I wasn't bothered, even though there was a pain creeping into my heart.

He made a move to step closer to me, but then his phone rang; the noise startling us both and he reached into his pocket and pulled it out. His jaw clenched and he stepped further away from me as he answered it. "Yes, Dad. I'm on my way."

He put his phone back into his pocket and paused for a moment, then he looked at me, opened his mouth, as if to speak, only to close it again and shake his head.

"See you around, Eve," he said without looking at me,

before walking away and leaving me alone and utterly confused.

I finished collecting the rest of the hymn books in a daze, whilst constantly watching the large doors in case he came back to tell me what it was that he wanted to say. What I said to him annoyed him, I wasn't so naïve and inexperienced that I couldn't see that, but I didn't understand why. Noah was cold and untouchable, everyone knew that, and yet, my words seemed to touch him. The most frustrating part was that they weren't even my words, they were Sister Theresa's. Still, I was the one that appeared to pack a punch when I delivered them, and I could neither understand nor rid myself of the guilt that I felt over hurting him.

I tried to get him out of my mind, but there was no escape, especially since everyone was talking about him. Noah was never at Sunday service, and his presence didn't go unnoticed. He stood out because of his looks, but also because of the vibes that he gave off. He seemed to be able to arouse the females around him, whilst simultaneously intimidating the males. He was a fourth generation, Founding Family Trueborn. He was part of our elite, but he'd happily step into the ring at his fight club and let you try to hit him without there being any repercussions. However, people rarely managed to hit him because he was so fast. Noah didn't just have a temper, he had the skills to back it up too.

It wasn't just the orphans that were talking. As we left the food hall, I walked past Sister Wren talking to Sister Theresa about it too. She was wondering, in fact, she was openly asking what might have brought about the change. I could feel Sister Theresa's eyes on me, and I braced myself as I passed them.

She was looking right at me with a very unimpressed

expression on her face, as she answered Sister Wren. "I dare say that we'll find out soon."

Sister Theresa was strong, but she had a heart, and it was clear to me what her heart was feeling when she spoke. Outwardly, her composure and tone gave off her usual 'stern vibes', but in her eyes, there was only concern.

4
_____

_S_chool was a great distraction because we were so busy preparing for the end. Monday flew by, and I started to put what had happened on Sunday out of my mind. I had successfully convinced myself that I had imagined any pain that I thought I saw on Noah's face, believing that there was no way that I could have that sort of effect on him. Like Seb had said, I was not "his thing".

"Right class, we need to bring forward the final date for your group coursework, it's needed by Friday," Miss Tatler announced as we sat down in her business studies class. It was the last class of the day.

"What?" Harriet screeched a little too loudly as she leaned into me. "Can you come over to my house later?"

"Is that allowed?"

She raised her eyebrows at me. "Why wouldn't it be?"

"We've been friends for six years and I've never been invited to your house."

"I've never been invited to the orphanage."

I laughed at her, before quickly looking down again when Miss Tatler glared at me. "Do you want to visit the orphanage?" I asked, screwing my face up a little. There really wasn't much to see.

"I'd love to see where you live. Maybe we can get ready together for the end of school party?" she whispered, with excitement written all over her face.

"Wouldn't you rather get ready with—"

"Don't say what you're about to say." She glared at me. "You are my friend and I want to get ready at yours. And for the record, the only reason I haven't invited you to mine is... well, firstly because my parents are weird, controlling, awkward and somewhat embarrassing to be around. Especially when friends are over. It's like they have to remind everybody of their superiority, or something." She rolled her eyes a little. "And... well... also because I wasn't sure how you'd feel about the whole parent and family thing." She looked at little concerned.

"Oh, I'm pretty sure I'm not allergic to them."

Harriet exploded into a fit of giggles.

"Girls!" Miss Tatler shouted, silencing us both once again.

We calmed down and got on with our work, but a few minutes later, Harriet leaned close again. "Besides, you passed the Noah test."

"What's the Noah test?" I whispered back, as my heart started to creep up into my throat.

"Do you know how many friends I can't invite over because they make such tits of themselves when they see him?"

Oh, God. I'm pretty sure I made a tit out of myself, but I was glad that Harriet hadn't noticed.

"You were fine with him, so I know you won't annoy him, which is good, since most people just tend to piss him off and put him in a shit mood."

I was desperate to ask her if he would be at her house that evening but didn't know how to do it whilst still appearing like a non-tit, and so I agreed, and prayed to the God that Rose kept assuring me existed, that he wouldn't be there.

~

"Dad, Miss Tatler has brought a project forward, so Eve needs to come to ours tonight," she told her father as we got into the car.

"Hello, Eve, I've heard a lot about you. Will you be joining us for dinner?"

"Oh…"

"Yes," Harriet jumped in, preventing me from bowing out.

Pulling up to the house was intimidating. I'd seen it before, but only from the outside. It was in a part of The Beneath that was filled with tall town houses and dated back to pre-wall times. This was the area where all the Founding Families lived and as such, it wasn't somewhere I would venture very often.

The front door was opened for us, and I stepped into a large hallway that was very finely decorated. In truth, I didn't really have the vocabulary to describe exactly how it was decorated, since I lived in a room that was whitewashed. The only contrast in colour was provided by the cross above the door, and the only time we expanded on that was during an artistic phase that Vic went through three years ago. Her creation only lasted half a day before she was made to paint back over it in the purest white.

Harriet led us upstairs to her bedroom and closed the door. I just paused for a moment and took it all in. She had a double bed covered in pillows, a gorgeous dressing table, posters on the wall and colour. Lots of colour.

"You OK?" She was staring at me with a slight frown.

"Just taking in bedroom heaven." I sighed as I ran over to her bed and threw myself on it.

After a few hours, we'd made good progress on our project and I was finally feeling a little less like an alien in her home.

There was a knock at the door. "Dinner will be ready in half an hour," a lady in uniform told us.

"Thanks, Jill," Harriet replied politely, and for the first time that evening, I felt like I had something in common with her, since we both had ladies in uniform prepare our dinner for us.

"Can I use your loo?"

"Fourth door on the left," she said, without even raising her eyes from her laptop.

I closed her door and had only walked two steps when I crashed into a human wall. The wall had hands and it wrapped them around my waist to help me regain my balance. My body told me who the hands belonged to before my eyes did, because the intensity of the energy coursing through me could only be caused by one person.

"This is a nice surprise." I looked up and saw Noah smiling down at me, with a wicked look in his eyes. "What brings you here?"

"Harriet… we're doing coursework."

I kicked myself for sounding so much like a schoolgirl. Although, standing there in my uniform; it's not like he'd forget it. "I'm just going to the bathroom."

I stepped back and he released his hold and moved to the side.

"Third door on the right," he told me, as I scurried away counting the doors.

I got to the door, opened it and stepped inside. I reached out, expecting to find a cord dangling from the ceiling, but then I heard a switch flick, and the light came on. It took me about three-seconds to realise that I was standing in a bedroom and as I turned to make my exit, Noah walked in behind me and shut the door. He leaned against it, folded his arms across his impossibly broad chest, as a teasing smile spread across his face.

I shook my head at myself as I remembered, "Harriet said it was the fourth on the left."

"I guess she was sending you to the bathroom then."

"This is your room." I nodded at him as a shaky breath and a smile that I couldn't contain escaped me.

"It is." He stepped closer to me. "Since you're here I thought we could continue the conversation we were having in church?"

"What would you like to say?"

I tried to move away from him, but somehow didn't manage to send the message to my feet. He was standing so close to me that I could feel the warmth of his body and the heat started to rise from my own as he brushed my hair away from my left shoulder.

"The problem with you, Eve, is that you have a nun sitting on this shoulder, and an angel sitting on this one."

He brushed his finger across my right shoulder. It was such a gentle movement, and yet it sent vibrations right down to my core.

"I thought that was supposed to be an Angel and the Devil?" I smiled, because I knew he liked it when I challenged him, and that fed my desire to do so. I didn't realise until then, that desire was so much stronger than fear.

He shook his head. "Not in your case. You have Sister Theresa on one shoulder and then a little version of yourself on the other."

He looked at me sincerely, but I couldn't help but laugh at him.

"Now, I think I know what little, angel Eve is thinking." He fixed me with his darkest look yet and it suddenly felt like my underwear was sticking to me. "What I'd like to know is what Sister Theresa is telling you."

I looked down and sucked in as much air as I could. I needed the purity of the oxygen to clear the filth from my brain, because it was the only way that I was going to be able to keep my head. I looked back up at him and then glanced over to his bed, and his eyes darkened even more as they followed my gaze.

"Shall we just do this now?" I gestured to the bed. "That's what you want."

He clenched his jaw, wrapped his arms around my waist, pulled me close, and then his warm breath tickled me as he whispered in my ear, "But then I'd have to explain the screaming."

"Noah?"

A woman's voice almost went unnoticed, but I startled when she started knocking at the door.

"For fuck's sake!" he hissed, as he moved us both and put me against the wall next to the door.

He opened it and it pressed against my right side a little, as I was hidden from view. I stood there trying to catch my breath, realising that I hadn't inhaled since Noah whispered in my ear. My heart was beating so loud, that I was sure that whoever was on the other side of the door would hear it.

"Mum?"

"Are you eating with us before you go to The Dome?"

Ruth Joyson. I hadn't heard her speak before that day.

"I was planning to."

"Good. Word of warning; Harriet has a friend here and she's a pretty little thing, so please be on your best behaviour."

I had to stifle my laugh, but Noah didn't. He laughed at her gently and closed the door in a dismissive action, before stepping closer to me.

He leaned in and moved a strand of hair behind my ear, once again setting my skin on fire. "You are way more than pretty." He brushed his thumb across my full lips, stepped away from me and opened his door. "Straight across, on the left."

"What?" I managed to squeak out as I peeled myself away from the wall.

"The bathroom."

Dinner was delicious but horrendous, given the small talk that Harriet's parents felt that they needed to make, and also because of the effort required to not look at Noah. He disappeared before the rest of us had finished and I was disappointed not to see him upstairs when I collected my things from Harriet's room. I was just saying my goodbyes at the door, when he came downstairs in smart black trousers that hugged his muscled arse and sat comfortably against his groin. His white shirt appeared to be glued to his body, and my jaw nearly hit the floor as I took him in. I'd only ever seen him dressed casually before and that was painful enough, but dressed up all smart, took him to a whole new level.

"I may as well drive you, since we're both leaving," he said, as he checked over his reflection in the mirror.

He said it casually, for the benefit of the people around us, but I didn't miss the glint in his eyes when I caught sight of his reflection.

As soon as I got in the car, I could smell his aftershave and the scent was truly intoxicating. Every part of me was drunk on him, and every part of me yearned for him to reach out to me; but he didn't. He did nothing and said nothing for the entire journey.

I hid my disappointment, and when we pulled up outside St Martins, I made a move to get out.

"Wait…" His hand was on mine. His touch was intense, but his manner was awkward, as if he didn't really know what to do. "What are you doing now?"

"I'll probably track down my brother to make sure he's not been in trouble."

I laughed a little, but I was only half joking.

Noah gave a small laugh too, but then looked at me with such vulnerability that I thought my heart was going to implode. "What I wouldn't give to be important to you too."

he week continued just as busily as it started, and Harriet and I worked on our project in the library during lunch times. It took all my strength not to ask her about Noah. I just couldn't get the look on his face and the words that he spoke in the car out of my head. I knew I couldn't say anything to her though, because Harriet was happy thinking that I wasn't interested, and she didn't need, or want anyone else fawning over her brother. I was her friend, and he was just her brother. Just her brother who I couldn't stop thinking about, that I dreamt about, that I visualised when I was in the shower, and who I so desperately wished had taken me up on my offer in his bedroom. He was just her brother who had my heart and stomach permanently in knots.

Sunday came by in the blink of an eye and for the first time in years, I was nervous about singing. Staring at the wall was what always got me through it; a coping mechanism that kept the fear at bay. However, I was very aware of the possibility of Noah being there again, and I didn't know if I could trust myself not to look. I knew where the Joyson's sat and unfortunately, it was right in my eye-line.

I didn't look while Father Thurleigh was reading, and I didn't look as we sang along with the congregation. Then I stepped up to my mark, a little ahead of the rest of the choir, and I took deeper breaths than usual as I told myself, *stick to the wall,* on repeat.

The music started, and Sister Maria waved her baton, giving the choir their cue to sing. I listened to the choir and I watched her baton dancing along to the rhythm of the music. Then when it gestured towards me, I opened my mouth and sang. I looked out to my spot at the back of the wall, and I sang perfectly to it, but then my heartbeat quickened. I felt my eyes falter, as they slowly moved across to the left, then down a little, until they found what they were searching for.

He was watching me intently, perhaps even a little in awe, and then I forgot to breathe, and I forgot to sing, until Sister Maria's baton swiped angrily against her wooden stand.

For the second week in a row, I was on Sister Maria's shit list, and was once again given the task of collecting all the hymn books. I put them all in a pile outside the door of the storeroom at the back of the church, and once I'd collected them all I started to move them onto the shelves in the room. I had been waiting for the same feeling as last time to hit me. The feeling that let me know that he was there, but it didn't, and I gave up on the idea of seeing him that day.

Trying to ignore my disappointment, I turned to pick up the last pile and then jumped out of my skin when I saw Noah standing in the doorway holding it. He walked into the small room, kicked the door shut, and put them on the shelf with the others.

"Seriously! Can you stop scaring me like this?" I

growled, as I once again tried to get my startled heart under control.

"Sorry." He grimaced a little. "And sorry for distracting you."

"It's not your fault."

"So, it wasn't me that you were staring at?" He stepped closer. "It wasn't me that made you forget what you were supposed to be doing?"

I felt the fight in me wavering, it had been for days. "You know it was."

He stepped even closer, but channelling the final bit of resistance I had, I put my hand up to stop him.

He sighed and clenched his jaw. "What exactly did that nun say to you?"

"What I needed to hear, Noah. All you want to do is sleep with me. That's it."

He looked down for a moment and I could see that his jaw was grinding a little. Then he stepped forward and looked right at me with a pained expression on his face.

"I'm not going to lie; I want to have sex with you," he said, with the familiar, unapologetic look on his face. "I'll gladly tell you what I want to do to you, Eve. I could tell you what I was thinking when you got into my car, on that rainy day. I could tell you what I wanted to do with your mouth while I watched you eating pizza…" He gave a small, almost challenging smile, but I didn't feel like I could rise to it. "I could tell you what I want to do to you right now."

He was waiting for a response, but I was frozen on the spot. Part of me wanted to hear it and my body was reacting to him in a way that it had never done before, but I was also petrified, and he saw it.

"I could tell you. But I don't think you're ready… not yet. Besides, that's not all I want."

He got my attention, once again.

"I came here, because something about you intrigues me, and because I've been thinking about you non-stop for over a week — and that's not me." He shook his head, reinforcing his point. "I want you to like me too, because for some reason I need you to like me. I want you to sing in my club one day, because I think people will pay a fortune to hear you. I want all of you."

He stepped even closer and wrapped an arm around my waist, setting my body alight. He was looking me in the eyes the entire time.

"I'm coming for you, Eve." He pulled me against his body and the sensation made me gasp. "But if you want me to stop then all you need to do is say it."

I nearly fell apart there and then. My body was yearning for him, but my head was screaming at me to take him up on his offer — to tell him to stop. I needed to keep my guard up and to keep my head, and yet I was frozen, a helpless deer trapped in the dazzling headlights.

He lowered his head towards me, a little. "Tell me to stop."

I lost the ability to speak.

He moved closer, still. "Tell me," he gently commanded, and even though my head was screaming at me to say it, my body was telling me the exact opposite.

He moved so close that his lips were brushing mine. "Say it," he whispered against them, and then I finally managed to find the strength to speak.

"Don't stop…" The words flooded out of me without any thought and his lips landed firmly on mine.

I didn't think about techniques like I did when I was in his car; I just followed his lead. When he sped up; I did too. His tongue touched mine, I reached for his in return, and when he grabbed the back of my head to hold me firmly in place, I let out a gentle moan and he had me pinned against the wall in an instant.

I have no idea how far I would've let things go that day in the musty, old storeroom, but it didn't go any further than our kiss. Our passionate, all-consuming, life altering kiss, because we both jumped at his phone vibrating in his pocket, and he stepped away from me panting to answer his father's call.

I couldn't concentrate on anything for the rest of Sunday. I stared at the wall when my friends were watching television, and I just twiddled with my pen when I should've been concentrating on homework. At dinner, I moved food around my plate but couldn't eat it because my stomach was all over the place and I wasn't sure I'd keep anything down.

I was excited but I was also scared and confused. I didn't know what any of it meant. I didn't know if it would end with that kiss, or if that kiss was the start of something, because Noah didn't say a word before he left the storeroom after his father summoned him. He just looked at me in his indecipherable way, kissed me gently and left me breathless.

Maybe he didn't like it? Maybe I was a really bad kisser and I'd put him off? I had no idea, and not knowing was making me feel as crazy as the need to kiss him again was.

I was also petrified of facing Harriet, as it felt like I had betrayed her trust a little. We only had business studies together on Mondays and thankfully, it was the last lesson of the day, so I had time to pluck up my courage. For the rest of the time, I just hid in the library revising, hoping that nobody would ask me to join in with them. My sisters had already questioned me a million times as I was unable to concentrate on anything they were saying to me. I just put it down to exam nerves. Suddenly, I was lying to everyone that mattered.

I only had a few months before my time at school would end, and it felt like we were on auto pilot, and just doing what needed to be done before taking our exams. Miss Tatler was in a stricter mood than usual, and so Harriet and I barely got the chance to speak during class, but that didn't stop me from having palpitations every time she cleared her throat. I just kept thinking, *This is it; she's going to ask me something,* but she didn't. I guess on the outside, I was managing to come across as completely normal. I was still a complete mess on the inside. I even hung back a little after school in case Harriet was there waiting for him again, but she wasn't, and I walked home alone hoping every car that passed me would be his, but it never was.

By Tuesday, I started to think that Noah must have lost interest in me, since he hadn't got what he wanted. That thought kicked me in the gut and left me feeling bruised all day, but it also made me feel relieved. If one kiss had caused such emotional turmoil, I dreaded to think how I'd feel if we'd done more. If it had gone further, would he have just left me standing there, trying to put myself back together again? How do you put yourself back together after a hurricane has ripped through your heart?

However, I wasn't alone in life, because I had Adam, and he gave me a great distraction from my pain, especially when he and Seb got into another argument at lunch time. I had no idea what caused it and the teachers intervened before it got physical. All I could do before they were dragged out, was give my brother an exasperated look, letting him know that he was going to be in serious trouble later. At least Seb would be finishing when I was, and school would perhaps become the one place where Adam didn't have a target on his back.

By the end of school, I'd persuaded myself to forget about Noah. That was until I walked past Harriet in the hall. She was on her phone and I heard her say, "Thanks Noah, see you in a sec," before she hung up her phone.

My heart started to rise again as the realisation that Noah was going to be there, hit me. I couldn't face him, I wasn't strong enough, and so, I sped up a little to make sure that I avoided him. I didn't look at the cars lined up outside, I just caught up with some of my friends from St Martins and walked out of the gates. As soon as I did, I saw the crowd gathered on the pavement next to the fence, a little further along, and I knew what it meant. There was a fight.

Why was the world against me?

I started to panic as I realised that it was going to slow down or possibly even prevent my escape, but then I heard a voice I knew. John's voice shouted, "Get off him, Seb!" and my heart leapt into my throat. I went into auto pilot and ran over to the crowd and pushed my way through, knowing that I was going to find my brother on the other side.

I wasn't wrong. Adam was on the ground, Seb was above him, holding him down and hitting him whilst his friends held Adam's friends back, preventing them from helping him. I didn't even think. My brother was being beaten and my protective instincts just took over. I launched myself at Seb at full speed, sending him flying, and when I landed on him, my bare knees bashed painfully against the pavement.

I turned to look at my brother, who was lying on the ground with blood pouring from his nose, and rage overtook me. Red was all I could see. I hit Seb with all the force that I could, right in the face. It caught him off guard, but he expected and blocked me when I went for him a second time, and he shoved me backwards onto the ground. I quickly jumped up and put myself squarely, and firmly between him and my brother. There was no fucking chance of him touching him again. If he wanted him, he would have to go through me.

"Move out of the way, bitch!" he shouted at me furiously, as he rubbed the spot on his face where my fist had made contact.

"No!" My blood was boiling, and my body was shaking, but I stood my ground and raised my chin in defiance. I wasn't going anywhere.

He stepped closer to me. He was so close to my face that I could feel his breath and see his eyes practically bulging out of their sockets. "Move! Or you'll get a fucking slap too!"

I didn't move an inch, but he did. A figure suddenly moved between us, grabbed hold of Seb, and launched him into the wire fence that surrounded the school. I watched as it bent inwards under his weight, and as he bounced off it again and hit the ground. He righted himself quickly and jumped up to face the person that had pushed him, but he stopped in his tracks when he saw Noah standing in front of him.

Everyone went silent. Nobody made a sound. All I could hear was my heart thumping and the blood pulsing in my ears. Adam groaned and I turned to look at him again, but his friends were there, picking him up off the ground, so I turned back to look at the two men before me. Noah had his back to me, but I could tell from his posture and the way his shoulders were moving as he took short, sharp breaths, that he was absolutely furious. Seb saw it too, and he was visibly shitting himself in response.

"So, you're a big man, are you?" Noah seethed.

Seb didn't reply.

"The big man, picking on a little boy and threatening a girl?"

Seb still didn't answer.

"If you want to see how the big men play then I can take

you somewhere. Do you want to see how the big men play? Do you want to see how I play?" he asked, in an eerily calm manner, as he stepped closer to him.

"No…" Seb managed to squeak out, looking around him to see if his friends would support him; they didn't.

"No? Not as big as you like to think then?"

Seb frantically shook his head in response.

When Noah turned around, I could see the rage in his eyes, that was no doubt mirrored in mine. Our eyes locked for a moment, and then he looked down my body, pausing at my knees. I saw his jaw clench and I looked down to see the blood pouring from my right knee. I hadn't even realised. When I looked back up at him, he was looking at Adam and I once again followed his gaze towards my defiant and bleeding brother. Then we looked at each other again, before he turned back to Seb.

"If you, or anyone else, touch Adam Matthews again, it will be me that you deal with."

Holy shit.

"And if you so much as breathe in her direction again…" Seb followed the direction that Noah's hand was pointing in, and his frightened eyes landed on me. "Then I'll fucking kill you."

Seb looked stunned, and so was I. I looked at the people around me and they were just as shocked as I was. Then I looked down at Adam, and even though he was in pain, I could see confusion and concern in his eyes when he gave me a questioning look. Nobody knew why, but it was clear that the Matthews siblings were now under the protection of Noah Joyson.

Seconds later, the crowd started to disperse when a police car pulled up and Scott Legion and another officer stepped out. Scott was a fourth generation Founding Family Trueborn, like Noah, but he was four years older and already working his way up the ladder of the force that his family created.

"Noah?" Scott asked, sounding surprised and a little amused. "What are you doing here?"

"Just helping my sister's friend, Scott. Everything's under control," Noah replied seriously, whilst never taking his eyes off Seb.

His "sister's friend". He gave them all a legitimate and innocent reason for why he had acted.

"I can see that." Scott glanced at me with curiosity, and then he looked at my brother. "Are you taking care of that too?"

Noah turned around and looked at Adam again. "I'll take him to Jimmy."

Scott walked over to Seb and stood before him with his arms folded.

"I'm not sure if you just got really lucky, or really unlucky," he said, gesturing towards Noah. "But if I catch you involved in anything like this again, then you'll be down the station faster than you can blink."

Seb nodded at him. I was surprised he was still able to function given how much he was still bricking it. Yet, he knew that in the grand scheme of things that he had got lucky. The Other Side don't police us, but they do expect basic laws to be followed, but then so do The Council. We don't have a jail, but we have a police station with a few cells. People will be sent through the gates to The Other Side to stand trial in their courts from time to time, and some have even been sent to jail there. However, that's only done as a token gesture in order to stop them from looking in too closely. Most of the time, you're not going to be handed over to face a jury of your peers. Most of the time, you stand before the Founding Family elders that make up The Council, and most of the time you take whatever punishment they deem appropriate.

"Time for everyone to go!" Scott barked, and the obedient masses did as he ordered.

Scott and Noah started talking quietly and I went over to my brother, who was still surrounded by his five best friends. It was only us and Harriet still standing there, and she bent down towards Adam when I did.

"Who's Jimmy?" I managed to breathe out.

"I've got no idea." Her breath hitched. She was clearly shaken by the events that had just unfolded.

My spine tingled as Noah approached, and he stood behind me and looked at my brother's friends.

"I can't fit you all in my car. I'll take these three," he continued, gesturing to Harriet, Adam and me. "But you'll have to make your own way back."

They all looked shell shocked and somewhat in awe at the fact that Noah Joyson was actually speaking to them, and John was the only one who could find his voice. "That's fine, I'll help you get him in."

They pulled Adam up and put him into the back of Noah's car.

Harriet sat in the passenger seat and I sat in the back with Adam, who had been given a shirt to bleed into. Noah picked up his phone and made a call.

"Where are you?" There was a slight pause. "OK, I'll be there in twenty minutes, I need your help with something."

"You know, you can just take us back to St Martins," I told him, and he looked at me in the rear-view mirror. "The nuns can handle this."

He didn't say anything. He just started the car and pulled away. He dropped Harriet off at their parents' house, and then we drove off again. He pulled up at the disused warehouse that was once a thriving paper mill and got out. He opened Adam's door, helped him out, and I slid over to his side so that I could support him too. We walked through the main door of the warehouse and it looked just as derelict as I was expecting, but then Noah took out some keys and unlocked a door that led to a stairwell. We had to support Adam down three flights of stairs, and through another locked door, and then we were in what I took to be a gym, at first glance. Then I looked closer and saw only a ring, and I realised that it was where the fights took place.

A man appeared from a side door, he was in his thirties and he smirked a little when he saw us, but then he quickly came over, reaching out to take my place in propping up Adam. I followed them into a changing room, and they continued past the lockers and benches into another room. It smelled sterile, there were cupboards, sinks and a table in the middle. They lifted Adam so that he was sitting on the edge of it, and the man, who I could only assume was Jimmy, looked at me, and then back to Noah and gave another smirk. Then he took the shirt that Adam had been given away from him and examined his face.

Adam winced as he touched him, and I instinctively moved closer. Jimmy pulled a light that hung from the ceiling down and switched it on, moving it closer to Adam's face.

"How bad is it?" I asked him with concern.

"I've seen worse." He continued to study him. "The nose is broken but I ought to be able to reset it. The teeth are fine, as is the rest of the face, so, yes. Just this nose," he said, seemingly satisfied with his assessment.

He went to a cupboard and took out some pills and then fetched a glass and filled it with water. He handed both to Adam.

"We'll wait until these have kicked in. It'll hurt like a bitch otherwise." He smiled at Adam reassuringly and I instantly felt like he was a man to be trusted. "Your boyfriend is going to be a bit out of it for the rest of the night, but he'll be fine."

I opened my mouth to correct him, but Noah beat me to it. "He's her brother."

They shared a knowing look, with Noah making it clear that he wanted Jimmy to drop it. The two were obviously close and Jimmy seemed unfazed when he looked at me and gave a slight smile again, before looking down at my bloodied leg.

"I take it you'll be seeing to that?" he asked Noah, with the smile still present on his face.

Noah nodded and gestured for me to leave the room. As he did, Adam turned to me and did his best to give me a reassuring smile, but I could tell that he was still confused about what this all meant. He didn't know about the time I'd spent with Noah, and I knew that his questions would soon follow.

Noah picked up a first aid kit and we left the room. As soon as he closed the door, he took my hand in his and led me to an area where there was a row of sinks. He lifted me up, sat me on the unit without saying a word, and then examined my knee more closely.

"I can deal with this."

He said nothing, only smiled and shook his head a little as he ran the tap and wet some cotton wool. I flinched when I felt the cold water against my cut knee, but quickly reminded myself that my brother was going through much worse.

"Thank you for what you did back there. I've been protecting my brother all his life, but you just made him untouchable."

"I made you untouchable," he said, never taking his eyes off my knee, which he was cleaning meticulously.

My heart started to pound at an uncomfortable speed. Not

even an hour ago I'd convinced myself that Noah wasn't interested in me and that I, in turn, should forget about him. Yet there I was, letting him tend to my wounds after publicly warning people away from me.

I was nervous, but I needed to speak. I needed some clarity and I needed to understand him. "You seem angry. I'm sorry that you felt the need to get involved."

He threw the cotton wool into a nearby bin, put a plaster gently over my cut, then he placed his hands on the unit, either side of me and looked right at me. "Angry, doesn't even come close, Eve." He said it quietly, but his jaw was clenching. "I just watched the girl that I'm crazy about put herself in harm's way and nearly get hit by a bloke three times her size." His eyes sparked with rage. "Angry. Does not come close."

My head and my heart started spinning once more, as the fact that he said he was crazy about me went around my head on a loop.

He gave a little laugh. "You weren't lying about the fiercely protective part, were you? He'll be feeling that right hook of yours tomorrow."

He seemed impressed, but then he ran his thumb over my red knuckles and a dark look washed over his face again, and I could tell by the way his jaw clenched that anger had taken hold once more.

I didn't fear his anger, but I wanted to take it away. "What can I do to help?"

"I think you know."

He leaned into me, and I took a deep breath to steady myself as his lips closed in on mine. We kissed passionately for a few minutes and then he pulled away and I instantly felt deprived of his touch.

He let out a deep sigh. "Eve, I've tried to put what

happened on Sunday out of my mind. I've tried to put you out of my mind."

I looked down so that he couldn't see the pain that his words had caused.

"I'm being selfish right now, I know I am, but I can't help it. The situation with my family is complicated and I would have to keep you a secret." He sounded horrified at the thought, but I was just confused. "You deserve so much more than that. The right thing, the fair thing for me to do is to just let you go. To let you get on with your life without me in it…" He looked down for a few moments before looking back at me in pain. "But I just can't make myself do it."

He leaned in again and rested his forehead against mine, we both closed our eyes and stayed like that for a few minutes. It was hard to focus on anything other than his touch, but I tried to take in what he had said to me. The fact that I'd have to be a secret was plaguing me the most. It wasn't surprising really. It was the basis of my conversation with Sister Theresa, and it was the fundamental difference between us. He was a Trueborn from one of the Founding Families and I was an orphan from St Martins. I wasn't the sort of girl that his parents would want him to bring home. I wasn't the sort of girl they saw in his future. Perhaps in a different world, a world where we were free to choose, or free to leave; it wouldn't have been an issue, but we lived in The Beneath, and we didn't get to leave.

He sighed deeply and opened his eyes, and the pain in them made my heart hurt too. "You have to be the one to tell me to stop," he said in the same pleading way that he had spoken in the storeroom on Sunday. "You have to be the one to tell me to leave."

Even as he said the words, his lips were moving closer to mine and I completely forgot how to breathe.

"Tell me to leave," he pleaded, moving closer still.

Just like before, I couldn't say a thing.

"Tell me to go, Eve," he whispered, as his lips once again brushed mine.

I knew the right thing to do — the safe thing to do and to say. It was the thing I'd been preparing myself for all day, but I was already in too deep and I was already falling in love with him. As he rested against my lips waiting for me to speak, I placed both of my hands on the side of his face, gently cradling him, and whispered, "Don't go."

I pulled him closer, kissed him deeply and he reciprocated, wrapping his arms around my waist, pulling me even closer. Then his hands were on the back of my head, making sure that I wasn't going to escape, and that I wasn't going to change my mind. That wasn't going to happen because my body was acting on instinct. It was acting on desire and on passion and I couldn't have stopped myself even if I wanted to try... and I didn't want to try.

I wrapped my legs around his waist, and I felt him against me. He was hard, and I was flooded with a sensation and need that I'd never felt before. It was passionate. It was frantic. It was almost clumsy in our desire to be as close to each other as possible, and to touch as much of each other as possible. Then just like before, it came to an abrupt stop when Jimmy cleared his throat and apologised for interrupting.

6

$\mathcal{N}$oah asked Jimmy to give us a few minutes, and judging by the smirk Jimmy gave him, it was clear that he understood without explanation, that Noah had a raging hard on and needed to calm down. Once he was able to turn without poking someone's eye out with his dick; the two of them carried Adam, who was completely out of it, back up the stairs to Noah's car. I got into the back and they gently manoeuvred him in so that his head was resting on my lap. I looked down at him and the tears started to spill over. His nose was taped up and swollen, but I could see the cuts and bruises. He looked so small and fragile, lying in my arms, even though he was just as tall as me and was no doubt going to overtake me soon.

Looking down at Adam, like that, always made me wonder what it would be like to have children. It was supposed to be the most love you'd ever feel, and it scared me to think that I could possibly love anyone more than I loved Adam.

How could you function? How could you cope with the fear of losing them?

Noah got into the driver's seat and turned to me, reaching out for my hand. He felt warm, and he felt comforting, but I wasn't at ease.

"I've seen Jimmy put much worse back together before. It'll take time but he'll be fine." He smiled reassuringly but I was still struggling to believe him.

I smiled back at him, but I couldn't stop the tears from falling again as soon as I looked down at my brother. I didn't get the chance to hold him often, not since he was a toddler, when we'd snuggle together at bedtime. I used to stay with him in the nursery until he fell asleep. However, at the age of twelve, he'd show me affection occasionally, but only if we were alone. I knew he loved me though. Adam always proved his love through his actions, with his cheeky mouth and when he took a slap. He wasn't supposed to take a slap for me though. I'm the big sister and it was my job to take care of him. That's the promise I made.

We didn't say much on the journey back to St Martins and when we pulled up, we saw Adam's friends waiting on the steps, along with my roommates. They recognised the car and started walking over to it, and Noah quickly turned to me.

"I've put something in your bag. Keep it hidden," he told me quietly but urgently, before my door was opened and helping hands reached in for Adam.

It took a few of his friends to lift him out and as soon as they did, my girls came over and pulled me in for a hug, and it suddenly hit me how drained I felt. Pain, fear and a seriously passionate snogging session really takes it out of you.

"Are you OK?" Rose grabbed me by the shoulders and looked me over. "Everyone has been talking about what happened. Sister Theresa has read Seb the riot act, but in truth I think he was already scared out of his wits." She glanced towards Noah, who was now leaning against the passenger door. "Thank you for looking out for them."

Noah nodded to her and was about to speak, but then Sister Theresa came thundering out of the doors.

"Yes, thank you for your assistance Mr Joyson." She smiled curtly. "But we can take it from here."

She looked at me and my friends and gave us a silent instruction to go indoors with the others. I turned to Noah and he gave me a small but amused smile, he'd never really had to deal with the Sisters before and he clearly found them entertaining.

"Goodbye, Eve," he said, smiling at me knowingly.

"Bye, Noah, and thank you," I smiled back at him and had to rely on my sisters to pull me along, because my body didn't want to leave him.

He got into his car and left, we all went inside, and my friends were instructed to go about their business, and I followed as Adam was carried to the infirmary. Once there, his friends were also dismissed, and I waited alone in the cold corridor so that the Sisters could examine him for themselves.

I sat there for half an hour completely lost in my thoughts, trying desperately to focus, and think through everything that had happened, so it startled me when Sister Theresa opened the door. I stood up to greet her and she silently invited me into the room. We walked over to Adam, who had been cleaned up and put in a robe. He looked like he was resting peacefully, at least, and yet, I couldn't find any ease.

"James Sanderson always was good with broken bones." I gave her a questioning look. "Jimmy..." she clarified, before continuing, "and it would seem that under his current employer he's had the opportunity to perfect his skills. Your brother will be fine," she told me, and I was instantly filled with relief.

Sister Theresa didn't sugar coat things. If she was telling me that Adam would be fine, then she was telling me the truth, and breathing suddenly hurt much less.

We walked over to his bed and I sat next to him and took hold of his hand, taking advantage of the fact that he couldn't object and shove me away. "I remember the last time we sat like this."

"Oh, so do I," she chuckled. "I could not believe you went with him."

"I couldn't exactly let him go alone."

Adam was six, I was ten, and he sneaked out of his room and into mine in the middle of the night.

"I want to see the stars, Eve!" he'd whispered with excitement oozing from him as he jiggled on the spot.

I had tried to shrug him off and send him back to bed but he wasn't having any of it. It was an unusually hot summer, the nights were warm, and I had a hard time saying no when he had that glint in his eyes. I also knew that if I didn't go, then he'd go alone, and so I got up and we both sneaked out of the orphanage in our pyjamas.

It was around two in the morning and the whole of The Beneath was asleep, but the stars were very much awake and shining brightly. I pointed up to them, but Adam pulled me along the path, and I ended up letting him drag me all the way to the park.

"What are you doing?" I asked him, as he started to climb a tree. There were some lights in the area, but not enough to really see what we were doing.

"I want to see the stars."

"You can."

"No. The stars behind the wall," he argued, as he continued to climb higher.

He thought that the lights that shone from the tall buildings on The Other Side were stars, and my heart completely broke for him. The lights may as well have been stars, because just like the ones that shone down from the sky, they were much too far away to reach or touch.

"I see them!" he shouted excitedly, but then he slipped and came crashing to the ground, breaking several branches and his arm on the way down.

I carried him home, trying to be brave and not show my fear as he cried uncontrollably. Then I got back to the orphanage and screamed for help until my throat hurt, and when the lights came on, the Sisters descended.

Sister Theresa cleared her throat, bringing me back from my memory. "You need to be aware that not all promises can be kept, Eve."

"I can keep mine."

"Some promises aren't meant to be kept," she clarified. "Some promises break all on their own. You cannot be with him all the time. There will come a time when you will not be able to protect him."

I looked up at her quickly, ready to fight her claim, but when I saw that her eyes were watering, I realised that she was trying to help me, not chastise me, and I felt my own tears forming and quickly looked away.

She cleared her throat again. "However, if the rumours circulating around these corridors are to be believed, it seems that your brother has just received some quite substantial protection."

I continued to look at Adam, I didn't dare meet her questioning gaze.

"And just what is that going to cost you, Eve?"

I couldn't prevent the huff that escaped. "Nothing."

She moved closer and put her hand on my arm and looked at me with compassion, with the full force of the heart that she hides away. "On the contrary, my girl, it's going to cost you everything."

After a few more minutes, she suggested that I leave Adam to rest and sent me to get some food. I did as she asked and went to meet my friends in the food hall. Everyone was already sitting, and they stared at me as I walked in. Normally that would make me feel uncomfortable, but with everything that had happened, it just pissed me off.

I was still in my school uniform, carrying my bag; I had a large plaster on my knee, and I may as well have drawn a target around it, because people's eyes quickly shot to it, before they all whispered about how the story of what had happened must be true.

My roommates waved me over and I went and sat in the middle of them, trying my best to hide from the questioning eyes. Occasionally, I would feel someone watching me and I'd look up to see who it was, but it seemed that as much as they wanted to stare, and as curious as they all were, nobody wanted to look me in the eyes.

My sisters knew better than to question me there, because they knew that if there was anything to share then it would be done in the privacy of our room. So, they guided me there after dinner instead of congregating in the communal areas, like we usually did. After my time with Sister Theresa, I didn't feel like I had the energy to talk, and so I started to get my wash bag and pyjamas together in a pile on my bed, getting what I needed in order so, I could sleep in the bed next to Adam.

I knew what was coming though, and so, I waited for them to speak. I was half expecting for them to be buzzing about the fact that they'd been that close to Noah, given how they reacted last time; but they weren't. They were shaken and angry about how badly Adam had been hurt, and the threats that Seb made against me. They were also confused. Confused and concerned about why Noah would stick his neck out for us, like he did.

"Is there anything that we should know?" Sarah spoke, but she was voicing their shared concern.

"Not that I can think of," I replied, with my back still to them, because I didn't want them to see me lying. "I'm just going to go and shower and then stay with Adam."

They closed in on me for a group hug without saying a word, something that would usually feel so warm, but after how it felt to have been touched by Noah, it felt empty. Then they left the room and I'd never felt so alone.

Slumping onto the bed, I noticed my school bag and remembered what Noah had told me in the car, so I opened it up and saw a mobile phone and a charger sitting at the bottom. Excitement fluttered through me once again as I held it in my hands. I didn't own a phone, only a few people in St Martins did, and they were only the older ones really. They were in their training, had their own money, and some sort of life outside these walls. I switched it on and touched the screen and saw that there was a message to read.

This is how we can keep in touch. It only has my number in it & you can contact me whenever you want. I know what I'm asking you to do is shit. Keeping this a secret... I'll find a way to change that. This is your last chance to walk away. There will be no repercussions. Adam will still be safe. But if this continues any longer, I'm not going to be able to let you go. Noah xx

I sat on the bed and held the phone close to my chest as if it would be able to give me some sort of clarity. The entire day had been insane. This whole thing was insane. Getting involved with Noah, was insane. He was giving me a way out again, and this time I didn't have him touching me and clouding my judgement. He said Adam would still be safe. I didn't need to be with him to make sure my brother didn't get hurt. Yet, as that thought ran through my head it became clear to me that that wasn't why I was doing it. It never was. Noah's protection order on Adam came after he had already gotten under my skin, after we'd already kissed. Keeping Adam safe was a bonus to being involved with Noah, not a prerequisite.

Noah Joyson. I closed my eyes and pictured his face — the face of the Noah that I knew, because he seemed to be different to the Noah that everyone else described. He wasn't cold and he wasn't distant, but angry – I had seen glimpses of that. I had seen that side of him, and yet it didn't scare me, because I'd seen something else in him too. I'd seen his vulnerability, even though I'd dismissed it at the time.

Noah was loved and wanted by many people, but always for a reason. Women wanted him because of who he was. His family wanted him to conform and provide. Yet Noah, didn't feel like he mattered. He told me himself that he wanted to be "important to me". Noah wanted something that he had never had in his life. He wanted to be loved without conditions. He yearned for unconditional love and he'd come crashing into the world of the only orphan that already knew how to give it.

For the first time in my life, I'd had a taste of passion, and it had woken something up inside. I was sixteen and inexperienced. I was one of the unwanted and Noah was making me feel like I meant everything to him. It was scary, but it was also intoxicating, and I didn't want to give it up. I didn't want to give *him* up.

I looked down at the phone again, took a deep breath to push the remaining butterflies away, and sent my reply.

I don't want you to let me go… Eve xx

I showered in a haze and even though I wasn't sure my brain would let me; I did eventually fall asleep in the bed next to my brother. The drugs knocked him out all night, but he woke up groggy and in pain. When the Sisters came to check on him, I went off to get some breakfast, and was immediately hit by the buzz in the air. There was more gossip? Or perhaps it was still just about Adam and me. Laura saw me and frantically waved me over. I quickly learned exactly what was going on.

It seemed that what Noah told me was wrong. Seb didn't feel any pain from my punch the next day. In fact, Seb didn't feel anything for the next few days. Because while I was sleeping next to my battered brother, somebody dragged Seb from his bed and beat him so badly that he earned himself a two week stay in a private, guarded room, in the hospital on The Other Side.

I guess he wasn't so lucky after all.

It was obvious to everyone that it had been Noah, but it was never confirmed. Nobody was ever punished for it and when Seb eventually came around, he said that he never saw who it was.

The guilt chipped away at me, because as much as I hated Seb for what he had done to Adam, I knew that if it had been Noah, then it was done because of me, not because of Adam. Everyone knew that Noah was a loose cannon when he lost it, and I could see that anger building in him when we were at the warehouse, but at the time, I thought I'd helped to subdue it.

When I went back to Adam that morning to check in on him before I went to school, John was sitting there with him, filling him in on the details. Adam laughed about it. At least as much as he could before wincing in pain, but as soon as John left, his smile faded.

My inexperience with boys wasn't solely because of Adam. It was mainly down the lack of prospects within my circle. However, Adam didn't always help, and he had inter-rupted potential 'hook-ups' in the past. Yet Noah, what was he going to do to chase Noah away? There was nothing he could do against Noah, and I could feel the nerves radiating from him when I sat on his bed.

"What's going on between you and Noah Joyson?"

"Nothing. I'm friends with Harriet, like he said," I smiled, trying to come off as convincing as possible.

He frowned at me. "Liar."

I let out a long breath. I knew that I had to give him more, but I couldn't tell him the truth. "He's trying to keep me sweet because he wants me to sing at The Dome, when I turn eighteen."

"That's more believable, but you're still lying."

"You have nothing to be worried about, will you at least believe that?"

He turned away from me, clearly taking it all in, but even-tually, he looked back and gave me a weak nod. We — or mainly I, made small talk for a bit, but he was clearly annoyed by the fact that I was keeping secrets and he didn't give me much more than grunts in return. So, when it was finally time for me to go to school, he dodged the kiss that I tried to place on his head, and I left him to rest and wallow in his indignation.

7

*O*ver the next few weeks, Noah and I contacted each other by phone constantly and met up as much as we could. It was always stolen moments in his car, parked up at the warehouse that nobody really went to until after dark. It wasn't exactly glamorous, but I didn't need glamour. It was new, it was exciting, it was all I could think about, and I wanted to be with him whenever and wherever I could. Nothing felt more real than the feeling of being in his arms. Nobody, not even Adam, had ever made me feel so wanted, or so equal.

Noah was nothing like I had expected him to be, and the cold, guarded exterior he wore around others completely disappeared when he was alone with me. He relaxed, he was funny, and so smart, which surprised me a little. I don't know why, given how much he had achieved at such a young age. I think I had always put it down to his family name and the fact that people were scared of him, but it wasn't. He was always thinking, always planning and always listening. I never really felt like I had much to say about myself, and yet Noah hungered for my every word.

He hungered for my body too, and things were always heated between us. We were never together for long before things turned physical, but he took it slowly with me. He knew that I was a virgin and it seemed more important for him to make it pleasurable for me, than for himself. Even with my lack of experience, I could tell that he was holding back a lot.

When he started to explore my body more, he asked me how I liked to be touched, and I hid from him in embarrassment. It took about five minutes for him to peel my hands away from my flushed face and he was laughing at me the entire time. When he finally succeeded, I had to confess, that sharing a room with five other people, along with the rather regimented shower facilities at St Martins, didn't really offer much opportunity for self-exploration. So, he suggested that we should explore together and that's exactly what we did.

I may have barely been touched by a boy before, but I wasn't scared the first time that we did more than just kiss and grind against each other in our clothes. It's like I could feel that more was going to happen before I even got in his car, because I was so ready for more to happen. It was after school, and he undid my blouse and kissed my breasts as if they were providing him oxygen. He looked at me like he was going to devour me there and then, and I was desperate for him to, but he didn't even take off my bra. Instead, he caressed my neck with his mouth, as his hand rested on my thigh, before slowly moving up and rubbing against my underwear. I was so turned on that I grabbed a fistful of his shirt and started grinding against his hand.

Nothing had ever felt so good, until he pushed my underwear aside, and started rubbing my clit with his thumb. He was sliding over me with ease because I was so wet, then he pushed his fingers inside, started moving them rhythmically, and I felt like I was going to climb out of my skin.

Noah had woken up my soul with his words and his first kiss, and then he went on to wake up my body — and I just couldn't get enough. There wasn't a time when we were together that I didn't end up writhing and crying out as I climaxed.

After a few weeks of receiving so much pleasure, I was ready to do more, but when I straddled him in his car and tried to undo his belt, he moved my hands away and held them by my side.

"As much as I want you, and believe me, I want you," he growled into my neck. "I refuse to let your first time happen in the back of my car. You are too special for that."

I smiled darkly and bit my lip a little as I pushed my hips into him, because I absolutely didn't care where it happened. I just wanted it to happen.

"Eve…" he growled into my chest. "You are seriously testing my strength here."

He rested his chin on the cushion that my full breasts provided and looked up at me as I ran my tongue over my top lip in one slow and agonising movement.

"Oh, fucking hell…"

He looked so pained and I started to enjoy the power that I had over him, but he wasn't going to give in. He put his hands on my hips, pushed me away from him a little, and held me there so that I couldn't move.

"I assure you, that I think about being inside you pretty much 24/7," he groaned again. "It's torture! I'm crazy about you, but it isn't happening here, but soon. Trust me on that."

He pulled me close again and kissed me, letting me feel the force of his need with his tongue. I wanted to tell him that he already made me feel special, and I almost blurted out that

I loved him there and then, but I didn't dare, and I didn't want to scare him away. Although all the messages he was sending me suggested that running away was the last thing on his mind.

I knew what was on his mind because it was bulging out of his trousers. So, I used my newly found sexual bravery instead.

"Show me what you like."

A wicked grin spread across his face. "You want to play?"

"I want to play."

I went for his belt and he didn't stop me, but then he lifted me off his lap so that he could pull down his trousers. When I finally saw what had been waiting for me all this time, my body tingled with excitement, and when I licked my lips it was an involuntary action. I wasn't trying to tease him; I was just so desperate to have him. I couldn't take my eyes off him as he took hold of his penis and started to rub up and down. He grabbed the back of my head and pulled me into a deep kiss as he moaned into my mouth.

I lowered my hand, and wrapped it around his, following his movements and learning what he liked. Then he let go and I took over, responding on instinct and moving faster as his body started to shudder and his grip on my hair tightened. Then I got a taste of the pleasure and satisfaction that followed when he completely came apart at my touch.

$\mathcal{T}$he end of school finally came around and I was so excited to be done with that part of my life. I was even more excited about the party that Harriet was hosting at one of her family's clubs, and true to her word, she came to the orphanage and got ready with me. She seemed completely at ease in my room full of crazy girls, and if her surroundings offended her, she didn't let it show.

Laura and Sarah, who both apprenticed as dressmakers, had been working on my outfit for weeks, and Harriet insisted on lending me a pair of shoes to go with it. When I looked in the mirror, I almost didn't recognise myself. I had never worn anything so grown up, sexy, or revealing and it made me feel a little nervous. I was more than comfortable showing my body to Noah, but the idea of other people being able to see so much, made me feel a little vulnerable.

The dress, however, was amazing and once I put it on, I didn't want to take it off. It may have been new, but it felt like me, like the me that I was becoming. The "sexy little angel" that Noah said I was. It was black, a simple cut with some lace detail around the top that kept it from showing too much cleavage. It hugged my body, highlighting my curves perfectly and was shorter than anything I'd ever worn before. With the heels added, I felt like I was all legs.

"You look amazing!" Sarah beamed at me. "I mean seriously gorgeous — you are definitely going to pull tonight."

"She will if my cousin Tyler has anything to do with it." Harriet gave me a pointed look and all the girls huddled around her, desperate for the gossip.

Tyler liked me. That was news. He was in my year, but I never really had anything to do with him, but then the only man on my radar was Noah.

I continued to study my reflection in the mirror, trying to make myself feel more at ease. The others still appeared to be conspiring against me, but then a pillow whacked me in the head. I turned around and every single one of them, including Rose who had been caught up in the hysteria, were puckering their lips at me.

I laughed at them all. They were too ridiculous and far too lovable, but I also felt the twinge of guilt that pricked at me every time I hid something from them. Every time I made an excuse for missing dinner or to sneak off to use my phone in secret. I turned back to the mirror one final time and gently brushed a finger over my glossy lips. They hadn't been kissed all day and they were missing his touch. Noah hadn't said anything about being at the club, but I hoped that he wouldn't miss the opportunity of me being out and about, to get in a sneaky kiss.

"Do you think I'll be able to sneak this past Sister Theresa?" I ran my finger over the hem of my dress that was a good few inches above my knee.

"There's so many people going to this party tonight, I'm sure she won't notice." Vic smiled in encouragement, and she probably would have been right, but we hadn't taken into account the Adam-factor.

"Are you seriously going out dressed like that?" he asked as I passed him in the hallway on the way out. He looked so horrified that I instantly burst out laughing.

"Wow! I finally know what it's like to have a dad."

"He has a point."

Sister Theresa's voice crept up on me from behind. I slowly turned around to face her and turned into a pleading teenager, all but getting down on my knees to grovel before her.

"Sister Theresa... Laura and Sarah worked so hard on this dress, and I love it! It's a party and a lot of the children from the Founding Families will be there, and I'm sure they'll be way better dressed—"

"That's quite enough." She raised her hand to silence me. "I have no intention of interfering." Then she moved closer to me so that only I could hear. "Just remember to keep your head."

"I will. Thank you, Sister."

I kept my reply humble, but in truth, I was ready to fling my arms around her neck and hug her. However, knowing that wouldn't go down too well, I turned and forced a hug on a very unimpressed Adam instead, and left for the party.

We walked into the club and I was instantly hit by the buzz in the air and the hairs on my arms stood on end. You could feel the vibrations, even though there was no music playing. I had never been anywhere like it before, and I couldn't believe how amazing everything looked. Everyone around me was just taking it all in and I knew that they were all feeling the same. What we orphans were feeling in particular, wasn't just about our first night of freedom in an actual club. It was much more than that.

The night was to signify the end of life as we knew it, and the club, with its bright lights, seemed like a rainbow to those of us that lived amongst white and grey. There may not be treasure at the end of it, but there would be a new life. A chance to shape our own destiny and to become more than just the children of sinners.

Once everyone had arrived, Harriet's father gave a speech, welcoming and congratulating us for completing the first chapter of our lives. It felt genuine, like he was proud of us all, and I know that I wasn't the only orphan in that club to wonder what it would be like to have parents — just for a moment. He was still giving his speech when I felt my phone vibrating in my bag, so I carefully opened it up so that I could read it without being seen.

You look good enough to eat xx

Noah... My body started to vibrate in a whole new way, and I looked around the room to try and spot him, but the lighting created so many dark areas, and there were too many places where he could be hiding.

My phone vibrated again.

And I'm very hungry xx

I had to bite my lip in order to prevent my smile from giving me away, but I couldn't escape the heat rising within me, along with the thought, *tonight could be the night.*

I tried to find him again, but then Mr Joyson finished his speech, the music was turned on, and I was dragged onto the dancefloor with a group of my friends. I was desperate to find a sneaky way to reply to Noah, but every time I moved in a different direction somebody else wanted to talk, hug or dance.

Eventually, I made it to the toilets, and when I got into a cubicle and checked my phone there was another message from Noah.

When you're ready, go to the top floor. Behind the large speaker on the left there's a corridor leading to a door, it will be unlocked. Don't worry about security — nobody will stop you. I'll be waiting xx

I was in a club, at the first proper party that I'd ever been to, and so I should've wanted to make the most of it and to dance with my friends. However, unlike school leavers on The Other Side, we weren't going off in different directions. We would start along the paths of our chosen occupations, but it's not like anybody was moving away, and, other than Harriet, my closest friends all lived with me at St Martins, so we would have two more years of being together. It's only my sisters that I won't be seeing every day when they move out in a year.

At the end of the day, it wasn't even a debate that I needed to have with myself, because more than anything else, I wanted to be with Noah.

I'm ready now xx

When I got to the corridor on the top floor, I saw a security guard standing in the opening and I started to panic, but then he looked at me, nodded, and stepped aside. I walked past nervously, almost stumbling in my heels, opened the door, then almost screamed when a pair of hands grabbed mine. It was just Noah. He led me past a few more doors, wearing his beautiful smile that made me float. Then we reached the door at the end and he pulled me inside, before locking it behind us. He immediately pushed me against the wall and kissed me, making sure I could feel just how hungry he was.

"I didn't mean for you to come straight away. You can go and enjoy your party if you want?" He kissed me again, feeding the longing, growing inside me. "Besides, I've been enjoying watching you dance in this very sexy little dress."

He looked me up and down and when he pushed his hips into me, I could feel just how much he appreciated the view. "You're absolutely breath taking."

He started kissing me again, claiming my mouth and feeding the need that his touch always awakened.

I reluctantly pushed him back a little. "I wanted to come now and where have you been watching from? I couldn't see you."

He smirked, pulled me further into the office and showed me the wall covered in monitors. I laughed a little and turned to check out the rest of the room and felt the butterflies start to flutter when I saw that a sofa bed had been made up, and the area had been surrounded with candles.

"Does your office always look like this?" I teased in attempt to hide my nervousness.

"No." He smiled as he took my hand in his. "This is just for you... if you're ready?" His eyes flicked to the side and for the first time since I'd met him, he was nervous too.

"I'm ready... But there's something I wanted to ask you, because we haven't talked about it." I looked down as my own nerves got the upper hand.

"What's that?" he asked, then my skin burned as he pushed my hair behind my ears.

I was still unable to look at him, so he gently cupped my chin and lifted my face so that I was looking at him again. Then his gentle kiss and loving smile was all the encouragement I needed.

"Well, it's just that I know that you've been involved with quite a few people, and we've not talked about whether..." I paused, because I was not only scared to ask the question, but also to hear the answer. "Well, I just wondered if you were seeing anyone else?"

He let out a little laugh, as if he was relieved by my question, and he leaned in and kissed me with tenderness. Before pulling back and cupping my face with both hands.

"I know that I have a reputation. I have a few in fact… and I'd be lying if I said that they weren't deserved." He let out a shaky breath and almost looked like he was about to apologise. "But since the day that you got into my car with rain dripping from you, completely unaware of how beautiful you looked, I've only wanted you." He looked me in the eyes as his thumb brushed along my bottom lip, sending tingles to my core. "I've not been with anyone else since I met you, and I have no intention to. There's nobody else like you. Nobody compares and I honestly don't ever see that changing."

I took a deep breath and started to tell myself, *keep your head, Eve… Keep your head.* I felt like I was about to crumble, and that he was the only thing holding me up, and yet, he was the one looking vulnerable, as he said, "I'm in love with you."

"Don't say it if you don't mean it," I blurted out in a single breath.

"I wouldn't. I've never said it to anyone before because I've never felt it before. But I do… I love you."

All thoughts of trying to keep my head went out of the window, because my head had already relinquished any control that it had to my heart, and Noah had stolen my heart. I wanted to say it too, but suddenly felt afraid of making it known. So, I gestured for him to bend down to me a little, and then I leaned into his ear so that he couldn't see my face, and whispered, "I love you too."

He pulled back and smiled at me, as if all his Christmases had come at once. "Don't say it if you don't mean it."

"I mean it." I held his hands and started walking backwards towards the bed that he'd prepared for us, bringing him along with me.

I didn't leave that office for a few hours, and when I did, I felt like a wobbly mess; walking like a new-born foal, with no control of my legs. My hair was tangled, my makeup was non-existent, and I was relieved to be in a darkened club.

Like always, my pleasure was Noah's priority. He explored every part of me with his fingers and his mouth, and I orgasmed twice before he slipped on a condom and pushed inside me with a gentleness that reinforced his confession of love.

"Make sure you tell me if it gets uncomfortable or if I do anything you don't like."

I nodded at him, but I didn't feel in the slightest bit nervous. I was ready to experience all of him and I wanted him to take what he needed from me too. He stayed slow until I let him know my discomfort had passed, and I wanted more. I moved my body with his and then started to move quicker. He understood, and started to thrust into me harder and faster, and my body seemed to respond on its own, tilting up to allow him deeper. It still wasn't enough, and as soon as I saw that he was really struggling to hold himself back, I wrapped my legs around him and whispered in his ear.

"I love you, Noah. This feels so good, and you don't need to worry about hurting me. I want you to fuck me."

I had no idea where my braveness came from, but I felt so safe with him, that even though what was happening was new, it felt right, natural and where I was meant to be.

"Oh, God… Eve," he groaned out as he kissed me with more urgency. "I fucking love you!"

Then he let himself go.

He stopped holding back, and I felt the full force of his passion and his desire for me. It was my first time, so I followed his lead, allowing him to reposition and guide me as he took us both to new levels of pleasure. After we both came, we collapsed in a heap, panting and sweating. I had no idea how sex was supposed to feel. Some of my older friends had boyfriends and talked about sex being good, but most agreed that their first time had been a bit of a shambles; but my first time had been amazing.

"Is it always like this?" I asked him, whilst still trying to catch my breath.

"It's never been like this… never."

I rolled into him so that I could hold him close and feel his heart beating next to mine. I lay there, trailing my fingers along his skin, following the tattoo that started on his shoulder and stopped just before his elbow. The design was fascinating to me. Symbols from times long forgot, that represented strength and power. That's what he told people when they asked. However, the part of the design that always fascinated me most was the smaller symbol that stood for equality. He never said it out loud, but I knew what it meant. He didn't relish in his status, and he didn't see me as inferior.

He watched me quietly, savouring the utter perfection of the moment, before leaning in to kiss me. Then we continued to kiss until I felt him harden against me once more.

$\mathcal{I}$ started my new life in the salon, and my sexual awakening at the hands of Noah continued to blossom. I was growing in experience and leading the way more and more, and it felt so good when he lost himself in the pleasure of it — when he lost himself in me. Being important to someone; being loved by someone like Noah, someone who seemed so at odds with the entire world, created a confidence in me that I'd never had before. Noah Joyson loved me, and I'd often lose track of time, as those words travelled around my mind on repeat.

There were times, in the salon, when I'd overhear conversations between girls, getting ready for a night out at one of his clubs, chatting hopefully about bumping into him. They'd giggle about what might happen if they got the chance to get with him and would repeat what others had said, that he was good, but he was cold.

Noah qualified as an eligible bachelor in The Beneath, and if that wasn't the appeal then the challenge he presented was. Everyone wanted to reach the unreachable. At first it made me angry; the fact that these girls were trying to take what was mine, and I'd have to resist the urge to pull too hard on the strand of hair that I was cutting. Noah, however, just laughed when I told him, and reassured me with his touch that I was the only one that he wanted.

After a while, I no longer felt angry about their hope, but instead I felt hurt by their words. Hurt on his behalf at least, because they were wrong about him. He wasn't cold, and he wasn't distant. He was one of the warmest people I'd ever met, and that's saying something when you call Rose a sister.

I was Noah's girlfriend and that filled me with elation, and yet, I was also his secret, and that part always stung. That part brought me off my cloud with a thud. I had asked him why we couldn't let his parents know, and he repeated what he had told me before — that there were "complications". I never pushed it too much because I could tell that whatever the complications were, the situation was eating at him. Even though Noah was different with me, I knew what he was capable of and I didn't want him leaving me angry. I'll never forget the day they brought Seb back to the orphanage, because I've never seen a face or soul, quite so broken.

Noah had a dark side, and I wasn't ignorant of that fact. Sometimes he'd sit silently, lost in his own thoughts, and I'd see his jaw clench and a harshness settle in his features. I would reach out and touch him, and when he to turned me, I'd smile, and he'd be himself again. However, after five months together, my smile was no longer enough to calm him. It wasn't enough to chase the demons that shadowed him away, and one day, things changed.

I could tell that something wasn't quite right when we had lunch together in the warehouse. We always met in the warehouse. We were always hiding from everyone except for Jimmy. Noah barely ate, he barely looked at me and he barely spoke. I asked him if he wanted to talk about it, but he never did share what was torturing him. So, I didn't push, and went about the rest of my day, with a feeling of dread in the pit of my stomach. I called him before I went to bed, but he didn't pick up, and as I still hid my phone, I couldn't wait long to see if he called me back. He didn't, and I went to bed, still unable to shake my unease.

I woke up startled in the middle of the night when I felt a hand over my mouth, which stopped the scream that almost escaped. I was gripped with fear and about to lash out, but then I felt his breath against my ear.

"It's me, calm down," Noah commanded in a gentle whisper.

I pushed his hand away so that I could question him, but he put a finger over my mouth. "Come with me… quietly."

He picked me up and carried me out of the room, without making a sound.

Once in the dark hallway, he set me down and led me by the hand. I had no idea how he knew the layout, but he seemed to know where he was going, and we ended up in the laundry room. He opened the door, pulled me in, and then silently closed it. I stood in the dark, shaking a little from the cold, and from the lingering fear caused by how he woke me, and then the light came on, and the fear took hold again.

He wasn't my Noah. He was the other Noah, the dark Noah that I caught glimpses of occasionally, before the Noah that I loved returned. He always returned, and yet, standing before me in that room I could see that he was different. He wasn't cold, he wasn't distant, he just wasn't there.

"You scared me." I wrapped my arms around myself as some feeble form of protection. "What's going on?"

He didn't say anything, he just walked towards me, and as he did, I instinctively backed away. I had never been afraid that Noah would hurt me before that night, but the way he was looking at me left me shaking uncontrollably. I jumped when I felt myself reach the wall, and as I did, he pressed his body against mine, grabbed a fistful of my hair, and then his lips landed forcefully on mine.

I was pinned to the wall, unable to move, and unable to push him back as he invaded my mouth. I was barely even kissing him back, and when I opened my mouth more it was because I was struggling to breathe, but he used that opportunity to deepen the already aggressive, and intrusive kiss.

He let go of my hair and moved both of my hands so that they were above my head and then held them in place with one of his. I always thought that if I was ever in a situation where I feared for my safety, I would fight back. That I would kick, hit, scratch and scream, like I did when I protected my brother; but I didn't. I was shocked to the core and I was afraid, but I remained silent, and I remained still.

I knew that my face must have been etched in fear and my heart was about to burst from my chest. I didn't understand what was happening. All I knew was that it was Noah, and Noah loves me. Noah loves me and he wouldn't hurt me, that's what I kept telling myself. That's what I told myself while my hands were being held high, and that's what I told myself as I watched his free hand reach into his pocket and pull out a condom.

He held it between his teeth, pulled down his trousers, then used his free hand and teeth to tear the packet open. I swallowed hard as he lowered his hand down to himself and put it on. Then time seemed to stand still as I searched his eyes, trying to find a glimpse of the man that I loved. I couldn't see him, and I felt the fight starting to build in me. I couldn't hit him, but my legs were free, so I could kick him. I could kick him hard enough to send him backwards and I could scream blue murder and wake the entire orphanage up.

I was about to do it, but then I saw him. He was still there, but he was in pain, and the urge to fight him became over-powered by my desire to soothe him. He was lost and he needed me to help him find his way back. I wanted to help him find his way back.

Whether he sensed my acceptance, I'm not sure, but he released my hands and pulled down my pyjama bottoms. I took a deep breath in as his hands moved down my body and as he planted more, forceful kisses on my stomach. I flinched a little when I felt his hot breath against my clit, and even though I was scared, a surge of pleasure shot through me as he stroked me with his tongue. He did it a few times, but then pulled away, because he wasn't trying to pleasure me, he was lubricating me. I breathed out my relief then, feeling a little safer, in the knowledge that there was enough of him still there, and that he was trying to make it easier for me. There was enough of him still there for him to not want to hurt me.

He moved back up and looked me in the eyes as he cradled my face in his hands. "I love you."

I let the gentleness of his words flood through me when his hands became hard as they moved down my body, and I clung onto them desperately, as he lifted me up and pushed into me. I closed my eyes, trying to focus only on breathing as his deep, hard thrusts almost winded me, and I tried not to tense up when his hand grabbed at my hair and pulled my head back, exposing my neck, which he then buried his face in as he muffled his groans with hard kisses. The wall kept me upright, but I held onto his shoulders for support, digging my nails in whenever my back rubbed too painfully against it.

It was over quickly, and the moment he came, I felt him come back to me. His grip loosened and his kisses softened. He slowly pulled out of me and gently guided my feet back to the ground. Then he pulled up his trousers, not looking at me once, walked over to a row of washing machines across from me, and slid down to the floor with his head in his hands.

I bent down and, with shaking hands, put my pyjamas back on. My legs felt like they were about to give way, so I lowered myself so that I was sitting against the wall where he'd just taken me. I hugged my knees into my chest, and I rested my head on them for a moment, trying to catch my breath and trying to convince the tears that they weren't needed.

After a few minutes, I'd caught my breath and I looked over to Noah, who hadn't moved from his spot. "Did I... have I done something to upset you?"

His head snapped up and I could see the devastation on his face. He got up and quickly came over to me. He started to reach out, but then he stopped himself, as if he didn't know if I'd want him to touch me.

"No, Eve," he said with guilt all over his face. "No. Please, don't think that. You are not the cause..." He slumped back a little and put his head down in shame. "You're the cure."

He moved so that he was sitting next to me, leaning against the same wall.

"I have a darkness in me. I always have. People call it a bad temper, but it's always felt like more than that." He was staring at the machines in front of us as if they could give him his answers. "I get lost. I get so angry and I don't know how to find my way back and people get hurt..." I followed his eyes as they looked down at his hands and saw that both sets of knuckles were red and swollen. "I lost it tonight... and someone got hurt."

"At the fight club?"

"No... No, the people that step into that ring do so know-ingly, and we have rules. There's always people there that will stop things from going too far." He looked down at his hands again. "This was something else…" He looked right at me and I could see the sadness and regret in his eyes. "There was a point, a moment, when things could have gone way too far. And even though I was long gone... I thought of you. You just popped into my head and I stopped. I stopped myself. But it didn't get rid of it. I knew that I needed to be with you. I knew that I needed all of you in order to get rid of it. In order to be me again."

I swallowed hard and he tentatively reached out to hold my hand. His touch was soft again, almost pleading.

"I'm so sorry… did I hurt you?"

I turned to look at him and as I did the tears that I'd tried to keep away came spilling out. "A bit… yes." He looked down in shame. "But Noah… that wasn't the worst part for me. You scared me! I was scared of you."

"I love you so much, Eve… but I need you too." His own tears fell. "I need you in a way that isn't fair on you. You're the only one that can reach me. You're the only one that can stop me from losing myself and I can't promise you that this won't happen again."

I sat there holding his hand and closed my eyes as I tried to process what he had said. My body was sore, my heart was heavy, and my head was a complete mess. He loved me. He needed me. It might happen again.

As an orphan, I never got to see what healthy relationships looked like. I didn't have parents to guide me, or to show me how things should be, and more importantly, nobody showed me what an unhealthy relationship looked like. Nobody showed me when you should run a mile! The nuns taught us morals, but they were committed to their God. The rest of us just muddled through and tried to find our way. If my life had been different, then maybe I'd have been able to see it for what it was. Perhaps I would've recognised that it was toxic. That to be a man's anchor, his cure, a vessel that he would need to use physically in order to stop himself from hurting others was not acceptable.

I didn't have that though. I knew love. I loved Adam, and he loved me. I loved my friends and the roommates that I claimed as sisters... and I loved Noah. The connection that we shared wasn't like anything I had with the other people in my life. It was all consuming for me, as well as for him. I wanted and loved him on every level and he clearly needed me more than anyone else ever would. When you grow up as one of the disregarded; as a child that was so easily cast aside, the peace you feel from knowing that somebody out there loves you that much, isn't something that is easy to give up. It's not something that you want to give up.

When I focused on what had been done in that room, on the act itself... I realised that it was the fear that upset me the most. He warned me that it could happen again, but at least I would know what to expect if it did. I would know that he didn't want to hurt me.

I tightly squeezed my eyes as I argued with myself — my head versus my heart, because I knew, on some level I knew it was wrong. I knew I shouldn't let him do it, but I also knew that I loved him too much to leave him. Too much to leave him to fight his demons alone. Not only that, but Noah was mine, just like I was his, and if I was the only one capable of stopping people from getting hurt — then surely that made it my responsibility?

When I opened my eyes, I still wasn't sure which part of me had won the battle, but then I looked at him and I saw the fear and vulnerability on his face. Then I remembered what he needed. Noah needed unconditional love, and I loved him without exception.

I pulled the hand that I held in mine towards my lips and kissed each red and swollen knuckle. I released it gently, and did the same with the other hand. Then I looked him in the eyes and told him, "Next time, come to me first."

He leaned into me and started kissing me gently and I reciprocated willingly. He was my Noah again and I wanted to feel his touch and to forget about how the other Noah had felt. My heart was yearning for him. I started to move backwards, and he followed me down, kissing me constantly until he was lying above me on the floor. He paused for a moment and looked at me as if I was the most precious thing in the world.

"I love you so much, please let me make it up to you."

He lifted up my top and started to kiss and caress me with such gentleness that it almost tickled. His lips brushed against my skin as he made his way down my body, but then he paused and moved back up so that we were face to face. "Promise me you'll be mine forever?"

"I'll always be yours, Noah."

He smiled, his relief and love written all over his face, then he kissed me, before removing my pyjama bottoms, once again. Then his mouth was on me, and he made sure that I felt pleasure where there had just been pain.

10

J spent two years being the secret girlfriend of Noah
Joyson. Although, it wasn't a complete secret,
because Noah had people more loyal to him than they were to
his family, and some of them knew but his family were still
unaware. All of them, including Harriet, which was one of the
things I hated most. Even though it was school that connected
us, Harriet was a good friend and we still spent time together.
Going to her house was the worst, because if Noah was there
it felt like I was lying to her face when I acted as if I barely
knew him.

Some people like the danger of keeping a secret, but I
hated it. Noah has a darkness in him, but I didn't want to stay
in the shadows. I wanted the world to know about us, and for
the world to see him the way I did, and although I didn't push
it, I never really understood why they couldn't.

Then there was my family, specifically Adam, who has
never been the easiest person to hide something from, on
account of the fact that he has always been able to tell when
I'm lying. He's never told me what my 'tell' is, because he
thinks if I know then I'll work on it. So, Adam got suspicious

and one day after six months of, "sneaking around" he followed me after work. He kept his distance, but he saw me get into Noah's car and he followed us on a bike that he'd "borrowed" to the warehouse. It took him a while to pluck up the courage to approach the car, so by the time he came over and banged on the window, shouting for me to get out, I was already half undressed. I hastily tried to re-dress as I asked him to wait a minute, but he opened the door and ended up seeing much more of his sister than he needed to.

He was so angry with Noah that he actually tried to go for him! It was almost comical to watch him attempt to land a blow on someone far bigger and much more adept at fighting than he was. Yet, I also felt a sense of pride, that my little brother would try so hard to defend his sister's honour against Noah, of all people. It was one of those rare occasions, when I knew the little shit actually loved me.

Noah blocked a few of the punches, but then just put his hand on Adam's head and held him at arms-length, while I put my top back on; at which point I stood between them and tried to get him to calm down. We explained everything to him; how long it had been going on, why it was a secret — which he didn't understand — and we impressed upon him the need to keep it that way. He left that warehouse upset and angry and when I got back to St Martins my roommates were waiting for me, because in true Adam-style, he'd gone straight to them and told them everything.

They were hurt that I had been keeping secrets from them, but more than anything they were worried. I may have only been a year younger than them, but they treated me like a little sister, which is why they ranted at me for half an hour about how it was a bad decision, that Noah should "man up" and tell his parents, and how I deserved more than to be a secret fumble in the back of a car.

I knew they were right, even without them knowing about the late-night visits. However, I also knew that whatever the issue was with Noah's family, it was more complicated than any of us realised. I had asked more than once in those first six months and it was always the same. He always told me vehemently that he only wanted to be with me, and he promised me that he'd find a way to change the way things were. I didn't know what it was that needed to change, but I knew that it was the thing that brought out the other Noah... the dark Noah.

Dark Noah, or the Other Noah as I often called him, appeared at times, during the course of those two years. The hand that silently pressed against my mouth in the night no longer scared me, and I knew that the lost look in his eyes was only temporary. I found my voice, and I used it. If there was ever a moment when it got too much, I would tell him, and he would listen. It no longer felt like something that he was doing to me. It was something that we were doing together, and I even learned to enjoy it... sometimes.

It was rough sex, rougher than I'd like to do on a daily basis, but it was still Noah. I knew the driving force was need, desire and in a fucked-up way, even love. He allowed me to reposition myself, to find pleasure in it, and the more I came with him, the less he tortured himself afterwards. Even though I found a way to make it bearable, I didn't want it to happen at all. Because when it did, there was a moment in time when he wasn't my Noah anymore. It also meant that something had happened to cause it and that someone had somehow hurt him, and I didn't just want to bring him back from that hurt. I wanted to protect him from it too.

Eventually, my roommates saw how much I loved him, they accepted it and they even helped to keep it a secret. Of course, Sister Theresa knew, because that woman knows everything. One day, she invited me to her office and handed me a small glass jar. I looked at her bemused and she told me that I was to provide her with a urine sample. I did as she asked and once satisfied that I wasn't pregnant, she started talking to me about contraception and what my options were.

When I saw Noah the next day, I told him that the condoms could go, and he practically pounced on me. I had no idea that it would feel so different, and so much better without them! It was like there was no barrier between us at all. It was warmer, more intense, more passionate and it felt like we completely became one. Afterwards, Noah slumped next to me, completely breathless but smothering me in kisses, before laughing, "I think I love Sister Theresa, a little bit."

Just before my eighteenth birthday Noah surprised me one evening by driving me to The Dome. I was in no way dressed for it; but was excited, because I thought it meant that he was finally bringing us out into the open, but he wasn't. Like he had said from the start, he wanted me to sing there.

"David, my eldest brother will be in there tonight. I'm sorry to ask but you're going to have to play a part, you can't be my Eve in there." He clenched his jaw and gently tucked my hair behind my ear. "But you need to get used to that anyway because you'll see them all the time when you start singing here," he added, giving me a cheeky smile.

I "needed to get used to it". Those words suggested that despite his promises, we weren't about to tell his family any time soon. That stung, again. I looked down, because it hurt to see his smile and how he appeared to be able to make light of it.

We hadn't really talked about being a secret for a while; not since we fought about it the last time, almost a year before. It was our one-year anniversary and I asked him if we could finally tell his parents about us. I got the same response, or no response which it felt like, because he only ever said the same thing. I ended up telling him that it wasn't good enough and he had a meltdown. I couldn't believe that he was mad with me about it and so I yelled, right back, before getting out of his car.

I started to walk back to St Martins, and he followed me, shouting for me to get back in so that we could "talk about it". Then we got to a more populated area and I just stood there, on the pavement, daring him to make a scene in the street with people watching. He pleaded with me quietly to get back into the car and talk to him, but I was far too angry and continued to march back to St Martins, where I proceeded to cry my heart out in my room.

That had been our first fight and I wasn't sure if it meant it was the end of us. I didn't want it to end. I knew that my options were to stay a secret, for reasons that I didn't understand and keep the happiness that he brought me. Or be without him and feel the pain and emptiness that I felt that evening when I thought I'd lost him. He came to me that night, as I suspected he would, but he didn't ask me to help him find his way back. He just held me close while I cried in his arms.

Eventually, I stopped crying, but then I looked at his hands and my heart broke again as I realised why he didn't need me to help him. The answer was written over his red and swollen knuckles. Somebody had been hurt. The darkness inside him hadn't been chased away by the light that he found in me. It had taken hold, it had been released, and it had found its satisfaction on the broken and bloodied body of someone that didn't deserve it. As quickly as my tears had dried, they started to fall all over again, as I realised something else. That it was my fault.

That was then. That was a year ago, and still nothing had changed.

"I promise you that it won't be like this forever," he assured me, sensing what I was thinking. "And when you're here we'll be able to see more of each other."

"I don't recall agreeing to sing here." I pushed the pain away and gave him a challenging glare.

"Well, let's go and take a look, then shall we?" He smiled as he got out of his car.

I followed him in and was immediately struck by how grand and somewhat intimidating it was. I knew The Dome was said to be something pretty special, but it went beyond anything that I'd imagined. Walking into the main reception area felt like you were walking into a different world. A world of possibilities, a world where dreams come true, and a world that I didn't belong in.

The dome shaped ceiling, looked like it was reaching up to the sky, trying to touch the stars and although the room was full of people, seated around candle-lit tables and chatting happily, it had a sense of calm to it too.

It was a Thursday evening, and I was surprised to see how busy it was. Some people in The Beneath had done well for themselves, but not many were well off enough to visit The Dome frequently, but then I remembered who else it served, and I couldn't help but stare and wonder who in the room was from The Other Side.

Noah took me over to the bar and we leaned against it. "What do you think of the place?"

I rolled my eyes at him and smiled. "I think you know it's pretty impressive."

He smiled with the pride that he deserved to feel, considering that he was the driving force behind its success. Then he nodded towards the stage as a very smartly dressed man appeared and made his way to the piano. The people at the tables applauded him, and as they did a woman came out dressed in a beautiful blue ball gown and glided over to the microphone. I realised that I recognised her — Kate, she was two years older than me, and I took her spot as lead soloist when she left St Martins.

I laughed a little. "You appear to have a thing for singing orphans."

"No. I have a thing for you," he smiled back. "But I do have an eye for talent."

Kate started singing and it almost took my breath away. She was comfortable and confident, and she completely owned the stage.

I watched her in awe before turning to Noah. "You realise when I'm at church I'm supposed to be a singing robot?"

He laughed at me in response.

"I pick a spot at the back of the wall and that's what I sing to."

"Perhaps you could sing to me?"

"Only if it's a song about heartbreak and sorrow," I smiled, only half joking.

"I'd prefer one of happiness and hope." His smile held a hint of sadness.

"I'm not as good as she is Noah. You can't give me her job."

He turned to me, fixing me with a more serious look. "Actually, you're better, and definitely more beautiful. Besides, you wouldn't be replacing her, we mix the acts up. Nobody sings every night and there's room for you both."

We continued to watch her, standing as close as we could without raising questions, and I started to imagine myself standing where she was, singing so enigmatically and openly to an audience of our elite. Not just to them, but also to people from The Other Side. I started to look around, wondering again, if I could spot them in the audience, but then I noticed Noah move away from me a little and I felt the tension radiating from him as I followed his gaze towards the man walking toward us, smiling.

David — Noah's eldest brother by eight years. I'd never met him before, but I knew who he was. Everyone knew who the members of our five Founding Families were. David was handsome, the entire Joyson clan was attractive, but he was nothing compared to Noah. Nobody was.

"Noah," he said, reaching out to embrace his brother. Then he turned to me and looked like he was thinking for a moment. He smiled. "I know you, you're the soloist from St Martins!" Then he looked me up and down in a way that made my skin prickle all over.

"David, this is Eve Matthews," Noah said with formality, and we both reached out to shake hands, with David holding onto mine that little bit too long.

I looked at Noah and the way he clenched his jaw suggested that it hadn't gone unnoticed.

"Is my little brother trying to lure you over to the dark side?" David asked me with an amused smile on his face.

If only he knew.

"Trying to," I replied smiling, and doing my best to keep my tone light, even though the situation I found myself in was horrendous, and David was creeping me out.

"I guess we finally know why he started going to church," he said, looking down at my chest a little too indiscreetly. "And if you don't like it here then I'm sure we could find a place for you in The Cell," he added, with a smile that sent a chill down my spine.

The Cell: a place well known to all, but not somewhere I was ever likely to go to. It catered to the darker needs of The

Beneath, and to its patrons from The Other Side too. Exotic dancers, burlesque performances, very few clothes, but no touching. Never any touching, or so they told us. I'm sure David meant it as a compliment in a seedy way, but still, the insects crawling over my skin seemed to multiply and I had to stop myself from shuddering.

Noah sensed my discomfort. "Did you need me for something, David?"

"No, I was just after an introduction..." Sleaziness oozed from his smile. "So, what will it be Eve, are you joining the team?"

"I'm not sure."

"You will."

What an unbelievable cock.

"Noah always gets what he wants eventually, well, most of the time."

He gave Noah a pointed look, then he smiled at me again and walked over to a table of very well-dressed people and started inflicting his version of charm on them.

"Was your brother just flirting with me, or is he always like that?" More insects crawled across my skin.

"He was flirting." Noah spoke through gritted teeth. "I'll have to see if he feels like coming to the fight later, I owe him a rematch anyway."

I stifled a laugh. "Why? Did he beat you last time?"

Noah laughed as if what I said had been the most ridiculous thing in the world! "Not a chance, but I might let him get a slap in before I take him down again."

I made him smile but he was still tense, but then it seemed to fade away when he turned to me.

"All I'm asking you to do is give it a try. We've got people that can help work on your nerves and stage presence, and if you hate it then you can quit."

"Yes, and apparently I could get a job in The Cell." I smirked.

"Not a fucking chance." He was less than amused, and I couldn't help but laugh at him.

A couple of weeks later, I turned eighteen and the next chapter of my life was officially starting. I was leaving my home, that's what St Martins was, after all. I was leaving the sanctuary of the Sisters and I wasn't actually sure how it would feel to no longer have them watching over me. Sister Theresa, in particular, had always taken quite an interest in my life and I'm not sure I'd ever admit it to her, but part of me would miss her guidance.

Then there was Adam. He was a massive pain in the arse, used up far too much of my time and energy, especially when it came to keeping him out of trouble. Yet, he was still mine, and I loved him regardless, and it would be so weird not seeing him over breakfast. At least I knew he would be safe, just like he had been for the last two years.

Besides, he'd already suggested that he'd be coming over as much as possible for movie night. It was a tradition that we started when he was ten and he had no intention of ending it. All the films that we get to watch are censored by The Other Side. They all contain messages of the harmonious family, the doting wife and the loyal, hard-working husband. Most people would make a quick exit from the TV room when they came on, but not us. We found the hypocrisy of it all hilarious. The very existence of The Beneath was testament to the fact that it was utter nonsense. Men cheated, women had relations without being married, and we paid the price. All of us. I think Adam and I found them so amusing because in our case, our parents fucked up twice.

So, no, I probably wasn't going to get the opportunity to actually miss Adam, and two days after my birthday I moved out of St Martins and into a house with Laura, Vic, Sarah and Hannah, and one week later, I started working at The Dome.

It started off as training really, they had an amazing coach called Izzy who helped me find, and work on my style, and I liked Samson, the pianist right from the start. He was funny and very flirty, but it didn't feel threatening like with David, because it was clear that he was like that with everyone. If anything, he helped to put me at ease.

It also wasn't as tricky fitting it in around the salon as I thought it would be, given that the shifts there varied too. Noah seemed to always be around when I was. He had his own office but would often bring his laptop out to one of the tables when I was practising on stage. To anyone else, it just looked like he was checking on his new act, but every now and then he'd flash me a smile of encouragement and my heart would flutter. Or better still, he'd point towards the direction of his office with his eyes before disappearing, and that was my cue to follow him so that we could be alone.

After a few weeks, it all started to come together. I had a date to start performing and I'd got used to being around his family. I had spent time with his parents when I'd been with Harriet, but never really with his brothers, or the uncles and cousins that all had a hand in the business. Still, they all seemed friendly enough, towards the newbie. Then there was the added bonus of getting to spend more time with Noah behind the safety of a locked office door.

I started to feel like I actually belonged there, and I started to be hopeful, that once his family knew me better then we could stop hiding. I just had to prove to them that I was good enough. That's what I thought I needed to do — show them that I belonged in their world and that I belonged with Noah.

One Saturday afternoon, during a rehearsal, Samson

asked me if I played the piano and invited me to sit with him on the stool. I knew that Noah was at one of the tables with David and Rory (the middle brother) but I didn't think anything of it, because everyone knew Sam was harmless. We sat there, attempting to play duets, laughing away, when I felt a presence behind me, and I turned to see Noah staring at Sam as if he wanted to beat him senseless there and then.

Thankfully, Sam had no clue, but sensing the danger, I asked to speak with Noah in his office and we both walked away. He went in first and I pulled the door shut behind me and watched as he walked over to the far wall and rested his head against it, breathing heavily.

"You do realise that I interact with other men on a daily basis?" I was a little incredulous. "And I'm sure that you know that Samson is harmless."

"Yes," he said to the wall. "I just hate that he doesn't know that you're off limits." He turned to me. "I hate people thinking that you're fair game."

I sighed at him and rolled my eyes a little; he was the reason that nobody knew.

"I know what you're thinking." He smiled but his sadness shone through.

"Of course you do, because it's the same thing that I've been thinking for the last two years." I went to him, wrapped my arms around his neck and pulled him in for a kiss. "I'm not sure you deserve it, but I love you."

He picked me up and moved me over to his desk and trailed kisses along my neck, awakening the need in my body that was always brimming at the surface and always just for him.

"Promise me you'll be mine forever?" he pleaded in his familiar way.

"Forever," I promised, and as his love burned through me

our kisses became more intense and he started to push me backwards so that I was lying on his desk.

"Two years, 'ey?"

We both jumped up to see David standing in the doorway.

I didn't lock the door. Oh, fuck! I always lock the door.

David let out a deep, disappointed sigh as he walked in and closed the door behind him. I slid off the desk and leaned against it and Noah stood a little in front of me, staying close as if to create a barrier between me and his brother.

"Two years? Forever?" David cocked an eyebrow at Noah. "What exactly has been going on?"

Noah stood facing him, and his stance made my heart swell, because it was a stance that I recognised well, a stance I saw in Adam all the time. It meant defiance. Noah wasn't scared of his brother, and he was prepared to defy him… finally.

"Eve is my girlfriend and we're in love."

"You fell in love?" David asked, laughing a little in disbelief. He rubbed his hands down his cheeks, looking up to the ceiling and shaking his head, before looking back to Noah. "Well, that was a fucking stupid thing to do, wasn't it?"

11

David was kind, or perhaps concerned, when he suggested that I went home so that they could speak, but before I left, Noah pulled me in close.

"This changes nothing," he promised me, but I could see from the look in his eyes that it wasn't me that he was trying to convince.

I walked home in a bit of a daze, and when I walked through the door, Vic smiled at me and I burst into tears. I couldn't quite believe it happened and I blamed myself for forgetting to lock the door. If only I'd remembered to lock the door. I'd wanted them to know about us for so long, but it wasn't supposed to happen like that. I had a plan.

Then there was David, and what he said, I just couldn't shake it, and I was torturing myself about what it might have meant. Why would falling in love be so bad?

I thought being out in the open was what I wanted, and there we were, his family knew, and all I wanted to do was go back into hiding. To be back where they couldn't touch us. Where they couldn't take him from me.

Vic was the only one home and she tried her best to

console me, but I could tell that she was a little relieved. Even though my sisters all supported us, they only did it because they knew how much I loved him. They were never happy with his reasons for keeping our relationship secret, and now it had come to a head. It would go one way or the other, and they'd have my back either way. They'd hold my hand and guide me through the heartbreak if it came to it.

Vic spelt it out for me; the Joysons will either accept our relationship and we'd move on happily, or it would end, and I'd move on alone. "It will hurt but you'll heal… eventually, you'll heal."

That's what she thought. The others thought it too, but I knew better. There would be no moving on. Only Noah and I knew the depth of our love, and only we knew how I met his darker needs. How I kept his demons at bay. I didn't think I'd ever be able to love anyone else after loving Noah, and even if I could, I knew that there was no way Noah would let me.

When the rest of my housemates came home, Vic filled them in as I tried to get hold of Noah for the tenth time — but there was still no answer. I was lost and I didn't know what to do with myself. I couldn't eat dinner, I couldn't focus on TV and I didn't know whether to get ready for bed or wait up in case he called for me. Eventually, I went to bed, but only because the girls dragged me upstairs.

I felt completely helpless and completely alone. Only, I wasn't alone, because they all brought their bedding into my room and stayed there with me, and for the first time in over a year, we all shared a room again.

Noah broke the silence the next morning when he sent me a message saying that he was on his way over. It was Sunday and I should've been going to St Martins with the others for the service, but I stayed back and waited for him. My stomach was in knots the entire time and I just kept pacing the room. I had no idea what to expect and I was in bits. I was trying to prepare myself for heartbreak because I didn't dare hope. Hopes can get crushed and I was already crumbling, but then, the spark of hope started to ignite, when I opened the door and saw him smiling from ear to ear.

He walked straight in, wrapped his arms around me and lifted me into the air. I could barely allow myself to believe it, but it was true, they'd accepted us. They were annoyed about the secrets and lies, but in the end, they saw how much he loved me, and they accepted it. That's what he told me, and I don't think there was a moment in my life where I had ever been happier.

"I promised you forever," he told me, as he almost suffocated me with his kisses and carried me up the stairs.

Meeting Noah's family as his girlfriend was nerve-wracking, to say the least, and it was two days before my first performance at The Dome, so I was already a bit of a wreck. Yet, it was fine, more than fine in fact. They were warm, they were welcoming, and I started to see a future with them as well as with Noah.

Harriet was ecstatic, literally bouncing around on the spot happy. I thought she'd be mad at me for keeping secrets, but I guess, like Noah, she understood the reason for it. After all, it was her family too.

"Honestly, Eve, I'm so freakin' happy, you don't even know," she gushed as she pulled me in for a hug. "I can't believe he's managed to do this!"

Harriet was in the audience with the rest of her family for my first performance and they gave me a standing ovation, along with everyone else. In spite of my nerves, my first evening singing at The Dome was a great success. There were a few times when I felt like I'd messed up a bit, but the audience didn't appear to notice. Sam told me that I was a natural, and Noah was so proud that he looked like he was on the verge of crying.

I became popular, the nights when I was singing were in demand, and after a while I settled into it, I loved it, in fact. I was always scared to be seen when I sang in the church, but I guess that could have been down to the songs that we were singing and the fact that I was supposed to be a carbon copy of the rest of the choir.

Even though I was a soloist, it was never supposed to be about me, but that wasn't the case in The Dome. There I was encouraged to not just be myself, but to find myself. I'd never felt so free or so alive, and when the crowd went still, and Sam played his melodies, for the first time in my life, I was singing with all of my heart.

After a year together, as an 'official' couple, Noah took me to a flat that I'd never been to before. It wasn't massive or even that grand, but it had everything you could need, and it was cosy and homely. I liked it instantly.

"Could you see yourself living here?" he asked me, with the glint in his eyes that always made me melt.

"I think I could lower my standards," I'd joked.

He pulled me close and then dangled some keys in front of me. "Do you think you could see yourself living here with me?"

Life was good, more than good. My life was mind-blowingly amazing! We know our limitations in The Beneath, so we tend to keep our aspirations low. Friends, an occupation that we enjoy in the long term, good health, love, and not forgetting a family to call our own; are all we hope for. Yet, I felt like I'd surpassed that. I had everything I'd ever hoped for with a sprinkling of icing on top.

I was singing in The Dome, which wasn't only something I adored doing, but it also paid more than I ever thought I could earn. I was becoming pretty good as a stylist too, I had great friends, a brother that was safe, and I had Noah Joyson. I had his love.

There were some downsides to being with Noah though, and even working at The Dome, and that came in the sleazy shape of David. Noah's family were always nice to me. Harriet seemed different, a little lighter perhaps, and as she didn't really like the wives of David and Rory, she clung to me whenever we were all gathered together. David, however, I couldn't really put my finger on him.

Some days, I thought I'd catch him looking at me in disdain, and I assumed that he didn't think me good enough for Noah. Other times, he would look at me in a way that would make my skin crawl, just like the first night he stared at my chest. Then there were occasions when he almost looked sad for me. I didn't understand him, and that made me uncomfortable, so I avoided him as much as possible.

Unfortunately, that wasn't always possible, because when I was at The Dome, he was one of my bosses, and that meant showing a level of courtesy and respect, especially in front of the paying guests.

I popped to The Dome to see Noah one evening. I'd been working at the salon all day and he was going to be working most of the evening, and that, alongside the plans I had with Adam, meant that I wouldn't see him. It was just supposed to be a quick visit to steal a moment or two with him, which ended with me naked on his desk, screaming my head off. We'd been together over three years in total and we still couldn't get enough of each other.

ROXANNA C REVELL

I planned to make a quick exit, as Adam was meeting me at reception. He didn't necessarily need to meet me there, but I still felt like I needed to keep tabs on him. He may not have been touched since the day Noah put him under his protection, but he was still a little fucker. He pushed people to their limits from time to time, as if testing them, or daring them to see what would happen if they did.

I left Noah's office and walked along the back of The Dome's main hall on the bar side. The stage was still empty, but the audience was seated, and I stopped to speak to Bobby and Emma behind the bar, which was something I regretted doing when I heard my name being called. The hairs on the back of my neck stood on end, and I turned to see David standing by a table, smiling and waving me over. I looked at the people he was with and knew immediately that they were from The Other Side.

I knew how to spot them. Noah had shown me one night when we sat in a dark corner in each other's arms. There was usually an older married couple, or sometimes an older man with a woman who was clearly his mistress, but the consistent thing was their security. They always brought security with them, and they always stood out like a sore thumb.

However, the table that David was with that night was different as they were a table of two couples, one older and one younger. There didn't appear to be a guard with them, but you could tell by the way that the younger woman took in her surroundings with such fascination and intrigue that she wasn't one of us. Being there wasn't a treat like it would be for any family from here. It was an adventure to her, a step into the dark, the dangerous, and the unknown.

I groaned inwardly as I dutifully walked over to them. I hated having to schmooze with them, but I couldn't avoid it if David was calling me over. So, I took a deep breath, painted a smile on my face and tried to discretely straighten myself up, so that it didn't come across as obvious that I'd just been shagging Noah's brains out.

As I got close, David put an arm around me, and I had to fight the need to recoil.

"This is Eve, she's one of our singers," he smiled as he squeezed my side, and I chewed on my tongue as I attempted to charm them with my smile.

The older man stood up to shake my hand. "I'm Henry Southwold, this is my wife Gwen, my son Ethan and his girl-friend, Gabriella," he gestured at each one as he said their name, and I smiled at them all in turn.

I had to stifle a laugh when I noticed that up close, Gabriella didn't just seem intrigued, she was also a little pissed.

"Mr Southwold owns a number of hotels in Havensmere," David told me.

Havensmere — I sometimes had to remind myself what it was really called, because we only ever called it The Other Side.

Henry was looking at me intently, but I had absolutely no idea what the appropriate response was. "Congratulations, that must be quite an achievement."

He smiled at me as if I'd handed him a gold star, but in truth, I didn't really care in the slightest about him or his hotels. Havensmere, and the people in it — the people that were supposed to be better than us, held little appeal to any of us. They were allowed in so that we could take their money, not so we could build bridges.

"We were hoping to hear you sing actually," Henry continued. "Our friends came last week, and they were full of praise." He smiled so genuinely, that I was starting to think that he could possibly be a nice man.

"Thank you, but tonight you have the pleasure of listening to Kate."

He was still staring at me, so I smiled at the rest of the table too in order to avoid his gaze. "She's fantastic, I'm sure you'll have a lovely evening."

"What will you be doing this evening?" Gabriella asked, overly enthusiastically, and the younger man next to her almost choked on his drink.

"Gabbi…"

"I'm so sorry, Ethan," she giggled, brought on no doubt, by the wine in her glass. "It's just that I find this all so fascinating," she went on, clearly not realising, or caring that she was actually being offensive. "I just wondered what you do with yourselves here, that's all."

Her voice trailed off as she looked at the faces around her and realised, for the first time, how inappropriate she was being.

I pursed my lips to stop myself laughing, because I actually found her amusing, and I'd met her type before. They were the type that made people here resistant to The Other Side being allowed in. The type that made us feel like we were in a circus. I turned to David and could see that she was irritating him too, but he still gave me a look, reminding me to be on my best behaviour.

"Well… I'm going to be spending the evening with my brother," I smiled. "We're going to be watching movies, so not all that interesting really."

I was almost apologetic. Poor Gabbi, what a disappointment my response must have been.

"Oh, I beg your pardon," the older woman said, speaking for the first time. "For some reason I thought you were an orphan, which family are you from?"

Oh, lovely, I was suddenly worthy of her attention.

David shuffled a little, but I didn't break my smile or my eye contact with her. "You were right the first time. I'm from the St Martins' family and I am an orphan."

Her smile faded, and in her embarrassment, she turned red and blotchy. "Oh, well, when you said about a brother, I thought you were talking biologically."

"I was." Keeping up my false smile was starting to make my face hurt.

"Eve and her younger brother Adam, are quite a rarity here," David stepped in. "They're unique, in fact, full blood siblings orphaned four years apart."

They all looked down as if what was being discussed would be embarrassing for me. It wasn't. I knew who I was, and I had no problem with it, but I was embarrassed for them. For them and their complete and utter ignorance. I continued to smile and then I locked eyes with Henry. Henry wasn't looking down. Henry hadn't taken his eyes off me.

"I thought you'd left."

My body relaxed as Noah appeared next to me. His arm replaced David's and he moved me away from him a little.

"Believe me, I would like to leave," I whispered into his ear.

"Speaking of rarities," David announced, "allow me to introduce you to my youngest brother, Noah."

Noah may have opened the doors to The Other Side, but he didn't tend to mingle with them. He took their money and made sure no rules were broken, but he left David and Rory to greet and charm them. You could tell that they knew who he was though — everyone did. The youngest of the Joyson brothers was in charge, whether you saw it on a daily basis or not. He didn't just make the rules that they had to stick by when they visited; he'd been known to enforce them too. More than one man had been sent back through the iron gates in a worse state than they had arrived in and not just from alcohol.

So, yes, it was true to say that to be from The Other Side and in the presence of Noah Joyson, was a rarity, but then, he wasn't there for them. Still, he played the part of host, and when Henry stood to shake his hand, he greeted them with grace and charm. I felt a flush of pride for being the one that he still held close. The older woman fanned herself as if she was meeting a celebrity, Ethan looked cautious, Gabriella looked like she'd just wet her pants, and Henry seemed to be looking at the arm that Noah held firmly around me.

"I hope you all have a wonderful evening," he told them, then he turned to me with an amused smile. "I just saw Adam chatting Meredith up on the CCTV."

There was no way of stifling my laugh at that. Adam had been trying to charm his way into Meredith's pants for months. She's three years older than him, but Adam has always looked older than his years, and her resistance was starting to waver.

I turned to the table and gave them my first genuine smile. "That's my cue to go. It was very nice to meet you, have a lovely evening." Then I turned to Noah and gave him a gentle kiss on the lips. "I'll see you at home."

I walked away and didn't look back, and when I got to the reception area, I spotted Adam leaning against the desk, treating Meredith to his most endearing smile. Poor Meredith! She wanted to resist him and had told me months ago that she wouldn't go near him because he was younger than her, and my brother.

However, Adam was good-looking, he had filled out, he was self-assured, he was bloody persistent, and I knew that she was intrigued. I told her that I didn't mind if she went out with him, because I liked her and she'd probably be really good for him, and by the way she was playing with her hair it was clearly only a matter of time before she caved.

They turned when they heard me coming and I smiled at them both. "I'm your date tonight," I reminded him.

"How could I forget movie night with my big sister?"

I reached out to him and he rubbed the top of my head. Like I always knew he would, Adam now towered over me.

Meredith laughed and shook her head at us. "How can you watch those movies?"

"Because they're fucking hilarious!" we replied in unison, before we all burst out laughing.

Adam treated Meredith to one final smile, and I watched in amusement as she flushed.

"I'll see you soon," he winked at her.

Yes, just a matter of time. I really hoped he'd treat her better than the others.

Then he turned his back to me, and I jumped onto him for a piggyback.

I didn't turn around when I heard Meredith ask, "Can I help you, sir?"

So, I didn't see who watched us leave, laughing at the jokes that were only ours. I didn't see their sad smile, and I didn't see them turn away with tears in their eyes.

12

*S*o, that was my life. I was a singer at The Dome, I'd been living with Noah for one and a half years. We'd been together for four and a half years, and every time he asked me to promise him forever, I happily obliged. I never even had to think about it, because I was his forever, just like he was mine.

Adam developed a flare for mechanics during his later years at school and he was starting his apprenticeship under the Manners. I knew that he was seeing Meredith, although they were both keeping it quiet, and he and John were making plans to live together, when they were to leave St Martins. John had always been high up on my list of favourite people, and I was grateful that it would just be the two of them. John didn't encourage Adam's antics and I knew he had his back, no matter what. John loved Adam, in more ways than he'd admit, in more ways than Adam knew, and in more ways than would ever be reciprocated.

The Other Noah seemed to have disappeared. Noah was content with his life with me. He was at a place of peace and he stayed in the light. He still ran the fight clubs, because they were profitable, and he enjoyed getting in the ring on occasion. Sometimes it was to release his own aggression, and other times it was for the sport. It wasn't just that though, he felt that he needed to remind people what he was capable of, but the violence that came from the once overwhelming darkness, seemed to have been defeated.

At least, it was for those first two and half years that we spent out in the open, but six months before Noah turned twenty-five it came back. It came back, and shook me to my core, because I'd completely forgotten how to deal with it.

I arrived home late, after a performance at The Dome and he was sitting on the bed waiting for me. The lights were dim, so I didn't see it at first, and I just flittered past him, stroking his head on the way to the bathroom to get ready for bed. I was just changing out of my clothes when the door opened, and he was just standing there naked, staring at me. I giggled at him, at first, excited by how insatiable this man of mine was, but then I looked into his eyes, and I realised that he was back. Or more specifically, that my Noah was gone.

"Noah… what's happened?"

I felt the nerves starting to take hold, and I reached out to stroke his face, but he moved away from my touch. He said nothing, but the turmoil within was reflected by the tightness in his jaw, and I sucked in a breath and tried to get my head in gear and get prepared as he reached for my hand.

He pulled me out of the bathroom and then lowered me gently onto the bed, but I knew that gentleness would not continue. It had been a while, but it became familiar all too quickly. The fistful of hair, the relentless and somewhat ruthless thrusting of his hips against mine. The growls of pleasure and pain that he buried in my neck, and the guilt and remorse that followed after he released his demons. Then, just like before, like all those times, all those years before; he wouldn't tell me why. I cured it, I knew that, but I still had no idea what caused it.

It started to happen almost weekly, but I didn't allow myself to find enjoyment in it like I had before, because I knew what it meant. It meant that there was a problem, something was eating at him, something big, and something that he wouldn't share. How could I help him if he wouldn't let me in?

I started to think that it was me, and I started to resent it, and one night I pushed him halfway across the room when he came into our bed in the early hours. His heart was pounding, and his breathing was short and rapid. I knew what was coming, and I didn't want it. I shoved him hard, switched the light on, and looked at the version that I hated of the man that I loved, dead in the eyes.

"You will not touch me again until you tell me what the fuck is going on!"

He said nothing. He just got off the floor and walked out. The anger that I felt quickly turned to pain as I watched the door close, and that night I held his pillow close as I cried into it, no longer convinced that forever really existed. I went to The Dome the next afternoon and was immediately hit with an overwhelming feeling of guilt as soon as I saw Noah. There was no hiding what he'd done after I sent him away, because the dark bruises had taken over his hands, just like the darkness had taken over him.

A week went by without us spending much time together, or even talking much, and I started to truly believe that it was me. I was the problem. Noah didn't love me anymore and the fact that I worked for him made it complicated for him to break up with me. That's what was happening. That was my explanation for it. I couldn't face my friends, so I stayed in the flat most of the time, just hoping that he'd come back and talk to me. To set me free from my agony one way or another.

Then two days before his birthday, Noah's mother, Ruth, came to our home. Ruth had always been friendly with me, even back when I was no more than Harriet's friend. I spent Christmases with the Joysons - bringing Adam along too, and she always made me feel like I was part of the family. She always made me feel included and important.

However, that was not the case when I invited her in that day. She still looked like Ruth. She was immaculate, and her dark blonde bob didn't have a single hair out of place, but she was different with me. I sensed it the second she walked through the door. She was cold and guarded, but also nervous.

"Eve, I think you know that things aren't right between you and Noah, at the moment," she said, as I handed her a drink. "Honestly, it should never have come to this. We didn't think it would last this long."

To her credit, her surprise at least, seemed genuine.

"Are you actually dumping me on his behalf?"

"No…" She cleared her throat. "And yes."

I couldn't believe what I was hearing and any hurt that I had been feeling was replaced by confusion, astonishment, and a growing anger. I sat down on the stool across from her because I wasn't sure that my legs would hold me up.

"What exactly are you saying?"

She looked so uncomfortable and it took a while, but she eventually looked at me with sadness in her eyes and spoke two simple words that completely destroyed my life, "Time's up."

"What do you mean?"

She cleared her throat. "I'm sorry to have to be the one to tell you this, Eve. Believe it or not, but I like you." She smiled a little as if to reinforce the sentiment. "Noah should have had this conversation with you a long time ago, but he's been too busy trying to find a way out."

"A way out of what?" I snapped, as more anger started to replace confusion.

"Of his obligations... He has obligations. We let him delay them, we gave him until his twenty-fifth birthday."

"Ruth!" I pleaded. "Please, just tell me!"

She looked down at her hands for a few minutes and I sat there in silent agony, waiting for her to speak. Then she did, and I wished she hadn't.

"Noah has been betrothed to Jane Green since he turned eighteen."

I felt the floor fall from under me. There was nothing there. I was just floating.

"When we found out that he'd been in a relationship with you for two years, we told him to end it. But... well... you know how he is, how he gets, so in the end, all parties agreed to give him three years." She shuffled in her seat. "We gave him three years, Eve," she repeated, when she saw that I was struggling to take it all in.

"We thought he'd get you out of his system, but all he's done for the past six months is try to get out of the engagement." She was starting to sound as if it was all just an inconvenience and an irritant to her. "But he can't, and he will be marrying Jane in a matter of months."

My world fell apart. Right there, in that moment. Right in front of Ruth and the drink she was bringing up to her mouth — the drink I made for her, though I could no longer remember making it. The rug had been well and truly pulled from underneath me. My happiness was exposed as nothing but a lie, and the future that I'd envisioned, my future with Noah came crashing down around me.

I reached too far, and I flew too high, and the time had

come for me to come tumbling back down. To pay the price and to crash and burn.

"Naturally, you'll still have your job at The Dome. I know you'll need some time," she continued, as if it was nothing more than a business transaction. "This flat is yours too. Truly, Eve, I do think a lot of you, and I know that you love him."

"What are you doing here?" Noah raged at his mother as he came through the door.

He came rushing over to me, but I couldn't even look at him. I was rooted to the stool because it was the only thing that felt real and focused on the clock on the wall in front of me because it was the only thing that wasn't spinning. I was frozen, but time was moving. I knew that because I could see the hand on the clock ticking as each agonising second passed. I focused on that truth, that reality, and on the smudge mark that I'd been meaning to clean off it for weeks.

"Eve…" Noah grabbed hold of me and turned me to face him. "Don't listen to her!"

"Why? Is she lying?"

He said nothing but the look of devastation on his face was all the confirmation I needed.

"She's not lying, is she?" I didn't need him to answer. "You are the liar! You have lied to me every day for the last five years!"

"It's not like that! I don't want to marry Jane. This isn't my choice. I've been trying to make them see reason, trying to make them understand that they don't have the right to dictate."

"This is how we do things," Ruth countered. "You know this, Noah, you've always known this."

He turned from me to face her directly. "Yes, but I stupidly thought that having already seen two of your sons in unhappy marriages, you might just work out that the way we do things is FUCKING SHIT!"

"Don't talk to me like—"

"Eve is the best thing in my life, and I love her! Why can't that be enough? Why can't I just be happy?"

I sat there stunned and in silence, as they continued to argue, Noah was getting angrier and angrier and that only seemed to make Ruth more resolute. She was a strong woman, clearly stronger than I'd ever realised, but I could see that he was starting to scare her.

Usually, I'd try to intervene and calm him, but I realised in that moment, that all of the anger that Noah had felt during the entire five years that we had been together, was because he knew what was coming. His family were his demons, his family caused the darkness, so as far as I was concerned his mother deserved whatever came her way.

Then so did Noah, he deserved my anger.

"Every time you came to me to help you when you were lost..." They stopped and turned to look at me. "Every time the darkness took over and you came to me — your cure." I shook my head at how ridiculous those words now felt. "You had the chance to tell me what was going on. Every time I asked you what was wrong, you had the chance to tell me. In the early days, when I kept asking why we needed to be a secret, you had the chance to tell me." I looked right at him and let the tears fall. "You had the chance to spare me from this pain... but you chose not to."

"Eve..."

"It's actually my fault too, when you think about it. You told me that you were being selfish. While Jimmy was fixing Adam's nose and you were making my heart spin out of control, you said then, that you were being selfish. Do you remember?"

He nodded, and as he did a tear slowly slipped down his cheek.

"You even gave me chances to walk away. But how could little, Orphan-Eve possibly do that when the untouchable, Noah Joyson was making her feel like she meant everything to him?"

"Eve, please. There's still time, they could still see sense."

"Noah…"

I turned to look at Ruth as she spoke for the first time in a while. She actually looked sad, and that surprised me.

"Now is not the time for false hope. Now is the time to say goodbye."

"FUCK YOU!"

She startled at the force of his words.

"No, Noah, fuck you," I breathed out, as I started to stand up. "Fuck you, fuck your family, fuck Jane Green and her superior fucking family, fuck this flat, fuck singing at The Dome… FUCK EVERYTHING!"

I started to walk towards the door, but he grabbed my arm and pulled me into him. He was crying, something I'd never seen before, even in his darkest moments.

"You promised me forever," he pleaded as his tears started to mingle with mine.

I pulled away from him and did my best to hold back my tears, because they were blinding me, and I needed to see clearly.

"Yes… but you never had the right to ask me for it."

Then I walked out the door and away from the man I'd spent five years loving. I heard the shouting and the banging, and I knew the flat which was once my home was now receiving the brunt of Noah's anger, and I ran. I ran down the steps and out of the door, and all the way to St Martins.

I crashed through those church doors in the hope of

finding Rose, but as I reached the back corridors it was Sister Theresa that I found. She turned and looked at me and as she did, she saw the complete and utter heartbreak behind the tears, and she looked like she was holding back her own as she opened her arms to me. I fell into them helplessly and she held me silently as I completely fell apart.

13

She knew. Of course, she knew. Sister Theresa always knew everything and, looking back, she tried to warn me, in her own way. "They have their own rules," she'd told me, right at the start. If only I'd listened. If only I was able to keep my head. If only I'd managed to keep my feet on the ground, but it was impossible because Noah kept lifting me higher and higher. He had me floating on cloud nine from the start. What chance did I ever have?

Rose was eventually brought to me and it took some time, but I managed to fight through the tears enough to tell her everything. She couldn't believe it. She was still a nun in training, and she did her best to master her emotions, but she was furious, and after having a rant of her own she sat down and cried with me, taking on my pain as if it were her own.

She called my other sisters, and we all hid away in Rose's room. Unlike Rose, they had no qualms about showing their feelings and in the end, I had to beg them to stop. I was drained. I was totally spent, and I couldn't deal with their anger too. So, they just sat with me quietly, then made plans to go to the flat to get some of my things for me, and when they came back, they looked afraid, and I knew why.

"How bad was it?"

They all just looked at each other and it was clear that none of them wanted to answer. They didn't need to, my home had been trashed, I knew that, because I heard it happening.

They offered me to stay in the house that I once shared with them, but I opted to stay with Rose at St Martins. It felt safer there, like I could hide away behind an army of nuns that would happily and easily chase away anyone that tried to trespass. So, they stayed with me and just like the last time my heart was breaking, we once again shared a room.

I stayed hidden away for two days and they were the loneliest two days of my life. Rose stayed with me as much as possible, but she had her duties and her training. She called Della at the salon to explain what had happened, and that I needed some time off, but it turned out she already had an idea what had happened, because Noah had gone in looking for me.

"He was in a state," she told Rose, but I couldn't find it in myself to care because he deserved to feel it.

I really wanted my brother. I wanted his easy smile, his stupid jokes and for him to make me feel like I mattered again, but I'd begged everyone to try and keep it from him for a while. I didn't want him to see me so broken because I knew that he'd want to defend me. He'd go straight to Noah and I couldn't let that happen. Noah was a loose cannon and it scared me to think what he might be doing. When Noah suffered, other people suffered too, and he no longer had me to bring him back from it, but I couldn't let that be my problem, I just couldn't.

His parents did this, it was their doing and it was their problem. I needed to stay angry. I needed to try to figure out how to heal my own wounds. I couldn't take on Noah's too, and yet, whenever I closed my eyes, I saw his tears and my heart broke for him.

I should have known — or remembered, that nothing stays a secret in The Beneath for long. Three days after I left him, Noah tried to get into St Martins. Sister Theresa blocked his path and he'd argued with her. People heard, Adam heard, and he and his friends went to investigate.

Noah saw Adam and assumed that he knew what had happened and begged him to talk to me on his behalf. Adam came straight back into the church and tracked me down; barging into Rose's room with panic etched on his face, and as soon as I saw him, I broke down again.

I gave him a brief outline of what had happened, and he ran straight back out, screaming that he was going to kill Noah. I ran straight after him, begging for him to stop, and then we got outside, and I saw him. He looked broken, and angry but as soon as we locked eyes he softened. He tried to speak but then Adam pounced on him.

"YOU BASTARD!" Adam screamed as he pushed him against his car.

John and I ran forward at the same time and grabbed hold of Adam. I was petrified of him getting hurt, but Noah didn't do anything to retaliate, he didn't even defend himself. Adam was swinging at him and he didn't even raise a hand to block him.

John pulled Adam back and I put myself in front of him, to try and push him away from Noah. Then more of Adam's friends got involved and they managed to drag him away. I'd been so focused on getting Adam out of harm's way, that I hadn't realised how close I was to Noah, until I felt his hands on my waist.

He turned me so that I was face to face with him and I couldn't stop my tears from falling. I missed him. I was furious with him, but I missed him, and I loved him. You can't turn off five years of love in three days no matter how much you might want to.

"Eve... please talk to me," he pleaded, as he held me close.

"TAKE YOUR HANDS OFF HER!" Adam yelled, and I turned to see him struggling against his friends again.

"You need to go," I told Noah, then I tried to pull his hands off me, but he wouldn't let go.

"We need to talk."

"What about?" I snapped. "What will talking change?" He looked down. "Nothing, Noah. It changes nothing, so just go."

I tried again to break his hold.

"Please, let me go..." I begged.

I couldn't stop the sobs from escaping, and I put my head down to try to hide my pain.

Noah released his hold on my waist and moved his hands to my face, and as he gently cupped it, he lifted my eyes to meet his.

"I love you and you love me... that has to mean something?" His own tears escaped and cascaded down his cheeks unchecked.

"Not to the people that matter."

Then right on cue, those people pulled up in their car, quickly followed by two police cars.

Sister Theresa turned to Adam's friends. "Take him inside."

They dragged him away before Scott Legion stepped out of his car.

I tried to move away from Noah, but he moved his hands from my face and wrapped his arms around my waist in a vice-like grip. His parents stepped out of the car, quickly followed by David and Rory. They looked at us both, then back to each other with a mixture of concern and annoyance, and I started to feel afraid.

Noah didn't even acknowledge his family.

"Let me go," I whispered.

He just shook his head and then finally looked at his family with what could only be described as pure hatred.

"Thank you for coming so quickly, Sergeant Legion," Sister Theresa stepped forward. "As you can see there has been a bit of a disturbance. Nobody has been injured but I would like Noah removed from the area as soon as possible, please."

Scott cleared his throat and looked at Noah's father, Robert. Scott may be on the police force, but it was The Council that truly held the power in The Beneath. Robert was part of The Council, and he held more power than Scott did, no matter what rank he held or the uniform he wore.

"Noah, time to go," Robert ordered. "Eve, please step away."

I just looked at him, raised my arms and gave a slight shrug, showing him that I wasn't the one stopping me from moving, and Noah responded by pulling me even closer.

"Eve has asked Noah to leave, repeatedly," Sister Theresa added, letting them know that I wasn't at fault.

"Noah!" Robert demanded with more aggression.

Noah turned to face his father with a look so cold, that it stabbed at my spine. "Make me."

A feeling of dread washed over me as I looked up at his face and I started to shake when I saw that the darkness was about to take over. I looked to the side, just slightly, and made eye contact with Ruth, and the same fear had clearly taken over her too. Things were about to get ugly, and we both knew it.

David stepped forward then, clearly trying to mimic the commanding presence of his father. "Seriously, Noah, this is embarrassing. All this hassle for some little tart."

Noah let go of me and then the sound of his fist colliding with David's face seemed to reverberate through my body. Then seconds later the sound David's body made when it hit the ground did the same thing.

People were moving quickly, but it felt like it was all happening in slow motion. Noah was on top of David, landing more blows on him, and Rory was on Noah's back trying to drag him off. He managed to pull him away from David but then Noah turned around and hit him too, sending him flying backwards and stumbling to the ground.

Ruth was screaming, Robert was barking orders that fell on deaf ears, and I just stood there completely unable to move.

I'd always known what Noah was capable of. I always knew that helping him tackle his darkness stopped people from getting hurt. I knew he was feared. Yet, that was the first time I'd ever seen why, and it was as magnificent as it was terrifying. He was relentlessly and ruthlessly battering his own brother, but not because he wanted to. He wasn't thinking, he wasn't enjoying it, and he wasn't considering his next move. In fact, he wasn't there. He wasn't my Noah, and he wasn't their Noah either.

The four police officers on the scene jumped into action. Scott managed to get some cuffs on Noah, and between them and the rest of the men that were still standing, they managed to drag him into the back of a police car. It contained him but it didn't subdue him, and he kicked and kicked at the door and window, raging at them all. I couldn't take my eyes off him, and I couldn't stop the tears streaming down my face. Then Sister Theresa's hand suddenly appeared on my arm.

"Go to your brother, Eve." She saw the look on my face. "You are not responsible for this."

Noah was taken to the police station and locked up for a few days. He wasn't arrested, he was never going to be, they just needed to put him somewhere where he couldn't do any more harm while they tried to get him to calm down.

David was conscious but badly injured and he was brought to the infirmary. The infirmary was attached to the orphanage, but it serviced the whole of The Beneath. The nuns had internal access so that they could move between the orphanage and infirmary quickly and easily, but visitors and patients gained access via an external entrance.

I knew the code for the internal door, and I used it later that evening, after visiting hours were over to go and see David. I'd never really liked him, but I hadn't enjoyed seeing him getting beaten like that, and even though Sister Theresa said it wasn't my fault, I still couldn't help feeling responsible.

I found him in a private room and I quietly let myself in. He was awake and he watched me walking over to him. He was clearly in pain, but I couldn't feel sorry for him, because he was looking at me like I was something he had stood in. I didn't really know what I was hoping to gain from my visit, but his attitude towards me pushed any guilt that I was feeling far away.

"Come to gloat?"

"Why? Have I won something?"

"I guess not." He laughed a little, but then he winced in pain and put his hands on his ribs.

I stood close to the bed and looked at him with more calmness than I felt. "You called me a little tart."

He said nothing, but he looked at me in a way that clearly showed that he meant it.

"Well, that was a fucking stupid thing to do, wasn't it?"

14

I wanted to stay hidden in Rose's room as much as I could, but my presence in St Martins was no longer a secret, so there was no point. Adam made me eat dinner with him in the food hall, but it was horrendous, because everyone stared, and everyone whispered. One evening, I told Adam I couldn't deal with it, and got up to walk away.

"Not everything is about you, you know?" He gave me a big smile. "They all want to shag me, that's all. Can't get enough of this!" He wiggled his eyebrows and ran his hands down his body.

Such a cocky little shit. It worked though, and I treated him to a rare smile.

"You're gonna get through this." He took hold of my hand, something he rarely did in public. "You're the strongest person I know, and besides…" The cocky grin came back. "You have me."

"I'm not sure I'd know what to do without you," I breathed out, and then I felt the tears start to spill over again, and I ran back to hide in Rose's room.

A week went by and I tried to avoid the gossip, but I kept hearing snippets. People were absolutely loving the drama. Nothing that interesting had happened in years and I couldn't step out of Rose's room to even go to the toilet, without hearing something new.

I tried to block most of it out, but it was impossible not to listen when I heard two girls talking about how Noah had been locked up again because he went on the warpath and filled a few more beds in the infirmary.

I felt so guilty. Nobody knew what I did to stop this from happening. Nobody knew the part I played in keeping them safe. I bore the burden that came with that responsibility and I couldn't shake it off, no matter how many people told me it wasn't mine to bear. I knew it wasn't, not really. His family had orchestrated this. They gave me my marching orders, it's not like I chose to leave.

Still, I had left, and it was over, and I knew at some point I needed to figure out what to do with my life. Sister Theresa made it clear that I could stay at St Martins for as long as I needed to but being back there was driving me a little crazy. My sisters no longer had a spare room, but they offered to let me stay until I found a new place. Then there was the salon. I knew I needed to get back there, because I was letting Della and my clients down, but it all just seemed too much.

I had to think about finances, since I would no longer be living rent free, or receiving my wage from The Dome. There was just so much to get my head around and I was nowhere near ready and nowhere near capable of doing it. How can you focus on reality when you have no grip on it? How can you plan for a future when you no longer feel like you have one? How do you clean up the tiny pieces of your shattered dreams, and how can you trust your own instincts when they failed you so badly?

It was hard to know what was real and what was fake, so when Harriet showed up one Saturday morning and found me in the garden at the back of the church; I wasn't sure whether I wanted to see her. However, she ran over and wrapped her arms around me and we both burst into tears.

"I'm not going to ask you how you are doing," she said as she wiped her tears away. "I'm so sorry about all of this."

"Did you know?" I held my breath, waiting for her response, afraid to hear that my friend might have been in on the lie too.

"When it was first planned, yes, but that was years ago. Noah always objected to it and when I found out that you two were together, and that my parents were OK with it, I assumed that it had been called off."

She shook her head and was clearly struggling with it too. "Noah has always been the exception. He's always managed to change things and I honestly thought he'd done it with you. I thought he'd paved the way for the rest of us, that's one of the reasons why I was so happy! I swear, I had no idea that they'd just given him more time, I really didn't."

She was telling the truth. That was one worry to cross off my growing list, at least.

"I know that Noah should have told you, I do. But I know that he didn't because he's never stopped fighting them, he never stopped fighting for you."

I let out a shaky breath. "And now he's just fighting…"

"I've never seen him like this, Eve. He's a complete mess. I'm freaking out! Nobody knows what he's going to do next."

"He doesn't know either, Harriet… he's not in control right now."

The tears began to spill over again — will I ever be able to think about him without them falling?

"You love him, don't you?"

"I really wish that I didn't, but yes, I love him so much."

She pulled me close and held me there as I cried in her arms, until her phone rang, and she cursed when she saw her father's face appear on the screen.

"I'm sorry, but I have to go…"

She looked apprehensive, like she didn't really want to leave me. So, I wiped my tears away and gave her a small smile, letting her know that I wasn't about to completely fall apart, and she turned to walk away.

"Who have they chosen for you?" I had to ask. I had to try to understand their ways.

"Oh…" She flushed a little. "Daniel Legion. What do you think?"

I did my best to smile at her, but I shuddered at the thought of her being so closely connected to his grandfather, Commander Legion. He was worst of the worst.

"He seems nice enough, but you could do better."

She laughed a little then pulled me in for another hug and I had to persuade myself to let her go. She had always been a friend, but her family would no doubt pull her away from me, and I wasn't sure if we'd ever be that close again. A small part of me wondered if I was the lucky one, because I'd been deemed of no use to them and released. Yet, Harriet would continue to be trapped and would no doubt be playing by their rules forever.

That thought however, was soon kicked aside when my aching heart reminded me what I'd lost.

I'd lost everything.

15

$\mathcal{T}$he next day, Adam and I were both given a free pass to miss Sunday service. It's not something Sister Theresa would normally encourage, but she understood that I still couldn't face it, and she was keen to keep Adam away from anyone that went by the name of Joyson, too, "For everyone's sake."

We played pool in the games room while we listened to the choir and congregation singing along and he did his best to try to make me smile. That seemed to have become his personal mission over the past two weeks — finding a way to make me smile. We didn't speak much, other than to try and psych each other out when we were taking a shot, and for once, it worked, and I managed to take my mind off things, for a short while at least.

We were alerted to the end of service by the sound of multiple footsteps running along the halls, and we decided to retreat to Rose's room. I remembered the weird energy that we all used to have when Sunday service was over. So many children and teenagers having to be on their best behaviour for a few hours, always seemed to bring element of carnage and chaos afterwards, and I was definitely not on their wavelength.

Unfortunately, our plans were changed when we were stopped in the hallway by Sister Theresa, who was wearing the frown that was usually reserved for my brother, not for me. A feeling of dread overwhelmed me as she gently pulled me aside.

"Eve, there are some people in my office who have requested to speak with you." She seemed nervous. Sister Theresa was actually nervous. "I have told them that I would do them the courtesy of taking you there, but I assure you, that you will be free to walk out of that office whenever you wish to."

"Which people?"

"The Joysons and the Greens — Noah and Jane's parents."

My heart rate doubled, and it was Adam that spoke up. "What do they want?"

"To talk. What do you say, Eve? I'll stay with you, if you wish?"

She put her hand on my arm, to reinforce her words. She would be there for me, that was good. I had no idea why they could possibly want to speak to me. Noah's parents I could understand, but Jane's?

Sister Theresa squeezed my arm, reminding me that I needed to give her an answer, and I let out a shaky breath as I nodded at her. It had to be done. I had to go. I knew the people that I was about to face, and I knew that if they wanted to speak to me, they'd find a way to do it eventually. Better that they did it here, on territory that they didn't rule, and with the most fearsome woman in the whole of The Beneath by my side.

"I'm coming too!" Adam stepped next to me, staying so close that his arm was brushing against mine.

She didn't turn to face him, but I saw her give a small smile. "I assumed you would, Mr Matthews. So, let me advise you to mind both your tongue, and your manners."

I turned and gave him a pointed look, reinforcing Sister Theresa's warning, but the shrug that he gave me in return didn't really fill me with encouragement that he'd listen to either of us.

It took a few minutes to walk to her office, and as we did, I started to think about Jane. I should have seen her as my enemy, as the reason my life was ruined, and yet she'd barely crossed my mind. She was only two years older than me, so I'd seen her around, but we'd never had any reason to interact. We did not travel in the same circles, and the Greens in particular, came across as if they thought that they were a cut above the rest. Something I saw first-hand, on the few occasions that I had seen her parents at The Dome.

Derek and Elizabeth Green were somewhat condescending towards me, but I had always put that down to me being at the bottom of the hierarchy. However, it dawned on me, as I walked into Sister Theresa's office, that their attitude towards me was probably more to do with the fact that I'd stolen the heart of their future son-in-law and delayed all of their precious plans.

I almost swallowed my heart when I saw them waiting and could barely make eye contact with any of them, but they just watched in silence as the door was closed. Sister Theresa's office had a large desk set against a rather oppressive stained-glass window. On bright days, it would form a colourful halo around her head, but there was no sun shining that day, because the four people sat at the table in the corner, brought only darkness.

They were all sitting on one side and there was one chair on the opposite side, waiting for me. Sister Theresa went and sat behind her desk, and Adam dragged another chair over to the table, letting it scrape across the floor, forcing Elizabeth to wince and cover her delicate ears.

I could just imagine what they were thinking, *Insolent little bastard,* and I had to hold back a smile, as we sat down and faced them together.

Ruth shuffled awkwardly. "We had hoped to speak with you alone."

Adam beat me to the punch. "Anything you have to say to my sister, you can say to me."

"Right," Ruth swallowed. "Eve, I'm not sure if you've ever officially met Derek and Elizabeth before—"

"What's this about? Why are you all here?" I wasn't in the mood for pleasantries.

Ruth cleared her throat and looked at her husband, but he didn't seem inclined to speak, so she took the lead.

"We have a problem, and we need your help." Her porcelain skin started to turn pink. "To be quite frank, we did not foresee the fallout that would follow from your relationship with Noah ending."

"You mean you didn't reckon on him going around beating the shit out of everyone?"

Adam's response was laced with sarcasm. I gave him a warning look and at the same time, Sister Theresa cleared her throat, a wordless reminder for him to heed her previous advice.

"We thought that Noah had calmed down over these past few years," Ruth continued, unfazed. "But we realise now, that it was you."

"If you're planning on asking me what it takes to stop the darkness from taking over Noah, then I should tell you now, that's a conversation that Jane and I should probably have privately."

I looked over to the Greens and gave them an apologetic smile.

Derek looked ready to explode. "Jane will be his wife and she will be treated with respect!"

"Lovely. Remind me why you're all here again?" I raised my eyebrows at them.

"Noah needs to marry Jane!" Robert barked, turning even redder than Derek.

Ruth placed her hands on his, and took over again, bringing her special blend of calmness and coldness back to the table. "We, Founding Families have a plan. We map out our alliances, and Noah and Jane marrying forms part of a bigger picture," she smiled, as if that was a reasonable explanation.

"You mean avoiding inbreeding?" Adam smirked.

I gave him a nudge and he shrugged his shoulders at me innocently.

"So, what do you want from me?" I asked, interrupting, and taking the attention away from my brother.

"We believe that the only way that Noah will participate is if you are part of the plan, and we're here to propose an arrangement." Ruth's eyebrows twitched a little, suggesting that she wasn't quite as calm as she seemed.

My mouth opened but I was unable to form any words. I looked at Adam, and his blank expression suggested that he was just as confused as me, but I turned to Sister Theresa and saw that she looked absolutely furious. She, at least, seemed to know what was coming.

Ruth cleared her throat and brought my focus back to her.

"We want to give you your life back, Eve." They were kind words, but her smile sent chills down my spine. "You're such a talent, and you're missed at The Dome… and Noah misses you. We are offering for you to live in your flat and be with him…"

I shook my head in astonishment. "You just said that he must marry Jane."

"Yes, he must, and if he agrees to do so then he will be permitted to keep you… as his mistress."

She was calm. How could she say that to me and remain so calm?

Adam burst out laughing! "This has to be a joke?"

Robert slammed a hand on the table, and it jerked forward at the force. "This is no joke, young man, and it's not a decision we've come to lightly and there will be rules."

"Oh, please, do tell me these rules, Robert, I can't wait to hear them," I practically snorted.

"You will be with Noah, and you will continue to love him. He will be permitted to stay with you on some days, but he will be with Jane for the majority of the time. You will continue to meet his needs and you will be discrete about it."

He pointed at me, just to make himself clear.

"You will sing at The Dome and lead the life that you led with him before. But Jane will be his wife. She will be the one on his arm in public."

"And I'll be expected to go back to the shadows."

"Yes." He sat back and folded his arms.

There were times, in Bible studies when a passage seemed farfetched and I just couldn't quite take it in. I never really questioned or challenged them, because that was never the point of our studies; we were just supposed to absorb it. So, there had been moments in my life before, when I heard something that seemed beyond ridiculous, something that I didn't quite have the capacity to process, but nothing more so than what had just been put to me.

It wasn't just me, either. Adam leaned back in his chair and just gaped at them with his brows furrowed as he tried to make sense if it. Adam always had an answer for everything, but he met his match that day.

They sat there, saying nothing, but not looking in the least bit unfazed as they waited for my response. Eventually, my brain reconnected, and I managed to form some words.

"And what do Noah and Jane think about this?"

"Jane will do as she is asked!" Derek responded with a fist on the table.

"They don't know about this?" I was stunned, utterly stunned.

Ruth stepped back into the fray. "We've come to you first. If you agree to this, then I'm sure Noah will too."

"Fuck me, Adam. If this is what it means to have parents, then I'm glad we're orphans!"

He shook his head in disgust, as he edged closer to me. "That makes two of us."

"If you don't mind me asking…" Sister Theresa joined the conversation for the first time. "But as part of this arrangement of yours, what would happen to any children that Eve might conceive? Would they be welcomed into the family?"

My heart started to race again. Why would she think to ask that?

Robert almost jumped out of his seat, clearly enraged by the suggestion. "Eve will not have my son's children! That will be a condition. Noah will be expected to be a proper husband to Jane. She will have children. Eve won't."

That was like taking a bullet, and we were done. I glared right back at Robert, pushed down the bile that was starting to rise and spoke with as much firmness as I could muster, while my body was shaking all over. "Yes, well, thank you, but *Eve*, doesn't want to have anything to do with your arrangement! Are you aware that you're all fucking insane?"

I stood up and tried to step away, but Ruth stood too, reached across the table and grabbed my arm.

"What life do you think you're going to have, Eve? Do you think you'll have the chance to marry and have children?" She looked at me with sadness, but I knew it was all fake. "Every man out there will be too scared to go near you. And if anyone did, what do you think Noah would do to them?"

"He'll move on."

"You know that's not true. He won't let you go. You love him." More fake smiles. "It isn't perfect, but we're offering you a chance at happiness."

"This isn't about my happiness; this is about control. You can't control everything, and you don't control me!"

I snatched my arm out of her grasp and pulled Adam out of the room before he could say his piece too.

Of all the things I was expecting when I walked in the room, being asked to be a mistress was most definitely not on the list. Talk to Noah and try to get him on board, was number one. Go back to The Dome was on there too, what with me making them money, but mistress? They most definitely blind-sided me with that one.

They were offering me scraps. I was good enough to sleep with Noah, but not to marry him. They wanted me to keep him sane. To do what was necessary to keep him happy, and I was supposed to do it all without complaint while he went off and made babies with his wife. No fucking way!

Adam was glued to my side for the rest of the afternoon. Neither of us said much, but I knew his protective instincts were in overdrive. I was just in a bit of a haze. Neither of us could quite believe what had happened, and we just kept looking at each other and shaking our heads; repeatedly asking the other if we'd dreamed it.

We went to dinner, but I was still too wound up to eat, and just spent most of the time staring at my plate and asking myself how things got so fucked up. When I eventually pulled myself out of my own head, I noticed that Adam was constantly sending messages on his phone and had a rather lovely smile on his face.

He looked so adorable when he was happy, and I couldn't help but smile with him. "Go and see her. There's no point in us both being miserable."

He tried to act like he didn't know what I was talking about and put his phone back in his pocket.

"Go and see Meredith."

He looked down a little and laughed, then the adorable smile retuned as he got up and kissed me on the top of my head, before walking away.

I didn't really want to be around anyone other than Adam, but John, being the beautiful human that he is, kept me company for a bit, until the film came on. It was getting late, but I figured that Rose deserved her room to herself for a bit, so I settled into the sofa. I tried to stay awake, because I wanted to avoid dreaming, but eventually, I drifted off involuntarily, listening to the voices on the screen and the lies they told about happily ever after.

I woke with a start when I thought I heard a voice urgently saying my name. I brushed it off as just being the TV, until I felt hands on me.

"Wake up, Eve!" Rose shook me again and I jumped up in a panic. "Come with me, we need to go!"

My heart was beating out of control from the shock of her waking me, and it took me a few seconds to process what was happening, but when I did, the first thing that struck me were the tears in her eyes.

She pulled me along, and it was only when I almost stumbled that I saw the bag that she held in her other hand. It was an overnight bag — my overnight bag.

"What's going on? Where are we going?"

She didn't reply, she just pulled me quickly towards the door, and then to the police car waiting outside, with the rear door held open.

"Rose!" I demanded, as she pushed me inside.

She got in the car with me and handed me my ID card, gripping my hands firmly as she did. The door shut, the car started moving and Rose's tears fell.

"We're going to Havensmere General." She almost choked on the words.

Havensmere General — the hospital on The Other Side.

Fear took hold of me and I felt like my throat was about to seal shut, but I needed to speak. I needed to know. "Why?"

Rose looked down as more tears fell, then she drew in a sharp breath and forced out the words, "It's Adam."

16

The police car drove at speed towards the iron gates, and we were then ushered through them. I couldn't even focus on what was happening, so Rose took charge and kept pulling me along. The guards at the gate led us towards two police officers in Havensmere uniforms, and they opened the door to their car and once again, Rose pushed me in. They were our escort, or more specifically our guards, but I barely looked at them. I was barely blinking, barely thinking and barely breathing.

Once the car started moving, I finally found my ability to function. "What do we know?" I breathed out.

Rose was still holding my hand and I felt her grip tighten. "Adam and Meredith were attacked in the street."

Oh, God, no!

"By Noah?"

"I don't think so. I've only received a bit of information, but my understanding is that there were three of them, three masked men." Rose was afraid and she was never afraid. "Meredith was knocked to the ground and Adam..." she paused and closed her eyes, but the tears spilled over. "Adam was beaten up by them all."

I couldn't stop the cries escaping me. Adam, my Adam, my brother! This couldn't be happening.

"How bad is he?" The shaking started as the words came out.

"I honestly don't know. Sister Theresa went out with the infirmary ambulance, but she knew straight away that it was more serious than anything we could cope with!"

I broke down as the image of my brother covered in blood invaded my mind, and Rose undid her seatbelt and wrapped herself around me as I cried uncontrollably in her arms. I knew this would happen one day. Adam had spent five years winding people up knowing that he had the protection of the great, Noah Joyson. Everyone knew that we'd broken up and now somebody, three somebodies, had decided the time was right to teach him a lesson.

Suddenly I was angry.

"He shouldn't be here. We need to take him back to St Martins!" I raged. "They don't care about us here. They won't help him. We need to bring him home."

She held my gaze, and I felt the intensity of her words. "Eve, he needs to be here. We can't help him at St Martins right now. They will take care of him, they will," she assured me as she gripped my hands.

We sat silently for a few minutes and I just stared out of the window because it was the only thing to do. The Other Side was bright, everywhere was lit up, and it all just seemed a blur of colour as we quickly passed through. Though that could have been because of the tears.

"What about Meredith?" I felt bad that she had only just occurred to me.

"A bump to the head and a few grazes, that's all," she

assured me. "But she insisted on going with him and I believe she's going to be interviewed at the hospital."

I nodded, genuinely relieved for her, but then another thought hit me straight in the heart and I almost doubled over. "I told him to go out tonight. I told him that we didn't both need to be miserable and that he should go and see her…"

"Look at me!" Rose spoke with more force than I'd ever heard her use before. "This is not your fault, Eve. It's not."

I swallowed hard and shook my head at her because that was getting harder to believe. "I've been hearing that a lot lately."

We pulled up to the hospital and our doors were opened for us. Rose came around to my side and grabbed hold of my hand again. One of the police officers led the way, whilst the other walked behind us. I turned to look at him and he looked at me without any expression, as if I wasn't worthy of thought, and I couldn't help but scowl at him.

"Do they really think that we want to run off to find Mummy and Daddy?" I was speaking to Rose but loudly enough for the two men to hear.

Rose turned to him and apologised with her eyes, as she told me, "They're just doing their job, Eve."

The officers cleared the lift for us, and as they did, we became a spectacle for everyone to stare at. They knew who we were, it was clear from the robes that Rose wore, and I just glared right back at them all, making sure they could see my contempt for them. One of the officers spoke, checking which floor we needed to go to, and then he pressed a button. I watched the red numbers change, moving up one floor at a time at a painfully slow pace. It was far too slow and it gave me too much time to think.

"I can't lose him…"

Rose pulled me in and wrapped her arm around my waist, as the tears flowed freely, once more.

We were taken to a waiting room and Meredith jumped up as soon as I walked in. I grabbed hold of her, while Rose went over to Sister Alice for an update.

"Where is he?" I whispered urgently against Meredith's ear.

She pulled away so that we could speak properly. "I'm not sure exactly, they're checking him over, seeing what needs to be done and they won't let us in."

I was still holding her, and I could feel her trembling.

"He's on his own?" I asked, panicking again.

"Sister Theresa and Sergeant Legion are with him," Sister Alice clarified, trying to remain calm. "We don't know the extent of his injuries yet."

I was about to let go of Meredith, but she suddenly grabbed hold of my arm, looking me in the eyes as she spoke. "I need to speak to you… alone." Her eyes widened as if to convey the importance of her words.

I turned to one of the officers and gestured to the door. "Can we step outside for a moment?"

He looked at his colleague for conformation and then opened the door for us. Meredith pulled me a little further down the corridor, with the guard following close behind; close enough to hear. I scowled again, making my annoyance clear, but he just looked at me as if he was devoid of emotion like before, and he clearly wasn't going anywhere.

I turned back to Meredith and looked her over. She had a bruise and graze on her forehead and one of her hands was sporting a bandage, but other than that she looked relatively unscathed.

"Are you OK? What happened?"

She looked down and swallowed hard, and when she looked back up at me, I could see how afraid she still was.

"We just went out for a walk… that's all. We weren't even out for that long. Then all of a sudden we were just jumped on by three men!" Tears filled her eyes, and she started shaking again. "I got knocked down, but Adam was dragged into an alley and... and they all just started hitting and kicking him."

Neither of us could contain our cries, and I had to put my hands over my face and tightly squeeze my eyes shut, in order to escape the image of feet stamping on my brother, as he lay helplessly on the ground.

Meredith pulled my hands away and when I looked at her, I saw that her tears had been replaced by fear, once again. "That's what I told Sergeant Legion. That's what I was told to tell him."

I looked at her questioningly, but she continued before I could speak. "That's what the man who spoke to me told me to tell the police. What he told me to tell everyone… except you." She pushed back her sobs as she forced out her last words. "Because that's not what happened."

What was she talking about? My face asked the questions that my mouth was unable to articulate, and she held my hands tighter and spoke again.

"There were five of them…"

What the fuck? My heart slowly made its way up my throat.

"They dragged both of us into the alley. Three of them held Adam, one held me, and then the other stood in front of me and told me what I needed to do, what I needed to say," she said, as her voice started to crack. "Then I was thrown to the ground and my head was turned to face Adam, and that's when it started… that's when they attacked him!"

"Meredith…. what the hell?" I blurted out. It just didn't make sense. "Did you see them? Did you recognise his voice?"

"No… they were all in black and wearing balaclavas. But Eve, listen…" she said, and the fear was back in her eyes. "When they were making me watch… the man that spoke to me bent down and told me that there was something else that I needed to do."

"What?"

"I can still smell his breath…"

"Meredith… please…" I begged her.

She swallowed hard and drew in a deep breath. "He said to make sure that you get the message…"

She immediately clasped both hands over her mouth as she gagged.

"I don't understand… what message? What did he say?"

I could barely breathe.

"That's it," she said, shaking her head. "As they were beating him up, he said, 'make sure Eve gets this message' and then he told them to stop and they all just left!"

I played her words over in my head on repeat, trying to figure it out, and then my heart plummeted to the floor as it suddenly sunk in.

Adam was the message. Adam being hurt was the message. It was orchestrated, it was ordered, which meant that it was approved by The Council. There were five of them, and no doubt it was one man from each of the Founding Families. The attack wasn't about Adam. It was about me. It was about my refusal to go along with their plans.

I was burning up, and my stomach churned, making me feel like I would throw up there and then, so I closed my eyes and leaned against the wall and did my best to breathe through it.

"Adam said they asked you to do something." Her voice was almost a whisper.

"Please don't ask me, Meredith... please don't..." I breathed out, before struggling to draw more air in.

We heard heavy footsteps approaching, and I slowly turned to see Scott Legion walking towards us. He looked calm and professional, and if I had not still been in shock, then I think I would've hit him there and then. I wanted to hurt him. I wanted to hurt all of them, but I couldn't. I couldn't, because they had just shown me how far they were willing to go to get what they wanted, and I knew that beating up my brother was just the start.

Scott put his hand on my arm; the feeling repulsed me, and I looked down at it, before looking up at him with pure hatred written all over my face. He didn't miss it, but his only reaction was to calmly take his hand away. I never prayed, but I prayed in that moment for God to make my thoughts a reality, so that I could will him to die on the spot, writhing in pain.

"How are you, Eve?" he asked me in the way a decent policeman would ask. Except he wasn't. Nothing about him was decent.

"How is my brother?" I asked through gritted teeth.

He didn't even falter. "I believe they are bringing him out shortly." He turned to Meredith and asked, "Have you done everything you needed to, Meredith? I need to take you back."

Everything she "needed to," his words weren't lost on me. What a bastard! What a complete and utter bastard!

I clenched my fists and held them firmly against my side in order to stop myself from beating him senseless. I glanced at his hands, trying to see if he had been one of the five, but there were no marks on him. Then it occurred to me that he probably wouldn't dirty his hands on my brother.

"What are his injuries?"

"I don't have all of those details."

"Surely you need them, so that you know what to charge the people that did this with when you find them?" I glared at him, expressing my fight in the only way that I could.

"I assure you, Eve, that we'll do everything we can to apprehend the people responsible for this." He smiled, it was a rare sight and there was nothing genuine about it.

He turned to Meredith and became authoritative again. "Meredith, I need a moment alone with Eve. Please return to the waiting room and get your things."

Meredith looked at me and I gave her a slight nod, letting her know that I'd be OK, and she pulled me in for a hug before doing as she was told. Scott watched her walk away, but I never took my eyes off him, and as soon as Meredith was back in the room, he turned back to me and looked startled for a moment when he saw the anger radiating from me. I was glad of that, I wanted him to know, I wanted him to feel it and I wanted him to let the others know too.

Still, he was a Legion, and so he righted himself quickly, put his hand in his pocket and pulled out a mobile phone, which he then held out to me.

"You're going to need this."

I looked down at it; it wasn't my phone because I'd left that in the flat when I walked out and hadn't seen it since. It wasn't Adam's phone either, because his had a big crack down the screen. I looked up at him and he gestured with his eyes for me to take it.

"Why exactly do I need this?" I asked, as I took it from his hand.

"When it rings, you need to answer."

I couldn't believe what he was saying to me, and in front of a police officer from The Other Side too. I glanced at the officer, he was staring at the wall ahead, but there was no way that he wasn't listening, because Scott wasn't even attempting to be discrete. Fear blended with my anger at that point, because his indifference towards their officer, only served to remind me who had absolute power in The Beneath.

I swallowed hard and channelled the anger again. I didn't mind him seeing me angry, but I would never give him the satisfaction of seeing me scared.

"Of course… I wouldn't want anyone to have to leave me another message."

He was about to respond, but then we both turned as we heard the sound of wheels squeaking as they rolled along the floor at speed, with multiple footsteps hurrying along beside them. I knew straight away that it was him, I just felt it, but then I saw Sister Theresa amongst the doctors, and I ran to them, holding my breath.

I tried to get alongside them, but they ushered me out of the way, and all I saw was a mass of dark hair, machines, and tubes. They moved so quickly, it was hard to take everything in, but the thing I didn't miss was the tube coming out of his mouth and breathing for him.

I'd been pinned to the wall by the speed in which they passed, and I was about to collapse to my knees, when Sister Theresa put her arms around me. I could barely breathe, and I could hardly even see her through the tears that were blinding my eyes. It was bad. It was so bad. My knees started to buckle, and she guided me down to the floor.

"Oh, my God!"

She shushed me, gently. "It's not as bad as it looks, Eve."

"Can he breathe?" I choked out, as the words almost got

stuck. "That tube… can he not breathe for himself?"

"The doctors have heavily sedated him to aid his recovery, the apparatus is only temporary."

She was trying to reassure me, and I did my best to remind myself that Sister Theresa didn't lie.

"Come on, let's get you to Rose. They need a few minutes to get everything set up and then they'll come and talk to you," she said, as she tried to pull me up.

I stood shakily and she guided me back to the waiting room. I was crying, my blood felt like it was flowing too quickly, and I thought I was going to be sick. I just kept thinking that it couldn't be real. I was having a bad dream because the films were still on in the background and they were creeping into my thoughts.

That must be it. I must still be on the sofa in the TV room, because I couldn't be on The Other Side. Police officers went there because there was a collaboration between the forces, and really hurt or sick people went there, and I wasn't sick. I wasn't hurt. I closed my eyes tightly, hoping that I could wake myself up and that when I opened them, I'd be lying exactly where I was when I fell asleep.

Yet, when I opened them, I was still in the hospital corridor, still being guided towards the waiting room by Sister Theresa, and the officer who seemed familiar, but not, was no longer looking void of emotions, like I must have dreamed before. He was looking at me with sadness and concern.

Then I realised that something felt different and I put my hand behind my back and touched the phone in my pocket. Then I saw the dream, no, the memory of Adam being rushed past me. The door to the waiting room was opened and Rose got up from her seat and rushed to meet me. I tried to step forward, but a black fog started to take over my vision and two strong arms caught me from behind as I fell to the floor.

17

"She's not been taking care of herself," I heard a voice say. "I should have made sure she's been eating," the voice said.

It was Rose's voice.

I tried to follow it, and I tried to open my eyes and find my way back, but it was still so dark, and they felt too heavy.

"She's been under a lot of stress these past few weeks, doctor," Sister Theresa added. "She just needs to get her strength up."

"Eve? Eve… can you hear me?"

"Rose…" I swallowed, trying to lubricate my throat, as I managed to slowly force my eyes open.

It was too bright. I had to keep blinking, and my head was throbbing.

"Adam!" I cried out, as I bolted upright, making the room spin again.

"Slowly, Miss Matthews — you need to take it slowly," a woman's voice instructed. She was all in white, but she wasn't a nun, she was a doctor.

"I need to see my brother!" I argued as I tried to get off the bench.

She put her hands on my arms and guided me back down. "I understand, Miss Matthews, but you just fainted. You need to drink something, and I understand that you most likely need to eat something too."

Rose passed me a drink. They were all looking at me and I realised that I had no choice, so I held the cup for a moment, and then I quickly drank it when I realised just how thirsty I was. Then a sandwich was put in front of me, but I pushed it away.

"You need to eat," Rose insisted.

"No, I need to know how my brother is!" I tried to stand up again, but Rose held me.

"Eat something first…"

"No, Rose! I will eat anything you want me to eat, after I've seen my brother." She looked down a little, and guilt kicked at my heart. "I promise you I will eat after I see him."

They all looked at each other questioningly, and the doctor finally gave her approval, before reaching out to help me. I was dizzy and my legs felt weak, but I wasn't going to let that stop me, I needed to see him. I walked a couple of steps and suddenly felt like something was missing, but what? I reached for my back pocket and felt for the phone that I'd been given, but it wasn't there.

I started to panic and looked on the floor around me. I needed that phone. Then I heard a man clear his throat and I followed the sound towards the police officer that I'd seen before. We made eye contact, but then he looked down quickly, then he looked back at me, before looking down again.

I followed where his eyes led. He was standing with his hands behind his back, but he had moved one hand out a little to show me the phone that he held in it. I looked back up at him, concerned that he'd taken it from me, but he just nodded at me and followed us out of the room. I realised that it was him that caught me, and he must have grabbed the phone at the same time. Why would he do that?

We got to the door but then the doctor paused and turned to me. "You need to be prepared for what you're about to see. There are lots of machines and tubes, but mostly because of the sedation," she said, in a professional but reassuring manner. "It can be quite shocking to see."

I nodded weakly and continued to breathe deeply as the door opened. The first thing that struck me was the constant beeping sound, which I realised was the rhythmic beating of his heart. It was steady and it was peaceful, but it was still a machine. Then I heard the pump pushing the oxygen into his body and I wanted to be sick again. A blue curtain was closed around his bed and we slowly walked towards it. I had been so desperate to get to him, but as soon as I got into his room I could barely move. Seeing him would make it all real. I knew it was real, my head was still hurting too much for it to be a dream. Still, seeing him and touching him would destroy any hope I was still clinging onto, that it might not be.

I walked around the curtain and doubled over, and Rose rushed to me and lowered me to the floor, concerned that I was going to faint again. It wasn't that. I just couldn't breathe. The pain of seeing my brother covered in wires and bandages stopped the air flowing into my body. He looked so helpless and so lifeless, except for his chest which was moving up and down as the machine pumped air into his lungs.

The beeping... listen to the beeping, I told myself on repeat.

The beeping was his heartbeat, that was real. He was doing that by himself. He was keeping his heart beating and he wasn't giving up. I finally inhaled a deep breath and then let out a loud cry and burst into tears.

Rose wrapped her arms around me and held me tightly as I cried, but after a few minutes I gently pushed her away, took a deep breath in and wiped the tears away. I needed to be stronger. I needed to face it, all of it, and I needed to be strong in order to be able to deal with what would be coming next. I needed to be strong for Adam.

I looked at Rose and, understanding what was going on in my head, she gently helped me up. I turned to look at him and I forced myself to take him in. He was covered in bruises. His right forearm was in a cast and his left hand was bandaged. There didn't seem to be a part of him that hadn't been hurt. I wanted to touch him, but I was scared to hurt him, so I turned to the doctor and the tears fell once more.

"I understand that he looks bad, but your brother has actually had a lucky escape," she smiled, with assurance. "His injuries are significant, but not life threatening. There's nothing that won't heal, in time."

I let out a deep breath and looked at him again. I wanted to feel relieved, because what she told me was positive, but I couldn't, because he hadn't been lucky. It wasn't down to luck. It was down to the fact that the people that did it had been meticulous. They had a goal. They knew their objectives, and they knew just the right amount of damage to inflict. It wasn't a random attack, or a mugging gone wrong because things like that rarely happened in The Beneath, and it wasn't someone looking to settle a grudge. The people that had a grudge against him, wouldn't have been as controlled.

It was exactly what Meredith had told me. It was a message.

I tried to swallow but my mouth was too dry. I managed to croak out, "Can he hear me?"

"Not while he's under sedation," the doctor told me. "We sedated him because we couldn't tell the extent of his injuries and we were concerned about swelling on the brain." She saw the alarm in my eyes. "There's none… we plan to bring him out of the sedation tomorrow."

"How long will he need to stay here?"

"We will reassess again once he's out of the sedation, but I anticipate that it will be a few days before he'll be well enough to be transported to St Martins."

"A few days?" My body started to heat up again. "So, I'm just supposed to leave him here?"

"Eve…" Sister Theresa moved towards me. "You can stay with him. Rose brought some things for you and there's a bed there."

She pointed towards the pull up bed in the corner, near the window and then Rose put my bag on it — the bag I saw her carrying when she woke me up.

"There's a private bathroom through there." The doctor pointed towards the door in the other corner. "And of course, it's our practice to have two guards at your door."

I laughed dryly and shook my head. "No expense spared for the orphans, hey? Are two guards really necessary?"

She cleared her throat. "Well…. there are two of you."

"I don't think he's going anywhere, do you?" I gestured towards Adam.

She probably didn't deserve it, in fact, she definitely didn't deserve it. She was looking after my brother and the guards were doing their job. In truth, it wasn't really them that I was mad at, but they were there, they were strangers, and they were part of the world that had put us in this fucking situation in the first place. I needed to vent my anger somehow and they were an easy target. My own people hurt my brother in order to hurt me, and there was nothing that I could do to them in return.

"Eve…" Rose started to walk over to me.

I didn't need her to say any more and I gave her a look that communicated just that. I knew I was being unreasonable, she didn't need to tell me, so instead, she held out the sandwich and led me to the chair by the bed. She gave me a look, one she'd clearly been learning from Sister Theresa and I knew there was no point in arguing. I promised her I'd eat, and it was time to make good on that promise.

Sister Theresa led the doctor and officers towards the door and started to speak with them, but not very quietly. "She won't be any bother, and she's actually a very nice young woman, she's just very protective of her brother."

I forced down a mouthful of the somewhat dry sandwich. "You are aware that I can hear you?"

Sister Theresa turned to me and raised an eyebrow. She knew that I could hear her, she had meant for me to. Then she turned back to the others and said, "I assure you that he is her only concern."

The doctor left and the guards stepped out of the room, leaving the door open. I'd eaten the sandwich, which didn't improve the more I ate it, and looked around the room for a drink. Apparently, we got a private bathroom but no water machine.

I stood up and walked to the door.

"Where are you going?" Rose frowned a little.

"I need some water."

"I'll go," she said moving towards the door, but I waved her off.

"It's fine," I told her, continuing on my path. I needed to go and not just for the water. I needed to get that phone back.

I stood in the doorway and both guards looked at me, so I

turned to the one that held my phone and asked him if there was a water machine anywhere. He nodded to his right, gesturing for me to follow, and I did so dutifully, as he walked along the corridor and turned left. The water machine was there, and we were conveniently out of sight of the other guard. I filled up three cups of water, put them on top of the cooler, and then turned to him with my hand out, only to find that he already held the phone in his hand, ready for me to take.

I studied his face as I took it, but he'd gone back to being the blank slate that I'd first given the evil eye to when we arrived. Any hint of concern that I thought I'd seen in the corridor was now gone, but then I had been a bit of a bitch.

I took the phone and put it back into my pocket. "Thank you for catching me."

He nodded.

I picked up the drinks and turned back to him, expecting him to start walking back, but he didn't. He looked awkward, his Adam's apple was moving with the force, and then he looked to the side a little. Whatever he wanted to say, he was clearly struggling with it.

"I'm Officer Southwold… Ethan," he looked at me expectantly, as if that would mean something to me. It didn't, but I nodded at him in acknowledgment. "My partner is Officer Reynolds," he continued, "and we've been assigned to you and your brother for the duration of your stay. There will only be one of us on at a time, not two — your brother is not considered a flight risk."

My laughter interrupted him momentarily, but then he continued, "I will be taking the day shift, Officer Reynolds will be taking the night, and if you have questions at any point please feel free to direct them to either of us."

I couldn't help but shake my head in disbelief. Did they

really consider me a flight risk? I looked him squarely in the eyes. "Officer Southwold, did you say?"

He nodded in reply.

I glared at him. "I'm here because my brother was attacked tonight. I'm staying with him because he's my brother, my full blood brother and in my world that's a pretty big deal. I will stay here with him because his safety means everything to me, and when he's ready to go home, I will go home with him."

He looked down a little before looking right at me again. "I understand that you're not about to try and run off, Miss Matthews," he told me. "But I think we both know that the reason you're here is a little more complicated than that."

I was ready to tell him to mind his business. I knew he'd heard what had been said earlier, but it was nothing to do with him, and he could shove his self-righteousness up his arse! I didn't get the chance though, because he stood to the side and gestured for me to walk ahead of him, indicating that our conversation was over.

When I walked into the room Rose and Sister Theresa were standing at the bottom of Adam's bed with their hands entwined, and their eyes closed in prayer. They pulled away when they saw me, and I handed them both a drink. Then I perched on the edge of Adam's bed and I reached out and stroked his hair. It was a small, gentle action but as I did it, I remembered the last time I touched him like that. It had been when he slept soundly having been knocked out by some seriously heavy painkillers after Seb broke his nose.

I remembered how I sat by his bed and then I remembered his head resting on my lap in the back of Noah's car. A fresh wave of pain then hit me, as I remembered Noah's hand reaching out to me, reassuring me, and trying to take the pain away. Then my mind took me back to how he held me the last time he saw me. How he held me tight and refused to let me go.

"Eve, would you join us in prayer?" Sister Theresa asked, sensing that I was lost in my thoughts. "I know it's not something you generally partake in, and it may not give you answers, but you may perhaps find guidance."

I turned to her, she was smiling and held her hand out in hope.

"That won't be necessary." She lowered her hand a little. "I know why this happened and I know what needs to be done to make sure it doesn't happen again."

Rose stepped forward with a frown on her face. "Eve, I know you blame yourself, but…"

She paused when I sat up a little and took the phone out of my pocket and dropped it into the chair next to the bed. She looked at it, and then her frown deepened.

"Where did you get that?"

I let out a deep sigh. "A gift from Sergeant Scott Legion. When it rings, I'm supposed to answer."

Sister Theresa put her head down, walked over to my bed and let out a deep sigh as she slowly lowered herself down. Rose looked between us both and gave me a questioning look. I hadn't had a chance to tell her about my meeting with the Joysons and Greens. She'd been busy, I'd given her space and I didn't know how to say the words out loud.

"What's going on?" She shook as she spoke the words.

Tears pricked at my eyes. "This was a message, Rose."

"No, Eve, it was a vile attack by three—"

"Five," I said, interrupting her. "There were five of them." Her hand went to her mouth in shock.

"Meredith told the police that there were three because that's what one of the five told her to tell them," I continued. "But they told her to tell me the truth and…"

I paused to swallow down the sobs that were desperate to escape, then I sucked in as much air as I could and exhaled deeply.

"They told her to make sure that I got the message."

"What message?" Rose asked, in shock.

I could no longer hold back the tears as I gestured towards Adam. "This message! I told them that they couldn't control me this morning, Rose... and this is how they've chosen to teach me that I was wrong."

"What are you talking about?"

I turned to Sister Theresa and she looked right at me with acceptance and contempt, not for me, but for what she knew was the truth. She knew what The Council were capable of.

"Could you tell her, please?" I asked her, and then I went into the private bathroom, sat on the perfectly white, spotless floor, and wept my dirty, orphan tears.

18

*W*hen Rose came into the bathroom a few minutes later she was frantic, and she was furious. More furious than I ever thought her capable of.

"You can't agree to this, Eve, you can't!"

"This was my warning after refusing them once, Rose. What do you think will happen if I do it again?" I challenged her. "Shall we start planning his funeral now?"

She argued with me and I'd argued right back. She loved me and she didn't want me accepting the half-life that they were offering me, but I loved Adam and I would do what was necessary to keep him safe. I always had and I always would. Rose knew that, and so she let go of her anger and started to plead with me instead, hoping she could pull on my heartstrings.

It didn't work though, because I wasn't being driven by my brain or by stubbornness. I was already following my heart, and deep down she knew that.

"Rose, I've spent the last five years being in love with Noah. I'm still in love with Noah." I shook my head, trying to make her see. "I just need to focus on him and try to forget about his—"

"Wife?" she answered for me, with her hands on her hips.

Don't judge me Rose. Please don't judge me.

"Well, at least as his whore I won't be expected to go around for family dinners anymore," I replied, giving a bitter laugh.

"It's so unfair, Eve. You cannot live like that, it'll be torture!"

I couldn't help but laugh at that, because what part of our lives had ever been fair?

"Rose, you of all people should know that life isn't fair." She rolled her eyes at me. "Perhaps this is my test..."

"Don't use God against me! You don't believe that!" Her voice raised in anger again.

"Perhaps not, but you do, so maybe you should find solace in that?" I argued back, but then I couldn't take the pain in her eyes, and so I left her there and went to sit in the chair next to Adam's bed, making sure the phone was in reach.

"I think it's time for us to leave," Sister Theresa said gently as Rose emerged from the bathroom a few minutes later; her eyes looking redder than when I left her.

Sister Theresa put her hand on my shoulder. "I'm not sure if we can visit, but I can call the hospital and will keep in touch," she told me, and she placed a gentle kiss on my head. Then she moved over to Adam and gently kissed him. "Keep fighting Adam, keep fighting."

Rose went over to him next, kissed him too and then whispered something so quietly that I couldn't hear it. Then she walked over to me, smiled, took hold of my hand and gave it a squeeze. That was her way of telling me that I was forgiven.

After they left, I just sat in the chair and watched Adam, constantly hoping that he'd give me a sign that he was there, even though I knew that wasn't going to happen. I'd seen what a strong sedative did before, and I wasn't going to get anything from him until it wore off. So, I studied the monitors instead. I looked at all the numbers and stats, memorising what they should be and watching for any slight change. I did that for hours, and when my eyes got too tired, I sat back in the chair, closed them, and tapped my finger to the rhythm of the beeping — to the rhythm of his heart.

I woke up when the morning sun shone brightly into the room, and as my eyes opened, I had to shield them until they adjusted. I tried to move but was hit by a twinge of pain in my neck, and as I became aware of my surroundings, I realised that I had fallen asleep in the chair. There was a blanket on me, which I hadn't put there. I guess a nurse did it when they came in to see him during the night.

My legs were sore from having been bent awkwardly, and I had to slowly move them down to the floor before I stood up and tried to straighten myself out. I checked the phone, there were no missed calls. Then I went over to the monitors and saw that there was no change, everything was just as it had been when I fell asleep, including Adam, who was lying in the exact same position as when I last looked at him.

I still couldn't believe this had happened, that they would actually do this. I'd accused them of being controlling but I still didn't think they would do something like this. The Council were known for determining and enforcing punishments, but I didn't know they used these tactics to control and manipulate too; but then I guess people didn't talk about it once the message had been received. There was no doubt in my mind that this was about coercion as opposed to punishment. The level of Adam's injuries had been calculated. It was a taste of what would come if I didn't bend to their will and I had no doubt that worse would follow if I continued to resist.

I turned when I heard footsteps. It was another doctor, a man this time; Dr Thompson he informed me. He needed to take some stats from Adam before they started bringing him out of the sedation and so I decided to use the opportunity to take a shower and change. I didn't want to watch them poking and prodding him and I realised that I didn't smell too great either. Rose had packed everything that I needed, and I felt a twinge of guilt over how I had treated her the night before. She only wanted to do what she thought was right by me, I knew that, just like she knew that I only wanted to do what was right by Adam.

After I showered, I stood and looked at myself in the mirror. The shower had been hot, so I had to wipe the steam away and it took a few minutes for my blurry face to come into focus. "All of this hassle for me," I said quietly, as my image became clearer.

All of this because Noah loved me. I used to think that made me the luckiest person in the world, even when it meant dealing with his darker needs. Noah had been selfish, he had been utterly careless with my heart, and when he dropped it, it broke into a thousand pieces, and I thought my life was over. I wanted to hate him but instead, I found myself yearning for him. I hadn't fallen out of love with him and I couldn't imagine that I ever would, and now he was being handed back to me by the very people that took him away.

I started to wonder why I hadn't just accepted their offer in the first place. I would have what I wanted. We would be together again, and I would have the life that I loved back. Everything would be as it was before, except for the fact that Noah would be married to someone else and I'd be hidden away. On the nights that he wasn't with me he would be in another home, with another woman and he would be having sex with her.

Just the thought of it had me leaning over the sink and gasping for air, and I was reminded why I had refused them. It was because of that part. Sharing him and not knowing how she made him feel, always wondering whether he was enjoying her, and whether he would call out her name when he came inside her, like he did with me. Watching her grow his baby. A baby that should be mine, and then standing on the outside looking in, as they raised their family — something that I would never have. That part was going to kill me.

When I left the bathroom there was another doctor in the room and some breakfast had been brought in for me and put on the side. The second doctor didn't introduce himself and I didn't care enough to ask, but they told me that they were satisfied, and they would begin the process of bringing Adam out of the sedation, and that I should expect him to wake up in a few hours. I thanked them and as I watched them leave, I caught a glimpse of the guard. The shift change had clearly occurred as Officer Southwold was back, and when our eyes met, he looked away immediately. Obviously, I wasn't considered worthy enough of his courtesy that morning.

I sat in the chair, ate the toast and drank the coffee; it tasted like shit, but it was wet, and it was caffeine, so I swallowed it down. Then I just sat watching Adam and waited for him to wake up. He no longer had the breathing apparatus and so when I watched his chest moving up and down, I felt reassured that it was him. That he was breathing for himself.

I started to relax in the knowledge that he would be OK and then I started to get bored, and as my mind was no longer frantic with worry, it created space for the anxiety to take over in full force. I kept looking at the phone, waiting for it to ring and wondering whose voice I would hear when I answered it.

There were no distractions, there wasn't even a magazine for me to read, so I decided to start counting his heartbeats. I counted each beep until I reached one hundred and then I'd start again. However, that soon got boring too and it didn't subdue the churning in my stomach, so I stood up and decided to go and look out of the window, for the first time.

So, this is The Other Side.

Last night it had looked like a blur of lights. Yet in the light of day, it was just bricks, mortar, and tall, glass-lined buildings, that seemed to glisten in the morning sun. We didn't have those in The Beneath. It looked pretty impressive, but then I didn't have a lot to compare it to. I guess it's no wonder that they think we might want to escape our confines and live here, walking their clean streets and enjoying their freedoms. Even looking at it from above, like I was, it still held no appeal to me. Except for the last part; their freedom. That was becoming something that I did envy.

I was staring at the block of flats opposite me and could see that people were waking up and opening their curtains, letting the light of their world in. It was the start of a new day for them and I started to imagine all the things that they would be doing, but then the phone rang making me jump out of my skin.

I'd put it on the ledge so that I wouldn't miss it if it rang, and as I reached out with my hand shaking, I saw the words, 'Answer Me' on the screen. They saved the number as 'Answer Me' — the complete pricks! The anxiety that had been crippling me left and a determined anger took its place.

"Yes," I said with venom, hoping that the poison would seep through.

"Hello, Eve," Ruth replied with warmth. So, it was Ruth. It could have been worse.

"Ruth…" I replied with a coldness that I hoped she could feel. "Did you draw the short straw, or did you volunteer?"

"I understand that you're angry, should we rearrange for a better time to speak?" she asked with an air of professionalism.

"No. There's no point in delaying the inevitable, is there?"

She cleared her throat a little, she sounded poised, but I could feel her nerves radiating through the phone. "How is Adam?"

"Don't you even say his name! You know how he is!" I raged at her. "Who was it? David? Rory? Or one of your nephews? Whoever it was, you can tell them and the rest, that it was a job well done."

I was shaking with rage and breathing rapidly, but I knew that wasn't how the conversation could continue, so I put the phone down for a moment and tried to compose myself.

"Eve?" I heard Ruth say as I put the phone back to my ear.

"Still here…" I replied, then I reminded myself of the words that I should have listened to years ago; *keep your head, Eve.*

"Believe me, I am sorry that it came to this… but I assume that the message was clear? I assume that you understand?"

"Yes, I do. Your message was received loud and clear."

"When will you be returning home?" she asked, her business-like tone was back.

"They think he can be transferred in a few days," I swallowed hard and reminded myself to keep breathing.

"That's good. I'd appreciate it if you could contact me

using this phone on your return, so that we can arrange a meeting. It would be good to readdress the matter we discussed yesterday morning as soon as possible."

She was so cool, so in control, and I wanted to knock her off the pedestal that she had placed herself upon. "Still filling beds in the infirmary, is he?"

Bitch didn't rise to the bait.

"I'd like to be able to end this conversation with the understanding that you will be more agreeable to our offer this time." So calm. So cold. "That would be a good message for me to be able to pass on."

More messages. The venom returned. "I never realised what a cold bitch you are, Ruth, how did I miss that?"

"Eve…" she sighed, "please work with me here. Will you agree, yes or no?"

I swallowed hard and I paused. I knew what I was going to say because I decided the minute that I found out what really happened to Adam. Yet, the fighter in me, the orphan in me, and the part of me that I shared with Adam, couldn't let them have it without putting up a bit of a fight.

"Yes, or no, Eve?"

My heart was pounding, and I had to fight with myself to force out the word, "Yes."

Ruth breathed a sigh of relief and I heard her start to speak, but I ended the call and dropped the phone onto the bed. They had their answer and nothing more needed to be said until I had to meet them again.

I turned my back to the wall, leaned against it, and closed my eyes. This was happening, this was really happening. I was so nervous about what was to come next. I was going to have to face the people that hurt my brother. Or at least the ones that ordered it, and I was going to have to do it without showing them how much I wanted them all dead! Then there was Noah. I had no idea how he would react. I knew he wanted to be with me, but not like that. He would never have wanted that for me.

I slowly opened my eyes; I was now facing the door, that was always open, and Officer Southwold was standing on the other side of the corridor facing me. He looked right at me and I held his gaze. I knew that my expression was pretty blank, like his usually was, only it wasn't this time. He looked concerned, perhaps even angry and I just continued to look at him in my drained and emotionless state, until I heard Adam.

He was slowly waking up and I ran straight over to him and pressed the button to get the attention of the nurse.

"Adam, it's Eve, can you hear me?" His eyes were fluttering but he didn't respond. "Adam…" I stroked his left arm, and his eyes opened.

He was struggling to focus, and he looked like he was about to try to sit up, so I gently guided him back down. "Be still, Adam, don't try to move yet. You're in the hospital. You've been hurt, but you're going to be OK now." The tears fell, and my voice cracked as I told him quietly, "This won't happen again."

"Eve?" he croaked out.

"It's me, I'm here." I wiped the tears away and tried to put a smile on my face for him.

Then the nurse came in and started to talk to him and explain where he was, but he seemed too out of it to take it in. She told me that she needed to do some more assessments and then said something about a catheter, so I reassured Adam that I would be right back.

"Is there anywhere I can get a decent cup of coffee?" I asked Officer Southwold, as I stepped into the corridor. "I assume my money works here?"

He glanced into the room and thought for a moment, but then nodded and led me to the lift. Once again, he made sure that nobody else came in and I received the curious stares from the people of The Other Side.

"Who are you trying to protect? Me or them?" I asked him, with a small smile. It was easier to smile now that Adam was awake. He however, said nothing. "I never knew that I was so scary."

His wall of silence was unbreakable, but I thought I saw a slight smile, and then the door opened, and he led us out, this time staying right by my side.

Once at the café, we joined the queue and I again became a spectacle for people to stare at. I wasn't sure how they knew that I was from The Beneath without the nuns around me, but then if I was some sort of criminal I would've been in cuffs. So, I guess it was fairly easy for them to put the dots together.

One older lady in particular sat staring at me quite openly. She was sitting with a little boy, whom I took to be her grandson, and when I looked at him, I did a double take because he reminded me so much of a little Adam. I smiled at him and he smiled back, and then much to the older lady's alarm, he ran over to me and tugged on my hand.

"Hello," he giggled.

"Hello," I chuckled back, but then he was ushered back to his table and I was given the evilest of looks, by his dear grandma.

"It's OK," I told her with a smile. "We don't eat children in The Beneath." Then my smile soured. "We just take care of the ones you abandon."

She tutted at me, walked away and my smile widened. I'd been feeling so powerless and that tiny, insignificant, and potentially uncalled for moment, gave me the tiniest feeling of power back.

Officer Southwold cleared his throat and he gestured for me to move forward in the queue.

"I thought you weren't scary?" he asked in a hushed voice.

"I guess I'm becoming a product of my life."

I stood in the queue, looking at the back of the head of the woman in front of me. She had great hair and I couldn't help but wonder who cut it.

When we got back into the room, the doctor was with Adam explaining what his injuries were and what the next steps would be. Adam smiled at me and I went and sat on the bed with him, pleased to see that he seemed so much more awake than when I left him. We both listened as the doctor talked and as soon as they left, I turned to him and gently embraced him.

"Ouch!"

"Sorry. Is there anywhere that doesn't hurt?"

"I don't think so…" he said, groaning a little. "The doctors said that Meredith isn't here, did she get hurt too?" he asked me with concern.

"She just had a bit of a bump to the head and a graze, that's all," I reassured him. "She came with you in the ambulance, but they took her home again."

He smiled, relieved that she was OK, but then he looked at me and his smile faded. "There's something really important that I need to ask you."

My heart started to pound uncomfortably. He was going to ask me about the attack. I took a deep breath, but then he smiled again, and asked, "Am I still pretty?"

I let out my breath and smiled right back at him. He was still Adam. He was still my cocky little brother.

"You look almost as good as you did yesterday morning," I told him, laughing a little.

"Gorgeous, then!" he beamed.

I shook my head a little whilst smiling at him, it was always hard not to smile when Adam smiled, but I couldn't keep the fear from finding its way back in, and my heart pounded once more as I plucked up the courage to ask him, "What do you remember?"

"It's a bit blurry really... I remember that I was Meredith and that there were men all in black... but that's it," he told me, and it was clear that he was trying to focus his thoughts and remember more, but then he chuckled a little, and added, "I suppose I've had this coming for a while, haven't I?"

I stood up and walked away from him but soon felt so dizzy that I thought that I might faint again. Pausing for a moment, I then went over to my bed and sat down, resting my elbows on my legs, and my head in my hands.

"Eve... what are you afraid to tell me?"

God, I could never hide anything from him.

"Come here." He reached out his bandaged hand.

I stood up and slowly walked over to him, but I didn't take his hand. I stopped and stood at the foot of his bed instead and held onto the rail for support. I looked at him and the tears spilled out of me.

"This wasn't your fault, Adam... this wasn't because of you... It was because of me."

"What do you mean?" His face scrunched a little, and he gestured for me to come and take his hand again. "Why would this be your fault? There's so many people that have wanted to slap me, for years."

I went over to him, perched on the bed and I gently held his injured hand. "Do you remember what happened yesterday morning?" I asked him, and he looked away for a moment so that he could think.

"You mean our visit from the parents from hell?" he

asked, smirking a little, but then he saw me look down in shame and his smile faded. "You think this was them?"

"It was them," I told him shakily, unable to meet his eye.

"Come on… no, Eve. You don't know that…"

"I do, Adam. I know, because they told Meredith to tell me that this was a message. There were five of them, Adam — one from each of the families, no doubt."

He looked like he was going to try to argue, but I put my hand up to him to stop him.

"Sergeant Legion gave me a phone." I got up to show it to him. "Ruth has already called. This is my fault, and I am so, so sorry!"

I burst into tears and leaned into him. He remained quiet as he let me cry for a few minutes with his hand gently resting on my head, but then he spoke. "They did this to punish you for telling them where to stick their fucking ridiculous arrangement, didn't they?"

I took a deep breath, raised my head, wiped my tears away and then I looked him right in the eyes. "It wasn't a punishment, Adam, it was a warning," I told him through freshly falling tears.

He looked down for a moment. "A warning of what will come if you refuse them again?" he asked, and I nodded a little in reply. "They're not going to give up, are they?" He swallowed hard before looking right at me. "You said Ruth already called?"

I nodded again, then I looked away from him and he squeezed my hand tighter.

"Tell me you didn't agree to it," he demanded, and I put my head down as more tears fell. "Eve… Tell me that you didn't agree to it."

I pulled back my hand, moved away from the bed, and then I slowly turned to face him. "Of course, I did."

"No! You can't. It's insane, you said so yourself," he argued as his own tears fell. "Please, don't do this for me. I won't let you do this for me."

"Do you think I could live with myself if they hurt you again, or if they killed you because of me?"

Adam burst into tears. It was a rare sight to see my little brother so vulnerable and it made me rush over to his side and cry along with him. We stayed like that for a few minutes, both of us crying as I gently held him so that I didn't cause him more pain.

"Please, don't do this…" he pleaded, as he held me close.

I pulled away from him so that I could look at him and then I leaned down and kissed his forehead, and for once, he didn't pull away.

"It will be OK. I love Noah and he loves me… we'll figure the rest out," I said, shrugging a little as if it wasn't the big deal that it was.

Adam looked like he was going to argue again, but I stopped him.

"There's nothing you can say to change my mind. I made you a promise when I was four years old that I would always protect you and I don't intend to break that promise now."

He didn't try to argue again, because he knew that when I pulled that card out, there was no point. I made that promise when I was four and when I didn't know what it meant, but since then, I've walked that line knowingly and whole heartedly.

Instead, he gave me the silent treatment and so, I went to sit on my own bed and just stared out of the window. After a while, I looked over to him and saw that he was sleeping peacefully. I walked over to him and took hold of his hand. He was out cold, so I took advantage of the moment.

"Thank you for loving me, Adam, and thank you for

trying to fight for me… but it's my job to fight for you," I told him, as I placed a kiss on his head.

He slept a lot for the rest of that afternoon and when we did speak, we avoided talking about it anymore. I could tell that it was eating at him, but he knew that he couldn't change things. Later in the evening, the doctors came back to tell us that he could leave in two days. He smiled at them with gratitude, but as soon as they left, he turned to me and the smile faded, because he knew what I would do when we got back.

I slept in the bed that night. It took a while to switch off because now that Adam was no longer attached to a heart monitor, I didn't have the rhythmic and robotic beating of his heart to drown out the noise coming from the rest of the hospital. It was busy and it was noisy, and it was made worse by the constantly open door. Adam had been given sleeping pills to help him rest and I eventually fell asleep out of sheer emotional and physical exhaustion.

When I woke the next morning, the sun was blinding me again. As I started to focus on the room, my other senses came to life, and I became aware of the aroma of coffee — nice coffee. I sat up and looked at the windowsill next to my bed and reached out to pick up the hot cup of coffee. It was from the same café I went to yesterday, and as I took a sip, I discovered that it was exactly the same drink as the one that I had ordered for myself. I stood up and walked over to Adam with the cup in hand, and as I passed the open door, I gave Officer Southwold a small smile in thanks, and he gave a small nod in return.

The last days spent in the hospital were long and drawn out and we were both getting cabin fever. We were unable to discuss the elephant in the room and so all we could do was make small talk. The only light relief was when I found a book trolley in the hallway, which I noticed held a copy of

Pinocchio. I asked Officer Southwold if I could borrow it, he gave me an amused smile in response, and I had taken it back to Adam smiling brightly.

I read it to him while he was drifting off to sleep each night, just like I did when he was little, and each morning I woke up to a hot cup of coffee waiting next to my bed.

19

*S*ister Francis arrived not long after I'd showered, and I was surprised to see that she was unaccompanied. When I questioned her, she told me that the infirmary was busy in a very abrupt and disapproving manner. My eyes widened as I turned to Adam; Sister Francis, or the 'Jolly Nun' as we often called her, was always smiling, always laughing, even if she was just greeting you in the hall, she would do so with a laugh. Unfortunately, I was well aware who it was that had wiped the smile from her lovely round face.

Instead of feeling shame, it just made me more determined. People may not have been aware, but I took on the role of protecting The Beneath from Noah's dark side when I was sixteen, and I wanted to make it all stop. I didn't want the violence, not against my brother and not against anyone else either. Although, there were a few people that I didn't give a fuck about being hurt, but unfortunately, they were untouchable.

The nurses helped transfer Adam onto the stretcher, and then Officer Southwold escorted us to the ambulance bay.

Sister Francis seemed to be a bit jollier again in his presence, and she was chatting away with him in the lift. I hadn't really been looking at her, but Adam gave me a nudge and used his eyes to tell me to, and when I did, I realised that she was blushing! I smiled back at him and then looked at Officer Southwold properly for the first time since I met him. I suppose he was good looking, he had dark hair and eyes, much like Adam and me, but perhaps a little lighter and definitely minus the eyelashes and lips. He was tall and well-built and I'm sure that he got his fair share of women. He was also in a uniform and apparently, that suited Sister Francis down to the ground.

He helped us lift Adam into the back of the ambulance and then Sister Francis walked around to the driver's side, and he walked with me to the passenger door. I reached out to the handle and started to open it, but as I did, he put his hand on mine and pushed it closed again. He looked like he was having a serious internal battle, and clearly didn't know if he should say whatever it was that he wanted to, so I took the pressure off him by thanking him for the coffee that he'd left for me each morning.

He nodded a little and then asked apprehensively, "Are you going to be OK?"

"I'm not your problem Officer—"

"Ethan… my name is Ethan."

"I'm not your problem, Ethan. Once I'm through those gates you don't need to think about me ever again." He still looked torn, so I added, "And yes, I'll be fine… thank you for asking."

I smiled at him and then I climbed into the ambulance, shut the door and watched him from the wing mirror as we drove away behind our police escort. I saw him lower his head for a moment, but then he stood upright and watched us go until we were out of sight. I knew that he was listening to our conversations in the hospital, and I had been sitting there, thinking how it all must've been a great source of entertainment for him. Yet, it would seem that I underestimated Officer Ethan Southwold.

When we got to the wall, I was taken aback by how oppressive the gates looked. I hadn't paid attention to them the night Rose and I left, but they were old, heavy, impenetrable — unless you had the cash to bribe the guards. They were also noisy and tortuously slow moving. They creaked and complained as if it was painful for them to open for us, and even though I was going back to my home, those gates made me feel completely unwelcome.

My stomach churned with every creak and I realised that I was afraid. I was afraid to go through them and face what was coming next. I was afraid to see Noah, afraid of what he had done, of what he might do, and of not being able to compose myself when I saw him — and most of all, when I saw them.

I was too nervous to call Ruth, or 'Cold Bitch', which was what her number was now stored in the phone as. I preferred that much more to 'Answer Me'. I sent her a text message as soon as the gates closed behind us, and she replied immediately letting me know that a car would be collecting me from St Martins in two hours.

Two hours. They didn't waste much time. Two hours until I'd have to sit in a room with them again, and two hours until I saw Noah — my broken and lost Noah.

When we got to the infirmary we were taken to a private room. I gave them some space while they got Adam ready and assessed him for themselves and I used the time to look around the infirmary. It was busy and I couldn't escape the guilt. There were beds full of men showing various levels of injury, and all because the man that I loved had fallen apart, without me. I was the cure, and I was the glue that held the broken bits of him together.

People thought he was a bully. A violent thug that took his temper out on anyone that was unlucky enough to cross his path. A privileged, Founding Family Trueborn that was never held accountable for his actions. I understood that, and from the outside that's exactly how it looked.

Yet, to me, he was a beautiful soul that had a darkness inside him. A darkness born out of the pressures and constraints that his family put on him. He was a man born into power who had no power over the most important aspect of his life. He wasn't alone, because that was how it was in his family — in all their families, and most of them toed the line and played their parts, but it drove Noah to despair.

I couldn't look any of the patients in the eye and so I decided to turn around and go back to Adam, and as I did, I saw Rose walking onto the ward. We locked eyes and she smiled at me because Rose never held a grudge, and the relief I felt made me instantly feel lighter. We walked towards each other and embraced, squeezing each other, and when I whispered an apology into her ear, she held me even tighter.

"I should be able to get a break in about an hour and a half," she told me, "shall we have a cup of tea?"

"Oh…" I suddenly felt nervous. "I need to be somewhere."

She looked down and stepped back a little. "Right…" she replied, nodding in understanding. "So soon?"

"Rose…"

"I don't want to argue with you. I understand, and I will support you."

"Have you been speaking with Sister Theresa, by any chance?" I teased.

She had, of course. They'd talked it through, they'd

prayed, and they'd come to the conclusion that there was no choice but to accept it. What other choice would I have been able to make? So, instead of fighting me, Rose decided that the best thing that she could do was to support me. To be there for me without judgement or condescension whenever I needed it. Because she knew that there would be many times when I would need her… when I'd need her to hold me, without saying a word and make everything good again, in the way that only she could.

I left her and went back to her room where my wardrobe was in bags on her floor; she really was a saint to have put up with me in this small space for the past few weeks. I rummaged through the bags looking for something smart to wear and settled on black jeans, a fitted white top, and a pair of grey ankle boots. I put some make-up on for the first time in weeks and then I sat on the bed and watched the clock.

I took deep breaths, I tried to plan how I would act and what I would say, and I tried to find a mantra that I could use to stop the tears from falling when I saw him; but nothing felt strong enough. Then, I finally got a text from Cold Bitch letting me know that the car was outside.

Ruth was waiting for me in the back of the car, and even though the temperature felt icy, she smiled at me warmly, just like she used to — back when we were all living a lie. She even complimented my appearance and gently patted my knee.

"Thank you for doing this, Eve, you won't regret it."

You'd think I was her most favourite person in the world.

I just looked at her blankly, gave her the phone back, and asked, "What exactly am I about to walk into?" She raised an eyebrow in question. "Who will be there, and do Noah and Jane know?"

"The Council will be there."

"The Council?" I asked, as my heart started to beat more rapidly. "Is that really necessary?"

"There may not be a formal contract, Eve, but this is going to be considered as a binding agreement. Everyone needs to be on board, and everyone needs to know what is expected of them," she told me in a somewhat self-righteous manner. Then she ran a hand over her hair to smooth it. "This goes beyond the three of you... and no — we thought it best to wait until you were there before we told them."

"Poor Jane..." I said, under my breath, and then we spent the rest of the thankfully, short journey in silence.

We pulled up at The Dome and we walked through the front doors and into the main hall. I couldn't help but feel a twinge of sadness as I looked at the stage. I missed it. As we continued to walk, I realised that we were going to the board-room; it's a room I'd been in quite a few times and a space I'd always found stuffy and oppressive — except for the times when it was just me and Noah in there. I felt the nerves starting to take over, and for a moment I was tempted to just run away. I couldn't though. There would be no escaping it.

As we got closer, I could hear raised voices and the minute I heard Noah's, I felt like I might actually be sick, but then the door opened, and everyone went silent as we walked in.

Noah was the first person I saw, and my heart felt heavy as soon as my eyes settled on him. He looked like hell. He was angry and they'd been arguing, but he stopped in his tracks when he saw me. All I could see was the darkness, and my heart broke for him. He was still in control, but the dark-ness had taken over many times in the last few months, and it was clearly draining him. It was sucking all the life and colour from his skin.

I heard a female voice question why I was there, and I

assumed it was Jane, but I didn't look. I couldn't take my eyes off Noah, and he couldn't take his off mine.

He eventually spoke. "Eve! Are you OK?"

I cleared my throat and took a deep breath, determined to hold back the tears, because I couldn't let them see me cry. "Yes…" I started to reply, but a loud and intrusive voice cut in.

"Noah, Jane, Eve – please, all sit down," Commander Legion barked from the middle of the table.

Commander Legion is a man whose name was enough to send chills down my spine. He was grey all over, but still had a full head of hair, he was also large, well-built, and scary as hell. He was past retirement age, but he could still take on some of the younger men. I'm not sure he could take on Noah in a fair fight, but then he wasn't known for playing fair and everyone in that room, including Noah, knew that it was best to do as he said.

"What's going on?" Noah was asking him, but he didn't take his eyes off me.

"You, Noah. You're what's going on!" Commander Legion shouted as his hand slammed onto the table. "Making The Council get involved over a marriage dispute, it's—"

"Why is Eve here?" Noah demanded, daring to interrupt him.

"I'll let your parents explain," he replied, sitting down in one heavy movement, and pulling his chair closer to the table, making it shake in the process.

The entire Council was in a row along one side of the table, I had been positioned in the middle on the other side, Noah was at one end of the table on my left, and Jane was on my right — not that I'd even looked at her. I glanced at Noah's parents and then turned to Noah, who was yet to take his eyes off me. I tried to give him a reassuring smile, but then had to look down to compose myself and discretely wipe away the single tear that I couldn't stop from escaping.

Robert cleared his throat. "We need to find a way to move things forward," he said in his usual authoritative way. "We believe that we have a solution — it's one that hasn't been needed before and one we hope will not be needed again."

"What solution?" Noah glared at him.

"On Sunday morning, both your mother and I, along with Derek and Elizabeth, visited Eve to offer an arrangement. There are areas to still be discussed, but ultimately, what you need to know right now, is that if you marry Jane, then Eve can remain in your life... as your mistress," he said without apology.

Noah laughed darkly, Jane gasped, and I just stared down at the table.

"There's no way that Eve would agree to that." Noah's anger was rising, all traces of his initial reaction gone.

Robert was about to reply, but I spoke before him.

"I didn't, but I've since been... persuaded." I looked Robert dead in the eye, letting him know exactly what I thought of him.

He didn't fluster, he never did. "The incident with your brother was regrettable, but clearly necessary..."

"Oh, you fuckers." Noah started to rise from his chair.

He was quiet and, on the outside, he looked calm, but I knew that he was furious. "Adam... you're responsible for what happened to Adam," he fumed as he looked at each of them.

"No, Noah, you are!" Robert argued back. "You've given us no choice but to take action."

Noah put his head down and I could see the tension building, but I could also see him fighting it. Then he walked towards me and, taking my hands in his, pulled me from my chair and led me to the door.

"Where are you going?" Robert demanded.

Noah didn't even look at him. "We need to talk."

"Sit back down!" Commander Legion ordered, and I froze on the spot.

Noah turned to him without a hint of the fear that I felt. "You're about to dictate the rest of our lives. You can spare us five minutes." Then he led me out of the room.

He led me along until we got into his office, then he shut the door, pulled me into him and held me tightly. He was breathing hard, just like the last time he held me, but unlike the last time, I didn't try to push him away. I didn't try to make him let me go. I held onto him just as desperately and buried my head in his chest.

It felt so good to be in his arms again. I loved him, I missed him, and I needed him. I needed him to help me make sense of it all, and I needed him to take the pain away.

"I'm so, so sorry!" he said as he held onto me. "This is all my fault. I dragged you into this. I should have stayed away from the start… I'm sorry, I'm so sorry."

I couldn't say anything, I just cried against his chest; my tears soaking his shirt. He slowly tilted my head back, held it gently in his hands and wiped the fallen tears from my face.

"I love you so much, Eve," he told me tenderly as his own tears fell. "I know I'm fucked up! I… I can't even think about the shit I've done since you left… I just…"

"You got lost…" I said it for him.

"You are the only thing in my life that makes sense. You have been right from the very beginning. I never really knew who I was until I met you. I just tried to be who they expected me to be, but I've never been able to do it… then I met you and I was hooked. You saw something in me that nobody else did… you saw me."

"I love you so much, Noah, and I've missed you every second of every day."

The tears were still falling but I smiled at him in adoration as I ran my hand through his messy hair, and then down his fuzzy cheeks. "You need a shave… and a haircut."

He took my hand and kissed it. "I need you."

He leaned down and I kissed him without holding anything back. We had both been through so much pain, and we both needed each other to ease it. Nobody else could ease it. His hands went down my body and he cupped my bottom, pulling me into his groin and making me gasp, before picking me up and carrying me over to his desk. I wrapped my legs around him and pulled him as close to me as possible as the thrill and relief his touch provided washed over me. I was losing myself in him, just like he was in me. I was his cure, and in that moment, he was mine too.

It couldn't go further though, because we had to go back into that room, and we had to talk. So, I found his hands and pulled them away from me, and then I reluctantly withdrew my kisses, and rested my forehead against his.

"We can't do this now," I told him, whilst trying to catch my breath. "We do need to talk about this."

"I know..." he said, then he stepped away from me, ran his hands through his hair and let out a deep breath. "How is Adam?"

"He'll be fine… this time."

"I can't ask you to do this, Eve… I don't want to do this," he told me, shaking his head and clearly in pain.

"You haven't… they have," I shrugged. "And you have to… for me, for Adam — or next time it'll be worse!"

I started shaking once again.

He moved back to the table, rested his hands on either side of me and looked me right in the eyes. "This won't just be a marriage for show, Eve — they expect it all."

"I know… they will want their grandchildren." I tried to laugh but it came out as a sob that I quickly swallowed back down.

"I cannot stand in that church with her when it's you that should be my wife. It's you I'm meant to be with!" His anger started to rise again. "Having sex with her… I can't even imagine doing it. It would be a betrayal to you!"

I looked at him, and took a deep breath, trying to show him that underneath the emotions, I was sure about it, and that I knew what it all meant.

"Noah… I know this is going to hurt — I do. I know that thinking about you with her is going to tear me apart… but I can take it." He shook his head at me. "I can, Noah. I can take that over losing Adam. That's the reality I'm facing here."

"Eve... I just…"

"We'll be together… we'll still be us… won't we?"

"Forever," he replied, and he leaned in and kissed me again.

The door slammed shut making us both jump and in walked Jane.

"So, this is how it will be, is it?" she seethed. "You two sneaking off on your own? This involves me too!"

Noah turned away from me and walked towards the wall, keeping his back to her. She was right, I hadn't even given her much thought, but it affected her too.

"I know," I told her, looking her in the eye for the first time.

Jane is pretty, she's taller than me, athletic with short blonde hair, much like Ruth's, only lighter. All clean cut and proper, that's how she seemed, but then that's what she was supposed to be.

"What's wrong with me Noah?"

He didn't respond.

"I know I don't look like her," she gestured towards me, "but then, not many people do. You have never once thought about how your actions affect me, have you?" she demanded, but he still didn't respond.

"I was two years below you in school and I fancied you, just like everyone else," she continued. "And then I turned sixteen and was told that I'd be marrying you by the time I was twenty... and I was so happy." Her sad smile suggested differently. "Then that first gathering we had with all the families — when it was to be officially announced... you know I must have tried on five different dresses..." she confessed. "I was so excited to see you, but then you walked in drunk, with some random girl, and that was that."

"Jane..." Noah turned to face her, but she wasn't finished.

"You made it very clear that you didn't want to marry me," she continued, "but everyone told me that you were just rebelling, and you'd come around. But then at a time when I should've been preparing for our wedding, I found out that you were in a secret relationship!"

She glared at me and I could feel her hurt.

"Then you were given three more years and neither you nor anyone else even stopped to ask me how I felt about it!"

"I'm sorry," Noah said, and I knew he meant it. "I am. I know I've been nothing but a dick to you and you haven't deserved it — you haven't." He stepped forward a little. "There's nothing wrong with you, but I'm not attracted to you in that way, I'm just not."

Her face pinched as she looked down.

"But I don't dislike you. I treated you like shit on purpose because I thought your parents would want better for you and call it off."

She turned away from him for a moment, appearing to think, and then turned back to stare at him bitterly, before turning to me. "And now I'm just supposed to accept you?"

"No," I told her, and she let out a slight huff. "No, Jane, don't accept it. Go in there and tell them that you won't marry him. Go in there and tell them that you deserve better — because you do! You go in there and tell them you won't do this because I'm not going to." My tears started to fall again. "I did that once and I know what I risk if I do it again, Jane. They've shown me what I'll lose."

She walked to the other side of the room and we all stayed silent for a while, but then she turned back and stood closer to us both.

"How is this even supposed to work?" she asked me.

I let out a shaky laugh and crossed my arms across my chest. "I believe they had some sort of rota system in mind."

"And I'm supposed to accept my husband being in love with someone else? Sleeping with someone else?"

"Yes… Just like I'm supposed to accept that the man that I'm in love with, the man I thought I'd marry and have a family with, will be doing that with someone else."

Did she really want to compare hurt with me?

She shook her head at us. "I don't like this."

"Are you going to go in there and tell them no?" I raised my eyebrow at her, but inside I was pleading with her. Inside I was desperate for her to do the thing that I couldn't do — to get us out of this.

She looked down a little, before looking at me and shaking her head again.

I guess that's not going to happen.

I swallowed down some bile before turning to Noah.

"What about you, Noah?"

He looked at me in pain, as if begging me not the ask the question.

"Are you going to tell them no?"

He shook his head. He was defeated. He'd been fighting it for years and he was finally defeated. "No… I'm not going to let them do anything else to hurt you."

We made an unspoken pact there and then, that we would figure out a way to make it work together. When we walked back into the boardroom we entered together, and then we sat across from them, with Noah sitting quietly between his future wife and his future mistress.

We listened as they told us what would be expected and we all sat silently, nodding on occasion so that they knew that we understood. The only time any of us spoke, was when they reiterated what I had already been told about not having children of my own.

Noah started to object, but I took his hand in mine, and when he turned to me, he saw that I already knew, and had already agreed to that too.

Once they'd finished, Commander Legion took centre stage again, acting as an Official.

"Jane, do you agree to the terms of this arrangement?"

She looked at him and nodded in obedience. "Yes."

He gave her a slight smile and then turned to Noah. "Noah, do you agree to the terms of this arrangement?"

Noah turned to me and I gave him a gentle nod and then he turned to face Commander Legion, and with his jaw clenched, replied, "Yes."

The whole room seemed to sigh in relief and Noah's parents gave each other an accomplished smile.

"Eve—"

"I have one request... or demand," I looked him right in the eye, feeling more determined than afraid.

Robert scoffed, "You're not in the position to make demands."

"All three of us are giving something up," I said, gesturing to Noah and Jane. "We're all having to compromise, but I'm the only one being told that I'll never have a family of my own."

Robert looked at Ruth and she looked down in an attempt to hide her shame.

"So, you will not hurt what little family I do have, ever again."

I looked each and every Council member sitting at that table right in the eyes, and they all seemed to shuffle in their seats.

"Nothing like this will ever happen to my brother again," I told them. "I will do everything that has been asked of me, but if Adam so much as grazes his knee, I will hold you responsible. You will keep him safe, no matter what, or this deal will be over! One way or another, I will be gone."

20

They gave Noah and me a week to "recover" from it all, and to give themselves some time to do some 'damage control' within the community of The Beneath. However, the wedding would be taking place in three weeks, and for the two weeks prior, Noah and Jane would be expected to play their parts — without me. It was just the start of things that would be happening without me, and the start of all of the lies that would follow and the acts that would no doubt break me.

When we left that meeting room, we went back to our flat, and the first thing that struck me was that everything had been tidied. There was no evidence of the battering that it took the day I walked out the door. You'd almost think that everything had gone back to normal, were it not for the constant weight in my heart that reminded me that nothing would ever be as it once was.

It was time to try to adjust, but it was also time to heal, and so, I led Noah to the bathroom, sat him in the chair and fetched the hair clippers and his razor from the cupboard. We didn't speak. We didn't need to. Actions have always spoken louder than words with Noah, and he knew through mine that I was truly back and ready to look after him. Ready to comfort him with my unwavering and unconditional love.

He just gently held onto my waist, watching me, with those eyes that no longer seemed lost, while I straightened him out. While I started the process of putting him back together again. I ran the clippers through his hair, an action that seemed so familiar to me, because I'd been doing it for years, and once his hair was back to how he liked it, I took the razor and carefully started shaving his face.

"You're not tempted to give me a bit of a cut, are you?" he smiled as I rinsed away some of the hair and foam from the razor. "I probably deserve it."

"You probably do." I smirked, and he ran a finger down my side, making me shudder. "And if you don't keep still, I might just do it."

I wiped his face clean, caressing it with a warm, wet flannel, as I tried to push my heart back down to my chest. It felt so heavy, staring at the face of the man that was mine, and yet wasn't.

Trying my best to stay positive, to just enjoy the short time that we would have together, I forced a smile onto my face. "There. You look like you again, but you should probably shower too."

"Yes, we probably should." A wicked grin took over his face and he grabbed hold of me, lifting me off my feet and took me into the shower with him.

"Nooo!" I squealed in protest. "These are my only clothes!"

He didn't stop, he just laughed at me, switched on the shower, and I was helpless to do anything to stop him as the water streamed over us both, as we stood there fully clothed. He pulled his clothes off, and as he did, I removed my top and bra, but my jeans were soaked and stuck to my skin and I couldn't pull them down. Noah laughed at me some more and started to help me, but he soon realised that we were never going to get them off while I was standing in a small shower and getting wetter as each second passed.

"I didn't think this through, did I?" he said, still laughing.

God, it felt good to see him smile and hear him laugh again. This was the part of him that I wouldn't be sharing. The warm, carefree Noah that only ever came out with me.

He moved me aside as he washed himself and I just stood there, fixated on him in my semi-naked and soaked state. He looked so good; muscular, with abs to die for, and he had me throbbing from head to toe. I really needed to get my trousers off. It had been too long since he'd touched me, too long since he'd pleasured me and too long since he'd been inside me.

"Struggling with something?" he smirked, with a seductive twinkle in his eyes.

I smirked right back, knowing that he would be feeling exactly the same as me. "Hurry up or I'll start without you." I ran my hand down my wet, naked cleavage, feeling very satisfied when his mouth dropped open as his eyes watched the path my hand was taking before I made a quick exit.

Once in the bedroom, I lay on the floor and tried to pull my jeans off but still couldn't get them all the way down, and when Noah came in seconds later with a towel wrapped around his waist, he laughed at me even more.

"Help me!" I pleaded, and he crouched down and started pulling them down for me, pausing when he got to my ankles.

"Honestly… I'm tempted to just take advantage of you in your vulnerable state."

He pushed my legs inwards so that they bent at the knee,

ducked under my feet, which were still stuck in my jeans, and leaned over me.

"You could do anything to me right now and I wouldn't object." My breath hitched. I was so desperate for him that it hurt.

"That's good to know…" he said, as he started to follow the path that my hand had taken in the shower, with a gentle stroke of his finger.

He leaned down and kissed my hungry and demanding lips, before lifting me off the ground and putting me on the bed. I thought he was going to enter me straight away, but he didn't, instead he used the fact that my legs were trapped to tease me with gentle kisses on my breasts.

He saw my pain and started laughing at me, and I almost grabbed his hips and pulled him into me in response.

"Noah! This isn't fair. Please, just get in me now!"

His smile softened and held a hint of sadness, as he said, "I have a lot to make up to you for." I was about to reach out and stroke his face, but then his smirk reappeared, and my body flushed with glee, in response. "So, save your moaning for the orgasms that I'm about to give you."

I took in a deep breath as his head went low and he went to work with his tongue and his fingers, and because it had been so long since I'd been touched that way, he had me calling out my pleasure within minutes. He wasn't finished with me though, and he carried on until I was writhing underneath him once again, only releasing me when my moans subsided. Then he raised himself onto me, kissed, and sucked at my lips and tongue, as he thrust inside.

He was so desperate for his own release that it didn't last long, and within minutes he had collapsed on me panting. I lay there breathing just as hard, loving the feeling of having him pressed against me. However, I was also starting to cramp up, so I pushed against my soggy trousers and, with the last bit of strength my body still had, managed to get them off my feet.

I lay next to him and closed my eyes, finding a sense of peace, at last. I had him to myself for a week… just a week. I had a million questions going around my head, but I kept them to myself. They were questions that I was never going to like the answers to, so they could wait. They could wait until my week was over because that's when the next stage of pain was going to kick in anyway.

I started to turn away from him, but he pulled me into him, objecting at my departure from the bed. "I need to put my clothes in the dryer," I told him, as I tried to free myself from his grasp. "All of my clothes are in Rose's room and I can't exactly show up at the infirmary naked."

His smile was lazy. "Why not? It's such a good look on you." Then just like before, his smile faded, as he remembered why none of my things were in our home. "Shall I come with you and help you bring your things back?"

"Oh…" I hesitated. "I'm not sure that's the best idea."

He closed his eyes, and released a deep, remorseful breath. "Yeah… I'm probably not the most popular person there right now," he admitted. "I am sorry."

"Shhhh..." I put a finger to his lips. "You don't need to apologise to me, and the best way you can make it up to the people that you've hurt is to try and get the darkness under control so that it doesn't happen again."

He swallowed hard and gave a slight nod.

"As for sweetening everyone up, well… I think your parents are taking care of that."

He released his hold and I slipped out of bed and put my clothes into the dryer, before jumping back in with him.

Warmth radiated from him, and I pressed myself against his side, soaking it up.

He was lying on his back with his eyes closed and his hands resting on his head. He felt so guilty, I could see that. People thought he got his kicks from causing pain. They thought it made him feel all the more powerful — but it didn't. I knew that he wasn't in control when he attacked those men. He wasn't thinking it through, and he definitely wasn't enjoying it. He wouldn't feel such remorse and guilt, if he did.

As I rested my head on his chest, his hands moved away from his head and he wrapped them around me, and I lay there absorbing everything about him.

"What are you doing?" he asked me in amusement.

"Smelling you…"

He laughed at me. "I didn't put any deodorant on, do I stink?"

"No, you smell like you… it's my favourite smell."

He laughed again before rolling me over so that we were lying on our sides, facing each other. "I don't deserve you."

"I know," I pursed me lips, feigning seriousness, "it's lucky for you that I've got abandonment issues."

We both laughed and then he rolled me onto my back and pressed himself against me again. I could feel his heart beating against mine, and I wished more than anything that time would stand still and that feeling of completeness would last forever.

He stroked a finger along my cheek. "I've missed your face." He kissed me. "I've missed these lips and this beautiful smile." He kissed me again, then he moved down to my chest and cupped my breasts. "I have definitely missed these God-like creations!"

He buried his head in them, making me laugh, and his own chuckle sent vibrations through my soul.

He continued kissing each part of my body, telling each area how much he'd missed it until he got to my centre. He paused, pulled my legs apart and just took me in, smiling in approval. I laughed at him, but I didn't feel self-conscious. Noah was my first and only, and there's nothing he'd not seen or done to me.

"This…" he said, rubbing his thumb over my clit, and making me tingle all over. "This, I have quite possibly missed the most."

"I notice that you've not mentioned anything about my brilliant mind," I quipped back.

"Hush, woman!" he growled with authority, but then he looked back up at me with his heart-melting smile. "I'm admiring a thing of beauty here."

I smiled back at him and he flipped me over so that I was on my stomach and then he started to caress my bottom, before slowly and gently pushing his thumb into the crease.

"I've missed this too…"

I couldn't see his face, but I could hear the lust in his voice and my stomach did a summersault.

"Don't you dare!" I squealed. "I have to go into a church soon!"

"Are you sure?" he teased, as he reached for the drawer.

Moments later, I jumped at the sensation of cold lubricant being rubbed against me. He started to gently rub it in, and then his other hand moved from my bottom to my front, sliding over my wetness in an agonisingly slow motion. He started to rub his thumb against my clit and push his fingers inside, and I groaned in pleasure at his touch and buried my head into the pillow.

"Maybe…"

"Maybe, yes?" He gently pushed the thumb that was caressing my bottom inside. "Or maybe no?" he asked, as he pulled it out again.

He continued to rub around the edge and increased the pace with the fingers that were already thrusting inside me. The anticipation was becoming too much to bear and as the waves of pleasure washed over me, I breathed out, "Yes..."

He groaned his appreciation, as he always did when I let him have all of me, and he pushed his thumb further in, preparing me for taking him, continuing for a few minutes, until I gasped, "I'm ready..."

"On your knees." His command was breathy and urgent.

I moved into position, he pulled his thumb out, and then I tensed a little as he pushed inside.

"Relax, baby..." he gasped. "Tell me if it gets too much."

I focused on the heat that was starting to build in my clit and rise up to my stomach, and then I started to move with him. He filled me completely. He was everywhere and the pressure and pleasure had me calling out.

"You OK?" he rasped out.

"Yes..."

"I need more..." he groaned, breathing hard.

"Me too," I pleaded in response.

His thrusts from behind came harder and my body started to shudder as I started to lose control, and Noah slipped another finger inside as he felt my release building.

"Agh!" I cried out, as I came hard, soaking us both.

"Oh... fucking hell!" Noah called out seconds later, as he thrust into me one final time, before we both collapsed in a heap on the bed.

We lay there panting for a few minutes as I tried to get my trembling body back under control.

"I swear you were made by angels…" he breathed out, as he brushed gentle kisses over my shoulders.

Giggling, I replied, "I'm pretty sure angels don't take it up the arse."

"Then they don't know what they're missing," he laughed in response, as he nipped at my shoulder.

He pulled me over so that I was facing him and as he did, I caught a glimpse of the clock.

"Shit… I need to get back to Adam, he'll be worried…"

Groaning in reluctance, I climbed over him and rolled off the bed and into the shower. I stood under the hot water and Noah climbed in behind me, wrapping his hands around my waist and pulling me into him.

"It'll take more than a shower to wash that sin away," he chuckled into my ear. "Careful walking into church…"

He received a gentle elbow in his side, but I still laughed. "You're a bad human being."

His response was more serious. "I know… I'll work on that."

I turned to face him, and we held each other as the warm water washed over us. I didn't want to leave that shower, but I couldn't make time stand still, I couldn't make that week last forever, and I couldn't avoid facing Adam.

Sighing, I left him there in all his naked gorgeousness, retrieved my dry clothes and got dressed. Noah gave me my phone back. It was one piece which surprised me, and then he drove me to St Martins and told me to call him when I was ready to come home. It was hard to say goodbye again so soon, but at least I knew it wouldn't be for long.

I walked through the main doors of the infirmary and readied myself for a fight as I walked into Adam's room, but to my relief, John was with him and when he saw me, he jumped up and gave me a hug.

"It's good to have you back, too," he said, squeezing me tight. "You seem different…" He eyed me with suspicion. "How are you feeling?"

"Just relieved to be home and have the annoying one in one piece." I smiled as I looked over at Adam, then felt the blow when I saw that the smile that he was wearing for John had been replaced with a frown.

"Me too," John said, giving me a sad smile. "Do you want me to save you a seat at dinner?"

"Oh…" Nerves started to dance around my stomach and then I looked at Adam. He was staring a hole into the wall, ensuring that I was going to have to get out of that one by myself.

"Thanks, John, but I'll just sort myself out later," I smiled.

John squeezed my arm and left the room, without asking me anymore questions, which was good, because I had no idea what to tell him. We'd been told by The Council to be discrete, but I didn't really understand how that would be possible. I was moving back to my flat, Noah was going to be there with me for an entire week, and then after the wedding he'd be staying there again on my 'assigned days'. It wasn't like we didn't have neighbours, and we'd already given them quite a show. Still, I couldn't just tell John outright, even though he and everyone else would find out soon enough.

Adam clearly still didn't want to look at me, but I went over and sat on his bed anyway, knowing that at some point he'd have something to get off his chest. Regardless of his anger, I was happy to be with him and I was so relieved. Being back in The Beneath and in the infirmary made it all feel less serious, and he was looking so much better already. Though perhaps that was because I knew that I'd done what was necessary. I knew that I'd made him safe.

After an agonising few minutes, I decided to break the silent standoff. "Have you spoken to Meredith?"

"She's coming over in a bit," he replied.

He wasn't looking at me, but at least he replied.

I wasn't amused, but I let out a little laugh. "So, you're mad with me now?"

He finally turned to glare at me. "Did you have to sign on the dotted line, swear an oath, or just spread your legs?" he asked, in a tone so sharp that it cut like glass.

"Whatever it takes, Adam," I replied without hesitation or deliberation.

Still, on that note, I decided to leave him to it. It was shit, because I knew my brother and I knew that he wasn't really angry with me. He was angry with the Founding Families, and with himself and his complete and utter powerlessness to change a situation that was breaking his heart.

On some level he blamed himself. He knew it wasn't his fault that they targeted him. However, the fact that he was my weak spot, the fact that he was leveraged and used against me, and that he was the person that I was prepared to make so many sacrifices for, ate at him.

He also understood deep down that I had no choice but to accept their offer, because I had nowhere else to go and I couldn't escape them. Still, having Adam to protect added another layer of complexity. I bore the responsibility of protecting my brother but he in turn shouldered the guilt that came with needing to be protected.

Feeling somewhat deflated, I walked out into the corridor and saw Sister Theresa waiting for me. Our eyes met and she gave me a smile and gestured for me to follow her. She was the last person that I wanted to see given what Noah and I had just done. I followed her, expecting to be taken to her office, but she carried on walking, heading instead, for the last place I wanted to be — the church itself.

I took a deep breath and reminded myself that God didn't strike me down last time.

We were greeted by the sound of the younger members of the choir practising, and I couldn't help but smile at them as an innocent warmth spread through me. That was me once upon a time, when life was much simpler and a million times less painful.

Sister Theresa walked along the aisle, stopping when she was more or less at the middle row, and then she sat down. I followed suit, and we just sat there in silence watching the choir. I didn't prompt her. There was no point in pushing Sister Theresa, she'd say what she wanted to say when she was ready and not a moment sooner.

Her sigh broke the silence before her voice did. "I was informed a few hours ago that a wedding will be taking place here in a few weeks."

She was still staring straight ahead, but my heart started to beat more rapidly. I should have known she'd spare me the niceties and get straight to the point.

"Yes."

"They got their way then," she said with bitterness. "And you…" she sighed as she finally looked at me, "you will have some semblance of happiness, amongst many moments of pain."

I snorted out a sound that communicated the mix of shock and disbelief that her statement made me feel. "Thank you for that reminder," I said, shaking my head at her.

"I speak what I feel," she reminded me, but there was no need. I hadn't forgotten.

"And don't we know it," I smiled at her.

I would always respect Sister Theresa, but not living

under her roof meant that I too could be a little more forthright.

"I've always thought you'd make a wonderful mother…"

I almost choked. "Are you kidding me?" I turned to her, shaking my head in disbelief. "Why don't you just stick a knife in the wound and twist it, while you're at it!"

I let out a shaky breath and glared at her a little. She already knew how much pain I was in and that was the last thing I needed to hear.

"If all you want to do is make me feel even worse than I already do, then I think I'll just leave."

She put a hand on my wrist and squeezed it. Her touch was warm and gentle, in stark contrast to her cold and hard words.

"That's not what I'm trying to do, Eve. Quite the opposite, in fact. They expect you to not get pregnant."

"I'm aware."

"Accidents happen, and if one occurs then you need to come to me first."

"That's not going to be possible. I will be having a monthly coffee morning with Ruth, where I'll be expected to do a pregnancy test," I told her, unable to stop the bitterness in my voice, because I really didn't see how that part of the arrangement was necessary.

Sister Theresa just stared at me for a moment and I realised that by providing that little nugget of information, I'd done the impossible. I'd actually rendered her speechless. In any other situation I would have laughed. Or, run and told Adam what I managed to do.

"Hmmm…" she replied, deep in thought.

"What does 'hmmm' mean?"

"We only have one type of pregnancy test here and you

have access to many virgins," she said with a conspiring wink.

"What are you talking about?" I laughed in disbelief. Did she really just wink?

"Mrs Ruth Joyson, will get her negative pregnancy test each month, I assure you of that," she smiled.

I looked at her, mouth open wide and in complete and utter shock. "Sister Theresa, I did not know you were such a badass!"

"Please don't use that language here," she chastised me, reminding me who she was. "When I came here all those years ago it was to make a difference to the lives of the children brought here," she said, her smile and tone gentle once more. "My job doesn't end when you turn eighteen… I keep a piece of you all right here."

She tapped her heart, and as I smiled at her, tears started to sting my eyes.

"The Founding Families and The Council are the engine. They're the cogs in the machine — the drivers of this world that they created," she continued. "But this Church is the beating heart and guiding soul, and even they wouldn't dare to touch anyone under its protection."

21

*O*ur week together flew by, and we remained hidden away in our flat, except for when I went to see Adam, and Della at the salon. I felt awful about all the time that I'd taken off and was worried that I might not have a job to go back to. I'd put in a lot of hard work over the years and Della knew me. Perhaps she even doted on me to some extent, and to my relief, she told me to take the rest of the week off and come back the following Monday. She had no idea how much that gesture made me feel, because if she had asked me to go back sooner, it would have cut into the precious time that I had alone with Noah.

As it turned out, it wasn't just her affection for me that had smoothed things over. Sister Theresa had spoken to her on my behalf, and Ruth went in and hired Della, and the rest of the team to do the hair and make-up for Jane and her bridesmaids.

I tried and failed to hide the shock and pain that image created.

They weren't going to expect me to go along, but it had been made clear to Della that keeping me on was part of the deal. I'd say that Ruth risked arousing suspicion with that move, but Della just interpreted it as her trying to ease her own guilt. People were talking about me, specifically about how I had been lied to for years before having my heart ripped out and, being seen to be doing right by me was part of their damage control initiative.

"I wasn't going to get rid of you, anyway," Della smiled, as she ran a hand through my hair. "I've invested a lot in you, and you're worth every penny. But if Ruth Joyson wanted to put that sort of money my way, then I didn't mind letting her think she was calling the shots."

I had to laugh at her, because Della had no poker face, so I don't know how she thought she had fooled Ruth, but then, Ruth would never have believed that a mere stylist would have been able to get the better of her. Ruth's predictability was amusing, and she couldn't have been more wrong. I knew Della, and I knew she'd worked her fingers to the bone to get her own salon. As far as I was concerned, she was worth ten of Ruth. Della had grit, compassion, a hug for everyone, and a soft and squidgy heart that was breaking for me.

She looked at me with the saddest expression I'd ever seen, and it had me choking up on the spot. "I can tell her that we can't fit the wedding in."

"No… Please don't, it's an amazing opportunity for you and this place."

I absolutely did not want her missing out on the money because of me.

She nodded but smiled with caution. "How are you? Are you really going to go back to The Dome and continue living in that flat?"

She shook her head at me, her eyes started to tear up and her pain kicked me in the gut, because once again, I was going to have to lie to someone that I cared about. It was so stupid because she'd find out eventually. In fact, that's what made it all so much worse. Not just what I'd agreed to do, but the fact that I was having to lie to people that would find out anyway, and I feared the inevitable moment when their pity would turn to disgust.

"Della… it is—"

"Shit!" she answered for me. "It's completely shit! I can't believe this happened, you two were…" She paused when she saw my tears fall. "Eve…"

"I'm OK," I told her, but she saw me shaking and pulled me closer. "Yes… the situation is definitely shit." At least that wasn't a lie. "But I'll be OK."

It took a while to reassure her that I didn't need to stay in her home with her, but eventually, she released me from the warmth of her hug, and I went back to the flat feeling utterly undeserving of her kindness. As soon as I saw Noah, I burst into tears, ran to the bathroom and locked the door. Noah freaked out, and I managed to speak clearly enough to let him know that nothing bad had happened. He knew how I would be feeling and said nothing more as I continued to break my heart on the cold floor. When I came out, he was leaning against the wall next to the door.

He pulled me straight into his arms. "I'm sorry…"

"Don't… I don't want this week to be spent thinking about what's going to come." I took a deep breath and wiped the tears away. "It's just hard lying to people, and I hate imagining what they're going to be saying about me when they find out — which they will."

"There are things we should talk about," he said as he kissed the top of my head.

"I know, I just don't want to do it yet." I was on the verge of tears again. "I want this week to be just us. Talking about it makes me feel like I'm sharing you already, and I'm not ready to do that."

We didn't talk about it. We didn't talk about what vows he would say. We didn't talk about how he was going to handle consummating the marriage, and we didn't talk about what life would be like when he laid his eyes on his child for the first time. We just enjoyed as much time together as we could, pretending to be oblivious of what was to come, and never asking what was keeping the other awake at night.

Time flies when you're having fun. Or perhaps it flies when you're dreading what's to come? It came though, our week ended, and it was time for me to step back into the shadows, while Noah and Jane began the facade of what was to be their wedding and their marriage. There were parties, rehearsals, clothes to organise — all of it, and the whole of The Beneath was busy and buzzing.

I was glad to be back in the salon because it kept me busy, although it did mean that I couldn't escape the gossip. Della put a stop to it, but then I just received the silent looks of concern. Everyone knew that I had been Noah's girlfriend for five years. They knew why we broke up and the fallout that followed. They knew that the marriage was arranged, and that Noah still loved me. They saw me as a victim, someone who had been left behind and someone to be pitied, and once again, I was left fearing what they'd think of me when they learned the truth.

Noah played his part; he went to suit fittings, had meals out with Jane and her family, he went back to work, and most importantly, he kept control. Everyone that mattered was happy. Everyone thought that the rules were being followed, but every night Noah would climb into bed and hold me, and every morning he was gone before I woke up.

He came over the night before the wedding, as he had for

the whole two weeks, but instead of climbing in bed and just holding me, he kneeled on the floor next to my head.

"Are you OK?" I asked him, concerned that he was going to crumble.

He wasn't crumbling, but he looked so sad. "You know that nothing about this situation is OK... but I'm trying my best."

"I know..."

I pulled him close, and he didn't pull away from me as he continued to speak. "Tomorrow I have to stand in Church and say vows to the wrong woman..." I could feel his heart beating at speed against my cheek. "I'll be putting a ring on the wrong finger and putting one on mine that means nothing to me... nothing but lies and control."

He released me from his embrace and cupped my face in his hands. "Tonight, I want to do right by my own heart."

He took a small navy box out of his pocket and opened it, showing me the two rings inside; both white gold, but whereas one was a plain band, the other was finished with intricate, diamond encrusted flowers, which glistened in the light, illuminating his face. He took the plain band, held it for a moment and then passed it to me. I held it in my fingers, examined it, and noticed that it was engraved on the inside with one word — 'Forever'.

Then he took it back and held both of my hands in one of his as he took the diamond ring from the box. He released my right hand and held onto my left, then he showed me the inside of the ring, and I saw 'Forever' engraved there too.

He let out a deep, regretful sigh. "I wish I could put this ring on this finger." He rubbed my ring finger on my left hand. "That's where it should be..." He lowered my left hand and picked up my right. "But what this ring symbolises is more real and means more to me than anything else in existence." Tears formed in his eyes, as he asked, "Eve… will you be mine forever?"

The tears were streaming down my face and I couldn't form any words, so I nodded my response; but as he pushed the ring onto my finger, I managed to whisper, "Forever."

He smiled and then handed me the box. "Do you want to do the honours?" He held out his right hand, I took the ring from the box and as I slid it onto his finger, I said the only vows I would ever be able to say to him, "We're in this together… forever."

22

_____

THE MORNING OF THE WEDDING

NOAH

I dragged myself out of bed and opened the curtain a little; it was still dark outside, but not for much longer, and I really needed to leave. I didn't want to leave. I didn't want to leave the flat and I didn't want to leave her. Yet, I had to… I'd agreed to, and so, with a reluctance that almost paralysed me, I put on my clothes, and then I just stood there and took her in.

There was a little bit of light coming in from the hallway, enough to let me get a glimpse of her, but not to wake her. Watching her sleep had always been a guilty pleasure, because if I were to sit and stare at her while she was awake, she'd roll her eyes and most likely throw something at me.

She carried so much burden and responsibility on her tiny shoulders, and there were times when she struggled to shake it all off and fall asleep. Yet, once she'd drifted off, she'd be out like a log and I loved it. It was like it was her body's way of shielding her and giving her the rest that she needed. A forced time out, if you like, for a person that just didn't seem to know when to quit.

How the fuck did it come to this?

I. Did. Fucking. Everything! Everything they wanted and more and still…

I gground my teeth in an attempt to stifle the growl that wanted to break free. I wanted to scream so loud that the building crumbled. I wanted my parents to feel it in their bones while they slept! I wanted them to feel what I felt. All the pain and all the rage, and yet it wouldn't make the slightest difference if they did.

I showed them how I felt three years ago, when David came into my office and I was dragged in front of my entire, fucking family — the male half, at least. I cried in front of the lot of them. I cried and I begged, and after getting over the initial shock of seeing me actually show some emotion, my mum just scoffed at me and turned away. My own mother turned her back while her child was breaking his heart in front of her.

I should have known.

So, I changed tact, and I showed them the side that they didn't just turn away from. I showed them the side that they cowered from, the side that they created. Unfortunately, for my cousin, Tyler, that meant that his time had finally come.

I'd wanted to slap Tyler a year or so before, when Harriet let slip that he fancied Eve, but I'd let it slide because he was family, and if I hit everyone that fancied her, then there wouldn't be many people left standing. However, he happened to be at The Dome one day, when she was rehearsing and had commented on how she was holding the microphone, suggesting that soon it would be his cock that she gripped in her hands and brought up to her lips.

I don't know how I managed to keep it together that day, but I did. It was some poor fucker at the fight club that got it, but thankfully, not too badly. However, the day when he stood there next to my uncle and his brothers as they looked upon my agony in disgust... well, that day, it wasn't just about what he had coming to him — it also served a purpose.

He knew why too and the minute my eyes landed on him, he knew what he'd done, and he knew what was coming. He actually pissed his pants.

I was outnumbered so not much happened, but the fact that I'd turned on one of my own made them stop and think. I didn't exactly feel good about it, but then I never did.

The only person I didn't give a flying fuck about hurting was Seb. The state of Adam's nose, and the fact that he'd threatened to hit Eve, he got what he deserved.

My parent's called Jane's over and after a few hours of heated exchange, they gave me three years. Three more precious years. My entire family knew, all except for Harriet, who apparently couldn't be trusted with the truth because of her friendship with Eve, and for three years we all managed to hide it from her. If there's one thing that you know how to do, when you're born into the Founding Families, it's keeping secrets.

Harriet found out the truth after Eve did, and I've never been scared of my little sister until that day! She went absolutely ballistic at me and I thought she was going to hit me, but then her anger turned to tears, as she realised what it meant, and the disappointment on her face had me crumbling to the floor. I hadn't just let myself down, I had let Harriet down too, and she realised that day, that her future was also set-in stone.

I grabbed hold of those three years though, and I didn't waste them. I gave out the beatings when it was my turn to do so without complaint and I made them even more money than before. Then there was Eve; they got to know her, and they got to see what she was worth. To them, it may only have been financial worth, but that was all they valued, anyway. Then, six months before my twenty-fifth birthday, I went back to them and asked for their blessing to marry Eve, and they laughed in my fucking face. The look on my mother's face still makes my blood boil, and her favourite vase ended up paying the price. I argued and pleaded with them every day for six months, but they wouldn't budge. Then my mother took matters into her own hands… something she'll never be forgiven for.

Eve let out a little, sleepy murmur and I moved over to the bed and kneeled on the floor next to her. Even if I was granted eternal life, I could never do anything to deserve her love. Still, who among us is worthy of the love of an angel?

I went to see David when he was in the infirmary. What I did to Tyler years before may have been planned, but what I did to David, wasn't. I don't really see eye to eye with either David or Rory. They don't understand why I can't just do what's expected of me. "Marry who you're supposed to marry and fuck around on the side," Rory had told me once. That's what they did — both of them. Apparently, it was too much to ask to just marry the woman you wanted to be with and just stick with her. I'd never cheat on Eve — except, I will be — and I don't respect my brothers for doing it, but still, I didn't want to hurt either of them.

I apologised to David and he just stared through me for what felt like hours, but then he said, "You're the Devil, Noah." He was so cold and so calm, and his words cut straight through me like a knife. "You took an innocent young girl and turned her in to what you needed her to be and destroyed her life in the process."

I didn't argue with him, because at the time, I believed every word. Afterwards, I thought about it some more, and I realised that he was wrong. I never shaped Eve into what I needed her to be, because she was already what I needed her to be. What I did, was ask something of her that I shouldn't have, but I would have stopped if she had told me to.

I never would have forced her.

She didn't tell me to stop though, because she did what she always did... she saw me. She saw the pain behind the anger and the darkness, and she loved me despite it.

I reached out and stroked her hair, and she exhaled a moan again. I continued to stare at her in complete and utter awe. How was it possible to love somebody so much?

I had so many things to regret in life, but the thing at the top of my list was her. I should have told her. I should have told her from day one, so that she could choose whether I was worth bothering with... but I couldn't. I had never been interested in Harriet's friends. They were all immature and even if a few of them were pretty fit, they weren't worth the fallout with Harriet, or the neediness that would follow. Then one rainy day, Eve Matthews got into my car.

Everyone always said that the orphans had to grow up quicker, but it wasn't just that she seemed older than her years; she just knocked the air right out of me. I've never told her what I felt that day, because I'd hoped to say it on our wedding day. Well, not my first thought, because my first thought was, *Thank you for the early birthday present, Harriet!*

Fuck me, my cock was practically rubbing against the steering wheel for the whole drive to the restaurant, and she drove me crazy from that moment on.

The thing I wanted to say... the thing I've been saving, is the soppiest thing I've ever thought, but it's also completely true. It had been raining hard, and when Eve got in, she wrestled with her umbrella, and then the moment she looked up to speak to me, and the moment our eyes met, the clouds parted, and a tiny ray of sunshine broke through, and just shrouded her in a warm light. That, right there, was the closest thing to an epiphany that I'm ever likely to have.

Up until that moment, I planned on ending the evening with her bouncing on my cock, while I sucked on those perfect breasts. That all changed when the light shone on her. I still wanted her, but it made me see more and I almost lost myself in the warm depths of her eyes. I had to get to know her and I had to spend time with her, but every moment spent with her just made me crave more.

I let out a deep breath and squeezed my eyes tightly closed, before turning to glance at the clock. I needed to go. I wished I could stay. I wished for that more than anything… that's what I had resorted to — wishes. I wasn't a wisher, and I wasn't a dreamer. I was the person that made the things he wanted happen and always had been. Now the world had reminded me that I was nothing special, and that I was just another pawn. I'd lived like a God for too long and now it was time to pay my dues.

Still, at least I had an angel by my side. Eve's love was my salvation and her light guided me out of the darkness. Her light and her body.

I took her in one final time before forcing myself to leave the room. To leave the love and light of my life sleeping peacefully, while I walked knowingly into the darkness.

23

J spent the day of the wedding with Adam; he'd been funny with me for the three weeks prior but realised that I needed him that day and snapped out of his mood. That, or someone else reminded him that I needed him and that he needed to step up. I suspected the latter to be the case, but I didn't know if it had been Sister Theresa, Rose, Meredith, John, or all of the above.

Adam was out of the infirmary but still resting, so we stayed in his room trying to ignore the church bells and the organ. In hindsight, it was a really bad idea to put myself so close to the wedding, but I wanted to be with the person that I loved the most, especially since he'd been acting like that love wasn't reciprocated for weeks.

Adam tried to placate his guilt by being animated, charming and fun, and I played along in an attempt to keep the pain at bay. I left my ring at home, because it was too noticeable and clearly expensive, so I didn't know how I was going to explain it. I just kept rubbing the area where the ring had been, reminding myself that Noah was mine despite what was happening in that church.

I was utterly relieved when Vic and Sarah showed up later in the afternoon and insisted that I went to theirs, and when I got there, the others were waiting for me with a drink in hand. They put some music on and told me that I was going to spend the rest of the afternoon getting shit-faced! They didn't know what was going on, so they thought that they were just helping me through my heartbreak, which they were. The love of my life was marrying someone else, the fact that it wasn't real didn't mean that it wasn't happening. They just didn't know that I'd be a part of that marriage too.

As the evening drew in, we started to run out of alcohol, so Hannah decided that we should go out. By that point, I was loving the feeling of being with them and very much up for a party. My life was about to cross over into new realms of complexity, and I realised that I needed and deserved, one night of being carefree with my sisters. One night, where I didn't need to think about the rules. One night, where I didn't need to think about the consequences, and where I could make a complete tit out of myself and not worry about remembering it the next day. So, they dressed me up and we hit the town.

We started at Halo, which wasn't a late bar but always had deals on cocktails, and it's dark, which was perfect for me because I didn't really want to be seen. Unfortunately, it lacked a dance floor and we really wanted to dance. So, after a few hours, we headed to Saints.

Saints had only been open for just over a year and was a club that Noah more or less set up himself. I'd been there with him many times and I knew the security guards by name. It was also popular, and when we arrived the queue was already about thirty minutes long.

"Do you think you could use your influence to get us to

the front?" Vic asked with hope, as she looked at the mass of people in front of us.

I cringed a little. "I don't know…"

I really didn't know, because I wasn't sure if I still had any influence. As far as these men were concerned, I was Noah's ex-girlfriend. When I'd been there without Noah, they always looked out for me and we all seemed to get on. Plus, I was still a main act at The Dome, which tended to get me an element of special treatment. Ultimately, I worked for the Joysons, just like they did. However, I didn't know if they'd treat me the same and I wasn't sure that I dared put it to the test.

In the end, I didn't need to. "What are you doing standing out here?" A gruff voice called, and I turned around to see a familiar face walking towards me, smiling.

"Robbo! Do you think you can get us in?" I asked, giving him my most endearing smile.

He scoffed at me. "Like you even need to ask."

He gestured for us to follow him and he led us to the front of the queue.

The other doormen smiled as we passed them, but I didn't miss the questioning look that they gave each other. They clearly had no idea what they were supposed to do and it's not like they could call Noah on the day of his wedding to ask if they still needed to look out for his ex.

Like most people, they suspected that Noah still loved me, but nobody really knew how it ended between us — other than badly.

It's not like I needed to be taken care of anyway, because I had my four, fearsome sisters with me, and they were not about to let anyone else do anything to cause me more pain. So, we drank, and we danced. I necked shots, I slammed slammers and I desperately tried to keep the smile on my face, forget about Noah, the wedding and sex.

Oh God… I didn't dare to even let a glimmer of that thought enter my brain.

Unfortunately, in The Beneath, some things are impossible to escape.

At one point, I was inside a toilet cubicle and I could hear a group of girls talking about me. "It's so sad… I'm so sad for her… Can you believe that she's still going to sing there?"

They would have seemed sincere had their voices not hitched in delight at the gossip.

I could imagine what they were thinking; the orphan that dared to reach for the stars had come crashing down to earth. That's what they thought, and I didn't need the reminder. Unlike Adam, my wounds didn't show on the surface, but they were real and raw and they fucking hurt. I just hid away until they left and then tried to gloss over the pain as I reapplied my lipstick.

It wasn't just the girls that were curious though; the men were too. I was the girl that brought Noah Joyson to his knees. The one girl he stuck with over the many that he'd had, and that intrigued them. I'd get a nudge from one of my sisters when we were dancing, telling me to look in a certain direction and I'd see someone staring at me. I was encouraged to go for it and to have some fun, but I always shook my head and carried on dancing.

Anyway, I was having fun. Despite everything, I was having fun. I was losing myself in the music and was almost too drunk to focus on life. Then suddenly, my friends moved away from me, smirking, as a hand wrapped around my waist, and a hot body pressed against me and started dancing with me. I turned around to see a face I vaguely recognised.

He was an orphan, quite a few years older but I couldn't place his name.

"Hi!" he shouted into my ear.

I nearly gagged. He felt sweaty and smelled like vomit.

"I'm Richard, do you want to come and sit with me?" He gestured with an eager smile to where the darkened booths were seated around the edge of the dancefloor.

Through my beer goggles, he seemed good looking, but I wasn't interested or available. "No thanks," I shouted back, as I took his hand from my waist and started to move away from him, but he pulled me back and put both hands around my body.

"Oh... come on." He started to eat my ear and the bile began to rise. "I'm sure you could use some fun, right now."

Feeling repulsed, I leaned away from his mouth and tried to release myself from his grip, but he was not getting the message. Sarah saw what was happening and started to come back over, but before she could get to me, I was suddenly surrounded by three of the security team. They were all big men, and I knew they could fight. Noah tended to hand pick them from the fight club and the hands around my waist quickly disappeared.

As soon as I was released, I turned around to see Richard being dragged off with one arm behind his back. That answered that question then, they were still looking out for me. I wasn't sure if it was out of friendship to me, or if they were playing it safe and avoiding the risk of Noah's wrath — but I was grateful to them either way. Wiping Richard's stinky saliva from my ear; I turned back to face Robbo and thanked him, but he just smiled before following the others.

For a moment I felt a little concerned about Richard... but only for a moment.

"Don't do that to me again!" I scolded Sarah as she

reached me. "I just want to have fun with you guys. I don't want setting up with anyone."

I knew they meant well, but they needed to know that I didn't want that to happen. Not just because it couldn't happen, but because that wasn't who I was. They knew that and they all apologised, professing their undying love for me, as those that love you do, when they're pissed as farts! We had a wobbly group hug, but then another song that we loved came on and we strutted into the middle of the dancefloor, which was where we stayed until the lights started to come on.

It was one o'clock, my head was spinning from the alcohol, and the beat from the music was still playing in my ears, but none of us wanted the night to end, and so we followed the crowd to a late-night café and sat on the curb eating chips.

"Oh, my God, I've got the best idea!" Laura squealed. "We should go to The Cell!"

We groaned at her in unison. Laura had always been desperate to check out The Cell because it was secretive, and in her mind that made it seductive and all the more exciting.

"Come on…" she urged, trying to rally us. "It'll be fun, and Eve can get us in, can't you?"

I almost spat out a chip. "I doubt it," I told her laughing, that's the last place Noah would want me to be.

"Oh, come on," she implored. "The bouncers are clearly still looking out for you."

"Which is exactly why they won't let us in."

"We could try…."

My head snapped towards Vic and my mouth hung open in shock as I looked at all of their faces and realised what had happened. One by one, their curiosity had won them over. They were all intrigued, and if I was being honest, I always had been too.

"We'll get turned away," I warned them, but they jumped to their feet and pulled me up from the curb.

We didn't get turned away. I've got no idea how five pissed young women actually got into a club predominantly frequented by men, but we did. To my surprise, we weren't the only ones, and there were one or two tables that had women at them. Some accompanied by men, but one table was all girls, just like us. The hostess welcomed us and sat us at a table and we just took it all in.

The girls were buzzing, but if anything, I was more curious than excited. Noah had always hated the idea of me coming here, but from first impressions, I couldn't tell why. It was like I'd expected and yet not. It was dark, which meant private, and seductively lit, but it didn't feel seedy. I didn't really get any negative vibes, but then my senses were somewhat numbed.

The dancers were sexy, and clearly out to seduce for cash, but they didn't seem predatory or even vulnerable. Part of me always wondered if The Cell was where those that had no other choice would work, but all I could see were powerful women. They were more powerful than me, that's for sure and they looked like they were having fun.

After a few minutes of sitting there and staring in awe, the hostess returned with two bottles of champagne. She put one in a cooler, then started to open the other, and we all looked at each other with the same expression, that said, "How the fuck are we going to pay for this?"

"Oh… do you have a drinks list?" Hannah asked, trying to hide her concern.

"No need." The hostess smiled as she popped the cork. "It's champagne for you ladies tonight, and it's on the house," she said, giving me a smile and a nod.

They all turned to me and giggled, and once our glasses were full, they all gestured towards me in a toast.

Then Vic leaned into me and brought me back down a little. "They must seriously feel guilty if we're getting the VIP treatment," she shouted into my ear.

I smiled at her and hid my real emotions behind my glass so that they couldn't see the guilt I felt over lying to them, and fear in my heart over what was to come. In truth, I had no idea why everyone was being so accommodating. I knew that not all of these people would know about the arrangement. So, it was either that they knew that Noah still loved me and were playing it safe, or they had been told by the Joysons that I was to be looked out for. Needless to say, my friends were enjoying themselves too much to question it and so I tried to get back on their wavelength and enjoy our night, which was clearly now going to go on until morning.

I felt apprehensive at first, like every single eye in there was on me, but after a couple of glasses of very expensive bubbles, I was dancing around the table with the rest of them. It wasn't easy to dance there but we were too drunk to care. I was completely in my zone, and had almost forgotten everything, but I was startled when Laura let out a scream!

I almost jumped out of my skin, but I quickly realised that it was more of an elated squeal, as one of the dancers took her hand, pulled her to the stage and pushed her up against the pole. We all burst out laughing as she tried, and failed to wrangle it like a pro, with the actual pro trying to guide her so that she didn't break anything. Then I felt a tap on my shoulder and the smiling hostess beckoned me to follow her, and my laughter got stuck in my throat.

I had no clue where we were going or why, and even with the copious amounts of alcohol flowing; I felt uneasy. She said nothing as she led me past the toilets and through a staff door and towards an office. She paused, knocked, and I heard a man tell us to "come in," and then she gestured for me to go in alone, as she turned and walked away. I watched her until she went from view, then placed my hand on the door handle, but I couldn't quite make myself open it. I had no idea who or what was behind the door, or why they wanted me alone.

My heart started to beat rapidly, as I debated what to do, but after about thirty-seconds I thought, "What the fuck else can they do?" and pushed the door open confidently, as if I did not give the slightest shit. I'm not sure what expression I wore on my face when that door opened, but Rick gave me an amused smile before giving me a slight nod, and I instantly relaxed.

Rick: the night manager at The Cell, and someone I'd seen on occasion when he had meetings at The Dome with Noah and his brothers. As far as I knew, he was a decent guy. I knew that Noah liked him, anyway, and even though Noah associated with the lowest of the low, he only liked those that he considered to be halfway decent human beings. Rick was in his thirties, and was one of the few at his level in the business that was not related to any of the Founding Families.

"Hang on a sec — she's here," he said, as he pressed a button on his phone.

He placed it on the table, stood up, put both hands in his pockets, and moved forward so that he was right in front of me. It would have felt a little unnerving were it not for the smile on his face and laughter in his eyes.

"Are you going to give me grief tonight?" he asked me, still smiling.

"I wasn't planning to…" I shrugged a little. "But if you're worried then why did you let us in?"

His smile never faulted. "The security at Saints informed all the clubs that you girls were letting off some steam

tonight… which is understandable." His smile faded then.
"And as you landed on my doorstep, it's now my responsibility to make sure you do that safely, as opposed to just
wandering off into the streets and into some random house
party."

"Oh… sorry…"

"It's fine." He was smiling again. "Anyway, there's somebody that wants to speak to you." He pressed a button on his
phone and handed it to me.

I took it nervously, expecting to see Noah's name on the
screen, but immediately felt pissed off when I saw David's
instead. I let out a loud sigh as I put the phone to my ear. "I'm
not going to cause Rick any trouble, so you don't need to
tell me."

I rolled my eyes dramatically at Rick, and he shuffled
on the spot in discomfort at the way I was speaking to his
boss.

"How are you doing, Eve?" David asked, almost
managing to sound genuinely concerned.

"Like *you* care," I scoffed.

He laughed a little. "Do you think we'll ever go back to
being friends?"

My laugh was a little darker. "I don't remember a time
when we were friends."

He sighed then. "I'm not your enemy, Eve…"

"You could have fooled me."

"I understand that you need this tonight," he continued, as
if I hadn't spoken. "I know this will have been a shit day for
you, but I'd like to make sure that this is a one-night thing as
opposed to the start of something?"

I wanted to laugh again, but the anger started to course
through me, and I couldn't quite manage it. "Don't worry,
David, I know my role and my place." I almost spat the

words out. "Tomorrow, I will go back to being the good girl who follows all your fucking rules."

"Good. Now, could you pass me back to Rick?"

I glanced at the phone and discretely tapped the speaker-phone symbol before handing it back to Rick with an innocent smile on my face. He still seemed a little shocked as to how I was able to speak to David the way I had, but he took the phone and put it to his ear.

"David," he said, letting him know he'd returned to the call.

"Rick," David replied, and then Rick startled at the unexpected volume of David's voice and moved the phone away from his ear. "Let her do what she wants... just keep her safe."

Rick was frowning at me, but I found the ability to laugh then. "Wow! You'd almost think he cared."

Rick softened a little. "What makes you think he doesn't? If nothing else, you make them a shitload of money." His smiling eyes reappeared as he shook his phone in my direction. "I thought you weren't going to give me any trouble?"

"Orphan's honour." I drew a cross over my heart to reinforce my point.

He let out a little chuckle as he turned towards to door. "Right... come with me."

I followed him back out to the main room, and he spoke to the hostess before taking me back to my friends.

"Ladies!" He smiled with an easy charm and I watched as Hannah blushed. "Would you like to follow me?"

They all looked at me, questions dancing in their drunken eyes, and I just smiled and shrugged at them, because even though I was no more in the know than they were, I knew Rick was under orders to let us have some fun. The hostess started collecting our drinks and then waited as we all got in line and followed Rick into another corridor that was full of doors. There were so many doors there and so many places to hide.

He led us to one, and held the door open for us as he gestured for us to go in. It was a small room, soft pink in colour and seductively lit, just like the main room, but it only had one small stage and a pole in the middle... as well as padded seating and mirrors all around. I guess people needed to get comfy when they were in there for a private show. I cringed at the mirrors a little, as I thought about how the guest got to ogle the dancer from every single angle.

However, the hostess then appeared, not only with our drinks, but also another two bottles of champagne, and I suddenly forgot what my issues were.

"If you ladies want to play with the pole tonight, you do it here," Rick smiled, then he left the room, leaving Hannah pining after him.

The girls were delighted, and we all did our best to dance seductively, but being completely wasted we looked like complete muppets. At one point, Vic managed to slide down the pole almost expertly, but then she couldn't stop herself and landed on her arse with a bang, leading to us all bursting out laughing. We must've been in there an hour, when Rick tentatively opened the door, caught my eye and gestured for me to follow him.

I was pretty wasted by that point and placed my hand on the wall to guide me as we walked. "Am I in trouble?"

He smiled at my drunken slur, but it didn't reach his eyes. "I hope not."

He led me further down the corridor to another room, but he didn't open it for me, he just gave a slight smile and walked away.

I was too drunk to be nervous and assumed that I was

going to find David on the other side, waiting to give me some grief. So, I almost staggered backwards when I saw Noah dressed in a dark hoodie and jogging bottoms, with his arms folded and looking very tense. I could tell he was struggling with his anger and I knew he'd had a tough day, but my heart suddenly hurt, and my drunken brain wasn't quite able to put the correct response together.

"Shouldn't you be somewhere else?" I raised my eyebrows at him as I made my way over to the stage so that I could get off my wobbly feet.

He put his hand in his pocket and pulled out my ring. "Shouldn't you be wearing this?" Then he came closer and put it back on my finger. "I went home to see you and you weren't there, and then I saw this in its box."

I put my hands up in a show of peace and tried to stand up. "Noah…" I swayed a little, so I put my arms around his neck for support. "How do I explain this ring? Where do I say it came from?"

He looked down a little and I cupped his face and kissed him on the lips that were no longer officially mine.

"It's just so sparkly…" I wiggled my finger around so that it caught and reflected the dim pink lights, sending flowery patterns around the room.

Noah wrapped his arms around me, and I felt his gentle laughter vibrating in his chest. He leaned into me and his breath against my ear, made my body tingle. "You're too cute when you're drunk. It's impossible to be mad with you."

That pulled my attention away from the sparkly flowers. I yanked his hands away from me, as I stepped back and glared at him. "And why exactly would you be mad with me?"

His arms flew out as he gestured around the room. "You're here!"

"So are you!" I shouted back. "Why aren't you at home shagging your new wife?"

My heart lurched as I spoke, because as soon as the words left my mouth, I knew I'd fucked up. His face just dropped, and he turned away from me. I knew I couldn't have hurt him more in that moment if I tried, and it made me feel like shit, yet how could I not say it? It had been plaguing me since the day I decided that I'd go along with their plan.

I could handle his wedding ring and I could handle him saying vows in Church, because none of that was real. However, the sex? They were expected to and were going to have sex. Regardless of how he felt about Jane, he was still going to get an erection, and he was still going to cum inside her, and in my mind, that meant that there was an element of pleasure involved. He would find enough pleasure in her to finish, and that's the bit that drove me to insane levels of insecurity.

He eventually turned around with his jaw clenched and his hands balled into fists that he held closely against his sides. "I cannot do this without losing it if you can't keep your shit together too." He was shaking, he was actually shaking. "You knew what this would involve. It's a job!"

He paused as the anger seemed to seep out of him, only to be replaced by sadness. He pulled me closer and held me. "I don't even remember it… I wasn't there," he whispered into my ear. "It's just going to be how it was with all the other girls before I met you. I'll just switch off and do it. It's mechanics, Eve — that's all. You and me… that's real!"

"And what if you start feeling something for her?"

"I don't hate her, and I don't want to make this harder for her either, but I don't think of her that way."

I pulled back a little, looked right at him and swallowed hard. "And what about when she gives you a baby?"

He rested his forehead against mine for a moment and then kissed me gently. "You have all of me. Jane just has an empty shell… Nothing and nobody will ever replace you."

I looked down as the tears fell and the pain kicked me in the gut. I knew it was hard for him too and it was inevitable that one of us would implode eventually. We'd put off talking about it, but it was never off our minds and it was too big to ignore forever. He lifted my chin up, wiped away my tears and kissed me again, and I responded by grabbing his head and kissing him back with more force. We stayed like that for a few minutes, kissing with both aggression and passion, but then I pushed him away, as anger suddenly flared up in me.

"I hate them all for doing this to us! That includes your parents."

He nodded solemnly in reply as he let out a deep sigh.

The mood had passed. Alcohol always tips you one way or the other, and it had decided to lead me down the path of anger and hatred, and I couldn't shake it. I couldn't look at Noah without seeing his family, so I turned away from him, wrapped my arms around myself and tried to stop the shaking that seemed to have come out of nowhere.

Noah came up behind me, rested his hands on my waist and leaned in close to my ear. "How you're feeling now… I know the cure," he breathed into me, and as the electricity shot down my spine, I pushed my body into his.

He kissed my ear, and then he stepped away from me. I kept my back to him as I watched him in the mirrors that lined the walls. He pushed his shoes off and then removed his clothes, whilst watching me, watching him via the mirrors the entire time. He saw the moment my body language changed… the moment anger turned to arousal, when my eyes became darker, and the throbbing in my clit had me shifting awkwardly on the spot.

Once naked, he sat down and I slowly turned around and moved, so that I was standing in front of him. His legs were spread, and he said nothing as he leaned forward and ran his hands up my legs. When he reached the top, he tickled my inner thigh for a moment, causing me to gasp, before he slid his hands further up and slowly pulled down my knickers.

I stepped out of them, and then he looked at me with an intensity that had my heart racing, as he asked, "Do you need anything?"

He ran one hand back up my leg, and when he reached my centre he smiled at my wetness. "Apparently not."

I pushed his hand away, moved his legs closer together and straddled him. I held myself above him, still not saying a word, but being completely unable to take my eyes off his.

He reached up and gently stroked my face. "You're feeling lost, aren't you?"

"Yes," I replied breathlessly.

"Let me help you find your way back," he pleaded, and then he put his hands on my hips and gently, but firmly pushed me down, not stopping until he was fully inside me.

He closed his eyes and clenched his jaw at the sensation, and I gasped and tipped my head back at the familiar and welcome feeling of him filling me. I hadn't expected to even see him that day, let alone have the opportunity to be with him, and my body started moving without any instruction from my hazy brain.

I started to ride him; slowly at first but then he tilted his head back and groaned, and all of a sudden, I just went for it. I dug my nails into his shoulders, and I bit his lip, and when he tried to retaliate, I pushed his head back and placed my hand around his throat. I was riding him hard and fast, giving him everything, and I was taking everything I felt out on him. I fucked him with the same level of aggression that he did when he came to me lost, and although I could see that he was struggling not to cum; I didn't get any pleasure from it because it wasn't me. I was angry, but not with Noah; my hate wasn't for him. I couldn't cure it with an orgasm because it would still be there afterwards, and so I slowed down.

Noah opened his eyes at the change of pace, and he saw the change in me too. He released the hold he had on my hips and brought his hands up to my face and cradled me.

I shook my head as my body softened. "I don't need to release my anger on you… that's not how I find my way back."

I was panting hard and I tried to lift myself off him, but he held onto me.

"Then how?" he pleaded.

"Not through anger… through love… through your love."

He pulled my face into his. "I love you, so much."

He kissed me, and kept me firmly against him, as he stood us both up, before lowering me gently onto the seat. He was on top, and he took charge, and as he cocooned me with his body and his love; I instantly felt the pleasure rising. My body came alive, I felt the hairs on my arms stand tall, then the heat started to rise from my core before it engulfed my entire body. I started to shake uncontrollably, and he held me together in his embrace, as I came hard, crying out his name. Noah quickly followed, crying out loudly and incoherently, then he just fell onto me panting. He planted desperate kisses all over my neck and chest making sure I knew who held his heart. I grabbed onto him and held him tight, as I pulled his mouth onto mine.

I didn't see the door open, but I heard the scream and we both turned with a start.

"What the fuck are you doing?" Vic shouted in shock and anger. "Get off her!" She waved frantically at Noah.

I started to try to rise up as much as I could with Noah naked above me, and still inside me. "Vic… this isn't what you think!" I pleaded but she just looked at me in disgust before storming out of the room.

The look on her face had been the look that I was expecting when people found out, just not so soon and not from one of my sisters.

I wriggled out from underneath Noah. "I'm going to have to tell them."

He started to quickly get dressed, and I could see his fear too. We were supposed to keep this secret longer than a fucking day. "Will they talk?"

"They didn't last time," I reminded him. "But does it matter? This isn't going to stay a secret for long."

Noah let out a deep sigh and pulled me close, his heart was pounding and not just from the sex and I had to repeat-edly reassure him that we could trust them. He didn't want me to have to do it alone, but I wasn't sure that he'd be left standing if I put him in a room with all of them, and so he was eventually persuaded to let me do it alone.

I went to the toilets to straighten myself up and then walked unsteadily back to the room where my sisters were. I opened the door, and they were all gesturing wildly as Vic told them what she'd seen. They turned at once when they saw me come in, and I felt like I was the size of an ant, as I shakily pulled the door shut behind me. I think I would have been less scared facing Sister Theresa, at that point.

I was expecting them to be angry with me, but they weren't. They were angry with Noah, but concerned for me, specifically, with the hold that they believed that he continued to have over me. They ranted on and on and I tried to explain, but they wouldn't let me. They just kept saying the same thing over and over again, never letting me speak, until I screamed at the top of my lungs and threw a bottle of champagne against the mirrored wall! We all jumped as the glass shattered and the panels crumbled one by one, revealing the baron black wall behind them. Then they all stood there, in stunned silence, finally listening to me as I told them everything.

I woke up at some point the next day, desperate for water and with a throbbing head. It took me a while to work out where I was but then I turned over and jumped when I saw Hannah lying next to me, staring at me. I was in her bed and in their home, and at any other time I would have laughed and called her a stalker, but my head hurt and the uncomfortable feeling in my gut reminded me that last night was more than just a heavy night.

The fog, blurring my thoughts started to lift, and as the events of the night started to unfold in my mind, I rolled back and lay there, looking up at the ceiling.

Hannah let out a deep sigh. "Did I dream what you told us last night?" she asked me quietly, it was barely more than a whisper.

I turned back to look at her and I could see the fear and concern written all over her face. "No," I croaked out in reply, and then I pulled the duvet over my head.

24

*I*t took six months for the whole of The Beneath to find out. I'm surprised it took that long, to be honest, and I'm very pleased to have been able to say that it wasn't my fault.

They were a horrible six months, for all of us, but Noah in particular felt like he was being torn in half. I tried to hide my pain and jealousy from him, but he always knew, and it couldn't always be contained. Even if I didn't say the words, he saw it in my face.

Then there was Jane, who would switch from being cold and bitter, to being the perfect, doting wife. It was hard for her too, I knew that, however, I couldn't help but feel like my heart mattered more than her ego. Jane was married to, and occasionally having sex with a robot. Noah was there, but he wasn't. He didn't want to make it horrible for her, so he was generous with her, but that only served to make things more confusing for Jane.

Jane had tried to keep herself emotionally distant and to treat it like a job, but she couldn't turn her emotions off when it came to the sex. Especially, as she was enjoying it, and as

ROXANNA C REVELL

far as she was concerned, Noah was too. She started trying to work that angle, and tried to tempt him, seduce him, even. She seemed to think that she had a way to make him happy, to make him hers, to make their marriage real, and to be rid of me. Unfortunately for her, Noah could tell what she was doing, and the harder she tried, the higher his wall became.

It took its toll on him, and I had to deal with the Other Noah more than once. Then, when I woke up to the fact that I was partially causing it, I gave myself a stern talking to. Noah hadn't wanted the marriage. He'd been fighting it since he was eighteen. He only agreed to it because I asked him to. Because I asked him to help me in my lifelong mission to keep Adam safe. I knew what it involved, and I still asked him, and he loved me enough to do it.

He loves me. He's mine. What we have is real. What we have is the truth. That became my mantra, and I repeated it over and over until it sank in, and I found a way to live with it.

The night that the secret came out was on one of my nights off. Not just a night off from The Dome but a night off from Noah. In truth, I didn't want a night off from Noah, but it was better to think of it that way, than thinking of it as what it really was — Jane's turn.

I went to Halo with Adam, Meredith, and John, which was a rarity for me. Usually, when I had the chance I'd escape with Harriet and my sisters, but things were still not quite perfect between me and Adam, so when he invited me out, I practically bit his hand off.

Meredith knew the truth. It was hard to keep it from her, after all, she was the one that was given the message, and she wouldn't drop it until we told her everything. She knew it was wise to keep it to herself, and even though John was as much of a brother to me as Adam was, I didn't want him to know. He may be able to keep a secret, but I didn't want to put anyone else at risk if they didn't need to be.

It was a fun night. Adam, as always, used my connection to The Dome to get some free drinks and we were all getting a little trashed. Dancing would have been good at that point, but we were cosied up in a booth and Adam and Meredith didn't really look like they were in a rush to go anywhere.

I'd grown used to seeing Adam with girls over the years, because he was never without one on his arm when we were out. I actually loved seeing him with Meredith, since she was the only one he'd ever cared about. I was a little envious of the fact that he was able to be open about his feelings in public, but ultimately, his happiness always made me smile. I turned to roll my eyes at John in mock-irritation over the lovefest happening in front of us, and he smiled back, almost convincingly. John has such a sweet smile, but it didn't cover his pain that night, and I felt that it was time to talk about why.

I dragged him to the bar, leaving Adam and Meredith to it. Well, we tried to anyway, only, I kept seeing John looking over with so much pain written all over his face, that it made me forget about my own.

After the second tequila slammer, I reached out and put my hand on his arm. "What are we going to do with you?"

He gave me a puzzled smile. "What do you mean?"

I stepped a little closer and looked him right in the eyes. "I know."

He shrugged his shoulders and furrowed his brow, genuinely not understanding my point, and so I gave him a reassuring smile, letting him know that he could always trust me. Then I looked over to Adam, he followed my gaze, and when we looked back at each other, I repeated, "I know."

He looked embarrassed and shuffled around a bit. He

started to speak, and the look on his face suggested that he was going to try to deny it, but then he looked in my eyes, that showed only love, and thought better of it.

"Does he know?" he asked, his eyes quickly darting over to Adam.

"Of course not," I scoffed. "That would involve him having some sort of a clue about anyone other than himself."

We both laughed and he nodded in agreement. My brother was a good person in the grand scheme of things, but things in his life often revolved around Planet Adam.

"What do I do?" he asked me with sadness in his eyes and I wrapped him in a bear hug.

I stood on my tiptoes and leaned into his ear. "He loves you, John," I told him with honesty, "but not like that. I don't think he'll ever love you like that."

John looked down and nodded in understanding. He knew it too. Adam loved the bones of John, but he was only attracted to women.

I gave his arm a little prod, snapping him out of his gloom. "We may live in The Beneath, but we're not entirely backwards here!" I laughed. "You aren't the only one. You just need to open your eyes to who else might be out there."

Heart to heart over; we ordered more tequila and then tried to spot any other gay men that might be in the bar. I had suspicions about a few, but according to John, my radar was well and truly off. After a while, Adam and Meredith announced that they were heading back to hers, and so John and I decided that we'd go to Saints to try to find some men. John thought that meant for me too and I played along, but it wasn't straight men that I was going to be hunting.

I was on a tequila high and ready to party with my third favourite man, but then we got outside, and we heard them. Everyone heard them. You see, Halo has a VIP area. It's great to be in. I'd been in there plenty of times and you can see everything that's going on in the main bar, but nobody can see you. So, little me, hanging out with the rest of the 'commoners' had no idea that Noah had been there with Jane, her brother Pete, and a few other friends. That is, until we got outside, and sobriety hit me in the face, as fear became the only thing flowing through me.

"This is supposed to be my night!" We heard a considerably drunk-sounding Jane shout as we stepped outside.

I recognised her voice and my heart started pounding. I looked further along the pavement, that was full people, all staring at the scene unfolding in front of them; Jane Joyson shouting at her husband in the street. Her friends were all around her, her brother was standing to the side, and Noah was holding the door to the car open and gesturing for her to get in.

"I'm not going anywhere with him… no, Pete, I will not be quiet!" she continued to shout, oblivious of the audience surrounding her. "He doesn't want to go home with me anyway, he wants to go home with her!"

She hadn't seen me, none of them had, they were all focused on Jane. Specifically, on shutting her up and getting her out of there. I turned to Adam and Meredith and they were both looking at me, completely unable to hide the fear in their eyes. I had no idea how to feel and no idea what to do, but I knew that if they didn't get her away soon, all the people on that street, the people that were staring with intrigue, trying to figure out what was going on, would soon find out.

I couldn't get involved. We'd accidentally found ourselves in the same bar and my presence had caused her pain. Seeing me would make it worse. Besides, I was supposed to be nothing more than Noah's ex.

Unfortunately, Jane then got me involved. "All you've done is stare at her, all night!" she shouted again. "It's supposed to be my night."

I watched as Noah tried to reason with her, but then he shook his head and turned to the side — to the side that I was standing on, and our eyes met. He paused for just a moment too long, and then Jane followed his gaze right to me.

"Oh, look. Here she is."

Every single person standing outside the bar turned to look at me.

"Go with her! We all know that's where you'd rather be."

I had two choices; I could either walk away or I could try to help. I had no idea which would have been the better option, I still don't. All I knew was that Jane was crumbling. Jane was about to reveal the secret, and we'd agreed to try to find a way to get through it together. It was the silent pact we made the day we gave up control over our lives.

I turned to Adam and the others. "You should go."

Adam stepped closer to me. "I am not leaving you here!"

John took my hand in an attempt to guide me away. "Don't get involved, Eve. Let's just all go."

"I'm already involved, John, and I need you to get my brother out of here."

Adam scoffed. "Oh, come on. What do you think they're going to do to me? This isn't your fault!"

John released my hand and spun round to Adam. "What does that mean?"

"I don't want to find out…" I replied, looking only at Adam. Then I turned to John. "Get my brother out of here… now."

Meredith guided them both away, I took a deep breath, and slowly walked along the pavement towards the carnage, with every single person watching every single step that I took. I didn't look at anyone and I tried to paint an expression on my face that suggested that it wasn't a big deal, but my God, it was.

Everything was about to turn to shit.

The girls with Jane scowled at me as I approached, and then got all huffy when I stood in front of her. I ignored them, because they were insignificant, and looked instead at the other people around me. Pete stepped back a bit, Noah looked like a caged animal about to explode, and Jane... Jane looked pissed as a fart, and well and truly broken. I turned to face her, which put my back to Noah, but I felt him move closer to me.

"Think about what you're doing," I told her quietly, but I was trying to speak volumes with the look in my eyes. She had to know what she was about to do would destroy everything.

"It was my night," she replied through gritted teeth and falling tears.

I put my hands out as a show of peace. "I didn't know you were here... but Jane, you need to go home."

I said it with kindness, but her response was the opposite.

"Don't tell me what to do, you stupid whore!" she spat in my face.

I felt Noah stiffen behind me. I knew that he wanted to stop her, but there were eyes on us and there was still a chance to stop everything from coming out.

I put my hands up again, not just to try to appease her, but because when the story was told by the people in the crowd, I wanted it known that I'd tried to play nice. "Fine. I'll leave," I said, turning to walk away.

"Yes, go back to your brother. I hope he appreciates how hard you have to fuck to protect him... oops, sorry..."

Sarcasm oozed from her drunken face. "I meant how hard you have to work to protect him."

What a silly bitch. She was snarling at me and I'd been drinking too, so it was a struggle not to bite back. However, I knew the only thing I could bite was my tongue, so I sucked it up and kept walking away.

Unfortunately, Jane wasn't done. "I feel sorry for you."

Her laugh was full of contempt, and I couldn't stop myself from turning to face her.

"Having to spread your legs for a man that's married…"

"Jane!" Noah barked out. "That's enough. Get in the car, now!"

She glared at him and let out a little huff, and I couldn't help but wonder why she didn't have this fight in her six months ago.

"She's pathetic, you know?" she growled at him. "The love of your life… your little mistress… she's pathetic… and so are you!"

The red flag was dangled in front of me and I couldn't hold back a second longer. I marched back and got right in her face.

"You didn't tell them no, Jane. You were the only one of us that could, and you didn't!" I reminded her. "I may be a mistress, but it's to a man that loves me. You, on the other hand… you married a man that doesn't love you, just because Mummy and Daddy told you to." I looked at her just as snidely, and asked, "So which one of us is really the pathetic whore?"

"Careful, Eve…" Pete chimed in as he stepped a little closer. "You wouldn't want Adam to have another accident, would you?"

The rage that I was trying my best to contain boiled to the

surface and I turned to face him head on. "Did you just threaten my brother?"

He just smirked at me, his superior attitude, glaring right at me. I started to move closer to him with my fist flexing at my side, but Noah grabbed hold of my arm and pulled me back.

"Leave it," he quietly warned me, and then he signalled with his eyes for me to look around.

I did, and I saw that every single person on that street was staring at us. Staring at us and questioning. They were already trying to put the pieces together.

I looked back at Noah and he leaned in close, so that only I could hear him. "Don't give them an excuse."

I knew what he meant. It hadn't been my fault, but if I said any more, and if I challenged them any more than I already had, then it was entirely possible that it would be taken out on me.

I looked back at Jane, who was now crying, with her head in her hands, and then I turned back to Noah. "I'm going home." I looked him in the eyes. "You know where I am if you need me."

He looked down and clenched his jaw, a flicker of shame crossing his face, as it always did when he thought about it. When he thought about what he needed from me when the darkness descended. What he knew that he would need that night.

I started to walk away, but then two cars pulled up, stopping with a skid. One was a police car driven by Scott Legion, the other was driven by David. My heart started pounding as the fear that had flowed before now crippled me. I'd hoped to be able to slip away but now the others were getting involved. Now, The Council was getting involved.

Scott and his colleague started clearing the crowd, who

walked away obediently, whilst craning their necks in order to get a glimpse of what would happen next. David then came over to Noah and grabbed his shoulder.

"What the fuck happened?" he asked him with a harshness that suggested he'd forgotten the beating he'd taken.

"This wasn't Eve's fault!" Noah replied in the same tone, with his glare warning his brother to remember it.

Jane cleared her throat. "This was me…" she said through her tears.

I breathed a sigh of relief. She could have thrown me under the bus and I was grateful that she didn't.

"I got upset… I started it."

David sighed and looked to Jane, and then to me. "Just take your wife home," he instructed, looking back at Noah. "I'll take Eve…"

"No!" Noah and I argued at the same time.

David let out a little laugh and raised his eyebrows at us both. "Seriously? What do you think I'm going to do?"

Noah looked at me and I could see that he was close to losing it, so I gave him a silent plea, begging him to keep it together, before I turned to David. "I'm fine on my own."

"Eve, can you for once, not see me as the enemy and just do as I fucking ask?" He glared at me, but he seemed more desperate than angry. "Noah and Jane need to leave, and I will get you home safely."

I looked back to Noah, who was hanging on by a thread and gave him a small smile of encouragement. Then I turned to David, nodded slightly, and then followed him to his car.

I turned to him as soon as he started the engine. "I didn't know they were there until we got out and Jane was already shouting in the street. So, don't go thinking that you need to teach me a lesson. Stay away from Adam!" I warned.

"The bouncers told me what happened, so don't worry about it," he said, never taking his eyes off the road.

"Good, because don't forget what will happen if you do."

He said nothing, he didn't even react. He just kept driving, keeping his eyes firmly ahead. Then when we pulled up outside my flat, he let out a deep sigh.

"Out of interest, Eve, where will you go? How will you leave, exactly?" he smirked. "We could kill him and there'd be nowhere for you to go."

I looked at him hard, trying once again to contain the rage that always flared up when anyone suggested doing anything to Adam.

"If you were to kill my brother… I would run myself a nice, hot bath," I said, looking him right in the eye. "I would take a sharp razor…" I put my wrist out towards him. "And I would slice, right here."

I put a finger against my wrist and as David looked down at it, I let the finger follow the vein along my forearm. "I would lie there, watching the blood pour out, feeling my life slip away… and in my dying moments I would be happy… because I would know that after I'm gone…" I paused for a moment and then looked him right in the eyes again. "Heads. Would. Fucking. Roll."

If he hadn't been sitting down, I think he would have stumbled backwards. He looked genuinely shocked and upset by my words.

"I truly hope that you don't mean that, and I would recommend not letting Noah hear you talk like that."

It was his turn to look me right in the eye. "I'm not sure you'd be able to cope with what he'd need from you…" he paused and looked me up and down, making sure I understood what he meant. "I think it would take quite a lot to bring him back from that."

I let out a bitter laugh, turned away and stared out of the window, feeling more exposed than ever before. I might as well have been sitting there naked, because apparently there were no secrets between us. I'd suggested to his parents that Noah's sexual needs went as dark as he did when he lost it, the day they came to the church. I hadn't really thought much about it since. I just assumed that they'd brushed it off as a weightless insult. Yet, David seemed to know the truth.

I turned back to him with a bitter smile, trying to act like I didn't care what he thought. "I disgust you, don't I?"

David looked at me with kindness and my stomach lurched. It was a look I'd rarely seen in him, especially aimed towards me, but it was definitely kindness.

"No." Then his face soured as he said, "He does."

25

----

*N*othing happened to Adam after that night. Nothing happened to Jane, except for the telling off that she got from her parents. Nothing happened to Noah and nothing happened to anyone else, because he came to me, like I knew he would, and he found his way out of the darkness, through me.

Unfortunately, enough had been said on that street for the few people that were there to put the pieces together, and the rumours spread. It would be more accurate to say that the truth spread like wildfire. Eve Matthews had agreed to be Noah Joyson's mistress in order to get him to agree to the arranged marriage to Jane Green; and Eve only agreed to do it because the Founding Families beat the shit out of her brother! That's how it went and there was no point trying to gloss over it.

So, instead, The Council went on the charm offensive, reminding the community of The Beneath of how and why they were so good for us. The school, the infirmary, local businesses, they were all given a financial boost. Business loans, new computers, medical equipment, you name it, they had it. People didn't forget, but they forgave. After all, what choice did they have?

As for me, I got a few looks for a while. People would stare and they'd whisper. Some people felt sorry for me, pitying me, and some judged me, thinking I was as pathetic as Jane said I was. Everyone had a differing opinion, but there was one thing that they all agreed on — that I was necessary. I was the glue that held Noah Joyson together, and my actions protected more than just my brother.

Noah and I were still expected to be discrete, and we couldn't go out for meals and be together openly in public — that was Jane's role. They still played the part, and nobody batted an eyelid, even if they had their thoughts, they weren't going to make them openly known. So, it all just became the norm, and after a while people stopped caring. The people that knew me and worked with me stopped giving me sympathetic smiles, and we all just got on with it.

Two years later, and we had found our groove, but then things started to change. When they first married, there was no suggestion of Jane getting pregnant. Their families figured that there would need to be an adjustment period, but after two years of marriage, grandchildren were starting to become expected, and I knew that Noah was being encouraged to sleep with Jane more than he was. More than the obligatory shag they had every couple of weeks in order to stop their families from interfering.

Once again, I had to repeat my mantra. *He loves me. He's mine. What we have is real. What we have is the truth.* It was easy to do because there was never any doubt in my mind that Noah still loved and needed me as much as he always had.

That wasn't the only thing that changed during those two years. The flow of illicit goods was starting to move from our side of the wall to theirs. Drugs were strictly forbidden on

The Other Side, but here, we had enough abandoned factories to get more than one marijuana farm up and running. Nothing was sold here. The Council liked to keep control of people too much to allow them to get stoned. Yet, through the guards, connections were made, the produce made it through the gates, and once again, the Founding Family pockets were lined with money from The Other Side.

I knew as much about it as most people did; and that was that the Manners and the Legions took care of it; but they needed people. Willing and brave young men to carry their goods through the gates and deal with whatever they faced once there; Runners they were called. It was risky, but they were paid well for it.

It wasn't just things on our side that had changed either. A new High Minister had taken power on The Other Side – High Minister Morgan, and he had big aspirations and the credentials to back them up. Morgan had been fundamental in making The New Order what it was. A state without a wall, without the divide. Now, he set his sights on Havensmere and St Martins, where it all began. He seemed to think that if he could reverse what was done here, then all the others would follow. A domino effect bringing about revolutionary change and equality for all.

He had a substantial following as there were many on The Other Side that felt guilty over the way that we were treated, and there were of course, those that wanted their children back. However, there was resistance too. Many didn't want to change the status quo. They feared what would happen if we were "set free". That perhaps we'd seek our revenge and riot in the streets. Of course, there were also those that didn't want the inconvenience of their illegitimate children showing up on their doorstep.

As if we ever would.

There was resistance in The Beneath too, more so, in fact, because none of us really wanted the change. We didn't have freedom to move, but it worked here, things worked. The Council and police force were as corrupt as they came, but as far as we could tell, that was pretty much how it was on The Other Side too. Besides, the wall didn't just keep us in, it kept them out, and most of us didn't like them all that much. Then there was The Council, who had no intention whatsoever of relinquishing their power.

Morgan quickly realised that it was going to be harder than he ever imagined, and so he took small steps. He wanted to stem the flow of babies being handed over and created a new male contraception that could be injected to prevent those pesky swimmers from being released into the wrong body. Fertain, it was called, and when regularly administered it was as effective as a vasectomy.

"Revolutionising men's relationship with contraception" is how he sold it, but no-one here could understand it. If they were so incapable of using condoms on The Other Side, then were they really going to regularly inject something into their testicles?

I was still at the salon, and The Dome, which was just making money hand over fist and keeping the Founding Families very happy. I loved singing there. It was a bit of escapism for me, it was right from the start. When I was on that stage all that mattered was my voice. It was nice to have people only think of me as a singer, even if only for a little while. Not the mistress or the whore. Not someone to be judged or pitied, but instead, someone to be admired and applauded, even respected.

David still insisted that I mingled with the guests. He knew I hated it and he had told me repeatedly that he didn't do it to piss me off. I was a "commodity" he told me once.

People didn't just want to see me sing from a distance, they wanted to get close, and they wanted me to make them feel like they mattered to me. I was supposed to boost their fragile egos and make them feel important.

"But they don't matter!" I'd argued, when he was giving me my 'pep talk' in my dressing room before I went on stage.

David and I had almost found an element of harmony to our relationship. He wasn't a friend, but he also wasn't the enemy. I think in his world, it was refreshing for him to have someone being honest, and I had no problem being honest with him.

He moved closer to me and handed me a different shade of lipstick to the one I was planning on wearing, and then smiled at the glare I gave him as I reluctantly took it.

"I know you don't realise this, Eve, but people are fascinated by you," he'd said genuinely. "The women are in awe and yet, jealous as hell, and the men want to get close to you so that they have something to wank over when they go back home to their boring and predictable lives."

I had nearly launched the curling tongs at him, but he just put his hands up in defence. "It's a game, Eve. Play the game and keep their money coming in."

It didn't make me feel any better about it, if anything it made me feel worse. I didn't want those rich men thinking that they could touch me. Although, there were times when I thought it would be funny if the sleazier ones tried to, because I knew that Noah would be the one to show them the error of their ways if they did. That is, if there was anything left after The Dome security team had finished with them.

They weren't all bad though, some were even tolerable, and one evening after my set, David escorted me through the applauding crowd. There were three people seated at the table we were heading to, all waiting expectantly; an older man, a woman of a similar age, and a younger man, who was, no doubt, their security. I focused on the smiling, older man, because I knew that he was the one David would want me to charm, and as we got closer, I realised that he seemed familiar, although I couldn't quite place him.

"Eve, this is Mr Southwold," David said, then he carried on talking, but on hearing the name 'Southwold' I immediately turned my attention to the younger man at the table. He wasn't security, he was their son, and someone I thought I'd never see again.

"Officer Ethan Southwold…" I smiled at him, as I put out my hand to shake his. "Surely as a member of Havensmere's law enforcement, you should be setting a better example?" I teased. "Isn't passing through the gates still frowned upon?"

His cheeks flushed a little and he beamed at me as if I'd just made his day, but he didn't get the chance to speak.

"You two have met?" The older Mr Southwold asked; Henry, I suddenly and quite randomly remembered that he was called Henry.

I looked back to him and caught the surprise on his face, and the alarm on David's. I smiled with grace and explained. "My brother had an accident a couple of years ago and had to spend some time at your hospital. I stayed with him, and your son had the unfortunate task of standing guard."

"Oh!" his mother said in surprise. "You never said, Ethan."

"It was work, Mother." He gave her a small smile, then he looked at me and a larger one appeared. "It was no bother," he said genuinely, but then he turned towards David and a harshness settled into his features, as he said, "And it was very enlightening."

Then his expression changed again, to a familiar one, the same one he wore when he stopped me from getting into the ambulance, and I realised that he had something that he needed to say. I had no idea what, but since he'd only shown me kindness, I decided that I'd give him the chance.

"Your son was a very gracious host," I said to his parents, then I turned back to Ethan, "and if memory serves, then I owe you a drink."

I gestured to the bar, and as he followed me over, I glanced back momentarily to see David looking horrified, and I couldn't help but smile a little. I did like the occasional moment of rebellion. I also saw one of the security team give me a questioning look and I gave him the signal to let him know that all was well. He looked a bit concerned because I'd never done anything like that before, and he knew Noah wouldn't like it. Still, he accepted my signal and spoke into his mouthpiece.

"Should I be concerned?" Ethan asked, gesturing towards the man now standing in position and glaring at him.

I laughed. "I think you'll be OK, but you probably have a time limit. What are you drinking?"

He smiled again before looking to the side a little. "You were absolutely breath-taking up there!" he blurted out, but he quickly composed himself again. "You look like you're happy. I take it life is treating you well?"

"I told you I'd be fine."

He smiled like a kid at Christmas. "I didn't think you'd remember me."

I shrugged as if it was nothing. "I always remember the things that take me by surprise," I smiled. "So, what are you drinking, and what is it that you want to say to me?"

He smiled knowingly. "Vodka and soda... thanks."

The barman poured his drink and handed it to him as I looked at him expectantly. He looked torn, just like he did outside the ambulance, but eventually he spoke.

"I'm training to join the Detective team… and I shouldn't be telling you this."

I took a sip of the drink that was handed to me, as I eyed him cautiously. "You haven't told me anything yet."

"I wasn't supposed to be coming here but my parents told me that you were singing, and I just had to," he said seriously, before quickly adding, "We know all about the Runners."

That wasn't what I was expecting.

"Then you know more than me," I replied, raising my eyebrows.

"We have good intel on the gangs that are opposed to them too…"

"What? They don't like people that exercise?" I kept the smile on my face in order to stop security from coming over, but in reality, I was completely confused.

"Not when they've ventured over from this side of the wall," he smiled a little too. "In fact…" his smile faded, "they want to put a stop to them, and they have a list of particular individuals that they plan to eliminate, if they pass through those gates again," he said with a pained expression.

"Why are you telling me this?" All of my smiling pretence was gone, as I feared what was coming next.

"Because your brother is on that list," he said, glancing at the security guard again.

There were no longer any smiles from either of us.

"No, he's not. Adam's not involved in that."

His hands moved towards me, as if he was about to touch me, but he quickly thought better of it. "He is, Eve, and I can tell you that with one-hundred percent certainty."

I swallowed hard, my body started to overheat, and I thought I might actually be sick. He looked so serious, so convinced, and this was Adam we were talking about. Of course, he was fucking involved in it. The only thing in doubt was how he'd managed to keep it from me.

I let out a deep sigh and a bitter laugh. "That fucking little shit!"

I shook my head and took a large gulp of my drink, and then I looked back up at Ethan, who had been silently watching me. "You came here just to tell me this?"

"Yes," he said, glancing down awkwardly.

"Why?" I asked in disbelief.

He let out a shaky breath of his own. "Because you were wrong. I didn't forget about you when you went back through those gates, and I didn't want the choices that you've made in order to keep him safe to have been in vain…"

"Mr Southwold." An authoritative male voice startled us both, and I turned to see that the security guard I'd reined in before, was standing right behind me. "I think it's time that you returned to your seat."

Ethan nodded at him, finished the rest of his drink, and started to follow him back to his table.

"Thank you, Ethan," I said before he was too far away, and then I went straight back to my dressing room.

As soon as I got there, I picked up my phone and started to call Adam, and seconds later David barged through the door. "What the fuck was that?"

Adam answered the phone, so I put a hand up to David and glared at him with such anger that he stopped in his tracks.

"Adam!" I yelled down the phone.

"What's wrong?" Adam panicked.

"You!" I growled at him. "You, are a fucking Runner!"

David raised his eyebrows and leaned back against the wall, clearly understanding where my rage had come from.

Adam started blustering on the other end of the phone, trying to deny it.

"Don't lie to me! I have just been told by someone from The Other Side... someone who knows what is going on — that not only are you a Runner, but you are also on a fucking hit list!" I became hysterical then. "You are known to the gangs over there, Adam, and if you step foot through those gates again, they are going to kill you! Do you hear me? This isn't a game. They will kill you!"

Adam started defending himself, telling me that he's good, that he's careful, but all that did was fuel my rage.

"This ends now!"

He growled down the phone. "You don't rule my life, Eve!"

"You are such a selfish piece of shit! You won't have a life if you don't stop because they. Will. Kill. You. No matter how good you think you are, if you go there again it will be the last thing you do. SO, THIS STOPS NOW!" I yelled, and then I threw my phone across the room and leaned against the dressing table for support as I tried to get my heart back under control.

I stayed there for a few minutes, with my eyes closed as I tried to calm down and then I opened them and saw David's reflection in the mirror. His arms were folded, and he looked seriously unimpressed, but he hadn't moved from his spot against the wall.

I gritted my teeth. "Did you know about this?"

He just shrugged. "Not my area."

"I need to talk to Noah." I pushed away from the dressing table and went to get my phone from the other side of the room, thankful that it still appeared to be in one piece.

David moved away from his spot and put his hand out to me. "You can't. He's with Jane and her parents."

I huffed at him. The one time that I'm the one that needed something and he was blocking me. "Then you call him and tell him that he needs to speak to whoever's area this is and tell them that Adam's running days are over!"

He nodded his agreement. "I will, but he's probably already been informed about your little chat, and will no doubt want to know how it is that you're so friendly with a police officer from The Other Side." He raised his eyebrows. "Are you feeling up for that tonight?"

I gave a small, bitter laugh because he just loved throwing that in my face at any given chance. What did he expect? I was his brother's whore, after all.

"Handling Noah… keeping him happy and stopping him from going over the edge is what I do, remember? It's the only reason you keep me around."

David looked like he was going to speak but I stopped him. I softened a little, after all, I really needed his help. "Could you please just speak to your brother, for me? Because I'm going to go and kill mine."

Adam was waiting for me at the door to his flat because he knew that I'd be coming. He gave me his signature, defiant look, and I'd never wanted to slap it off his face more than I had that night. I didn't though, I never would, but what I did was shout at him, a lot. He just shook his head and glared at me as I reminded him that he was only untouchable on our side of the wall. He was so adamant that he wouldn't get caught, that I literally had to bite my knuckles in an attempt to stop myself from beating some sense into his stupid, arrogant head.

Then his phone lit up and he gave me the death stare as he answered it. It was the call that I'd been waiting for. The call from either a Legion or a Manners - I didn't know or care which, but it was clear that they were telling him that he was out. He tried to argue with them, but they cut him off and it was his turn to launch his phone across the room as he shouted right back at me.

I just stood there and took it as he raged at me for being a "controlling bitch!" It stung, but not so much that I would change my mind and relent. He could be as angry with me as he liked, as long as he was alive.

Eventually, he told me to, "Just fuck off," so, I did. I think I'd taken enough of a verbal battering by that point, anyway, and was completely exhausted. When I got home, I just stripped off and climbed into bed, not even bothering with pyjamas. The sheets had been washed earlier that day and they felt lovely, but it still took me a while to switch off, but eventually I did, and not too long after, I woke with a start when I felt a hand stroking my face.

Noah switched the bedside lamp on as I jerked up so that I could see that it was him, and as my heart rate slowed down again, I sat up, rubbed my eyes, and pulled the duvet around my naked chest.

"I didn't know…" he told me, as he sat down on the bed. "But it's done, they won't send him through again."

I already knew, but it was good to hear it from him and I felt the weight slide off my shoulders. "Thank you."

He laughed a little. "They weren't all that pleased… apparently he's good."

"Of course, he is, this is Adam we're talking about," I huffed. "Give him a task that puts his life in danger, and he'll excel at it."

"Yeah, well, I told them that if you're not happy then I'm not happy…" then he looked at me and smiled a sad smile. "People don't like me when I'm not happy."

I put a hand on his shoulder and squeezed it. "They still like you, they're just scared shitless of you."

I smiled at that, because thank fuck that they were.

Noah took my hand from his shoulder and held it in his. He looked down and I saw the tension in his jaw before he looked right at me. "What do you need to tell me about Ethan Southwold?"

I shrugged a little. "He was one of the officers who stood guard when Adam was in hospital."

He didn't miss a beat. "You seem to have made an impression. He came here tonight just to tell you this… why?"

I fixed him with a challenging stare. "What are you asking me?"

His eyes darkened. "He wants you," he forced out through gritted teeth.

I bit my lip, unsure how to answer. I didn't know for sure, but Ethan certainly gave me that impression too, and there was no point in lying about it.

"Maybe," I replied, shrugging in an attempt to make light of it. "Or perhaps he just feels sorry for me. The door to that hospital room was always open, Noah. He would have heard all of our conversations. He knows why Adam was in that hospital… and yes… he appears to care, but what does that matter?"

"He won't be coming back here. The Southwold family are no longer welcome in The Beneath." He looked at me pointedly, as if expecting that to bother me.

It didn't… why should it?

"Noah…" I sighed. "He was kind to me at the hospital, and to be honest, I'm glad that he cared enough to come here tonight, because Adam would have been dead in a matter of days if he hadn't." I forced back the tears that tried to follow that thought away. "But that's it. Beyond that, he means nothing."

Noah still wasn't looking at me, and I didn't have the energy to lose him to the darkness, so I went on the offensive. I climbed out of the duvet and straddled him and as I did, he looked down my body in appreciation. He saw that my top half was naked when he came in, but the slight eyebrow raise he gave suggested that he wasn't expecting me to be completely naked.

I smiled inwardly because I loved the fact that I still had that effect on him.

I leaned into his neck as his hands ran up and down my spine, and gently started to kiss my way up to his ear. I was trying to calm him, but I could feel my own arousal growing.

"You, on the other hand…" I whispered into his ear, before leaning back and cupping his chin. I lifted his face up so that I could look him in the eyes, pressed my naked body against him, and he wrapped his arms around me tightly in response. "You mean everything."

26

PRESENT DAY

*I*t's been five years since I agreed to be Noah's mistress, and nobody really bats an eyelid anymore. There's been some good times, and some really bad times… but I had to accept that this is what my life was going to be, so I did. What other choice did I have?

Adam and Meredith are still together — I think — I can't keep up! They're still involved, but they've been on and off, so I have no idea where they are at this moment in time. They love each other, but Adam is as much of a pain in the arse as he's always been, and he pushes Meredith to her limit, and often ends up back on John's sofa or in his old room — if it's going spare.

John still loves him, even though he's been in relationships, it'll always be Adam for him. He came out to Adam not long after the truth about me and Noah was revealed. Adam didn't care because he loves John too, not in the same way, but he loves him. I do fear that there are times when Adam takes advantage of the situation, because he knows that John will never turn him away.

Sometimes I blame myself for the way Adam is. I took on

the role of protector right from the very beginning. Whenever he was in trouble that he couldn't talk his way out of, I intervened.

Then Noah did.

Other than the 'incident' five years ago, Adam is now and has always been protected, and everyone knows it. Especially Adam, and it's safe to say that there are times when it goes to his head. There are also times when he puts it to the test. Ever since I got him out of the Running business, it's like he needs to find new ways to rebel. New ways to endanger his life and new ways to piss me off.

The inner orphan is strong in this one.

We're good though. We're brother and sister, after all.

Growing up, I never got to see what sibling dynamics are like. Noah and Harriet's relationship reminds me of myself and Adam, but it's the other way around with them. Noah is the older, protective sibling, just like me, and Harriet is the little sister that he still feels like he's failed. He hasn't though because she actually likes her husband.

Harriet and Daniel married three years ago and she's happy with him, and we even get to do 'couple' things with them. It may be limited to dinner at our flat, but it's still something. Jane tends to avoid Harriet because she knows that her allegiance is to me, even though I don't really think of myself as being on a different team to Jane. We're on the same side, we were dealt the same, shitty hand, and I've never lost sight of who my enemies are.

Also, I never thought I'd say this about anyone born with the name *Legion*, but Daniel is OK. That's about as far as I can go on the positivity scale, because he looks too much like his grandfather, to be truly likeable, but I know he'll be good to Harriet. He seems to truly love her, but it also helps that Noah told him on his stag do, that he'd kill him if there was ever a tear on Harriet's face that was caused by him.

Morgan is still trying to end the divide. Fertain didn't really stem the flow of orphans coming here by any considerable amount, but he's still beating the drum. He still wants to open those gates and break down the wall. I don't ever see it happening, to be honest, but he's vowed to fight it until his "dying breath!" Given who his main opponents are on this side of the wall, he ought to be a little more careful with his words, especially considering what he's just done.

We laughed when we heard about Fertain, but his next phase 'Sanctuary' as he's called it, has rocked a few boats. He passed the bill two days ago allowing Havensmere to give sanctuary, "To any person or persons from St Martins, who considers there to be a threat to their life." That's what he said in the press conference and this time people aren't laughing. It's got people thinking. Nothing has been said out loud, but we're all beginning to question the way things are here. The Council knows it's risky, because all this time they've answered to nobody. Nobody has challenged their power or their methods for keeping peace and order, but that could now change. Feathers have been ruffled, and for the first time ever, we have someone else to turn to.

My life, over the last five years hasn't all been negative and turbulent, because there have been some lovely times too. Vic and Hannah both got married last year, and I had the pleasure of being a bridesmaid at both weddings. They were amazing days, and I was so happy for them! Jealous as hell, but happy.

Vic married a fellow orphan, so her ceremony was small, and relative-free, but Hannah bagged herself a Trueborn. Not a Founding Family Trueborn, but someone with an actual family — grandparents, uncles, the works. Knowing that it was my second time being a bridesmaid in a year, one of the groom's relatives happened to say to me, "Always the bridesmaid, never the bride," after having one too many.

He laughed a lot at the flippant and somewhat overused 'joke'. Then, on realising that those words were actually true for me, he slid away and cowered in the corner for the rest of the night. I just drank more and danced with John. John is always a great tonic for my moments of heartbreak and the only male that ever dares to dance with me, since Noah knows that he has zero sexual interest in me.

I'm also a Godmother twice over, and the thought, *Always the Godmother, never the Mother*, did pop into my head. If anyone else happened to think it too, they weren't stupid enough to share it. Still, it didn't stop me from going to the bathroom and crying my eyes out at both Christenings.

Marriage and babies; the two things I can never have, and the latter being something I yearn for more and more.

Noah and I are still the same — completely in love. I think there's still part of Jane and their families that would be delighted if our love wavered, but it hasn't, and I don't think it ever will. We spend as much time together as we can, even when we're not supposed to, stealing sacred moments whenever the eyes aren't on us.

A year ago, Noah and Jane's parents tried to "renegotiate" the terms of the agreement in an attempt to lessen the time that Noah spends with me. Jane is yet to conceive, and so they keep trying to persuade Noah to sleep with me less and Jane more, because they don't want him wasting all the good sperm on me. It has meant that he has been sleeping with her more often, and I still use my mantra to stop the visions of them together from creeping in. Especially, at night. They always seem to come for me when I'm alone in the dark.

Even if Noah has been with Jane more often than either of

us would like, it hasn't lessened his appetite for me. Still, much to their families' disgust there's still no grandchild.

We have limited tests available in The Beneath for this sort of thing, and that's not going to change. It was stipulated by The Other Side from the start, in an attempt to control the population in some way. There is no fertility treatment here, so if you don't get pregnant the old-fashioned way, then you don't get a baby. You can adopt an orphan, but that doesn't happen often and it's certainly not the Founding Family way.

As far as everyone can tell, there's no medical reason why Jane has not fallen pregnant. Everything is functioning and in working order with both of them. The families got so desperate that they even started to monitor when Jane was ovulating and suggested putting them on a schedule. Jane was mortified, Noah told them all to "Fuck off," and Sister Theresa had to intervene before her office descended into chaos. Ever the diplomat, she suggested that there was perhaps an element of stress involved, and that the families ought to take the pressure off and just let nature take its course.

That hasn't stopped them from monitoring us, and Jane and I both get our monthly meeting with Ruth. She holds her breath as we walk into the bathroom, waiting in hope for the outcome that they all so desperately desire; that is, for Jane to show her a positive test, and for me to continue showing her a negative one. Which I of course, always will, because that's what happens when you have friends that have taken the vow of chastity. Those backup tests give me the head start I would need if my contraception ever fails. A way to hide the truth long enough for me to take refuge in St Martins.

I have been singing at The Dome on Friday night for the past two years, but it's closed for renovation at the moment. I have an entire weekend off from performing, which I actually feel a bit sad about, but on the plus side it does mean that I'm getting a night out with my sisters, including Hannah and Vic, who are both getting a night off from parenting. I'm not at the salon until tomorrow afternoon, so that gives me a little extra time to recover from what I hope will be a pretty wild night. I need a wild night. A night to forget that my life is a complicated mess and always will be.

However, Vic has already put a spanner in the works by suggesting that she is going to struggle staying up past ten o'clock. Then there's also the added issue of the fact that whenever my nights out do start to get wild, I get a tap on the shoulder from a security guard and a private car to escort me home.

I was furious with Noah the first time it happened. I couldn't believe that he'd actually stop me from having a good time. It turned out that there was more to it than that though, because his father is involved too. Robert doesn't want anything to happen to his most lucrative singer. Especially, when she happens to be the key to his most lucrative son's sanity, and he has instructed security to step in if it ever looks like things are getting a bit "out of control".

Noah's hands aren't entirely clean in the matter though. He knows that he's done damage within The Beneath. In general, people love him. The security teams, the managers at the clubs all respect Noah and consider him to be in charge. Even within the general community people enjoy the world he's created for them. The money that comes in from The Other Side gets dispersed into the community and Noah is credited for most of it.

However, there are also those that have come face to face with the Other Noah and lived if not to tell the tale of the battering they received, but to remember it. Everyone knows what I mean to Noah, and he worries that if anyone did ever seek to even the score for the things he's done; they could do so by hurting me. So, if ever anyone is acting in a way that causes alarm, or if someone is too drunk to recognise me and tries it on, security steps in. I don't even bother to put up a fight anymore. I did at first, but I was literally carried out and put in a car like a disobedient toddler. They don't mean me any harm or even any disrespect. I get along with all of them. However, they answer to Robert Joyson in a professional capacity and Noah in a personal one, and they don't want to experience the wrath of either of them. I wouldn't want them to either.

Tonight, however, I am just going to try and put all of that to the back of my mind and revel in this very rare occasion, when I'll be out with all my sisters. Minus Rose, who technically is allowed to come out and play with us but generally chooses not to. Harriet will be joining us too. I think of her as one of my sisters, and in another world she could have been. If only I was good enough to marry her brother.

Adam and his clan will be joining us too, and I'm not sure yet if that's a good thing, but it has the promise of being a seriously fun night. That is, if the two mums in the group don't fall asleep in a corner somewhere, and I don't end up in bed alone, unsatisfied and incredibly irritated by midnight.

Harriet picks me up and as I get into her car, she pulls me in for a hug. "How long has it been since we did this?" she beams at me.

"Too long! Being married to a Legion has made you boring," I tease.

"Oh really?" She gives me a wry smile. "Why don't you look in that bag by your feet and see how boring I am?"

I do as she requests and burst out laughing when I see six bottles of The Dome's most expensive champagne at my feet.

I bite my lip and do a little jig. "And just what is the punishment for theft these days?"

She laughs at me. "I'm not sure it's classed as theft when it's from your own family... but I might let Daniel punish me later... if he's lucky!"

I laugh with her, but I never escape the stab of jealousy that always pricks at my heart whenever I'm around people in happy, ordinary, and fully functioning relationships — which is pretty much everyone I know, except for Adam.

We drive to Sarah's where we get ready and down the very much appreciated, stolen champagne, and then we head out to meet the boys at Halo. They're already here when we arrive and have clearly been on the beers for a while. I don't see Adam, but we all greet each other with a round of hugs, as we always do. We're family, after all. John is by the bar, waiting to be served but he moves over and lets me take his place, knowing that out of everyone here, I'll get served the quickest.

He pinches my bum and I give him a gentle slap, before he pulls me in for a bigger hug than the rest. He has always been my favourite. Except for Adam, of course, who is now coming out of the toilets with the biggest grin on his face... it's only eight o'clock, surely, he's not found trouble yet. He makes a beeline for me and his smile turns into a laugh as he pulls me in for a bear hug and lifts me off my feet.

"You'll never guess who I just saw in the bogs. Seb!" he tells us, without waiting for a response. Then he bursts out laughing. "And he really does have a tiny, little shrimp dick!"

John and I burst out laughing too, because that is and will always be one of the funniest things, I've ever heard him say. Even if it conjures up a rather disgusting image of Seb's penis, that I really don't need in my mind. Adam goes over to the group to share this new piece of information with them too, and one by one they all crack up and pull him in for a hug.

I'm still grinning from ear to ear when John nudges me and then leans in closer to me. "It's true… he really does."

A wide grin spreads across his face, and when my eyebrows shoot to the ceiling, he follows it up with an innocent smile.

My draw drops to the floor. "No. Fucking. Way."

John raises his eyebrows and gives me a nod in confirmation.

"Seb is not gay, no way." He must be winding me up.

"He most definitely is," he says, still smiling knowingly.

"I never would have called that," I say, shaking my head and taking a sip of the drink that has just been handed to me. "And why the fuck would you go there?" I scold him.

"It was a gin night…"

Ah… I nod my head a little, in understanding. John only drinks gin when his heart is hurting, and when it's hurting it's usually because of his feelings for Adam.

I give another little laugh trying to take him back to a happy place. "Still… I did not see that coming."

"Well, you're not that clued up when it comes to men, are you, Eve?" he says, as he gives me a challenging smile.

"I'm not sure how to take that."

"Well, clearly you have mad skills…"

I almost choke on my drink. "Mad skills?"

"Erm… Noah Joyson…" he says, as if I'm missing the obvious. "The man everyone wanted but couldn't have, fell in love with a sixteen-year-old virgin."

"I'll have you know that he loved me before I slept with him," I tell him, as I prod him in the shoulder.

"What are you guys talking about?" Adam asks as he bounces back over and takes his drink from the bar.

"Your sister being an amazing shag," John says with an innocent smile, and then we both burst out laughing at Adam's horrified expression.

"Oh, fuck that!" Adam retorts, as he starts to walk away, but I grab his arm and pull him back.

"Don't you disappear. We need to talk."

"I don't need sex tips, thanks, I'm a great shag too," he replies, with a cocky grin.

Yeah, I don't doubt that. I've heard him at it, and I really don't need the reminder. I shake off the memory and give him a firm look. "Meredith…"

"No," he says dismissing me.

"Adam, we can get this out of the way now, or I can bug you about it all night? Your choice."

I give him a sweet smile, but he knows that I mean it, and he rolls his eyes and nods towards an empty booth. We sit down opposite each other, and Adam moves into his stand-offish pose because he knows that he's going to get a grilling.

"What's going on with you two?"

He just shrugs in response.

This is how our serious conversations always start, or my "interrogations," as Adam calls them. It's the dance we do, and it makes me smile, because it's utterly pointless because he always shares in the end.

I continue, undeterred. "You clearly love her, and for some mad reason she loves you too. So why do you keep—"

"Fucking it up?" Adam interrupts.

"Yes!"

Adam sighs and starts to fidget, then he drinks some of his drink and then fidgets some more. He's holding out on me more than he usually does, which means that I'm involved, and that has me panicking.

"Is it my fault?" I blurt out. "Is it because I've always been too controlling, and you need to rebel?"

He looks at me and laughs little. "To some extent," he replies, and though he's smiling in order to soften the blow, I know he means it.

"Look, Adam, I just want you to be safe… I know you don't get it…"

"I do get it, Eve!" he almost shouts. "You're my sister. This relationship works both ways."

"But it's different for me."

"How?" he asks, shaking his head at me.

I look down a little and take a sip of my drink and try to force back the tears that want to escape. Adam and I are close, and we talk. Yes, I piss him off and he drives me insane, but we talk. However, I've never told him what I'm about to tell him.

I take in a deep breath and get ready to lay my cards completely on the table. In truth, I don't know why it's taken me this long.

"You have always had me, Adam. You came into this world and immediately had a sister. You knew that connection and that love straight away." I pause for a moment and he nods a little, but then looks down as his own emotions threaten to betray him too. "I had four years of being alone. Four years of being just like everyone else… and then you came along. This little baby was put in my arms and it changed everything. It changed me."

I can no longer hold back the tears as the memory of that day hits me. "It's not possible for me to just do nothing when you put yourself in danger — it's just not. I will always be the four-year-old girl, holding this magical baby… that just wouldn't stop crying," I add to lighten the tone, and it works, he laughs too.

I take another deep breath. "Protecting you is ingrained in me. It's part of who I am, and I won't ever stop. I'm sorry… I just don't know how to."

We sit quietly for a few minutes, just drinking our drinks and taking it all in, then Adam breaks the silence.

"You've never told me that…" he nods a little, as if I'm less annoying now that he understands me better, but then a grin spreads across his face, as he says, "I always thought you were just a control freak, to be honest…"

"Fuck off," I laugh along with him too.

He shuffles a little again, because this is the next stage in our dance, and it's his turn to lead now. His eyes dart around the room, before he takes a deep breath and looks right at me.

"I feel guilty, every single day that I'm with Meredith," he says without even attempting to suppress his sadness. "I can have with her what you will never have… marriage… babies… everything. Everything that you will never have… because of me."

I jump forward because I cannot let him think that. "Not because of you, Adam, it's because of them!"

None of this has ever been his fault.

"You live a half-life in order to keep me safe."

I reach out for his hand. "If you didn't exist, they would have found another way. They would have just used someone else to get what they want… it's what they do."

He looks down again as he clears his throat, then he swipes a hand across his cheek, trying to wipe away the tear that I wasn't supposed to see, and downs the rest of his beer. I take a huge gulp from my own glass, because this conversation has gone way deeper than I ever expected it to. I look at

Adam and I can see that my words are sinking in, but the frown on his face suggests that he's still blaming himself.

I can't let him own this. It's not on him.

"I love Noah, you know that, and you love Meredith. I want you to live a full life and I want you to have babies so that I can spoil them rotten and be their most favourite person in the world," I say with a big grin, because I want that for him more than anything.

He finally smiles at me, killing the tension that has been surrounding us.

"Right," he stands up because our heart to heart is clearly over. "You can get another round in. We need to take advantage of Cinderella and her status, before the clock strikes twelve and the three blind mice come to take you home."

He walks away laughing and I grab his arm and follow him. "I wouldn't let them hear you say that." I gesture towards the visible members of the security team, who are all seriously massive.

He turns to me, spreads his arms out wide, before gesturing towards his body. "What are they going to do to me?" He grins. "I'm untouchable."

We re-join the others and after a few more rounds we decide to head to Saints so that we can dance, but at half past ten Adam comes over to me and engulfs me in a rather sweaty bear hug. He still smells good though, so I squeeze him tightly and breathe him in. Drunk Adam gives much better hugs than sober Adam.

"I'm going to see Meredith," he shouts in my ear.

"Yay!" I shout back, as I do a little dance of joy. "Go and make me a niece or nephew."

His head tips back as he bursts out laughing. "That's a weird thing to say to your brother, you know."

I shove him a little. "I'm not interested in the details. Only the outcome."

He shakes his head at me, with his beautiful smile spread across his face, and my heart starts to glow. *Be happy, Adam*, I think to myself, all I want is for him to be happy.

He must see the tears forming in my eyes, because he pulls me in for another hug. "I love you... You know that don't you?" he tells me, and I almost choke up at.

I pull back so that he can see how touched I am by his words, but the solemn look in his eyes makes me pause for a moment. I try to speak, but he just smiles again and starts to walk away. I make a move to follow him, but a hot hand grips my arm, I'm spun around and a shot glass it forced into my hand.

"Down it!" Hannah screams in my face.

I do as I'm told, and then quickly turn around again, but it's too late, he's already gone.

As the night progresses, Hannah and Vic — who are showing no signs of flagging — continue to own the dancefloor. Shots, shots, and more shots, and then the night starts to get messy. I start to get messy. I get messy and I get wobbly, but I stay on the dancefloor, because it's almost midnight and as Adam said, it will soon be time for my escort home.

I keep dancing, laughing, and bumping into the bodies of the other wasted people that think they own the dancefloor too. Then I check my phone. It's twelve forty-five, and nobody has stepped in. It feels weird now, and I can't relax because I feel like I'm just waiting for it to happen. I look around and can see that the security team are all around the dancefloor and it feels like their eyes are on me. I am more wasted than I've been in ages, occasionally someone touches me, and yet all they're doing is watching.

"Just have fun!" Sarah shouts in my ear. She's been

watching me, and she knows what I'm thinking. "Just enjoy the freedom, for a change."

She grabs my arm and pulls me over to a podium and we join the girls that are already on there, dancing. I don't look at my phone again and so I'm a little taken aback when the lights suddenly come on. The exits are all opened, and I join the sea of bodies that are leaving the club. Then I wait in the queue for a taxi, just like everyone else. I'm drunk and confused and I'm a little disappointed, because I could actually do with a lift home right now and my feet are killing me. I've never had to wait for a taxi before and I'm now learning that queuing is crap.

I eventually walk into my flat at about half past two, release my poor feet from the confines of my shoes and then hobble to the bathroom. I brush my teeth because the burger that I inhaled is leaving a horrible aftertaste, but my bed is calling, and I have neither the energy nor ability to clean my face. I'm going to feel like shit in the morning, so I might as well have the panda eyes to complement the look. I open the door and head to my bed but then I immediately stop in my tracks.

Suddenly I feel sober. The ground feels like it's moving beneath me, but not because of the copious amounts of alcohol I've consumed. No. It feels like it's moving because I'm scared. I'm absolutely bricking it, because the Other Noah is standing in front of me, looking darker, more lost, and more broken than I have ever seen him look before.

27

*N*oah shouldn't be here, neither version of him. He's supposed to be with Jane tonight. It feels like somebody is dancing along my spine with ice skates on, because as drunk as I may be, I know that something bad has clearly happened, something very, very bad. I ignore the voice in my mind that cares about my own safety and is telling me to just hide in the bathroom, and instead, I do what I always do. I put Noah's needs first.

I walk closer to him, breathing deeply in order to try to slow my heart that is beating out of control, and as I get closer, I see that he's been crying. Breathing is now a little harder to do because Noah never cries, not even when he's at the height of guilt. The only time I've seen him cry is when we broke up, but I've not done anything to cause this… have I?

I need to talk to him. I need to get him to talk. It won't stop what will inevitably follow, but he made me a promise years ago that he would always tell me what's happened. He can't always manage it before, but as soon as he's tasted his cure and comes back to me, he lets me back in.

I reach him and I rest my hand on his chest. His heart is beating even harder and faster than mine is. "What's happened?"

He says nothing, he just clenches his jaw as he continues to fight with himself.

"Please, talk to me," I plead, but it's no use, he's too far gone.

He needs actions, not words, and he needs me. I wrap my arms around his neck and lean up and gently kiss his cheek as I move closer to his ear. "It's going to be OK... I love you... I'm here for you," I whisper, giving him permission to take what he needs.

His arms wrap around me in a vice-like grip, he lifts me, then turns and slams us both down onto the bed, and as the air is pushed out of my chest, all I can think is, thank God, we were next to the nice, soft bed.

One hand fists my hair, and his kisses fall on me aggressively. He bites at my lip, a little too hard and I gasp in pain and dig my nails into his shoulder. That's my way of letting him know when he goes too far. He doesn't apologise, he barely breaks his stride and then both hands move to my strappy top and he rips it open. He actually rips it right down the middle! I look down at my exposed chest and then up at Noah in alarm because he's gone. He's long gone and I'm not sure if he's going to hear me tonight. I'm not sure he's going to pick up on my cues because I don't feel like he's even seeing me.

He leans down and starts kissing my chest, and as his teeth graze painfully across one of my nipples, I sit up and grab hold of his face. I hold him right in front of me and look him in the eyes. "Remember who I am. Remember that you love me."

He pauses, and then he comes back to me, just for a

moment. He pulls my hands away, leans down, rests his forehead against mine, and whispers, "I love you, Eve, I always will… please don't ever forget that."

Then he takes hold of my hands and presses them against my sides, and his need takes over as he lands aggressive kisses on my body, once again. He moves lower and lower, then releases me in order to remove the rest of my clothes and then it starts.

I close my eyes, try to relax and remind myself that it never takes long. The alcohol seems to have numbed my senses a little and it doesn't feel as uncomfortable as it probably should do. I decide to use my intoxicated state to go with him and to enjoy it, but I have to keep my eyes closed. I can't look at him. I can't see his face and enjoy it because there is no pleasure in his eyes. There's only pain.

I try to block the image of his tear-stained cheeks out and tell myself that if he's taking what he needs, then so can I, and yet I don't enjoy it. I can't, because I keep seeing the tears that he's cried, and I remember that what's going on inside him must be a million times worse than anything that will happen to me. I open my eyes again and see the broken and tortured, love of my life trying to find his way back, and then seconds later he growls out as his demons are released and he crashes onto me, panting hard.

I wrap my arms around him and kiss the top of his head, that is buried in my chest because he's not ready to look me in the eyes yet. Then I wait for his body to soften, for him to relax and for him to come back to me, but he doesn't. It doesn't usually take this long… Oh, God, what the fuck has happened?

"Noah…?"

He doesn't lift his head up; he keeps it buried in my body as he shakes it from side to side.

He's not ready to talk, so I don't push, I just lay here, holding him and stroking his head, trying to help him in the only way I can, but I'm seriously struggling to keep my eyes open. Seeing Noah may have been sobering at the time, but I have drunk a lot and it's getting harder to stay awake.

"Do you hurt?" Noah asks, still without looking at me.

"No." Although I'm sure I'll feel it in the morning. "Are you ready to—"

He flips me onto my stomach before I can finish my question, and at first, I think that it's my turn. That he'll pleasure me now, like he always does, but when he lowers his chest onto my back, I can feel that his heart is still beating at an insane rate.

It didn't work. He's not my Noah, yet... and then it starts all over again.

28

The first thing I notice when I wake up is my dry mouth, but that feeling is quickly overpowered by the pain in my head. I wouldn't have normally got so drunk when I knew I'd have to be in the salon today, but I never expected that I'd be staying out so late. That was weird.

Next, I feel my body, more specifically, the lower half and it does not feel good. I had to deal with the Other Noah twice last night and then after that, my Noah, or someone that more closely resembled him, insisted on making it up to me.

Honestly, I just wanted to sleep.

No, I wanted to talk. I wanted him to tell me what was wrong and then I wanted to sleep.

He wasn't going to stop until I came, and when I finally did, he moved us both into the fetal position and wrapped himself around me, resting against my back. I could feel his heart pounding and I asked him to talk to me, but all the response I got from him was the slow shake of his head from side to side. I tried to stay awake in case he just needed time, but alcohol and exhaustion beat me, and I fell asleep wrapped in his embrace.

We're still in that same position, only now he's resting peacefully. I lift my head a little so that I can see the time. It's ten o'clock, I need to be at the salon for one and I need to start trying to make myself feel human. Shower. Coffee. Toast — lots of toast. I also really need a wee… then I feel it. That pain inside, deep inside, that lets me know that I am going to feel more than just sore for a day. Great.

I start to pull away from Noah, and as I reach for his right hand to lift it up, I see the bruises on his knuckles. I didn't see those last night, I didn't see much beyond the pain in his eyes, but someone else did. Someone else felt pain last night, because apparently, he didn't come to me first this time. I'm not the only one who is going to be feeling the repercussions of last night.

I want to talk to him, but I'm scared to. I'm scared to know what was so bad that not only did he hurt someone, but he also couldn't find peace in me. Unfortunately, I think I already know.

I hold his knuckles gently and I kiss them all, just like I did the first time, like I do every time. Then I free myself from his hold, go to the bathroom, and then I hold my breath as I lower myself onto the toilet, because I know that this is going to sting.

Oh, holy fuck!

I bounce my feet on the ground and grab a hand towel to bite into as I empty the last of the contents of my bladder. I sit for a moment, wincing as the throbbing continues and then I slowly get up and hobble to the bathroom cabinet. It's not exactly the first time I've had cystitis and I tend to keep a packet of the over-the-counter sachets to hand. I reach for it and then fill a glass with water, but as I watch it dissolve, I know it's not going to work. This is going to be a job for antibiotics, which means I need to get to Rose before I go to the salon.

Shower. Get in the shower, wake up, wash all the cum away and try to feel human again, but paracetamol is needed first.

I take my time in the shower, mainly because I don't think I'm going to be able to do anything at a great speed for a few hours. Then once dried, I slip on my dressing gown and go to the kitchen. I decide I'll eat some toast while the coffee machine works it's magic and then take a cup to Noah and see if I can get him to talk.

Three glorious slices of generously buttered toast later, and I take two cups of coffee into the bedroom. Noah's not in bed… that's funny, I didn't hear him get up. I put both cups down on my dressing table and walk to the bathroom, only to find the door is open just like I left it and the bathroom is empty. There's not really anywhere he could be where I wouldn't have seen him from the kitchen, so utterly puzzled, I go back to our bedroom.

His clothes are gone, his shoes too. I call out his name. Nothing, and then I walk around all the other rooms, as realisation dawns on me. He's not here, which must mean that he left while I was in the shower? He never does that. He has never once gone anywhere without saying goodbye, especially after a night like last night when he's full of remorse.

He left without a single word, while I was in the shower because he still doesn't want to talk. He can't look at me in the light of day and negate on his promise to always tell me what's going on, but at the same time he doesn't want to tell me, so he's run off.

I grab his cup of coffee and throw it into the sink as my blood starts to boil and my heartbeat goes through the roof. I can't believe him. What a fucking coward! After what he put me through last night — the consequence of which is going to cause me pain for days — he's just buggered off to hide somewhere.

I stomp back to the bedroom to get some clothes, but then I stop and go over to the bed and slowly sit down as the anger is quickly replaced by pain. Not the physical pain that I'm already feeling, but the pain that hits you right in the heart, when you realise that you already know what's happened. For him to be as lost as he was, to need what he needed and to do what he did, it has to be something big, something life changing.

I guess Jane finally got pregnant.

I let that thought sink into my tired, hungover brain, which isn't capable of truly comprehending this new thought, this new reality, this new future. Because the future will be different now. Everything will be different now.

Somehow though, I have clearly managed to comprehend it, because the tears are streaming down my face and my heart is plummeting into the ground. The man I saw last night wasn't my Noah. He never fully found his way back, and now I'm wondering if he'll ever be my Noah again, not when he becomes 'Daddy'.

I sit for a while, not really thinking, but just letting the tears spill out. I need to think about it. At some point, I'll need to process it, but there's a more burning matter to deal with, right now.

I didn't need to explain to Rose why I had cystitis because she's not comfortable with that level of detail. She's not a total prude she's just not "sexually aware" — her words, not mine. She is, however, a trained nurse and she understands the biology of it all, if not the emotional complexity of the act itself.

Nobody has ever asked me what goes on between me and Noah on the occasions when he needs me as more than a lover. His family don't want to know what he's capable of and my family don't really want to know what I go through, not when there's nothing that they can do to change it. Rose did make me do a pregnancy test first though, and as it's negative, that means she doesn't need to do me a back-up test tomorrow before I head for my monthly meeting with Ruth.

I take the first of my antibiotics while I'm there and then I walk to the salon, hoping the fresh air will go some way to clearing my head. Then I make it through my gruelling, five-hour shift, styling hair, painting nails, and generally making people look amazing for their Saturday night out, on a mixture of painkillers, cranberry juice, and crisps. Della noticed the cranberry juice in the fridge and tried to send me home, but I refused. I need to be busy. I need to focus on cutting, styling, and highlighting, because if I go home all I'll do is think about Jane growing Noah's baby in her womb, and then I'll cry about the fact that mine will always be empty.

Eventually, I have to go home and after eating a massive pizza I decide to go to The Dome. I know people are still working while it's being renovated and I'm hoping that's where Noah will be hiding away. He's not answered any of my calls and I can see that my texts have gone unread. He has got to talk to me. We cannot hide from this and I don't know how I'll stay sane through the night if we don't deal with it now. My stomach is constantly in knots and I feel like I'm going to be sick all the time, and I can't spend the night not knowing.

I'm hesitant though because I'm scared. I need to know, but at the same time I don't really want to. Taking a deep breath, I use my key to let myself in through the side door and then head to the main room. There are a few people at the bar, including Meredith, and she gives me a weak smile as I approach.

I smile a little more brightly, certainly more brightly than I feel. "Is Noah here?"

"I've not seen him, but there have been a few people in and out the offices," she says as she continues to mix the cocktail that she's teaching the other bar staff to make.

She barely looked at me. I know she's busy, but she was standoffish, which isn't like her. Maybe she decided not to take Adam back last night? Well, that's my chance of having a niece or nephew to distract me from my miserable, half-life shot.

I try to keep my smile in place, but I'll have to try and talk to her later. "OK, I'll go and see."

I walk through the large double doors that lead to the offices and meeting rooms and head towards Noah's office. The door is shut and so I tentatively knock on it. There's no answer, so I knock again.

"Noah, it's Eve… are you in there?" I try the handle, but the door is locked.

"He's not here." David's voice startles me, and I turn to see him standing in the doorway to his office, a few doors down the corridor.

I take a moment to regain my composure because he doesn't need to know that there's a problem, and then I turn to face him, with a neutral smile. "Oh… Do you know where he is?"

"Don't you?"

I raise my eyebrows at him, because my normal self

would challenge him, and I need to seem normal. "Wouldn't be asking you, if I did." Then I shrug as I turn to walk away.

"Has something happened?" he asks, and as I turn to face him, I see his concern.

Feeling a little defeated, I let out a loud sigh and shrug my shoulders. "It would appear so, but I don't know what."

He steps forward a little. "Are you OK? You don't look great."

I shrug again and take the insult on the chin. Of course I don't look great, because I feel like I've just been run over by a bus.

"Just hungover," I tell him, and even though he knows it's a lie, he nods a little and goes back into his office.

None the wiser, I walk back to the bar and decide to tackle the next problem instead.

"Hey, Meredith," I say with caution, getting her attention. "I take it things didn't go well with Adam last night. I know he's been a dick—"

She huffs, a little and I see the confusion and irritation on her face. "I didn't see Adam last night."

"What?" I ask in surprise. "But he left the club early to see you."

"I was up reading until about eleven last night, and he definitely did not come to see me." Her eyes darken, she lets out a deep sigh and shakes her head. "I guess he got a better offer," she says and then she turns to wipe a tear away.

Oh, for fuck's sake, Adam! I let out a loud breath of my own, shake my head and stretch my hands out in apology.

"Meredith… I don't know what to say." Then I start to get angry because I can't believe he's done this again. "We talked last night. He loves you! We talked about how he'll stop messing things up…" I let out a frustrated growl. "I really thought that he listened this time."

She slams the drink that she was making onto the counter. "It doesn't matter, Eve, I'm done with him!" She says it with anger, but her tears are full of pain. "I can't keep doing this with him."

I nod at her because I'm surprised that she's taken so long to cut him off. "I know…" I reach out to her, but she shakes her head and walks quickly to the toilets.

All concern about Noah now gone, I walk out the door and pick up my phone and call Adam, but it keeps ringing until it connects to his voicemail.

"Where are you?" I practically shout down the phone. "I'm sorry, but I've just well and truly landed you in it with Meredith! But then if you'd gone to her last night, like you said you were, then it wouldn't have happened," I admonish him. "Adam…" I groan. "You two could be so great! Just call me… love you," I add begrudgingly.

Next, I call John because if Adam is hiding anywhere, it's more than likely to be with him. Only he's not and I can't help the anger boiling over, because if Adam isn't at John's then it would seem that he did indeed get a better offer.

"Shall I make some calls and see if I can track him down?" John asks, but he doesn't sound concerned. He knows Adam too well to be concerned.

I let out a shaky laugh. "What's the point, John? He'll show up when he's outstayed his welcome in whichever bed he stumbled into last night."

It is time to put this shit fucking day to an end, and so I go home, take more antibiotics and painkillers, and then I sit on the toilet wincing, for what I hope will be the last time for the night.

Then I sit for a while, staring at my phone, waiting to hear back from one, or both of the men that mean everything to me — my brother and my lover. These two men that I love so much, each in their own way, feel like the bane of my existence right now. I wouldn't be without either of them, but one of them has given me a urine infection, the other has given me a headache, and both of them make my heart feel like glass — fragile, easily shattered, and once broken, beyond repair.

29

$\mathcal{I}$ didn't hear from either of them before I went to bed and the first thing I do when I wake up is check my phone. Nothing. No reply from either of them. I let out a growl as I slump back into my bed. They are both in so much trouble! I wish I could just stay in this bed all day and hide away from them, like they are from me. Perhaps that's what I should do… just sack the day off and sack the pair of them off and let them come running back to me. Chasing them around is exhausting.

Unfortunately, I can't hide away in my bed because it's Sunday, which means Sunday service. I may never have embraced religion, but I always go because that church was my home, and those women that give everything to us all, without asking for a thing in return; raised me. However indifferent I am to their God; I love and respect each of those nuns completely.

I groan, admitting defeat and get out of bed, quickly popping a painkiller before I go to the loo. Going to church isn't all that bad though, because it guarantees that I'm in the same place as all my sisters and goddaughters at least once a week. That is always the silver lining, and so, every Sunday, almost without fail, I go, and today isn't going to be any different, regardless of how emotionally battered I'm feeling.

That thought perks me up a bit until I remember what else is due to happen today. It's 'that time of the month'. Not that, 'that time of the month', that's much more pleasant than what I'll be experiencing today.

Today, is the day when I sit in a room with Ruth Joyson and smile my fake smile as we go through the motions of pretending to be friends and enduring painful, but polite, forced conversation, before I hand her a plastic stick that says, 'Not Pregnant' on it. At which point, she smiles the only genuine smile that I ever see on her smug, self-important face.

I'm starting to feel the antibiotics doing their thing, and compared to Hannah, I'm the epitome of health, because she is struggling. The mums in our group hit it hard on Friday night and as Holly is currently teething, Hannah is clearly paying a hefty price for her one night of freedom. Mind you, Neil isn't looking too bright either, so halfway through the service, when Holly will no longer be appeased, I offer to take her outside to give them a breather. They get to close their eyes for a few minutes, and I get precious baby snuggles. I think I'm the winner here.

God, I love this girl and baby Mia too. If Adam isn't going to get his act together then I will have to dote on my goddaughters instead. However, if he keeps shagging around the way he does, I may end up with a new relative, anyway.

Pushing away the irritation that thinking about Adam currently causes, I take Holly outside. I sing to her and she starts to relax as she watches the leaves on the blossom tree in the church's yard, dancing in the gentle breeze. It takes a little while, but eventually, she settles, so, I sit on a bench as she sleeps against my chest, and I breathe in her beautiful scent and thank the world for her existence.

This also gives me an opportunity to access my phone, because Adam is not here, and as irritating as he is, I do need to track him down. It's not like he's always here, so it's not exactly unusual, but I am still so annoyed at how he's treated Meredith and I wouldn't be surprised if he's avoiding me.

I need to stay angry with him because it stops the other feeling from creeping in. I've been trying to avoid it, because I know I'm just being paranoid, but I can't shake the uneasy feeling that I've had since I found out that he didn't see Meredith. I just keep going back to the look on his face when he told me that he loved me when he left the club on Friday.

Straight to voicemail. I shake the chills away, because he's either fed up with me calling and has switched it off, or he's having too much fun to realise his phone is out of charge. Either way, he is seriously taking the piss this time! It wouldn't be so bad if it wasn't for the fact that he lied to me. That's the bit that's really getting to me. Of course, we keep secrets from each other, but he looked so sincere when we spoke on Friday. I just don't understand why he didn't go to Meredith.

Footsteps crunching in the gravel get my attention, and I turn to see Jane walking towards me.

Here we go.

I sit up straight to prepare myself for the news that she's no doubt about to share. I always wondered if she'd come to me and gloat when the time came. However, as she gets closer, I realise that she doesn't exactly look happy, and that relaxes me a little. Call me a bitch, but if she's not happy then maybe what I'm fearing hasn't actually happened.

She stands in front of me, looks at the baby in my arms

for a moment, as an unidentifiable emotion flickers across her face, before she straightens it again and looks me in the eyes.

"Friday was my night, Eve."

I let out a little laugh. "Hello, Jane. It's nice to see you too."

She huffs and folds her arms. "Maybe I'd be more pleasant if you stuck to the rules!" she snaps back. "Or perhaps you can tell me where my husband is hiding?"

Oh… so Noah isn't in church either? I don't sit in a position where I can see them when we're here, because I hate to watch them play the perfect couple, so I just assumed that he was here.

"Well?" she asks as she taps her stiletto-clad foot against the ground.

I really wish she didn't feel the need to treat me like some minion. However, I haven't got the energy to battle with her as well, so I shrug it off.

"I don't know where he is."

She scoffs a little. "Right… and what about Friday night? He disappeared around eleven o'clock after receiving a call and I've not seen him or been able to contact him since."

The feeling of dread starts in my stomach, but then quickly rises up to my heart, because this is not good. I thought Noah was just avoiding me, but apparently, he's avoiding everyone.

"I was out with my friends on Friday and I didn't get home until around two in the morning. But…" I start to feel a little nervous about what I'm about to reveal. "Noah showed up when I went to bed."

"Why didn't you send him home?" she demands, and her face reddens as her anger rises.

I raise my eyebrows at her, because I'm seriously not in the mood for her on top of everything else.

"Jane…" I try to remain calm, and I gesture towards Holly, in order to remind her not to shout. "You wouldn't have wanted him to be anywhere near you… trust me."

She shuffles a little, looks down, and then her hands drop to her sides in submission. Jane knows what I mean because she's seen for herself. She's not experienced it for herself, because Noah doesn't need or want her in that way. However, a few years ago, after having an argument, she followed him when he came to find me. I had been singing at The Dome and was getting changed in my dressing room when he just barged straight in, with that look in his eyes, completely lost and completely gone.

He came at me, pushed me against the wall and took his cure, there and then. Only, he didn't lock the door, so when Jane stood outside and heard his grunts and my gasps, she took hold of the handle, slowly turned it, and opened the door just enough to be able to see. She only watched for a few seconds, but that tiny glimpse into my world was enough to scare her into going to stay with her parents for a few days.

The girl clearly has more sense than me.

She looks at me now and she softens, then she lets out a deep sigh, and sits on the bench next to me. "That bad?" she asks with concern.

"Honestly… it's not something that I'd like to be repeated anytime soon," I tell her, and then I hold Holly a little tighter, to remind myself that there's still light in my world. "I don't know what happened… he usually tells me, but he clearly doesn't want to this time," I say, unable to hide my unease. "I don't know where he is. He left on Saturday morning while I was in the shower and I've not been able to contact him either. The only thing I do know, is that he hurt someone."

"What?" Jane sits forward a little, as the fear flashes across her face.

"Whoever called him away on Friday... wherever it was that he went, he hurt someone," I tell her shakily. "I saw the bruises on his hands."

She leans back against the bench and lets out a shaky breath. "Oh..."

We sit staring at the trees that surround the church, saying nothing for a while. The wife and the mistress, with our fragile but amicable alliance, but then she clears her throat. "You're seeing Ruth today?"

Irritation creeps in again because I'd almost forgotten about that. "Yes... Don't worry, I already know I'm not pregnant."

"She'll be happy then... at least you never disappoint her." She laughs dryly, and then she looks down at her tightly clasped hands.

"Oh... I wondered..." I start to say, and she looks up at me with a question in her eyes. "I just thought that maybe..."

She pins me with a cold stare. "You thought that I was pregnant and that's what sent Noah off the deep end?" She looks away, offended, but then she lets out a bitter laugh. "Well, I guess that would probably do it."

Suddenly, the doors to the church open and people start to spill out. Service is over so it's time for the next treat of the day.

Jane stands up to leave, but then turns to me. "She's lovely, by the way," she says, looking at the baby in my arms with a sad smile. "What's her name?"

"This is Holly," I say brightly, and I place a soft kiss on her peaceful, little head.

"You should probably give her back before Ruth sees you. She might think that you're getting ideas."

I look down a little and take a deep breath in. "My thoughts are the one thing they can't control, Jane."

She smiles softly and nods a little before walking away towards the crowd. She understands that, because it's times like these when we realise that we have more in common than we think.

I already need a wee as I knock on the door to the Joyson's house, so I'm hoping that I can avoid the chat and just do the test, so that I can start attempting to track Adam down. I'm worried about Noah too, but I'm going to have to wait for him to come to me. Given what Jane told me, he was probably called out to deal with Council business on Friday. Nobody dishes out a good kicking like Noah does. He doesn't enjoy it, but if you wind him up and then point him in the direction that you need him to be in, then he'll do the damage that you want him to.

Then he hates himself. I feel for him, I do, but I can't go chasing after him, because if he's not yet calm, then I can't give him what he needs.

Jill shows me into the front room where Ruth is already waiting. She doesn't acknowledge my arrival because she's focused on the news, and I take a look myself and see High Minister Morgan standing in front of a microphone, surrounded by a crowd, before she turns it off with a scoff.

"Have you seen this?"

I know her well enough to know that she's not looking for an answer.

"He's planning on coming here to speak to 'the people' to let them know more about how Sanctuary will work!" She's clearly annoyed and that always amuses me, so I have to hide my smirk. "The bloody nerve of the man!" she continues. "We take care of our own!"

That we do, in more ways than one.

She sits down and gestures for me to do the same, as she paints a smile on her face and the pretence begins. "How are you today, Eve? David said you looked unwell when you saw him yesterday."

"Hangover," I reply with a shrug.

"Oh," she says, then she looks a little uncomfortable and I know she's going to ask me about Noah. "I understand that Noah has done a disappearing act, I don't suppose you know where he is?"

Poor Ruth, she does so hate not being in control.

"Sorry, but no."

She starts to pour herself a drink and is about to offer one to me.

"Actually Ruth, I already need the loo and there's something that I need to do, so can I just do the test now?" I hold out my hand expectantly.

"Oh… of course," she replies, cool as ever. "I suspect you want to look for Noah?"

"Actually, no, I want to look for my brother."

She stands so quickly that it makes me jump, but then she straightens out her skirt and paints her false smile back on. "OK."

She goes to her bag, hands me the test and I take it to the bathroom.

Negative; like I knew it would be. I wipe it dry, hand it to her and she gives a small smile before throwing it in the bin and sanitising her hands. I'm surprised she doesn't save them as some sort of trophy, because me not getting pregnant is the one thing that's going her way.

I walk to the door, but before I open it, I hear heavy and determined footsteps walking along the hall towards me. I already know who they belong to, and I turn to see Robert looking as irritated by my presence, as he usually does.

He nods a slight greeting. "Are you going to look for

Noah?" he asks, then he raises his eyebrows, impatient for my answer.

I bite my cheek and try to remain calm because I truly hate this man, and whenever he's in my presence all I can think about is what he did to Adam.

"No," I reply with more calmness than I feel.

He scoffs a little and I suppress my smile. The fact that I always challenge him is a constant source of annoyance. He doesn't even try to hide it. "Why not?"

I let out a deep breath. "Because I need to look for my brother!" I tell him with my irritation also unchecked.

He looks down for a moment, before looking me in the eyes again. "What about Noah? Aren't you concerned about him?"

Does this man ever stop? I roll my eyes at him before fixing him with a glare. "Yes, Robert, I am," I say with contempt, and I step forward a little. "But, you see, Noah has you — his father, and he has his mother…" At which point Ruth comes into the hallway. "He has two brothers, a sister, aunts, uncles, cousins — he even has a wife."

I shake my head at them and their inability to take responsibility for their own son.

"But Adam? Adam only has me… we only have each other. So, I'm going to have to delegate the responsibility to you, when it comes to Noah. At least, until the antibiotics have done their job…" I look them right in the eyes so that I can revel in their embarrassment and shame, before telling them, "My brother is my priority, right now."

I open the door, but before I step out, Ruth steps forward. "Adam isn't all that you have, Eve. Don't forget that."

I scowl at her and close the door, shaking off the weirdness I feel whenever it seems like Ruth is trying to be

ROXANNA C REVELL

genuinely nice to me. I walk a little further along the street, and I start to smile a little because I have to grab these tiny moments of defiance when I can. It's childish, I know, but these people took my life. They took it, then they gave it back to me, broken, distorted, and limited, and I will never forgive them for what they did to Adam.

I call John to let him know that I'm on my way and before I can even knock on the door, he opens it. He's got his phone in his hands and he looks concerned. He loves Adam as much as I do, but he's usually cool and calm, so the fact that he's worried makes my gut churn more.

"Nobody knows where he is. I've tried the usual places he goes, but nobody has seen him!"

I step through the door and put my hand on his stomach, and I can feel his heart pounding from there. I push back my own rising fear and decide that it's my turn to be the level-headed one this time.

"Somebody has to know where he is. He's either got someone covering for him, or he's found someone new to play with."

John shakes his head. "I don't know this time—"

I stop him. I can't let him go down a dark path because I'll follow right along behind him. "John, this is Adam, he's done this before."

"He avoids you, not me!" John argues back.

He may as well have just slapped me in the face, it would have hurt less. "Cheers."

"You know what I mean..." he adds, stroking my arm. "He avoids getting into trouble with you, but he usually calls me to bail him out."

"He has to be somewhere. I'll ask around with the door staff and see if anyone has seen him." I wrap my arms around him and squeeze him tight as I fix him with a smile. "Come on, it's Adam. He's never at a loss when it comes to finding a bed."

John rolls his eyes because he knows that part is definitely true. "I guess so…" He appears to relax a little, then smiles, as he adds, "And it's not like anyone is going to hurt him."

I leave John smiling, but it was all a front. I am worried and I spend the rest of the afternoon and evening using every contact I have and speaking to everyone I can think of that may know where Adam is, or has been since Friday, but nobody seems to know. I try his phone repeatedly but it's still going straight to voicemail and his mailbox is now full. I'm trying my best not to freak out, but it's getting harder not to.

I know I told John that he's done this before, and he has, but not for ages. It's not just that either, he seemed so sincere when he said that he was going to see Meredith. He wasn't lying, I know it. He's a good liar, but not with me. It's not that he doesn't try, it's just that I can smell his bullshit a mile away. We know each other's tell.

I can barely eat dinner and when I go to bed, I do my best to try and sleep, but it's impossible, and my mind and my worry flitters between Adam and Noah. I feel completely powerless and the fear is crippling me. I know I shouldn't feel so afraid about Adam being MIA, because I know he'll show up, but with Noah it's different.

I've no idea what's going on, since my first theory was completely off, but I know it's bad. I knew it on Friday when he was thrusting into me and the fact that he's still avoiding me only serves to further fuel my dread. I've called him a few times too but he's not picking up. I want to help him. I want to hold him, to reassure him and to take the pain away. Still, I bolt the front door before I turn out the lights because I can't have him showing up here tonight. Not when the damage he did still lingers.

30

---

*M*y alarm is beeping at me and I slowly open my eyes to see that's it's almost seven now, and I can't dismiss it for a second time. I finally fell asleep at around three o'clock in the morning, and I have to be at the salon for half past eight.

The men in my life are driving me crazy, and my mind took me to some dark places last night. Thoughts always seem dark in the dead of night, but they usually brighten by the time the sun rises. Not this time, because the only message on my phone is from John, telling me he's heard nothing more.

While I was lying in bed, I was picturing Noah cosied up with someone else. I've been telling myself that he's finally sick of me and the life we lead and has moved on. I've even been imagining him coming to see me to tell me that this new, faceless woman is pregnant with his child. That bit made me cry. That bit still makes me want to cry.

Then there's Adam. My mind went very dark there. Darker than I know is possible, and too dark to revisit now.

I rush to get ready and quickly down my coffee before

heading out the door. At least being at the salon will give me something to focus on, and it's Monday, which means that Adam will re-emerge. He has a job, and it's probably the only thing he shows true dedication to. Not only that, but the people he's been partying with will need to get back to normality too. All will be revealed today, and I'll be able to bollock him for all the grief he's caused.

With that happy thought in mind, I pull the door shut, run down the steps and out the main door to the building, and then I stop to do a double take, because in my haste I almost didn't see Rose. Rose, who is standing next to Sister Theresa in front of a police car.

I take in the scene before me and see both Scott and Daniel Legion standing on the other side of the car, avoiding my gaze. That's not exactly unusual, but I look back at Rose and I see that she's been crying. No… she is crying.

My heart jumps up into my throat as I reach out to her. "What's wrong?"

She looks down, her shoulders start to shake, and she tries to try to talk, but she can't.

"Rose?" I say with even more concern as fear starts to take hold.

I turn to look at Sister Theresa and when I see that her eyes look red too, I start struggling to breathe. She puts a comforting hand on Rose's shoulder, then reaches out to pull me closer, before taking my hand in hers, and holding it firmly in place.

Rose takes a deep breath and looks at me, and through her tears, she manages to say, "We need to go to Havensmere…"

I let out a breath and shake my head. Not again. This wasn't supposed to happen again. The chills start to disappear as my blood starts to boil.

"How badly is he hurt?" I ask. Then I look behind her and glare at both of the Legion brothers.

Rose's tears fall with more force, she puts both of her hands on my shoulders, and I feel Sister Theresa's grip tighten. These three things have me shaking at my core.

"We need…" She looks down again.

"Rose…" I plead, because this is torture.

She looks up again and tries to gather herself, once more. "Eve…" she says, more clearly this time. "We need to take you to the morgue."

I laugh at her in disbelief and then I pull away from both of them. "No, you don't," I tell them, as I try to walk away, but both of them reach for me and stop me from leaving.

"They've found a body…"

"Stop it."

"The DNA test—"

"I SAID, STOP IT!"

Rose steps back a little as her tears take over and I just glare at her angrily, because what she's saying isn't true and I can't believe she's doing this to me.

"Eve…" Sister Theresa says gently, stepping in front of me so that I'm forced to look at her. "We need to go now, my girl…" She's being gentle but she's telling me, she's not asking me. "You need to formally—"

"It. Is. Not. Him," I force out through gritted teeth. "I'm not going. The test is wrong. I'm not going. I'm going to work!"

A wave of fury and pain takes hold and I try again to break away, but she has me in a vice-like grip. Her face crumples and I just stand here, helpless and shaking.

"I'm so very sorry, my little angel," she tells me as a tear falls down her cheek, "but you have to do this."

I feel like I step out of my body and watch from afar as

the door is opened and I'm guided into the car. I'm placed in the middle, with Rose and Sister Theresa on either side of me. Daniel looks awkward as he sits in the passenger seat and Scott looks devoid of emotion as he starts the engine.

It's not Adam. It's a mistake and we're going to clear this up. Mistakes happen in labs, I've seen it on the TV. Sister Theresa thought there was a mistake with Adam's DNA test when he was a baby. She had to send it off three times. That's what's happened. It got misfiled, and some stupid fuck has been careless and made a mistake. Adam will be at work, they'll see. It's all just a mistake. I reach into my bag and take out my phone and call my brother, because it's Monday morning and he will have got his shit together and gone to work.

He'll answer me this time.

He doesn't. It goes straight to voicemail, but that's OK. He's probably going to borrow a charger when he gets there. I take another deep breath and focus on Adam, walking to work as if he hasn't got a care in the world.

"It's not him," I say again, to nobody in particular. "He has no reason to go there. He doesn't do that anymore… it's not him," I tell them, and as a tear tries to fall, I wipe it away forcefully because there's no need to cry, because my brother is not dead.

Nobody says anything for the entire journey, and we all sit in silence, except for Rose, who is failing to contain her quiet sobs. I want to hold her and tell her that it will all be OK soon, but I can't make the words come out.

We drive through the gates and follow the Havensmere police escort. Then the car pulls up at the hospital, just like it did five years ago. Silently, we get out of the car and I choose not to hear what their police officers say to ours. The silence continues as we walk through the corridors that smell so sterile and feel so suffocating. I swallow hard, but still don't speak as we notice the sign on the wall that instructs us to turn left to reach the morgue.

We approach the three men ahead of us — two of them are in dark suits and one is in white, and I break my silence to tell Rose, once again, that it's not Adam. Then when we reach the men, Scott starts to talk to one of the suits and I look directly at the other, who is standing quietly and avoiding my gaze.

I keep staring at him until he eventually looks at me. Ethan Southwold looks me right in the eyes, with the knowing, resolute look that he gave me the last time I saw him. Then he gives me a sad smile and suddenly, all hope is gone. I grip Rose's hand tightly and look at her as my heart starts to beat at an unbearable rate. She grips my hand just as tightly in return and turns me towards the door that is being held open by the man in white.

She guides us into a room that is empty, except for a table with a white cloth draped over it. A white cloth, that has a large body hidden underneath it. I start to shake all over and pant as I struggle to breathe and hold back my tears. Rose moves behind me and wraps her arms around my waist, so that she's ready to catch me if I fall. The man in white places his hands on the sheet and starts to slowly pull it back to reveal the truth, hidden beneath.

At first, I just see a mass of dark hair. It could be anybody's hair, really. Then I look at the forehead, but there is a bandage covering the damage underneath, so I can't really tell. Then I see the eyes — they're closed, and his long, dark eyelashes are resting just above his high cheekbones.

We do have ridiculously long eyelashes, my brother and me.

Then the nose. It's different to mine, but then it has been

since Seb broke it. Then the lips, full and thick just like mine. Except they're a pale blue, instead of the pinkie-red that I'm used to seeing... because he's dead.

Adam. Is dead.

It feels like there's a long pause as it all sinks in. Then another as I try to breathe. I feel my legs start to buckle. My ankles lose their strength, and as my knees follow suit I crumble to the floor, bringing Rose with me. Then I draw in a deep breath and exhale it with a loud scream as the pain goes straight for my soul and tears through it as if it was made of the thinnest paper. Then I scream again and again as my heart shatters like glass, and the tiny shards rip my flesh as they mix with the tears that are flooding from my eyes and cutting their way down my face.

Once upon a time I had a brother, but now he's gone and I'm not sure that I want to be in this world without him.

31

ETHAN

I stand outside the morgue, waiting. We've done this before; Bennett and I have definitely been here before, but I know that this time isn't going to be like any other. Bennett is talking to the coroner about last night's football match. It's a conversation I would normally join in with, but not today. Today I cannot shake the nerves and they are making me feel sick to the point where I actually went to the toilet and wretched a few times, but nothing came out.

Once again, I'm about to see the woman that has fucking plagued my thoughts ever since I first met her. I should feel excited, and in any other situation I would be thrilled, because I yearn to see her. I've never yearned for anyone, but I yearn for her. Yet, today, I am dreading seeing her too, because there is no doubt that she is about to look upon the body of her dead brother, and I know the pain will be unbearable.

This woman, that I feel inexplicably connected to, like our lives are somehow entwined. This woman, that I have in reality, only met on three occasions, over the past eight years, and yet she means more to me than any girlfriend I've had. This woman... Eve... is about to fall apart.

I hear multiple footsteps further along the corridor and clear my throat to alert my colleagues, and they immediately silence and adopt their well-practised, respectful poses. I try to adopt mine, but it doesn't stop my spine from tingling, because she is going to turn the corner any moment now and I will finally see her face again.

It's been three years since I saw her at The Dome and warned her about Adam being at risk. This got my parents banned from crossing through those gates again — something that didn't go down well with my father. The Dome is where I first saw her, although I know she doesn't remember. I went there with my parents and Gabbi, who was my girlfriend at the time, and we met Eve, by chance. She wasn't singing that night, but she was there, and David Joyson called her over to our table. She seemed to float, or maybe I was the one float- ing, because I'd never seen anyone so beautiful. There was something familiar about her too, but I couldn't really under- stand why, and all I could do was sit there and stare at her.

Gabbi. I was so ashamed of her that night. My mother too because their behaviour was appalling. Eve — an orphan that both women had looked down on, had more grace in her little finger than my mother and Gabbi had combined. Eve smiled through their ignorance, and then Noah Joyson appeared, and I watched with envy as she seemed to melt into him.

I was absolutely gutted.

Noah had wrapped an arm around her, discreetly moving her away from his brother in a way that managed to seem both protective and possessive. He loved her, that was plain to see, and she clearly loved him too. I'm not afraid to say that I have never been so jealous of a man in my entire life.

I'd heard about Noah's reputation before I went there,

everyone had. You knew what the rules were when you crossed through those gates and you knew what would happen if you didn't stick to them. I wasn't expecting him to live up to the hype though, but he clearly did. I'd seen men with those model-type looks before, but they'd usually paid for them and did what they could to maintain them. That was not Noah Joyson though. He looked deadly and he was deadly. You got in his way and he knocked you down, end of story.

He may have been polite to us, you'd even think he liked us if you didn't know any better, and maybe it was just my training, but I could tell that he was dangerous. It just seemed to radiate from him. A quiet threat, always lingering in the background, and it was clear to see that Eve was the calm amongst his storm.

God, I hope he realises how lucky he is, and I hope he's spent every day of the last five years making up for what his family did to her.

Gabbi was an embarrassment in more ways than one that night. I could practically smell the reaction that he had on her. I did quite well out of it though, because we had the best sex ever that night, but in my mind, I was fucking Eve, and I had no doubt that Gabbi was fucking Noah in hers. We broke up not long after.

I next met Eve, three years later, when Adam had taken a battering. She was in no way the smiling hostess that I'd first met. She was scared and angry. She was so fucking angry, but she was still so beautiful, and her love for her brother only added to the appeal. I still cringe when I think about how I acted at the hospital, because I could have lost my job! I was only supposed to watch and listen. I shouldn't have put the blanket on her when I saw her sleeping in the chair, that first morning. I shouldn't have abandoned my post in order to take her to the café, and I definitely shouldn't have brought her a coffee each morning.

I just couldn't help it.

I wanted to be near her, I wanted to know her, and I so desperately wanted to save her. If I could have stopped her going back through those gates and into a life where she'd be trapped, I would have. I would have done it in a heartbeat... but I couldn't.

However, that has now changed thanks to Morgan, and now I can do something for her. Now I can offer her an alternative.

The footsteps get closer and they finally turn the corner, and as their figures emerge, my heart skips a beat, and my mouth goes completely dry. The first person I see is Sergeant Scott Legion, and I can't help the flicker of anger that starts to light up inside me, because I've never met anyone less deserving of the title. The corrupt fuck! They all are in St Martins though and everyone knows that The Council calls the shots. The police force is just a front, but Legion will no doubt soon be joining The Council anyway, and then his younger brother, walking slightly behind him, will follow.

I try to look at the officers, even though they disgust me, because it's easier than looking at Eve. It's hard though, because I can feel her and my eyes want to take her in, even if I'm not sure my heart can take it. So, I look at the two nuns walking on either side of her, instead. They're easier to handle than the Legions because I know they care about her. Sister Rose and Sister Theresa. The formidable team that are always by Eve's side when she needs them.

Sister Theresa certainly is formidable, that was clear when I met her at the hospital, and I have so much respect for her. You could easily mistake her for being the cold, no-nonsense type, but I saw her heart that night. The younger one, Rose, is clearly a Sister to Eve in more ways than one and is now walking by her side with her hand clasped in her own.

Thankfully, Bennett takes the lead and starts speaking to Legion, he is senior to me after all, and to be fair, the less contact I have with Legion the better. However, I'm running out of ways to avoid looking at Eve. I have to at some point, but I'm afraid to, because I know that she'll see the truth in my eyes, and I don't want to be the one to tell her. I don't want to be the one to destroy the illusion of hope that I know she'll be clinging onto.

Still, I look. Of course, I look. I was always going to look at her, just like a moth drawn to a flame. As always, her beauty takes my breath away, even in these circumstances. I look in her eyes and as expected, they are full of hope. I've seen that look so many times before; the loved ones of the deceased and their refusal to admit the truth. They walk down the corridor clinging on to the tiniest shred of hope, then they enter that room, and their hope becomes as dead as the person laid out on the table in front of them.

I really didn't want to be the one, but as soon as I look at her, I just can't fake it. I can't do anything to add to her denial, not when I know that her world is about to come crashing down. I swallow hard and it hurts to do so, and then I smile at her, or at least I try to. I try to give some sense of support in the only way I can, while standing in this corridor, with the people that have no idea how well I actually know her. People that cannot know how I feel about her, but it's my fucking smile that makes her see.

I just stand here watching as the hope disappears from her eyes, like a light slowly going out. Not instant, like a switch, but more like someone slowly turning the dial on a dimmer. The light slowly fading to dark as hope turns to fear.

She turns away from me and I want to pull her back, or go in there with her, or just do something other than stand here watching. She has Rose, at least. She has the person she needs most, and so I watch as Rose guides her in, and the door closes behind them. Then I count, because it is always the same; one, two, three, four, five, six, seven, eight, nine… ten.

Then I hold my breath and wait for it.

"Noooooooooooooooo!" Eve screams, and then she screams again and again, until the screams turn into uncontrollable, agonising sobs, as her heart completely breaks.

I have been here before, too many times and nobody ever knows what to do with themselves. It's the most awkward and uncomfortable thing in the world, to listen to somebody in so much pain, while you just stand here waiting. This time, however, it isn't awkwardness that I'm crippled by. This time I am utterly overwhelmed by the feeling of helplessness. Eve's pain seems to have its own energy. It's so strong that it's taken on some sort of form and it's spreading from that room and reaching out to touch me.

Jesus Christ, this is too much. This is fucking unbearable! I clear my throat and turn away from the others just in time to discreetly wipe away a tear.

I need to try to focus on something else, and so I turn and look at the others. Daniel Legion has turned away from us and is standing with his hands on his hips, with his head bowed low. Bennett is business as usual; hands folded across his front, and his eyes are closed while he sings a tune in his head in order to block out the cries. Scott's leaning against the wall next to the door, rubbing his temples. I try not to scoff because I'm pretty sure that his anguish is more to do with the fall out that is going to follow, than about any concern for Eve. Fucking dick!

I turn away before I do say something and see Sister Theresa on my right, with her eyes closed and her hands clasped in silent prayer.

More footsteps approach snapping my attention away from the only other person in this corridor that's feeling genuine pain, and I turn to see High Minister Morgan walking with purpose in his stride, followed closely by his Executive Assistant, Sharon.

I let out a discrete sigh, because Sharon and her drama are the last thing that I need right now. She beams at me, which I guess is understandable considering that I keep sleeping with her but it's not appropriate, and so I barely even look at her. Morgan does not usually come to the morgue like this, but then it's not often that we have someone from St Martins show up in Havensmere, dead. Still, I really hope that his presence is a sign that my request has been approved.

He reaches out and shakes my hand. "Detective Southwold." He nods at me and then he steps to the side and does the same with Bennett. "I take it that we have a positive identification?" he asks with remorse.

"Yes, it certainly sounds that way," Bennett answers in the same tone.

Morgan nods solemnly before turning towards Scott and reaching out his hand to him. "It's a pleasure to finally meet you, Sergeant Legion," he says, and you could easily believe that he means it. Morgan is a great politician.

Then he turns his attention to Sister Theresa, who is still standing in silence, and this time he puts out both of his hands and holds one of hers in them.

"Sister Theresa," he says humbly, "it is always a pleasure to be in your presence. I'm just so very sorry that it's under such terrible circumstances."

"As am I, High Minister," she replies with sincerity. "As am I."

Morgan holds her hand for a few moments more and then releases her and turns back to me. He then gestures to Sharon, and she takes a file from her bag and hands it to him. He passes the file to me, nodding in the process and my heart skips a beat in excitement. Thank fuck... Thank. Fuck.

"I've looked over your application and I am happy to approve it. Sanctuary will be granted to Miss Matthews, for the duration—"

"What?" Scott scoffs in disbelief. "Sanctuary? For Eve?"

He steps away from the wall and moves closer to us, and I almost want to laugh as he tries to hide the fear that just flashed across his face.

He shakes his head at us. "I can assure you that is not necessary."

"Miss Matthews will be granted Sanctuary by the state of Havensmere for the duration of the investigation," Morgan continues. "At this stage we do not know the circumstances of her brother's murder and cannot rule out the risk to—"

"Eve, is not at risk!" Scott counters. He is fucking incredulous. "I assure you that nobody is going to hurt her..." He pauses, appearing to have a change in thought, and he looks right at me. "On what grounds have you even based this application on?"

I stare the fucker down. "On the grounds of what I witnessed in a hospital room, five years ago, after the deceased was attacked."

"*Nobody* will hurt Eve," Scott says, he's starting to lose it and is now bordering on aggressive.

I guess he should have been a little more discrete five years ago then, shouldn't he.

"Did you ever apprehend the five... excuse me..." I clear

my throat as I give him a pointed look, I want him to know that I know. "Sorry. I meant to say the three people responsible for that assault?"

He doesn't even blink. He's better than I thought.

"There wasn't enough evidence and Adam was found here, this time."

"Yes, it is accurate to say that he was *found* here." I emphasise the word 'found' because the evidence collected so far, suggests that Adam wasn't killed in the place where his body ended up. "Her brother has just had a bullet put in his head, and we don't yet know who did it, or why."

"She won't accept it, anyway," he sneers, as he goes back to lean against the wall.

Sister Theresa clears her throat, and all eyes turn to her. She doesn't look at any of us though, she just stares at the wall in front of her, as if she's able to see through it and into that room.

"Eve was four years old when Adam came to us," she says, with a distant and faint smile. "We named him Luke, and did all the tests, and then to my complete and utter disbelief; we had siblings — full blood siblings." She shakes her head as if she still struggles to believe it. "I had that test done three times! I just couldn't believe it. But it was true, and so we changed his name to Adam — perhaps not the best choice, in hindsight," she says, laughing fondly. "We keep them at the preschool in the orphanage until they're five, and so I went to fetch Eve," she continues, "and there she was, playing Mummy to a little doll."

She laughs again and finally turns to face us with such a beautiful, and genuine smile, that seems to make the air feel warmer. "I walked with her to the nursery, holding her tiny hand, and I asked her if she remembered what it meant to be brother and sister — we teach them about family dynamics…" She pauses and her expression turns sour, showing us exactly how she feels about the divide. "We make sure they know how the world could be for them, once they set out on their own."

She clears her throat again. "I told Eve, that she had a brother and that I was taking her to meet him," she continues, "and then I watched her eyes squint and her eyebrows furrow, as she tried to make sense of it in a way that only a four-year-old can." She pauses again and chuckles at the memory. "She was the tiny bundle of dark hair and eyelashes," she says, with genuine fondness. "I knew she'd be a beauty, though… Do you know what she said to me?" She looks at us all once again. "She said, 'But my mummy and daddy knew it was wrong when I was taken away, so why did they do it again?'" She looks right at Morgan, before adding, "Out of the mouths of babes, as they say."

Morgan clears his throat, thinking that's his cue to speak, and no doubt he would love to start on about how he plans to change things, but he doesn't get the chance because Sister Theresa isn't finished.

"He was a screamer, baby Adam," she continues. "Causing grief, even then! But we sat her down and put him in her arms and she rocked him and smiled at him. She even sang a little… and he stopped crying." She lets out a shaky breath and a single tear falls down her cheek. "I sat watching them, completely enamoured by their interaction, and so I stayed quiet and I heard her make her promise to him… the promise that she has always lived by." Sister Theresa pauses and swallows hard, and I have to stop myself reaching out to her. "She told him, 'Don't cry now, Adam. I'm your sister and I'm going to look after you. I will always look after you.'"

Her head bows low and I hear her sniffle, and it's clear that she needs a moment to compose herself, and so, we give it to her. Nobody speaks a word, but it isn't silent, because there hasn't been a moment of silence since Eve saw her brother.

After a few minutes, Sister Theresa turns to face us again, and the look on her face makes it clear that she is going to be speaking with purpose and I brace myself in preparation.

"Do you hear that, gentlemen?" She gestures to the room where Eve is still inconsolable, and everyone focuses on her cries once more. "What you're hearing right now is pain... despair... complete and utter devastation in its rawest and purest form," she says with force. "And what will come next is anger, anger like nothing you've seen before — I assure you of that. Followed by the need to make sense of it, and to find someone to blame... and which side of the wall do you think she'll look to first?" She looks directly at Scott and Daniel. "I've known and loved that girl her whole life, but right now, I don't think I can judge what she'll do."

Still facing the Legions, she makes no attempt to hide her contempt.

"So, Sergeant Scott Legion, I suggest that you go and make whatever phone calls you need to make, to whomever you need to make them to. Because the one thing I know for certain, is that the Eve that is going to walk out that room is not going to be quite as compliant as the one that walked in."

The door to the room opens, and we all jump and turn at once, and Sister Rose walks out and gently closes the door.

"She wants to be alone with him," she says gently, and then her face crumples and her tears fall, and she walks into the open arms of Sister Theresa and cries.

"I'm sorry," Rose says, as she tries to compose herself. "I know I should be stronger."

Sister Theresa pulls her close again and holds her there.

"You cry as much as you need to, my dear Rose. This is a sad day… this is a very sad day."

I watch them for a moment, but when Sister Theresa's tears fall too, I feel my own threatening to spill over again. This is hurting me, but it's their moment and it's their pain as well as Eve's. I swallow hard and tear my eyes away from them, and then I have to stop myself from punching the wall, as I watch Sergeant Scott Legion, walking away with his phone pressed to his ear.

32

EVE

*M*y heart broke five years ago when I found out about Noah and Jane, and I thought that was the worst pain that I could ever feel. I was wrong. This pain is beyond comparison. It's beyond words. Beyond comprehension. There's a fire in my lungs and when I breathe out it feels like it's being extinguished, only for the flames to reignite and burn brighter, when I breathe in again. My heart feels like there's a rope around it, tightening and squeezing with every beat. It's fighting against it, trying to free itself... but it can't.

The biggest difference between this pain and the pain I felt five years ago, is that last time I knew I would carry on. Last time, I knew that I had to go on living, and I had Adam to live for. Aside from keeping Noah sane, my life's purpose has been my brother. Keeping him safe and letting his light shine. That was all that mattered to me. When I had to give up a part of my own future, the fact that I could share in Adam's, made that so much easier to come to terms with.

I don't have that now and I don't know how I'm supposed to continue. What is there left to go on living for? A broken world, a broken man, and a broken relationship.

This wasn't supposed to happen. Why did this happen? He was supposed to be safe. I made him safe. I fixed it. I took care of him. That was my job. He was supposed to always be safe! He was supposed to live and go on living through the children that he would make, that I would adore. He's not supposed to be dead. Why should I live while he is dead? He had everything to live for and all I'll ever have is the scraps that are thrown to me.

This wasn't supposed to happen. Why did this happen? Why, how and who? Who did this to him? How much pain did he feel and how scared was he?

Did he know?

Why didn't I know? Why didn't I feel it? We were that close.

He was part of me, he was all of me, so why didn't I feel it?

I slowly push myself up from the floor and away from the wall that I've been sitting against and I go over to him. I've never seen him so still and so quiet. I've seen him sedated twice but his chest still rose and fell, and his heart was still beating then. Now there's nothing. He's not there anymore. He's pale, cold, and broken, and dead and gone.

I pull the sheet back a little more to see his chest and all I see is bruises and I let out another loud sob. He did feel pain. This wasn't quick and easy. They didn't make it easy for him.

I look back to his face, there's only a mark on one side and the bandage on his forehead. I need to know. I need to know how. So, with trembling hands that I can barely feel, I move towards the bandage and start to lift it up, but then a warm hand is on mine, moving it away.

"Don't, Eve…" Sister Theresa says gently. "Don't look at that."

"What is that bandage hiding?" I croak out as the tears continue to fall from my face, soaking my sleeves.

"He was shot," she tells me quietly.

"After he was beaten first!" I cry out.

Why didn't they just shoot him? Why did he need to feel all that pain first? He didn't deserve this.

Sister Theresa reaches out and I crumble into her arms and break down again. She holds me so tight, as if she's trying to stop all of the pieces of me from coming apart, but it's too late. Everything has shifted, everything is out of place and this world doesn't make sense to me anymore.

"It hurts to breathe…" I croak out. "I don't want to breathe…"

She pushes away so that she can look me in the eyes. "Don't ever say that," she tells me firmly. "Don't you say that Eve. Do you think he would want to hear you say that?" she asks, looking at Adam.

"He's dead!" I reply as I swallow back tears that now taste bitter. "He can't hear, and he can't think, so it doesn't matter—"

"It does matter," she interrupts firmly. "Adam was a fighter! He loved you just as much as you loved him, and he would not want you to give up," she tells me with a strength that I don't think I'll ever feel again. "You matter, Eve," she says with compassion. "You matter to so many people, and we will not let you give up."

"Are you going to tell me God has a plan?" I ask with disdain.

Her face softens and she gives me a gentle smile. "No, Eve… I won't tell you that, because I know that won't bring you comfort, and on days like these, the world makes no more sense to me than it does to you."

Tears roll down her face and I watch them as they fall

onto her robes. Then I turn to look at the body that once homed one of the brightest souls this world has ever seen, and I take him in once more. Then I close my eyes tightly, because this isn't him, not anymore, and this isn't how I want to remember him.

I turn back to the woman whose soul still shines, and ask her, "What am I supposed to do now?"

"You breathe, Eve," she says, with a gentle smile. "You breathe through the pain and you take it one day at a time. And if that's too much, then you take it one hour, or one minute at a time." She squeezes me tightly. "You let the people that love you help, and then you remember where Adam got his fight from," she pauses, and I look her in the eyes and I see her love for me shining in them, as she says, "He got it from you."

I fall into her once more and she holds me there and we stay that way for a few minutes, until she clears her throat and takes a deep breath. "They need to speak to you now... Are you ready?"

"No..." I tell her honestly. "I'm not sure I ever will be... but I have to."

Still shaking, I step away from her and turn again to the table. I lean down and kiss him on his forehead. Then I whisper a new promise to him. "I'll find out who did this... and I'll make them pay."

Pulling myself away from him for the final time, I follow Sister Theresa out the door and I see that there are two more people in the corridor now. A man and a woman; High Minister Morgan; I know his face. He looks at me with sadness and remorse, but I don't understand why he's here. I glance towards Ethan, he looks genuine in his sadness at least, but it's the other suit that speaks.

"Miss Matthews," he says, with formality. "I'm Detective

Bennett, this is Detective Southwold," he gestures towards Ethan, but before he can continue Morgan interrupts him.

"Miss Matthews... I'm High Minister Morgan," he says with what feels like well-practised calm. "We are deeply sorry for your loss."

He puts his arm out and points towards the direction that we came in from and I follow him, with Rose and Sister Theresa by my side and the two Detectives — one of whom it feels like I'm not supposed to know — walking behind me.

We turn a corner and as soon as I see Scott and Daniel Legion, my heart starts beating faster. So, I take Sister Theresa's advice and I breathe through it. Through the pain and through the rising anger, and I remind myself that I don't know anything yet.

I'm led into a small room that feels even smaller when everyone fills it, except for the woman, who waits outside. Detective Bennett stands at the back of the room and Ethan and Morgan stand by two chairs on one side of the table, and Morgan gestures for me to take the chair opposite him. Sister Theresa sits next to me, Rose stands behind with her hands on my shoulders. I watch Scott and Daniel as they take their positions against the wall behind me.

We're from the same place. I'm one of them, Adam was one of them... and yet, they've not said a thing.

"Miss Matthews," Ethan says, and I turn to look at him. "Let me say, once again, that we are truly sorry for your loss," he pauses and clears his throat. "We will need to ask you some questions, but not today—"

"When did he die?" I interrupt him because I have questions of my own.

How long has he been gone?

How long have I been chasing a ghost?

"The autopsy puts the time of death between midnight

and approximately two o'clock on Saturday morning," he replies with a gentle nod.

I take it in and translate it into a language that makes sense to me. Friday night. After Adam left me on Friday night, when he was supposed to go to Meredith, somebody killed him. An image of Noah standing in my room flashes into my mind and I quickly push it away, because that's not possible. I guess that explains why I didn't sense it though… why I didn't feel him leave. It's because I was pissed as a fart and dancing with my friends. He was dying and I was dancing. I look down and remind myself to breathe as fresh tears burn down my face.

I wipe them away and look directly at Ethan. I need to know more. "He was shot."

"Yes."

"But he was beaten first…"

He swallows hard. "Yes. Eve… may I call you Eve?" he asks formally, and I realise that I was right. I'm not supposed to know him.

It's good that I can pick up on some things, then.

I nod at him, and he continues, "As his next of kin, we will need to ask you some questions. You may have information that you're not even aware of… but we won't ask that of you today," he pauses to clear his throat. "There is something else we'd like to discuss right n—"

"This is ridiculous!" Scott interrupts and I don't miss the irritation in his voice.

My head snaps towards him and I see him shaking his head, further fuelling the anger that I'm trying to subdue.

One of their own has been found dead here, on The Other Side, and that's the first thing he's said. I take in another burning breath and turn back to Ethan, he's scowling at Scott too, and it's Morgan that speaks.

"Have you heard of Sanctuary, Eve?" he asks me.

I look at him with a puzzled expression, but I nod, because I have.

"We wish to grant you a stay of Sanctuary, here in Havensmere, for the duration of the investigation into your brother's—"

"Murder." I say it for him.

He clears his throat again, before he answers, "Yes."

My heart starts to beat a little faster, but my body and reactions are still a little slow.

"Why?" I'm really confused, but I don't have the energy to react.

"Your brother was found here, but we don't yet know for certain that he was killed here," he continues, and the bile starts to rise. "We have assessed the potential risk to you—"

"What are you talking about? This isn't about me!" The bile that was rising has now been overpowered by anger.

"Eve," Ethan says, and I turn to him again. "Do you remember meeting me in the hospital, five years ago?"

I nod in reply, trying to remain calm, even though I want to run and hide. I know where he's going with this. I know what he's about to reveal.

"Do you remember that the door to that room was always open?"

I nod again.

"And do you think that it's possible that I heard the conversations that took place while you were there?"

I swallow hard and look down. He knows the answers to these questions, and I don't want to play games, but right now I trust him more than my own, and so I decide to follow his lead.

"Yes," I say, looking up at him expectantly.

"I did," he confirms, "and it was part of my duty to write down what I heard," he adds, almost with an apology.

"Can you, therefore, understand why I thought it necessary to apply for Sanctuary on your behalf?"

"No." I'm not ready to turn on them just yet. At least, not on Noah.

Disappointment flashes across his face and he looks down, then Morgan leans forward a little, bringing my attention to him.

"Eve, it's my understanding, from the information Detective Southwold provided, that you entered into an agreement to be a mistress to Noah Joyson."

His words make me feel ashamed. Hearing him say that makes me feel ashamed and yet he hides any contempt he may feel about the situation.

"It is my understanding that you only entered into this agreement because you believed that the assault on your brother, five years ago, was orchestrated by the Founding Families."

"That's what you're basing this on?" Scott laughs, and the sound sends chills down my spine. "What you believe that Eve believed, from conversations overheard five years ago?"

Ethan looks like he's about to jump out his seat, but he quickly lowers himself back down. "If it is the case that Eve believed it, then it suggests that she entered into the agreement under duress and for fear of her brother's life," he argues back.

This is ridiculous. This whole thing is ridiculous! Adam is dead and they're arguing about me.

"I have no interest in being a poster-girl for your political campaign," I glare right at Morgan, and they all turn to look at me again. "My brother has just been murdered... Why would I stay here on my own?" The tears once again stream down my face and Rose tightens her hold on me, as I try to remember Sister Theresa's words; "Breathe through it…"

I have to keep breathing. No matter how much it burns.

"I assure you that your safety is my priority — that's why Sanctuary exists," Morgan replies solemnly. "And due to the circumstances, we would allow one of the Sisters to stay with you for a few days," he gestures towards Sister Theresa.

She takes my hand in hers. "If Eve chooses to stay, it should be Sister Rose that stays with her."

"Eve," Ethan says again, and when I look at him, I feel the intensity of his gaze burning through me.

He wants me to do this.

"There will be two cars waiting for you when you leave here. One will be going back through those gates, and the other will take you somewhere safe."

"She'll be safe in her home!" Scott spits through gritted teeth.

Ethan looks at him without even attempting to hide his dislike, then he looks at me with a pleading look in his eyes. "You have the choice."

I have a choice… that's a first.

Everyone gets up to leave and I just stare at Rose in confusion and disbelief. Why would I stay here? I need my friends. I need Noah. Then I remember Noah as I last saw him, and I look at Scott and Daniel and see no hint of sadness. They just look pissed off. Scott does, at least. Daniel, though… Daniel looks scared and neither of them have spoken to me. Neither of them can meet my gaze.

I grip onto Rose's arm as we leave the station and as we walk down the front steps, I do see two cars, right next to each other, pointing in different directions. One could belong to anyone, but the other belongs to Commander Legion. They really have brought out the big guns. I guess they truly are scared.

My body takes me towards the car most familiar to me, but then the back door opens and out steps Ruth, and I stop in my tracks.

Ruth.

Why is it always Ruth?

Do they think that I like her because of our monthly meetings? Or do they think that as a female she's the best representative to meet with me? Clearly, they don't realise that I hate her just as much as I hate the rest of them, and I'm very aware that underneath her pretty face and friendly facade, that she is one cold bitch!

She walks towards me; the picture of empathy as she extends out her arms to reach for me. I step out of my body for a moment and watch as my right arm swings out, and my hand collides with her face, before the stinging feeling on my palm pulls me back in.

"Eve!" Rose gasps as she grabs hold of me.

Ruth regains her balance, her hand goes to her cheek and she looks at me in complete and utter shock, as Commander Legion comes forward to support her. She stares at me openmouthed, unable to speak, but neither can I, because I'm as shocked as she is. I don't even know how that happened.

Ruth composes herself more quickly than me. "Eve..." she shakes. "I know you're hurting, and we are all deeply sorry... I understand your anger—"

"What did I do wrong?"

My brain has now caught up with my body and I know why I slapped her. I slapped her because she's a cold, lying, bitch and she hurt him once before.

"Eve, no..." she replies, shaking her head at me. "No, don't go there... this happened here," she says, as she points to the ground at her feet. "We are going to get the answers and find out who is responsible—"

"You are responsible."

"No!" she says vehemently. "Please, come home, you need to be with Noah."

"Has he come out of hiding, then?" I ask, as angry, burning tears fall. Then something catches my eye and I see that Ethan is now standing by the other car, watching, and waiting for me to choose.

Ruth follows my gaze, and her eyes widen as she starts to panic. "Of course, he's going to be there for you. He loves you! You need to be with him," she implores.

I look at her and shake my head. All I can feel is the heat. I know my heart is beating at a painful rate, but it's the heat that drives me now.

"I asked you for one thing. Everything I gave up… and I only asked for one thing in return."

"Eve—"

"ADAM IS DEAD!"

She starts to put her hands out again but thinks better of it. "Eve…" she pleads, starting to seem a little desperate now. "This. Wasn't. Us."

"What did I do wrong?" I ask again, managing to force out the words, even though my throat feels like it's closing tight.

"You've done nothing wrong, Eve," Ruth replies, her tone laced with desperation.

I've never seen her desperate before, and for the first time in five years I start to feel a little powerful. They're scared about what I'm going to do because I can walk away from her. If I choose to; I can stay.

I look down, then at Rose. She's confused and scared, but she gives a small nod in support. I look at Ruth. She's petrified and even the Legions are on edge. None of them seem upset, they just look scared. No… they look like they're losing control. The fuckers didn't see this coming, did they? They should have though because I warned them.

I look directly at Commander Legion. "So, you'd say that I kept to my side of the deal… that I kept my word?"

He swallows hard, but his countenance is as stern as always. "Yes, Eve. You did."

I nod at him and they seem to relax, but then I look behind them to Sister Theresa, who has been watching in silence, and unlike them, she's seen me decide. She nods at me, then gestures to the car that Ethan is standing by. I look at him too and he puts his hand on the door handle.

I turn back to Commander Legion and let him see all of the hatred that I bare him. "Then watch me keep my word now."

I grab Rose and quickly walk towards Ethan, who has now opened the rear passenger door fully.

Ruth follows me gesturing frantically. "Eve! What are you doing? Come with us, this is crazy! Think about Noah…"

I turn and almost charge at her, but Rose pulls me back. "YOU WERE SUPPOSED TO KEEP HIM SAFE!"

I pause to recompose myself as much as possible, taking in as much air as I can. I have the power now. I get to decide. They can be the ones who are afraid.

Taking one final breath to calm myself, I manage to speak clearly. "I asked you. For. One. Fucking. Thing. Whether you pulled the trigger or not, Adam is dead, and you are responsible." I step a little closer to her. "Now you pay the price."

I look back to Sister Theresa, one last time. "Will you please speak to John and Meredith, for me?"

"Of course," she replies, giving me a reassuring smile.

I get into the car, pulling Rose in with me. Ethan shuts the door, and I hear him shouting at them "Back off!" before he gets into the car and instructs the officer at the wheel to drive. I don't turn around, but I hear them shout. I hear them plead, and I start to panic.

What am I doing?

I have no idea what I'm doing.

All I know for certain is that I want them to suffer too.

33

I can't stop shaking for the entire journey. I don't know if it's anger, fear, or adrenaline, but I just can't stop. I wrap my arms around myself in order to try to control it, but it's no use and even Rose doesn't manage to help as she pulls me close.

The journey is short, and we arrive at a hotel. I don't see the name, but it looks fancy and the car pulls down the street next to it and into the staff entrance at the back. Ethan holds the door open and for a moment I can't move.

What have I done? Why did I do this? I shouldn't be here.

He sees the fear and he sees the doubt. "Eve…" he says, as he reaches out his hand. "You can go home, whenever you want to."

As he speaks those words, I realise that right now, I don't want to go home, and so I take his hand and he helps me out of the car. We go in through a side door and there waiting for us, is another face that I recognise. It's been a while, but it's almost comforting to see another familiar face.

"Dad," Ethan says as he greets Henry. "Thank you for agreeing to this."

"It's no bother" he replies, as he looks at me with sadness in his eyes, and I suddenly remember that first meeting, all those years ago. Henry Southwold owns a number of hotels.

They lead us to a lift, and I watch as the numbers get higher and higher, until it reaches the very top. I guess they want to keep the broken-hearted and unpredictable orphan away from paying guests.

We step out of the lift and into a corridor so exquisite that it puts The Dome to shame, and then Henry lets us into one of the two doors that lead off from it. He takes us into what looks like a sitting room, though it's bigger than my entire flat. It's too much. This is too much. My brother has been murdered and they're putting me up in a palace. I look at Rose, and as always, she understands what I'm thinking and speaks for me.

"A much simpler room, would suffice," she tells them graciously.

"Actually, this works better logistically," Ethan replies. "There's only one other room on this floor and we need to keep guard—"

"I didn't ask to come here, this was your doing," I counter, as I feel the anger building up again.

He gives a gentle nod. "I know. But…" he pauses, as he thinks over his next words with caution. "But something inside you told you that you're better off here, or you wouldn't—"

"The only thing I know is that my brother was murdered!" I take another deep breath as the tears start to fall once again. "I don't know what to do... who to trust… or where I belong, right now," I say honestly. "I don't belong here… that's for sure." I almost scoff as I gesture around the room, taking in the décor, the detail, the giant television, and everything else designed to keep the rich happy when they pay a fortune to stay here.

"Eve…" Henry begins with similar caution. "I'll do everything in my power to make sure that you have everything you need, while you're here… and my son—"

"I'd just like to lie down," I say, interrupting him. "Can you show me to a room, please?"

He puts a hand towards me, but quickly pulls it back and instead, points towards another door, and then he leads me to a bedroom just off the room that we are in.

It's still ridiculously large and I barely look at my surroundings, I just go to the curtains and close them because it's too bright. I go over to the bed, pull back the covers, lay down, and then bury myself in them. I need darkness and I need everything, and everyone gone. I need to think. I need to figure this out and I cannot do that when they surround me… it's suffocating.

I continue to hide under the safe, warm covers, because everything is unfamiliar and unsettling and part of me wants to run back home. Back to Noah. Then there's another part of me that knows that I should stay here. Not just the part of me that knows that the Founding Families were behind this. Not just the part of me that keeps going back to how Noah was on Friday night. Not even the part of me that wants to punish Ruth and every single Legion on the planet!

It is all that, but also more.

I feel completely out of sync with the world. I have no grasp on reality, so being somewhere I don't belong and where I'm completely out of place somehow makes more sense to me than being somewhere familiar. If I were to go home, I'd find everyone exactly where they should be. Everything would feel normal, except for one gaping void. Except for the one person that is no longer there. The one person who made my life worth living... Adam.

A world without Adam's laugh, his bright smile and his stupid, cocky face just doesn't make sense to me. Better to stay in the world in which he never existed, than the world where he was once everywhere.

After a while, Rose comes into the room. I heard her talking to the others, but I don't ask, and she doesn't tell me. She gets into bed with me, pulls the cover back over us, holds me close and cries just as hard as I am.

When I wake up the room is still dark, but I can see that there's light outside. The position of the bed and the window is so similar to my flat, that for a moment that's where I think I am. I sit up and try to make out my surroundings as my eyes adjust to the dark. Then the weight of my heart pulls me back down to the bed and I curl up to shield myself from the pain, as I let out a loud cry.

Rose comes running into the room and I recoil from the light that she lets in. I want to stay in the dark forever. It feels like I will be in the dark forever.

Eventually, I run out of tears and I just lean against her, she's said nothing this whole time, she's just let me cry it out, but she's still Rose, still a caregiver — my caregiver.

"Do you think you can eat something?"

"No..." I know I should, but it doesn't feel right.

"At least come and drink something," she urges, as she pulls me up from the bed.

I see a clock by the door, and it says that it's two o'clock in the afternoon. I can't even remember what time we got here. "How long have I been asleep?"

"About three hours."

She hands me a bottle of water and sits me on the sofa.

I look around the room again, taking in even more of the things that I don't need. "What's been going on?"

"The detectives will come by in the morning to speak with you. There's guards outside, but this space is private," she assures me. "They won't come in without knocking."

I drink some water and then jump at the sound of my phone. Rose picks it up, her brow furrows and she immediately ends the call. It was Noah. I know that without asking.

"I've spoken to John."

"Oh, God... John!" I breathe out as fresh tears fall, and I'm hit with another wave of pain — his pain.

"He's devastated..." Rose confirms, as she wipes away her own tears. "Meredith too... they both want to speak to you."

I slump onto the sofa next to her and put my head in my hands as the tears fall with more force. I know I have to speak to them, but I don't want to. Right now, I'm in a bubble with Rose in this strange, alien place where I can almost convince myself that it's not real. Speaking to John... hearing his voice and his pain, there will be no denying it then.

I take a few deep breaths and look up at Rose. "That was Noah?" I gesture towards my phone, and she just nods at me. "Have you spoken to him?"

She clears her throat before replying, "Yes... he's devastated too. He wants you back there. He says that he should be the one looking after you..." she pauses and looks a little uncomfortable, before she continues. "He doesn't understand why you've chosen to stay here... and I'm not sure I do either."

I let out a shaky laugh because this is what Rose does. She's always so desperate to believe the best, when faced with the absolute worst.

"You know why, Rose. You just don't want to admit it."

I take my phone and water and go back into the bedroom and close the door. There are ten missed calls from Noah, and I know that he'll be going out of his mind. I will call him. I will talk to him, but I need to be a little stronger, and I need to speak to John and Meredith first.

Two hours later, I put the phone down and rest my heavy and hurting head against the pillow. The handset feels boiling hot and it's running low on power.

I spoke to John first. Meredith didn't seem as bad as John. She's heartbroken and torturing herself over the time they spent apart, but John… John was raised side by side with Adam, they were together right from the start. Best friends, brothers and in John's heart they were meant to be lovers, and I'm not sure that he'll ever get past this.

John begged me to go back, because he doesn't under-stand my choice either, but unlike with Rose; I didn't let on why I really chose to stay here — because John's there. He's behind that wall with them. He's angry and confused and utterly, unbearably heartbroken, and unlike Rose, he would lash out and I cannot let him do that. I cannot put him at risk.

There's another call that I need to make but I realise now that I do need to eat and somehow, I need to charge my phone first. I go into the living room and find Rose sitting quietly, but she stands up when she sees me.

"I should eat… and I need to charge my phone too. How—"

"We just need to call," she says, as she walks over to the phone on the wall. "Mr Southwold has said that they'll bring whatever we need."

True to his word and fifteen minutes later, the sandwiches we ordered are brought to the room, along with a phone charger. Not just that, but there is also a case with fresh clothes, underwear, and pyjamas that we're told should fit us.

Once again, I'm somewhat overwhelmed and confused by the treatment we receive, but my practical brain is grateful. At least I'll have clean knickers to wear tomorrow. Funny, how even now the thought of wearing the same knickers two days in a row would still bother me.

After forcing some food down and charging my phone, I take it back to the bedroom but I'm too nervous to make the call. I sit here, breathing hard as the sandwich threatens to come back up, because this call isn't going to be like the last calls. It won't be like with John and Meredith when we tried our best to console each other. I'm so scared of making this call, because this time I have questions and the answers are going to change everything.

The answers could destroy everything.

Eventually, I pluck up the courage and, breathing hard, I call Noah and he picks up immediately.

"Eve!" he breathes out, with panic and pain etched into his voice.

I burst into tears because I should be with Noah. I'm feeling the most pain I've ever felt, and he is the person that I should be with. Yet I know deep down that he's the person — that he's one of the people that I'm better off being far away from.

He tries to soothe me, but I can hear that he's crying too, and after a few minutes I take some deep breaths, and try to get my head back in gear. We need to talk, and I need to find a way to get the words out.

"Eve… I am so, so sorry… Please come home, please let me help you," he pleads. "Why did you stay?" he asks, as his voice breaks.

"I wish I was in your arms, right now…" I start to say, because even though I've made this choice, Noah's arms are where I want to be. Wrapped in Noah's warm, strong, protective embrace. Being soothed by the man that loves me more than anything. The man that would do anything to protect me.

At least, that's what I've always believed.

"Then come home! Please…"

"I can't…" I tell him through my tears.

"Why?" he pleads in response. "I know you're hurting, and angry… and I'm so, so sorry."

"Why are you sorry?" I ask, managing to put a little more strength behind my words as I remember what it is that I need to do. "Did you kill him?"

"No!" Noah practically shouts in response. "How can you even ask me that? I would never…" his voice breaks again, and I hear him taking a few deep breaths of his own.

I know he didn't kill him, that's not who he is, but I know that he knows something. "Friday night," I say firmly. "Tell me about Friday night."

He says nothing but I can hear him breathing, his breaths are shallow and fast which tells me that he's scared.

"Shall I be more specific?"

"Why are you angry with me?" He sounds so broken and it almost makes me stop in my tracks.

Almost.

"Who did you beat up on Friday night?" I ask, with my voice raising in line with my anger.

"You think I'd kill Adam?" The pain is clear in his voice.

"No…" I reply honestly. "But you hurt someone, and it fucked you up like I've never seen before, so it must have been someone that mattered—"

"I would NEVER. Kill. Adam… I've never killed anyone!"

He's being defensive and he's still not answered my question.

"I don't think you'd kill Adam, Noah, and that's not what

345

I'm asking you. Who did you beat up on Friday night?" I ask again, with more force.

"I don't remember..." he says weakly. No... he lies weakly. He's fucking lying.

"Yes. You do," I reply through gritted teeth.

"Eve... please, come home..."

"ANSWER ME!" I shout down the phone so loud that Rose comes running into the room.

"Eve... please..." he begs again.

"You're starting to sound like Ruth," I tell him with a coldness in my tone, that is a stark contrast to the anger I'm feeling. "And I know you're lying too."

"Eve... I love you," Noah says through his tears. "Please come home. We can talk properly when you're home."

"Why won't you answer my fucking question?" I ask desperately, as tears flood out of me again.

"Eve... I need you here... please come home," he begs, once again avoiding the question.

"Noah... for once this is about what I need... not you," I tell him, through my sobs. "I will be coming home... not today, or even tomorrow, but eventually, I'll come back. And when I do, we'll talk again."

"Eve!" he objects.

"We will talk. When I'm back." I tell him firmly. "I love you, Noah. I love you with all my heart," I say with honesty. "But I suggest that you make this the last time that you lie to me."

34

"What happens when you die?" I ask Rose, as we both lay in the dark, unable to sleep.

She lets out a small sigh. "I believe that all are welcomed in heaven," she says, and I can hear a slight smile in her voice. Her faith brings her comfort and right now I envy that. "Adam is at peace now. He's in a better place."

I say nothing, I just lie next to her feeling the tears fall down my cheeks, soaking the pillow beneath me.

"What do you think happens?" she asks me.

I let out a shaky breath. "Honestly? I think that he left his body, and then he came to find me… to find a way to let me know that he was leaving me." I choke back my sobs. "I think he tried to reach out to me, but I was having too much fun… it was too loud, and I was too drunk."

"Eve…" Rose protests.

"Then I was too busy being fucked by Noah," I add with more bitterness.

Rose sits up and turns the bedside lamp on and I have to cover my eyes while they adjust to the bright and unwelcome light. She pulls me gently towards her so that I have to look directly at her.

"I can't tell you what the soul does before it leaves... I wish I had those answers," she says gently and honestly. "But the one thing that I know without any doubt, is that Adam loved you," she says vehemently. "You were his hero! He wanted you to be happy and he would still want you to be happy."

"How can I do that now?" I ask her desperately. "I know The Council did this... do you think that they found out about the pregnancy tests? Do you think this is my punishment?"

"I will not allow you to blame yourself!" she says angrily. "We don't know anything yet. And... and if it turns out that it was them..." she pauses, and swallows hard, before continuing, "If it was them, then whatever their so-called justification would be... you, Eve... you could never have done anything to deserve this."

I close my eyes, but the tears still flow, Rose wraps herself around me, and eventually we fall asleep, holding each other tightly.

There's a knock on the door at ten o'clock and we know it's Ethan and his partner, as they already called up. I sit on the sofa in the new clothes Henry gave me, and Rose lets them in. My heart instantly beats faster as I see that it isn't just Ethan and Bennett that have come; Daniel Legion is with them too.

My defences immediately go up and I jump out of my seat. "Why are you here?" I ask, without even attempting to mask my hostility.

Daniel looks a little uncomfortable; he's probably the least offensive out of all of the Legions, and as Harriet's husband, I have spent time with him. However, he is still a Legion, he's still a Founding Family Trueborn, and right now, he feels like the enemy.

"This is a joint investigation, Eve. Both forces are collaborating, and you ought to have representation from one of your own, while being interviewed," he says formally, then he looks down a little before looking at me with what appears to be genuine concern. "How are you? We're all so worried about you."

Oh, I bet they are.

"I'm just brilliant, Daniel," I reply bitterly.

He looks down, then back to me and hesitates, before he speaks again. "When do you think you'll be ready to come back?"

"I'll come back when Adam comes back."

"Eve…" Daniel looks worried, genuinely worried, as he says, "Adam's gone… he's not coming—"

"I MEAN HIS BODY!" I shout at him, interrupting the dumb twat in his patronising train of thought. "When I find out who killed him, and when they release his body," I gesture towards Ethan. "That's when I'll come back."

"That could take weeks, Eve," Daniel replies in a pleading tone. "Noah—"

"Noah, is not her responsibility!" Rose snaps out in a tone more forceful than I can ever remember hearing from her. "If you want this case to be resolved quickly, then perhaps we should get started with the interview?" she asks, and it suddenly feels as if Sister Theresa is in the room with us.

In any other situation I would have applauded her boldness. I'd have rewarded her with a proud smile and a big hug. Instead, I just manage a small, grateful smile, because I couldn't do this without her by my side.

"Shall we sit?" Ethan asks, as he gestures towards the sofas.

I sit back down, Rose sits next to me, Ethan and Bennett take the sofa opposite, Daniel sits awkwardly to the side on his own, and all three of them take out their notepad and pen.

"This is a joint investigation," Detective Bennett agrees. "However, as St Martins... because St Martins..." he stumbles on his words, unsure how to continue. "Given the nature of the relationship between Havensmere and St—"

"Are you referring to the fact that St Martins sits behind a wall, because it's filled with inferior beings?" I ask with more calmness than I feel.

I was tempted to go with a more scathing tone, but sometimes calmness packs more of a punch, and I need someone to punch.

"The police force here is more experienced and better equipped to lead this case," Ethan replies, coming to his partner's rescue.

Bennett gives him a small nod and then he turns back to me, having regained his composure. "Eve, as we mentioned yesterday, we'd like to ask you some questions," he says with kindness and formality. They've definitely had more practise at this than Daniel. "Are you ready?"

I grip my hands together, take a deep breath and nod my head in response.

"OK... Can you tell us the last time you saw your brother?" Bennett asks, and all three of them ready their pens, awaiting my reply.

"Friday night..." I tell them weakly, before continuing, "we were all out on Friday night."

"Who is 'we all'?" he asks.

I take another deep breath as I fight against the tears. These are simple questions, but they take my mind back to just a few short days ago when Adam was still carefree and happy. When Adam was still alive.

"His friends…" I reply. "John, and his other roommates from the orphanage… and me and mine," I tell him, and I list their names when he requests them.

"How did your brother seem that night?" he continues.

"He was good…" I reply, shrugging a little. "We had a heart to heart about his girlfriend, and when he left, he told me he was going to see her."

"Can you remember what time he left?"

"I think it was around half past ten…"

"And what time did you leave?"

I let out a deep breath. "I stayed until the club closed… I don't remember the exact time, but we got food and I remember getting in after two."

"Was there anything about that night that stands out?" he asks me.

The fact that nobody escorted me home at midnight, I answer, but only in my mind… and Noah. Noah, waiting for me in the dark when he should have been with his wife. Noah crying and broken. Noah almost breaking me.

Bennett clears his throat and I realise that I'm yet to give a verbal response.

"I don't think so."

"Nothing stands out?" he asks, trying to prompt me. "Nothing seemed out of place?"

Everything was out of place that night. Everything was wrong.

I shake my head at him because I'm not sure that I can trust myself to speak, or that I can trust myself to lie convincingly.

More questions follow, simple ones about the time he left, and then really stupid ones about Meredith. Was that their angle? Meredith killing Adam in an argument. A fit of jealous rage! It was ridiculous and I made sure they could hear that in my tone when I responded.

After a few more preposterous questions, I can tell that Bennett wants to change his line of questioning, because he looks uncomfortable, once again. I'm sure he has the capacity to investigate or he wouldn't be in his job, but he seriously needs to work on his game face. Ethan seems to realise when his partner starts to stumble and covers for him by distracting me with a cough, or movement. I just wish he was the one asking all the questions instead.

"What do you know about the Runners, Eve?" Bennett composes himself enough to ask.

I can't help but glance at Daniel, who gives me a slight, concerned look in return. If there is anyone in this room that can answer questions about the Runners, it's him, not me. However, I know where this question is going, because I know, that they know Adam was involved, and I really can't be arsed with wasting time pretending.

"I don't know much, but I know Adam was involved in that," I reply with honesty. "But that stopped... years ago," I add with more force.

I glance at Ethan and he's looking at me, his face full of warning, as he turns his head ever so slightly from side to side. It's so subtle that I doubt anyone else even sees it, but I do, and I know what it means. I'm not to tell Bennett about him coming to me.

Bennett clears his throat again pulling my focus back to him. He looks a little surprised, like he'd not expected me to be truthful, and once again he's nervous.

"Thank you, Eve..." He shuffles in his seat before looking directly at me again. "You clearly believe that Adam was no longer involved... but can you be certain?" he asks, pursing his lips a little as he looks at me with condescension.

"Yes," I tell him firmly, clearly, and without so much as a quiver.

He clears his throat again. "How can you be so sure?"

This man is really starting to get my back up.

"Because I am."

"Eve… with all due respect, I need to ask for more than that," he says, almost apologetically. "How can you be so certain that Adam was no longer involved?"

"He was stopped," I tell him, bluntly. "By me."

"And he would listen to you?" The nervousness seems to have gone now, as if he's following a script and my answers are feeding right into it. Somehow, I'm giving him confidence.

"No." I swear I see him almost smile. "We argued about it. I told him to stop. He refused, but I went over his head."

"How so?" he pushes.

"Noah..." I tell him, while pushing away the pain that comes with saying his name.

"So, Noah… Noah Joyson, made him stop?" I nod at him in confirmation. "Your brother was that scared of—"

"Noah made the people that were sending Adam through the gates, stop," I quickly clarify. Why am I defending him? "Noah went to them, not to Adam."

There's a silence in the room for a moment and I use the opportunity to take another look at Daniel. He's actually sweating. He must be bricking it. All this talk about an illegal business that his family is involved in.

It's always been known that The Other Side doesn't really care about the illegal goods trade. They know the players on their side, they know the Runners on ours, and most importantly, they know that the guards at the gate are on the take.

Without them, the venture wouldn't even be possible. The police here could have stopped it years ago if they wanted to.

Bennett clears his throat again, bringing my attention back to him. "Eve, I'm sorry to have to tell you this, but we have reason to believe that Adam was still running goods—"

"That's not possible!" I interrupt aggressively. This, now sweaty, little man has gone from getting my back up, to pissing me, right off.

"Because nobody would go against Noah?" he challenges.

"Exactly," I reply through gritted teeth.

Bennett starts to try to speak, but I beat him to it. "What do you think about this, Daniel?" I glare at him, but I don't wait for his reply. "This is a joint investigation, so what have you got to add?"

Daniel shuffles in his seat and can barely look me in the eye as he says, "We're looking into the possibility that Adam was still invol—"

"That is shit and you know it!"

I can't believe what I'm hearing. Why are they saying this? Adam. Stopped. Running. There's no way he'd have got back into it. He wouldn't have done that to me, and *they* wouldn't have gone against Noah. I look again at Daniel and catch him sharing a look with Bennett and I realise that this isn't a joint investigation. It's a joint cover-up.

"I don't think I can do this anymore… can we end this for today?" I ask them calmly, trying to contain the growing rage that is desperate to be let loose.

They need to leave. Now.

Bennett clears his throat again, and I can't stop myself from rolling my eyes in frustration. What now?

"We understand, Eve… you've been very helpful. Thank you, for your cooperation," he says formally, and without feeling, but then his nerves seem to return. "We need to speak to you about Sister Rose," he says, and she and I both turn to each other. "High Minister Morgan acted without the approval of the other Ministers when he agreed that she could stay."

"I need her," I plead, as the tears start to build up.

"Unfortunately, we will have to take her back to St Martins tomorrow," he continues with apology.

"You could come back too, Eve," Daniel blurts out.

I just glare at him and give no reply. I cannot imagine being here without Rose and they've clearly decided to put this on Adam, but I don't know if I can go back. Not yet.

"It's something to think about…" he adds, and then they all stand to leave.

Rose walks them to the door, but I stay rooted in my spot by the sofa, but before the door is opened, I speak up. "Can I speak with you privately, Detective Southwold?"

Bennett turns to Ethan, then to me and I know that he's going to object, and so I add, "Please?" more gently, and then Ethan steps in.

"I'll meet you in reception," he says with authority. Bennett and Daniel leave the room, sharing yet another look.

Rose turns back to me and looks between us both. "I'll just be in the bedroom," she says, and I give her a weak smile in return, before walking over to Ethan with more purpose.

"What was that?"

He lets out a sigh and looks down.

"Ethan!" I say more firmly, and he looks me in the eye, completely unable to hide his guilt. "Are any of you even going to investigate this properly?" I ask in despair.

"Eve… there are things going on here that you don't understand," he replies quietly.

"Do you want to know why I stayed here?" I raise my eyebrows at him. "I stayed because I trusted you more than my own. Not Morgan, not Bennett... you!" I let out a shaky breath. "You can just take us both back now," I tell him in disgust.

"No! You need to stay."

I open my mouth to argue, but he puts his hand up to stop me.

"Morgan wants that wall down... more than anything, OK? And yes, he's going to use this situation to help his cause."

"By saying that Adam was killed here?" I ask in disbelief.

"Better here than in St Martins," he replies. "Look... if we close this case saying that Adam was killed on your side of the wall, smuggled through those gates and then planted here, people will be scared!" He shakes his head a little. "Morgan is playing on people's sympathies, on their guilt — that's what will get that wall down. But fear..." he pauses, as he becomes gentler. "If people start to fear what The Council is capable of, then they will want to build it even higher."

I put my hands over my face as I take in what he's saying. It's like what I thought when they first suggested Sanctuary. I'm a pawn. Worse still, Morgan is using my brother's murder to his advantage. I slowly lower my hands from my face, wrap them around my waist, and look at Ethan, letting my tears fall unchecked. "Will I ever learn the truth?" I choke out.

"Yes!" he replies with force, as he moves forward and grips my arms. "Morgan needs this to look real. We're going into St Martins with our best forensic team tomorrow. We have a lead on a warehouse and if there's anything to find, we will find it," he says, with the same vehemence as when he told me about Adam, years ago.

"We will find the truth," he continues, "because Morgan wants the truth... in case it's useful in the future," he admits, and he shakes his head at his words. "But… no matter what we find, the official report will say that Adam was murdered here," he tells me with regret.

I have no idea how to feel. I guess I never expected much from The Other Side, but I had put my trust in Ethan. Now I'll be forever in the dark and living among my brother's murderers.

Hanging on to the one last thread of hope I have, that there's someone willing to do the right thing, I ask him, "And what will you do with the truth?"

"I will give it to you," he says with a passion that takes me by surprise. "I will find out the truth and I will tell you the truth… I swear on my mother's life, that I will tell you the truth, Eve."

I let out a deep breath and the tears flow down my face once again. "Thank you…" I breathe out, barely forming the words

"Eve…" he says a little more cautiously. "This truth thing… it has to work both ways. You need to tell me what you're not telling me, about Friday night," he says pointedly. "It won't go beyond me, but if I'm going to get to the truth, then I need to know what you know."

I step away from him and walk back to the sofa and resting against the arm for support, I close my eyes and take deep, slow breaths in. I need to know the truth. I have to know who is responsible, and yet, in order to get those answers, I'm going to have to betray Noah. Noah, who has most likely betrayed me. I don't know how, or to what extent… and yet, somehow, I know deep down in my gut, that the man who owns my heart, knows who is responsible for breaking it.

I open my eyes and look back at Ethan; he's just watching me, waiting for me to decide. He says it won't go any further than him, which means that it will never go on record, and even if it does, they've already decided the outcome. This won't ever come back on Noah, so is it really a betrayal?

That question floats around the darkest parts of my mind as I stare blankly at the wall in front of me, but then another thought hits me. Adam. If I don't tell Ethan everything, if I don't get to the truth, then I am most definitely betraying Adam. I never did that while he was living and I'm not about to do it now that he's dead.

I turn to face Ethan once more. "Promise me, this will stay between us."

35

ETHAN

*B*ennett looks like an excited schoolboy and I can't help but feel disgusted with him. Unlike me, Bennett has never been through the gates before, has never stepped foot in St Martins, and the fact that we are going in with three police cars and two forensic units has him practically pissing his pants in excitement. To be fair, it really is quite the spectacle, and people are lining the streets, staring at us as we pass them.

I can't talk about the times that I've been here, since I've never been in an official, and therefore legal capacity. Still, I keep my cool and glare at him, reminding him of the person sitting in the back of our car. Sister Rose hasn't said a single word, but her eyes are still red, and her cheeks are still flushed after the teary goodbye that she shared with Eve, only half an hour ago.

Eve brings out the protector in me and seeing how hurt they both were, hit me in the gut. It took all of my strength to stop myself from reaching out to pull them both in for a hug. I have to put up a wall to Eve when I'm around the others. I can't let anyone see how invested I am, or they'll drag me off

359

the case and I'll never find out what happened. That's the only thing I can really do for her right now. Find out and tell her what happened to her brother.

We detour away from the rest of the convoy in order to drive to the church and as we pull up, I see Sister Theresa walking down the steps. I shake hands with her and then open the car door for Sister Rose, who immediately falls into the open arms waiting for her. The two nuns don't move for a few minutes, but then they speak quietly, so only they can hear each other, and turn towards the church. However, Rose quickly turns back, grabs me firmly by the arm, and looks at me with such passion, pain, and sincerity, that it knocks the air out of me.

"You will look after her, won't you? She shouldn't be on her own."

"I am sorry that you couldn't stay longer," I tell her humbly. These women have a way of making you humble. "And yes, I will make sure she is looked after."

I hate the fact that I'm leaving Eve alone for a whole day, but I know that she will be looked after. She'll have the things that she needs, at least, because my father will see to it himself. He offered her the hotel room the moment I mentioned it. I had planned to ask him, but I didn't even need to. There are other hotels that she could have been put up in, but I felt better having her in one that is linked to me.

My father isn't even going to charge the state for it, and I know how much that room costs. He cancelled the booking that was supposed to be in there so that he could give it to her. He's given her clothes, that she clearly has no idea of the price of, and I wouldn't be surprised if he goes and visits her for himself. My father has a soft spot for Eve, he always has, and he was all too willing to have her under his care.

I may have only visited The Dome a couple of times, but

both he and my mother went there almost monthly, well, until my interference got them banned. I always felt like my father wanted to find a way to smuggle Eve through those gates so that he could have her sing in his hotels. She's better than what he already has, and my mother always liked having something a little more interesting to share at her tea parties.

We pull up at the warehouse and I have to suppress a growl when I see that a few of the Legion's police cars are already here. Technically, I should call it the St Martins force, but it's run like a dictatorship by the Legions, and through them, the Founding Families and The Council.

The lab found some tiny fragments of an old type of paint in Adam's hair. Paint that hasn't been manufactured for decades, but when it was, it was only done in this particular warehouse. It was definitely not produced in Havensmere. I really hoped to make a bit of progress before the Legions could interfere, but that clearly isn't going to happen.

Fuck it. It's not like they can stop us.

Bennett and I enter the warehouse and I'm pleased to see that my team is unfazed by the hostile eyes watching them and is getting things set up. Screens are going up and the infra-red cameras are being prepared, ready to catch any signs of blood — and they will. They always do. If this is where Adam was killed — and my gut tells me that it is — then it would've been cleaned up, but I'm prepared to dig up the concrete and take it back to the lab piece by piece if we find even the slightest drop or smear of blood.

I may never be able to give Eve the reason, but I will give her the location, and I will not leave this shit hole until every last inch of this place has been checked.

As we walk towards the scene, I feel my spine bristle and my defences go up on instinct, as a familiar and unwelcome face turns, and starts to walk towards us. Bennett stretches his arm out to shake his hand, but I don't offer mine, and by the look on his face, Sergeant Scott Legion has no intention of extending the courtesy to me either. Bennett then continues to walk over to the other officers on the scene, leaving us alone, surrounded by the tension created by our mutual dislike of each other.

"It's quite a show, you're putting on here," Scott remarks.

If he's concerned about us being here, he isn't letting it show.

"Just doing our job," I quip back.

It would appear that we've decided to drop the niceties and openly acknowledge our dislike for each other, and that's fine by me.

"I understand you dropped Sister Rose back this morning. I'd hoped Eve would come with her... how is she?" he asks, and to his credit he seems to genuinely care.

"She's heartbroken and angry... as you'd expect."

He turns to me with a sneer. "And I bet you're just itching to take care of her, aren't you?"

This is the real Scott Legion. The corrupt, arsehole and the fucking bully that I know and hate. I'm about to let him know exactly that, but then I jump out of my skin as a car pulls up at speed, tyres skidding on the ground and brakes screeching. Everyone turns to face the black car, the seriously expensive black car — the type I could buy with my inheritance, but not my salary. My stomach lurches when the driver gets out and starts to march towards me. Jesus, he couldn't look more out of place next to that pristine car. Not in his current state anyway.

Noah Joyson looks like shit, and I almost want to smile in satisfaction. He looks like he's not washed, slept, or eaten in days, which he probably hasn't. Big, bad Noah can't function without the woman that he's never deserved by his side, can he? I would laugh in his face, but instead I find myself clenching nervously as he gets closer and I can see that he is absolutely furious.

We watch him approach, and then Scott leans closer to me and I can hear the smile in his voice as he says, "Well, that's you fucked!"

"I don't suppose I can rely on you to do your job and rein him in, can I?" I manage to ask coldly, hoping that he can't sense the fear that is starting to take over me.

I'm tall, probably as tall as Noah and maybe even a little broader than him. Yes, I'm definitely the better built. I work out and I can most definitely take care of myself. Yet, as Noah stops in front of me, with his eyes dark and wild, I'm not sure that even the gun resting by my hip will be enough to stop him if he decides to go for me.

The last time I saw Noah he was composed and calm, completely in control, but clearly dangerous. Now he looks wild, lost and a little unhinged. I suspect that only makes him all the more lethal.

"Where's Eve?" Noah demands.

Keep your shit together, Ethan.

"In a hotel room," I reply with bluntness.

"Why didn't she come back with Rose?"

I shrug at him. "You'll have to ask her."

"She's not answering my calls!" Desperation is starting to creep into his voice. "Give me the number for the hotel."

Is he for real?

"Not going to happen," I manage to reply calmly.

I don't feel calm, but I've always been taught that it's best to come across as calm in the presence of a wild animal.

Noah snorts out a little laugh, he clearly isn't used to anyone standing up to him. Well, he better get used to it, because right now I am standing between him and Eve, and I have no intention of moving.

He steps a little closer to me, and I can see the fury in his eyes. "You can't keep her forever; you do realise that, don't you?"

Shit. He's not desperate anymore. He's regaining control, which means he's making a play for power. Bring it on.

"She's going to come back through those gates, to me." He raises his eyebrows, challenging me, and I bite.

"Maybe—"

Fuck! His hands grab the collar of my shirt so quickly that I don't have the chance to react as the fucker pulls me closer, almost lifting me off my feet. He gets right in my face, I can feel and smell his breath, but it's his eyes that I can't stop looking at, because I swear, they just turned two shades darker.

"I know what you're thinking." His jaw is clenched so tightly that his mouth barely moves as he spits through gritted teeth. "I know what you want. But if you touch her it will be the last fucking thing you do."

"Back. Off!" Bennett says forcefully, and I finally manage to breath as I see the gun that he is pointing directly at Noah's head.

Why the fuck didn't I just reach for my own?

Officers from both sides draw their weapons, some pointing them at Noah and others pointing them at Bennett, like we're in some sort of gangland standoff. Bennett looks at the scene around him, specifically at the officers that are directing their weapons at him.

"I think you know that it would be very unwise of you to pull those triggers," he tells them, with not even a hint of a quiver in his voice.

Thank you, Bennett! He can come across as hard as fuck

when he needs to. That, or he just channels the sense of superiority that he feels that he has over the people around him. Either way, weapons are lowered, except for his, which remains focused on Noah, and yet Noah is still holding onto me and glaring at me with pure hatred.

"Noah," Scott says calmly, but with authority.

He didn't even reach for his own gun when the others did. It's like he'd expected the shit to hit the fan and was quite enjoying it.

"Go home," Scott adds, with more force.

Noah turns to Scott and smirks; he clearly doesn't take orders from him. Then he looks back to me and slowly releases me, before taking a few steps back. He glares at Bennett, who has now lowered his gun, but is still staring him down. Then he smiles unnervingly.

"It was good to see you again, Ethan. Please send my regards to Henry and Gwen," he smiles, as he walks back to his car and drives off a little more calmly than he arrived.

I try not to react, but I don't miss Bennett glance at me, and I know I will have some explaining to do on the way back, as Noah knew I would. It was the perfect parting blow. The fucking prick!

Exhausted. Mentally and physically exhausted; that's how I feel when I step into my office later in the evening. It has been a long day, most of it spent in that warehouse, and I still feel queasy from the smell of paint that lingers there. Not to mention the fact that I almost had my head ripped off... but it was worth it. The forensic team are quite certain that they've found enough traces of blood to be able to run a DNA test, and I'm certain that it will be a match to Adam.

I had to explain Noah's comments to Bennett, but I'm pretty sure he believed that it was only my parents that regularly frequented The Dome, not me. He knows as well as anyone, that the rich go through those gates, and I may be a working man, like him, but nobody ever seems to forget the money that I have waiting for me. He did push a little as to why Noah was specifically gunning for me, but I told him that Scott had named me as being the reason that Eve had been given Sanctuary in the first place.

"Fucking Scott!" Bennett had said, and then he didn't push it further.

Bennett had clearly enjoyed the drama, excitement, and even the danger, that had been his first experience of life on the other side of the wall. In fact, he was buzzing, even suggesting that we go for drinks, which he never does. At the end of a hard day, Bennett goes back to his wife.

I told him that I have plans with my parents, but what I really intend to do is oversee the evidence being signed in, then I hope, if it isn't too late, that I can check on Eve. Noah is a prick, but he isn't wrong. I want Eve. I want her so much that it hurts me physically. I want to hold her, I want to protect her, and I want to fuck her so hard and so good that she cannot even remember Noah's name.

Shit… I rearrange my crotch as just the thought of being inside her gets me hard.

She drives me crazy, and whereas I only used to feel it on the rare occasions that I was around her, now I feel it all the time and if anything, being close to her, and having her in reach, has just made it ten times worse. Noah said he'll kill me if I touch her, but all I can think is that at least I'll die happy.

Noah also thinks that I can't keep her, but that isn't technically true. Eve is on my side of the wall now. She has distance from her world and her messed up life with Noah, and I have the means and the contacts to give her a new life. She no longer has to go back through those gates. Not if she doesn't want to, and if she asks me... well, if she asks me, I will follow her anywhere.

All she needs to do is ask.

I finish with the lab team around nine o'clock and then I get in the car and go straight to Southaven — my father's flagship hotel, my inheritance, and the place where Eve is currently alone and hurting. I know my late arrival will look strange to the officers standing guard, but I'm going to tell them that I'm just checking in. I'm just making sure she's OK after a day alone.

Yes, eyebrows will be raised, but I don't really give a fuck. Besides, they'll get it, because I heard a few of them talking this morning, with one saying that he hopes "that she tries to make a run for it so that he has a reason to tackle her to the ground."

The people with him had laughed and I barked at them, reminding them to be more professional and yet, I'm the least professional of the lot of them. I'm the one abusing my position to make a late-night visit.

I walk into reception, which is busy and bustling, even at this time of night, and see Gemma, a bubbly blonde that always has a smile on her face, and usually a cock in her mouth — if the rumours are to be believed — wave me over.

"Detective Southwold, your father is still in his office and he asked that we send you in, if we saw you," she says with a blush.

She can blush all she likes, it's not happening. I know the reason women tend to want me is either for my looks or my wallet. It's one of the reasons that I'm still single — much to my mother's despair. That, and the fact that I met a beautiful brunette, eight years ago, and since then, nobody has been able to compare.

I glance at my watch. This is just another delay, but my father may have seen Eve today and it's possible he wants to tell me how she is, before I go in myself. So, I smile at Gemma and take the private lift to my father's rather excessive office. I knock on the door, I always do these days, and then I let myself in.

He's at his desk, as always. My father works bloody hard and I respect him for that. I can't say that our relationship has always been easy, but at least these days he can be believed when he says he's working late.

I make my way over to his sofas and land with a thud. I am suddenly very weary. "You wanted to see me?"

My father gets up from behind his desk and walks over to me with a bottle of bourbon and two glasses. A welcome sight, that is for certain.

"You could probably do with this after the day you've had," he says, handing me a glass. "Morgan filled me in. I understand you had a run in with Noah Joyson… you OK?"

I let out a slight laugh and take a sip of my drink. "The man's a psycho. But I'm good. He sends his regards, by the way."

"Right…" he sighs, as he sits down on the sofa opposite me. "And you're here to see Eve. It's a bit late, isn't it?"

I roll my eyes and frown at him because I didn't miss the unspoken meaning behind his words. "Her best friend went home today," I reply defensively. "I'm just making sure she's OK."

My father clears his throat and takes a larger than normal swig of his drink. "You have feelings for her, don't you?" he asks cautiously.

Guilty as charged.

"What makes you think that?" I ask, avoiding his gaze by taking a large drink of my own.

"Because I know you, and I know girls like her…"

I almost spit my drink out. "What do you mean by that? 'Girls like her'. Like it's her fault that I'm in love with—"

"Ethan… you can't!" he says shakily, but seriously. "I didn't mean anything against her… I would never… I just understand the allure, the attraction… but Ethan, you can't!"

He's shaking his head at me and he looks scared.

"I know! I get it. It would cost me my job. It would cost me everything I've worked for… but Dad—"

"That's not why you can't." He stands up and starts pacing a little, before downing his drink.

What the hell is wrong with him? I just sit and watch him, unable to hide my shock and confusion. He has only ever had good things to say about Eve. I know it's tricky, I know there are obstacles, but he knows that I can get around them.

He finally stops pacing, sits down, refills his glass, takes a few more sips and then looks at me. Guilt. That's guilt on his face.

"I understand, Ethan… I do, because it was just the same with Louisa."

I jump up, as my rage boils over. "Why the fuck are you bringing up Louisa?"

Why is he bringing up his ex-mistress? Why is he comparing Louisa to Eve? Just because Eve is Noah's mistress… Fucking arsehole, I thought he was above all of this.

I turn to glare at him again, but the stricken look on his face stops me in my tracks. My father doesn't look angry. He doesn't look resentful or hateful towards Eve, he looks like he wants to apologise. He looks sorry, he looks guilty and he looks like he's in pain, and my stomach starts to churn as I remember a time when he used to look like this every day.

I look away from him and stare at his desk, allowing my mind to focus on Louisa. It's something that I try not to do, but Louisa's face is ingrained on my brain, after I wandered into my father's office when I was eight years-old and found her straddling him naked across his desk. I didn't really understand what was happening, but from the reaction my mother had when she walked in behind me, I knew it was nothing good.

Louisa; dark hair, full lips, long lashes, beautiful... shit! No, no, no, no, no! Eve...

I turn completely cold as all of the air leaves my body. The room starts to spin, my gut churns and the bile starts to rise. I slowly turn to look at my father, and a slight shake of my head is the only response that I can manage, as realisation works its way from my brain and into my heart, crushing it in the process.

My father looks down, puts a hand to his face and starts to cry.

I turn away from him again, walk to the wall and start to gently but repeatedly hit my head against it, as I try to push the new reality away. As I try to make it so that this conversation never happened. I wish it hadn't.

I slowly turn around so that I'm leaning against the wall, rake my hands through my hair, and then let them slide down my cheeks as they get soaked by my tears.

Heartbreak. Denial. Disgust.

I turn to look at my father, and finally manage to breathe out, "You promised us there were no children."

36

EVE

*I*t's so hard to let Rose go. I don't want to let her go, I need her, but Ethan and Bennett are waiting outside the door and they won't be leaving without her. Part of me is tempted to just grab my bag and go with her. To go back to my home, my friends and Noah, so that I can just break down and let them save me. Among these strangers that are always watching me, even though they rarely come into the room; I feel like I need to be strong or I'm letting my side down. Not that I'm entirely sure who is on my side at the moment.

Rose pulls back and wipes her tears away. "Call me whenever you need me," she instructs me.

"I will," I promise her, while trying to regain my composure in order to make it easier for her to leave me.

"Eve… please don't do anything…" she stumbles on her

words, before trying again. "This isn't your fault... please don't punish yourself... in any way."

"I won't," I promise her. "Maybe I'll just fill up on fancy food and watch all of their TV channels," I say laughing a little in an attempt to reassure her, but also at the ridiculous amount of TV channels that they have here, literally — hundreds of them.

Rose still looks concerned, so I hug her again, and tell her, "I'm stronger than you think."

"No, Eve," she replies, squeezing me hard. "You're stronger than *you* think."

Then she lets me go and walks slowly to the door, taking the light from the room with her.

As soon as it's closed, I crash to the floor and burst into tears. I'm alone. I'm completely alone. I'm lost, I'm lonely and I don't know what to do. I'm in this posh hotel, in clothes that I know must also be posh, they keep bringing posh food that I cannot stomach, and all I want is to turn back the clock. That's the only thing I want them to bring me. Some magical machine that will turn back time so that I can grab hold of Adam and stop him leaving the club.

I decide to sit and think about that for a while, because I've got nothing else to do and it's better than crying. I'm not even sure what day it is. Should I be styling hair or practising my set, right now? I don't know, so yes, a time machine will solve everything.

If I were to travel back in time, there are two possible outcomes, first; I would keep Adam at that club with me, I'd give him more alcohol, get him dancing and shove a pretty girl in front of his face — anything to distract him. Anything to stop him from remembering his love for Meredith and leaving.

Fucking hell! The one time he decided to be loyal and do right by her and I encouraged it.

The tears want to fall again but I refuse to let them, so I take myself back to that night and think about my second option; to let things happen as they did. I let Adam leave, but I leave too. I follow him, unseen, and I go where he goes, always just behind him, always out of sight. I stay close and hidden, following him right up to the point where he meets the person or people that plan to kill him. I wait until I can see their faces and then I pounce. I surprise them from behind, take their gun and put it to their fucking head instead!

I let the anger flow through me, and I embrace the power that I feel from holding the imaginary gun in my hand, and from saving my brother, but then I see Noah's face. I see myself holding the gun to Noah's head and the tears start to burn down my cheeks. Not just in my imagination, but here, in this room. Then I slowly turn the gun towards my own head, I feel my finger gently squeezing the trigger... then darkness.

"Room service," a woman shouts as she knocks on the door, making me jump out of my skin and bringing me back to the room and reality. To the world where I didn't save Adam. The world where I cannot bring him back.

The woman walks in, with a smile that is both friendly and cautious, and I pull myself up from the floor, go outside to the balcony and close the door behind me. The balcony happens to be the size of my bedroom and living room combined, it is fully enclosed around the edge, and I can feel the cool air against my face. I'm on the very top floor and I can see everything through the high glass wall that forms a transparent barrier between me and a fall that would surely kill me.

I stand and watch the world, their world, and I remember the last time I stood and looked at such a view. I turn to my left, as if to look at Adam unconscious in his hospital bed; but there is no bed, there is no hospital and there is no Adam. I can fantasise all I want, but there's no time machine and there's no way to undo what has been done. The only thing I can do now is trust Ethan. Trust that he'll tell me if Adam was killed in The Beneath or not. I know where to go for the rest of the answers. I know who will be able to fill in the gaps, but after that... I have no clue. I only know that somehow, I need to make them pay.

I need to stay strong. That's what I tell myself at various points throughout the day, and so I do my best to distract myself from the pain. I flick through the TV channels, trying to focus on something, anything, but after a while I get frustrated or bored, or the pain wants to claw back its control, and I try something new.

I sit inside, I sit outside. I eat, then I eat some more, and then I lay on the bed feeling sick. At one point, desperate for some sort of relief, I even tried to masturbate, but it didn't work. I tried everything, but I couldn't even get close to an orgasm. All it did was leave me with physical frustration on top of my emotional anguish.

Unfortunately, it did get me thinking. Usually, I only ever think about Noah when I'm pleasuring myself. Even after all the time we've been together, he still does it for me. However, thinking of him was too painful and so I made myself think about Ethan and it gave me an idea.

I may not be in the headspace to be able to get myself off, but that doesn't mean that Ethan couldn't. I know I shouldn't, but the thought has crept into my brain and now I can't get it out. Ethan likes me, maybe even more than likes me and why shouldn't I? Noah has sex with Jane — yes, I agreed to that situation, but he still does it.

The more I think about it, the more it distracts me from my pain and all that does is convince me that I have the solution. I so desperately want to feel something other than pain and I want to be held by someone strong, someone that I can feel safe with and someone who cares. I start to picture Ethan's hands, strong and large, stroking my skin, gently thumbing my nipples as he works his way down my body, and once again, I trail my own hands down.

Ten minutes later and I still cannot cum.

It's half past nine at night and I'm sitting on the sofa, not watching the TV, having had my third shower of the day. Henry provided me with some cream satin pyjamas — a cami top and long bottoms that I'm wearing under a thick, towelled robe. It would almost feel like someone is hugging me, if it weren't for the constant pain in my heart reminding me that I'm alone.

Ethan has been in The Beneath today and I thought he would have come to see me, but that's clearly not going to happen. It's not that I want to see him just so that I can try to seduce him, although I've not yet managed to convince myself that I shouldn't. I also need to know what he found there. I need some answers. I need some progress.

Moments later a knock at the door startles me and as it opens, I get up to greet whoever is on the other side. "Ethan!" I say in surprise.

God, he looks like shit. Has he been drinking? It looks like he's been crying.

He walks in, barely even looking at me and goes over to the sofa. It looks like he's going to sit down, but he pauses and then just leans against the arm, facing, but not looking at me. I instantly feel my pulse start to quicken, because I know that this must mean that he's discovered something. Something that has clearly shaken him.

Pushing the unease aside, I walk over to him. "I didn't think you were going to come," I tell him gently, because right now he looks like he feels worse than I do.

He looks at me then and stands a little taller. "I shouldn't have come," he says shakily. "I'm sorry, I shouldn't be here."

He starts to walk away from me, but I grab him by the arm. "Ethan, you cannot do this to me!" I scold him. "You cannot walk in here, at this time of night, after where you've been, tell me nothing and then just leave. Ethan… what happened? What did you find?"

He looks at me, then to the door, as if he's having a battle with himself about whether he should stay or go. I don't know why he's in this state, but I am not letting him go. I lead us both over to the sofa and pull him down next to me as I sit. He doesn't put up a fight, but he's clearly still fighting with himself.

My tears start to fall, as I beg him, "Ethan, please tell me what happened today."

He looks at me, then gently removes my hand from his arm, clears his throat and stands up, putting space between us again. "I won't know anything until we run the tests… it'll take a couple of days. But we found traces of blood."

The food that I ate earlier starts to rise up and I take a deep breath and try to force it back down.

He gives me a moment, but then he continues, "It looks like at some point there was a lot of blood in an area on the ground, but it was cleaned up… not well enough though."

I put my hands over my mouth and burning tears fall. I know my brother was shot, I know there would have been blood, but thinking about it on the ground, and about some-body with a mop and bucket just scrubbing it away; has me heaving.

"I should go…"

"No!" I shout, jumping up. He cannot leave. I cannot let the pain take over again. "Ethan, can you please just stay with me for a bit?" I ask, as I move closer to him. "Please… I've been alone all day."

I reach out to him and he recoils from me. He looks so pained, so anguished and I have no idea why. He says he wants to leave, but he looks so torn and it occurs to me that maybe we can make each other feel better; not just me.

I slowly reach out to him again, as if I'm approaching a scared animal, letting my hand rest against his stomach, as I move closer. He quickly grabs hold of my hand and moves it away from his stomach, but he doesn't let it go. He's breathing hard as he pulls it up to his mouth and gently kisses it, and then I feel my body start to pulse at the core.

It was such a light, simple touch, but it fuels my need to feel more.

"I have to go," he says again, with the same pain in his voice and the same look of anguish on his face, but he hasn't let go of my hand, so I move closer and press my body against his.

"But you don't want to go… do you?" I ask him, as I let my free hand explore his chest.

He does feel strong, I knew he would.

He looks down at me and I can see the fight that he's having with himself, clearly on his face. "Eve… we cannot do this," he says desperately, but he still hasn't let go of the hand that he's now holding against his cheek, and he isn't stopping me from exploring his body either.

"You won't get into trouble. I won't tell anybody," I reassure him, while I press my body against his.

I wouldn't be this forward and I would have let him leave, if I wasn't so desperate, and if it didn't feel like he truly needs this too. I know he wants it because I can feel him hardening against me.

"Your head is saying no…" I lean in to kiss his chest, and as I do, I feel him harden even more, and the throbbing between my legs increases. "Your body is saying, yes… but what does your heart say?" I ask him, as I continue to breathe warm kisses against his chest.

He finally releases my hand, and as he does, he cups my face and looks me in the eyes, as if he's desperately searching for something. He looks so tortured by this, and I don't understand why he's making this more complicated than it needs to be. I just want him to fuck me. I just want him to fuck the pain away.

"My heart…" he chokes out. "My heart is telling me to take you from this world… to take you far away and stay by your side forever."

He's asking for forever. I can't promise him forever, but I can give him tonight.

"So, what's the problem?" I move one of his hands away from my cheek, bring it to my mouth and start to gently kiss it.

"We can't do this," he says again, and yet he makes no attempt to stop me.

"I think we can." I stand on my tiptoes, wrap a hand around the back of his neck, and as I pull him close, I whisper, "I'm going to kiss you, Ethan… stop me. If you really want to."

I press my lips against his and start to gently kiss him and instead of pulling away, he pulls me closer. He wraps his arms around my waist and pins me against him, then he gently pulls back and looks me in the eyes. "I love you, Eve."

He doesn't wait for me to reply, instead he kisses me now, passionately, and deeply, as he greedily pushes his tongue into my mouth. I reciprocate, with the same level of desperation, and I grind myself against his erection. He groans into my mouth, and just as I think he's about to take me to my room, he pushes me away from him, and I stumble into the sofa.

Breathless, I look at him in shock. "Why did you do that? I thought you wanted it!"

He bends over and I see him breathing hard, then he stands up tall and backs away even further before turning to look at me. He's crying. Why the fuck is he crying?

"I'm sorry, I shouldn't have done that…" He rakes his hands down his face.

I shake my head in disbelief and start to move closer to him, but he puts up his hand and shakes his head at me, warning me away.

"You don't have to apologise, I want to do this."

"No…. no… you just think you do," he says as fresh tears cascade down his cheeks.

He's rejecting me. He still has a fucking hard on and he's rejecting me.

"Ethan, it's just sex!" I spit at him.

He lets out a shaky laugh, but the look on his face suggests that I just stabbed him in his heart. "It could never be, 'just sex' with you, Eve… and it's not going to happen."

"I thought you liked me."

"I do."

"I thought you cared!"

A slap in his face again.

"I do care, Eve. I care more than you know, and I care more for you than you do for me."

Is that why he stopped it? Because he feels more for me than I do for him. God, I want to growl in frustration. I have just put it on a plate for him and he still won't take it.

"I have people that care about me, Ethan… I just really wanted you to fuck me, that's all." I know I sound like a bitch, but now my pride is hurting as much as my heart is and I can't help it.

"Eve… please… I don't want to add to your hurt and…" he looks down and shakes his head again. "I want you… I've always wanted you…"

"Are you going to fuck me?"

He shakes his head at me gently, as his eyes widen, and more tears fall.

"Then go." I glare at him, before turning to walk to the bedroom and lock the door as the tears stream down my face, soaking me in shame and embarrassment.

"You stupid, stupid girl!" I whisper to myself. "Of course, he doesn't want you, you're a broken, orphan whore!"

A cry escapes me as I continue to berate myself and then eventually, I hear the door to the main room open and then close. I unlock my door and step into the now empty living room, and then slump on the sofa. Then the realisation that I've just pushed away the one person that was prepared to help, slaps me repeatedly across the face.

$\mathcal{I}$’ve been sitting on the balcony watching their world since three o'clock, when I finally gave up trying to sleep. Every time I closed my eyes, I went back to kissing Ethan, back to Ethan rejecting me, and back to me pushing him away. How could I have been so stupid? All I wanted was a few minutes where I could feel good again, and I ruined everything.

I tried everything I could to get to sleep last night, but unable to switch off, and still completely frustrated, I let my hands slide down again, thinking about how Ethan's tongue felt in my mouth, how it moved, and how it would feel if he was brushing it against my clit. I felt his erection; he's big and I started to imagine him inside me as we thrust against each other, sweaty, panting and screaming, and just as I was finally about to cum, I imagined seeing Noah, standing in the corner watching us, broken and angry, and I stopped... just like that.

I didn't think about it at the time because all I could think about was blocking out the pain; but I cheated on Noah, last night. I have fucked everything up! All I wanted to do was feel something other than grief, and then I saw the state Ethan was in, and I thought I could make him feel better too. I didn't. If anything, I made him feel worse. I don't know what was going on with him last night, but all I've done is add to his pain, and made myself feel guilty on top of everything else.

I'm a silly, stupid, weak slut and I'm petrified that Ethan will no longer want to tell me the truth. If I were him, I wouldn't want to speak to me again. I should have just let him leave. He was trying to leave.

The unwelcome sun starts to rise, and I go inside and pull the curtains closed, because I don't want to watch it. The rising sun signifies a fresh start, a new day, brightness… life going on. I prefer the dark right now. People can't see the tears in the dark and I can't see my own reflection.

The phone rings at ten o'clock; I've showered and had some food, but I'm exhausted and not mentally prepared for what I hear. It's Bennett, telling me that their investigation into the gangs in Havensmere, has pulled up 'persons of interest'. Apparently, they have someone in for questioning and they have a lead on a location and are sending the forensic team in today.

I couldn't say anything to him. It's not that I couldn't find the response, because I knew what my response should be. I should have thanked him and gone along with the lie because that's what it is. They're building the lie that they are calling their 'case', and soon I'll be told that Adam was a Runner and killed by a gang on this side of the wall.

I'm prepared to go along with Bennett and Morgan's lie, as long as Ethan tells me the truth, but I couldn't say anything because my throat literally closed up on itself and all I could manage was some weird, guttural sound, before he went on his way.

God, I hope Ethan is still willing to tell me the truth, even though I already know it. In my heart, I know.

~

The TV is shit. How can there be so many channels, and everything still be shit? I'm about to call down and order some lunch but a knock at the door stops me. I pause and wait, because usually people knock and then enter, but not this time. There's another knock and so I go over and answer it, completely shitting myself in case it's Ethan.

"Mr Southwold?" I say in surprise and relief, as I step aside and gesture for him to come in.

"Please, call me Henry. Do you mind if I come in?" he asks, as he clasps his hands together in front of his body.

He seems nervous.

"It's your hotel," I shrug in response.

He walks further in and heads towards the table by the window and, not knowing what else to do, I follow him over, and we stand on either side of it.

"Are you comfortable here?" he asks nervously.

"Yes…" I reply quietly, then I clear my throat and remember my manners. "Thank you for having me," I add with more clarity. Sister Theresa would be proud.

"It's my pleasure," he says smiling, then he stops and shakes his head. "I didn't mean 'pleasure'... what a silly thing to say!" he chastises himself. "There's no pleasure here… I wish the circumstances… Adam…" he keeps pausing, he's genuinely struggling. "I'm so sorry for your loss, Eve… I truly am," he says as he chokes up. "But I'm happy that I've been able to offer some assistance... that's all."

"Thanks," I reply, as I feel my tears building up again.

We stand and stare out of the window, watching the world below. It should feel awkward. We're two strangers really, but I feel comfortable with his presence and his silence.

"What do you think of this place?" he asks, as he gestures out toward the view.

I've been staring out the window, but not really focusing on anything in particular, and so I shrug as I say, "It's shiny."

It's all I could think of and it fits.

He laughs a little then looks ahead, as he asks, "And what do you think of us?"

I narrow my eyes a little, and he sees the question on my face, and clarifies for me.

"I mean the people here... the people that let their children be taken away."

He looks down again, as if hiding his shame. Or possibly his pain.

"Oh..." I say, a little taken aback, how am I supposed to answer this? "I think... most of the time we're just getting on with our lives."

"Yes, of course..." he says, once again appearing to scold himself for even asking, and yet he's clearly not finished. "What do you think of your parents?" he asks, swallowing hard.

Does he really want to know this?

I look at him for a moment and I realise how vulnerable he looks, like he's desperate for any information I can give him, and then I realise that I'm looking at a man that has a child in The Beneath.

I take a seat at the table that we've been standing next to, and he follows suit.

"I can only really speak for myself... and for Adam," I add, shakily. "It's like it goes around in a cycle," I explain. "You start off feeling angry and resentful; not necessarily at your parents because they didn't have a choice. More at the way the world is," I tell him, and he nods in understanding. "Then you feel angry towards your parents, because they knew the consequences, but they did it anyway."

He swallows hard.

"In mine and Adam's case, that anger was doubled."

He looks down.

"Because they did it twice! Losing one baby wasn't enough to make them learn..." I give a small, bitter laugh. "Then there were times when Adam and I would talk about how in love they must have been." I smile as I'm hit with the memory of laying on the grass in the park with Adam, romanticising over our existence, and the tears spill over. "We used to say that they must have been so in love that they just couldn't help themselves."

As I smile at Henry, he smiles back, and his own tears fall.

"Then we'd go back to thinking that they were fucking stupid!" I add more bluntly. "I pity them... I pity her, at least," I say more sombrely. "I have two godchildren, and when I hold them... even though they're not mine, I can imagine the pain of having them ripped away and my heart breaks for her... this woman that I've never met. But in the end, I'm grateful to them," I say, and he looks at me with hope. "Because whatever their reasons were, they gave me a brother... they gave me Adam," I choke out, as the tears once again take hold.

"I saw you two together," he says, and once again I look at him questioningly. "The night we met at The Dome, eight years ago... David called you over, and after a while you went to meet Adam, and I followed... he gave you a piggy-back out the door!" he says, with a little laugh.

A sob escapes me as I remember all the times my big, little brother would carry me around, as if I weighed nothing.

"The bond between you... it was so clear... so strong..." He shuffles in his seat and wipes the tears that seem to keep falling away. "And on the one hand I was so happy for you both..." He pauses again and looks me in the eyes. "And on the other... on the other... I was devastated that I could never be a part of it."

Silence. We're silent again except for my heart which is beating out of my chest. He's looking at me, he's crying, and I'm petrified.

"I knew your names already..."

Oh, fuck!

"I knew you sang at The Dome..."

Oh, please, no!

"And as soon as I saw you, there was no mistaking it..."

Please, don't say it...

"You look exactly like her," he smiles through his tears. "You look exactly like your mother."

I push away from the table, run out to the balcony, bend over and gasp for air. This is not happening. This cannot be happening.

Henry follows me out. "I'm so sorry Eve. I know this is a shock... but I had to tell you."

I turn on him. "How can you know? How could you know our names?"

"Eve... you and Adam are the only full blood siblings," he says, as he holds his hands out in apology. "I paid to find out your names and I went there as soon as I was able to, hoping to see you—"

"YOU ARE NOT MY FATHER!" I shout, as the tears

stream down my cheeks.

"I have no right to that title… I know, but you are my daughter… and Adam—"

"Please, stop!" I say desperately, as I slump onto the floor and hug my knees to my chest. "Please… just stop."

He does as I ask, but I hear him move closer and he lowers himself to the ground too. He sits in silence, listening helplessly as I just sit and cry. I've just lost my brother and now Henry, who has dipped in and out of my life for years; a man I thought was meaningless, is telling me that he's my father.

"I'm sorry to have done this to you now," he says, with nothing but love in his voice. "But I know Morgan's plans — I fund them… and I know what they will say happened to Adam, and I know that your stay in Sanctuary will soon end," he says with regret. "They'll send you back through that wall to Adam's murderers… and I had to tell you, because you need to know that you don't have to go back there."

I lift my head a little, but I can't look at him and so I stare right ahead at the glass balcony wall. It's bright now, and our reflections are staring right back at me.

"You don't have to go back there… I can get you a new ID, I can get you everything you need to go far away from here."

God, he sounds like Ethan.

Oh. Fuck! Ethan!

I feel sick and I jump up, preparing to run to the bathroom, but Henry grabs me before I get to the door.

"Eve, please… I'm serious. You can choose."

"Agh!" I cry out, as I double over in pain. I need to speak, I need to ask him, but I can't catch my breath.

He lowers me back to the ground and holds me, and I let him.

"Eve…"

"Are you going to tell Ethan?" I blurt out.

"Ethan knows," he replies calmly, and then the world stands still.

Everything stops. I can't even hear my blood pumping. I slowly pull myself up so that I'm standing, and then I turn to him. "When did you tell him?" I ask, slowly.

"Last night."

"When, last night?" I ask, unable to hide my panic.

"He came here to see you last night, but I had him sent to me…" he explains. "I was worried about his feelings for you… so I told him—"

"I need you to leave… I feel sick!" I say frantically as I run back inside.

He follows me in. "Eve, please… I'm serious. I want to help you!"

I run straight to the bathroom, now completely unable to speak. I lock the door, then go straight to the toilet and throw up repeatedly, until there's nothing left inside, and the retching finally subsides.

This cannot be happening. All of this… how can it be happening?

My brother is dead… my Adam… Then I learn who my father is, and then I learn that I have another brother. A brother who just last night had his tongue in my mouth. A brother, that I fantasied about having sex with… a brother, that I tried to have sex with!

I move back to the toilet and wretch again, but nothing comes out. I wait for a while, but still nothing happens and so I slowly pull myself off the floor and clean up at the sink. I don't look in the mirror because I can't. I can't look in the mirror without thinking about Adam, and I can't think about Adam without thinking about Ethan.

Oh, fuck me, this is so messed up.

I haven't heard Henry, so I assume he's gone and as I open the door, I'm relieved to find that he has. That's good, because I cannot look at him right now, either.

I look around the room, just wondering what the hell I'm going to do with myself now, and then something catches my eye on the table by the phone. I walk over and pick up the envelope that has my name on it and pull out the note inside.

My offer still stands, Eve.
I can and will help you.
I can give you a new life.
All you need to do is ask.

Henry x

It feels like there is something else in the envelope, so I tip it over and two things slide out. One is a business card with Henry's contact details and the other looks like a photograph. It lands face down, but there's something written on the back, just one word... **Louisa**.

My hands shake as I slowly reach out to pick it up. My heart feels like it's rising out of my chest and I take a deep breath, trying to calm it.

It's just a photograph, after all.

I turn it over and as I do, I let out a cry, because it isn't *just* a photograph. It's a photograph of a woman, smiling, happy and beautiful. She could almost be me, expect for the fact that she looks like she has no cares in the world. She looks like she's free.

No. This isn't just any old photograph... this is my mother.

38

*A*fter staring at the photograph for about five minutes I burst into tears and run for my phone. I haven't turned it on since I last spoke to Noah, and it bleeps at me persistently, with Noah's name constantly flashing up at me. I ignore all of the messages and make my call.

I've lost track of the days, so I don't know what Rose will be doing, but I desperately need to speak to her. It rings a few times and then is answered cordially by a voice I cannot place and I immediately, and frantically ask for Rose. I receive a rather shocked and breathless, "Eve?" in return, before the line goes quiet.

A few agonising minutes later and I hear the sound of my call being transferred, before a voice that I could never forget, or mistake says my name, "Eve, my dear girl, I've been so worried!"

"Sister Theresa…" I answer, before bursting into tears.

She lets me cry for a few minutes without saying a word. In fact, she says nothing until I blurt out, "Everything is so fucked up!"

I tell her everything. Everything that has happened and

everything that will happen; what they will say happened to Adam. I tell her about Henry, and then with shame oozing from every word I speak, I tell her about Ethan.

Sister Theresa is Sister Theresa; non-judgmental, understanding, resolute, and she assures me that I'm not going to hell, since I was unaware that I was about to commit incest.

～

That was two days ago. For two days I've spoken to nobody except for Bennett, when he's called to update me on the case. Now he's on his way over with Ethan, to tell me about the arrest that they have just made. Ethan is on his way over to lie to my face and I feel like I'm going to be sick.

I'm taking deep breaths and trying to find my empathy and understanding. That's what Sister Theresa told me to try to do. She may have been concerned for Ethan's soul, but she had sympathy for his heart, and for what he must have been feeling, and she encouraged me to try to do the same.

I'm trying. I'm really trying, but the thought of standing in this room with him has my gut churning.

They knock at the door.

I move closer to the sofa.

They let themselves in and I stand on my jelly legs, trying to breathe and trying to keep calm as they walk over to me. I steal a cautious glance at Ethan, but thankfully he is looking at his feet.

As they get closer, I sit down and they both follow my lead, Ethan still looking at anything other than me.

Bennett clears his throat. "Eve… as you are aware from our conversations, I'm here to tell you that we have made an arrest," he says, with a formal smile.

I swallow hard and take in a deep breath. "Who?"

"A man called Joe Bailey," he says with confidence. "He's a member of one of the gangs that was impacted when the Runners became more prevalent."

Here we go.

Take a breath.

I knew it was coming.

"Adam travelled through those gates on that fateful night," he says with the hint of apology. "They found him, and they killed him."

I put my head in my hands and let the tears fall. He thinks I'm crying because he's just told me how my brother died, but he's wrong. I'm crying because this is a massive betrayal to my brother's memory, and I'm going along with it.

Eventually, I find the strength to look at him and force out the words, "Thank you for everything you've done, Detective."

He twists his hands a little. "We will be releasing your brother's body in three days and your stay of Sanctuary will continue until then—"

"I'd like to leave now," I tell him, and I see Ethan's head snap towards me out of the corner of my eye.

"That's entirely your choice," he says with kindness, then he stands and reaches out to shake my hand. "I need to report to High Minister Morgan now, but Detective Southwold can go over the details of your return," he says, as he walks away.

I'm now alone with Ethan and the tension in the air is thick enough to touch, as he slowly turns to me with the same tormented expression that he wore the other night.

"You shouldn't go back," he says, and with a shaking hand he pulls an envelope out of his briefcase and hands into me. "Everything you were just told is a lie. The forensic evidence is fabricated, and the confession is a lie."

"Why would someone confess to a murder they didn't commit?"

"Because when you're looking at an arrest for multiple murders and you're given the option to make them go away by confessing to one... you confess, Eve," he says vehemently.

I step away from him and keep my back to him for a moment, before slowly turning and looking him right in the eyes. "Why should I believe you?" I ask with a coldness that hits him hard.

"I promised you, Eve!" he replies defensively. "I know... I know things happened the other night... but I'm not about to break my promise to you."

I open my mouth, prepared to argue, but he stops me.

"Eve! You're smart. Use your head!" he almost shouts at me. "That envelope contains the truth..." he says more gently. "Adam was not a Runner. He was killed in the old paint warehouse in St Martins. He was lying on his side when he was shot. I can tell you what angle the bullet travelled, where the person that pulled the trigger was standing and how tall they are," he says, as his tears start to fall. "I just can't tell you who pulled the trigger, because I wasn't allowed to look into it any further."

My heart hurts and the tears fall as the image of Adam's last moments come crashing into my mind and it takes all the strength that I have to stop myself from crumbling. I take a deep breath and look at Ethan again. "How can I trust you now?" I force out.

My words knock the air out of him.

"Why would you ask me that?"

"Because of your tongue down my throat!" I snarl.

He rakes his hands through his hair, and I see the shame on his face. Good. He should feel it too.

"I shouldn't have let that happen… but you—"

I glare at him. "Oh! So, it was my fault?"

"You didn't exactly make it easy to say no."

No, I guess I didn't, but there is still one fundamental difference between us; I didn't know we shared DNA.

"Well, what can I say? Your massive, fucking hard on gave me the impression that you were up for it! You're sick, do you know that?" I spit at him.

He steps back as if I've slapped him in the face, but I don't let him speak. "Henry came to see me the next morning," I say, keeping my tone casual. "Or should I say, *Dad*?" I add with more force.

"YOU ARE NOT MY SISTER!" he yells, stepping closer again.

"According to him, I am."

Tears stream down his face. "You are not my sister!" he says a little more quietly, but with the same force as before. "You're just Eve… you're just you…"

"Just me, who happens to have the same biological father as you."

"I am not your brother! I am not looking to replace Adam."

"You. Never. Could!" I argue back, as the tears burn down my cheeks. "We may not have any familial ties, but biologically; I am your sister, and you knew this when you pushed your tongue down my throat."

"Yes, and you were loving it. What does that say about you?" he counters angrily as his tears fall too.

"I. Didn't. Know!" I reply through gritted teeth.

"And. I. Didn't. Care!" he replies in the same tone, sending me stumbling back in shock.

He shakes his head. "I didn't mean that. I did care… that's why I stopped. That's why I didn't let it go further."

"You shouldn't have let it happen at all."

"You cannot turn off years of lust… years of love, just like that, Eve!" he starts to defend himself. "I don't want you as a sister, I just…"

I let out a shaky laugh, unable to comprehend what I'm hearing, and he changes his direction.

"Don't go back there, Eve!" he says more urgently. "Stay here for a few more days and I can get you what you need to get away from here, away from all of it."

"What? And start a new life with you?" I laugh at him.

He bends over, shielding the pain in his gut, before he slowly looks up at me. "If you wanted me to, I would," he says, so full of hurt. "I'd stay with you forever if you asked me to… but either way, I will still get you what you need. You just need to stay—"

"Please arrange for a car to take me back," I say resolutely.

"Eve—"

"Fetch a car… please."

He steps away from me, finally defeated, and makes a call. It doesn't take long to make the arrangements and then he just stands with his back to me, breathing heavily.

Eventually he turns to me.

"Officers will be here to escort you in twenty minutes," he replies formally. "Hide that envelope… it has my number in it. Call me if you need me."

Then he walks out of the door without so much as a goodbye.

39

The car pulls slowly up to the wall, I step out on my shaky legs and pass through the gates, leaving Havensmere behind me. The Beneath looks just the same as before, only it feels bigger. I guess I have been cooped up in a hotel for... I don't even know how long it's been.

I start walking, then notice the police car parked to my right, and as I turn to look at it, Scott Legion gets out and starts to walk towards me, and although every part of me wants to recoil, I stand frozen to the spot.

"Welcome back, Eve," he says in a friendly manner. "I'm here to take you home."

"I'd rather walk," I tell him, and I start to turn away.

There's no way I'm getting in a car with him.

He rolls his eyes. "Eve... come on." He never really did have any patience for me. "There's no need to be like this, the case is closed."

"I've been stuck in a hotel room for days," I tell him, not wanting to let on to the truth. "I really would rather walk."

He nods his head and walks over to his car, no doubt making his calls to let people know that I'm back. I pass a few people as I walk to my flat; they stare or give me a sad smile, but I don't respond to any of them.

The climb up the three flights of stairs used to be easy, but I've not used these muscles for a while and my legs are aching by the time I reach the door to my flat. I hesitate as I put my key in, as I have no idea what to expect, and the thought of walking in and finding Noah waiting, has my stomach in knots.

He's not here. That's good. I've no doubt he'll be here soon, but I want him to walk in on me. I want to be sitting when he comes back in.

Ten minutes later and I hear footsteps coming up the stairs at speed. The key is put clumsily into the lock and he bursts through the door, looking completely dishevelled and desperate, and I react on instinct and run over to him. He grabs hold of me and pulls me into him, wrapping his arms around my body and holding me there, as if his life depends on never letting me go.

I have missed him. I've missed him so much. The pain and the anger cannot destroy the love that I have for Noah. Nothing has ever been able to destroy the love I have for him, but that won't stop me from having to do what's needed.

He loosens his grip, moves me back a little so that he can look at me, and as he cups my face, ever so gently; tears start to form in his eyes. "I have missed you so much, Eve... I've been so worried," he says, his voice breaking.

"I've missed you too," I tell him with complete honesty, then he leans in to kiss me and I let him.

He kisses me gently, as if he's being a little cautious, but I have missed this man so much and he's the only one that can take the pain away, even if only for a little while. I reach up, grab hold of his neck and pull him into me, and as I do our kisses deepen and the need that has been plaguing me for days intensifies. His hands are in my hair and when I let out a little groan, he pulls it so that my head tips back, and he lands forceful kisses on my neck.

Everything inside me comes alive. I push my hips against his and he picks me up and pushes me against the nearest wall. I forget everything as I lose myself in his touch, in the need to feel him, and for the pain to go away. I tug at his shirt and he steps back to pull it off, and seconds later his lips are on mine as his hands explore my body.

Then something clicks in my mind, and I slow down as I remember that the pain is here for a reason. The pain is here because Adam is gone, and Noah needs to give me answers.

"Stop," I whisper into his neck, and he lets out a groan in objection and continues to trail his kisses along my collar bone, sending shivers down my spine in the process.

Focus, Eve.

"Stop," I say again, and this time I move his head away from me and hold it in front of my face with both of my hands.

He's panting and I can see that his need is almost taking over, but my needs matter more right now. "We're going to talk," I tell him, as I push him away from me.

I pick up his shirt and hand it back to him and he holds it for a moment, looking down at the floor, but then he slowly puts it on and turns me, with a look of fear on his face.

"Eve…" he starts to say, but I put my hand up to stop him.

I know this is going to hurt us both. Seeing Noah in pain always awakens my need to soothe him, but I stay resolute, and I stay strong, because I am going to get the fucking truth. Even if the truth ends up breaking us.

"Before you say a single word, there are things you need to know," I tell him, and he nods gently. "I know what the police say happened is a lie and I know why they're lying. I also know that Adam was killed in the old paint warehouse." His jaw clenches. "I know he was beaten up before being shot in the head. I know that you were called away from your house on Friday night. I know that you beat somebody up and I know that whomever it was that you hurt, must have mattered to you."

He turns away from me and walks over to the window in the living room, his shoulders slumped in defeat.

"The last time we spoke you lied to me," I tell him, and I see his head nod a little in confirmation. "I told you to make that the last time, Noah, and that had better be the last time."

"What do you want me to tell you?" he asks quietly, while still staring out of the window.

"I want you to tell me that you didn't come to me and fuck me like you did, after watching my brother be killed!" The tears stream down my cheeks. "I want you to tell me that the hands, that you then used to make me cum... that I kissed better in the morning... aren't the same hands that beat my brother!" I plead. "That's what I want to hear, Noah. But only if it's true... you only say that to me if it's true."

He turns to face me, and I see the tears streaming down his face. He looks so helpless and it takes all of my strength not to go to him.

"If I tell you the truth... I lose you," he almost whispers.

I step closer to him. "No, Noah... Telling me the truth is the only way you stand a chance of keeping me."

40

FRIDAY NIGHT

Noah

I know I'm shit to be around when I'm in a bad mood and Jane avoids me most of the evening, but that's probably because she knows it's her doing. Partly her doing, anyway. Eve is having a night out, and even though I know the club security teams will always watch out for her; it always puts me on edge. So, I really didn't need Jane telling her mother that we haven't had sex in weeks; the result of which led to an hour-long lecture from my parents reminding me about my responsibilities.

Now I'm going to have to head to the fight club at some point later to make sure my temper is let loose on someone that knows how to take a hit, and around people that know when to rein me in.

Unfortunately, it also means that the deed will have to be done.

When we were first married, I tried to make the sex nice

for Jane. I thought it was the least I could do, but that stopped years ago. Going down on her, tasting her... it makes me feel sick now, just thinking about it, and hearing her groans of pleasure made my skin scrawl. Feeling Jane shudder beneath me sent shivers down my spine in the worst possible way, and it felt like I was betraying Eve, even more.

It also confused Jane, and I didn't feel good about doing that. I'd dealt her enough shit over the years, so we just drew a line. We agreed that would stop, and now we just do what needs to be done. It put a stop to her pointless attempts of seduction too, because she finally realised that Eve is the only woman I want. She has been for a decade and will continue to be forever.

I turn as I hear Jane walk into the bedroom, I throw the lube onto the bed, she switches off the light, undresses, then I give her a quick fuck and leave her wholly unsatisfied as I take a shower.

I know she deserves more; she deserves much better than me. I also know that I'm a selfish piece of shit, and probably one of the worst people to walk this earth. If only I could fake it, like my brothers. They just seem to be able to go along with our family's plans without argument, even when it's clear that they hate it, but I've just never been able to fake anything.

I do, however, take comfort in the fact that Jane prefers things the way they are now, too. I'm the stud and she's the broodmare. It's a physical transaction, an exchange of fluids, that's it. Completely meaningless and completely pointless. I made sure of that, but unfortunately, I still have to play my part in order to prevent any repercussions.

I stand in the shower, washing Jane away from me and thinking about what I can do to change things. I'm always thinking about it, especially after sleeping with Jane. I have

the power to make anything happen, I always have, that's
what made me stand out from my brothers and take the lead,
and yet I am stuck in the shit, fucking situation. In this
marriage and in this lie.

My phone starts ringing, and I quickly turn off the shower
and reach for it, hoping to fuck that something's not happened
to Eve.

Worse. It's David.

Not even bothering to repress my irritation, I answer, "It's
ten thirty, what do you want?"

"You're needed," he replies, in the same tone. There's not
exactly much love lost between us these days. "Get your arse
to the old paint warehouse — now."

"Have someone else deal with it."

I do have plans to kick the shit out of someone tonight,
but it's going to be in the ring. Not the fucking warehouse and
not when I'm already on the brink.

"It has to be you."

Then the fucker hangs up.

"Fuck's sake!" I growl.

I head into the bedroom and put on my black tracksuit,
because if I don't go on my own accord, they'll only send
someone for me.

Twenty minutes later, I pull up to the warehouse. It's
nothing like the old paper factory, where the fights are held.
It's barely still standing, stinks of chemicals and harbours too
many ghosts for my liking. It's as far away from civilisation
as you can get in The Beneath, which is why it's The Council's chosen location for dishing out their more severe punishments. The people brought here don't always leave, but given
that they've requested me, it means that tonight, they will.

They'll receive a severe kicking, but they'll leave with
their heart still beating.

I get out of my car and I'm a bit taken aback to find that it's not just The Council elders that are waiting for me. It looks like a full-on Founding Family gathering — of the men, at least, and one that I've been excluded from, until now.

Why the fuck would they do that?

I pause, as an uneasy feeling starts to creep into my gut, but I try to push it off as I head over to David. I'm about to ask him what's going on, but he just hands me a pair of black leather gloves. I look to my right and see that the old barrel is burning, ready to dispose of them once I'm done. I've never known why they do this, it's not like anyone is going to get arrested and we need to burn the evidence.

David still hasn't looked at me and I let out an irritated breath. This is not going to be fun.

"What's going on?" I ask.

I turn when I hear a commotion and the answer emerges in the form of three men dragging another into the middle of the crowd that has formed. His arms are held behind his back and he has a sack over his head. I can't help but laugh when I look back at David; they really do like the dramatics.

Fuck it. I just want to get this over with.

With gloves in hand, I walk over to them, and as I get closer, the sack is pulled away and Adam is shoved to the ground. The men that were holding him step back to join the circle that has been formed, like a ring of men forming a rope around a boxing ring.

Adam. Fucking Adam? This is a line that was not supposed to be crossed!

I glare at them all in turn, as the rage burns through my blood. I bend down and pull him back up to his feet and give him the once over; he seems fine other than being shit scared.

I zone in on David. "What the fuck do you think you're doing?"

Commander Legion steps forward. "This little runt is guilty of skimming profits and he needs to be punished," he says, without the slightest hint of any emotion.

I groan inwardly because I should have known this was going to happen. Adam still has a hand in the illegal goods trade, I know this, Eve does too, but he's not going through the gates anymore, and she's trying her best not to stress about it, so I haven't got involved.

I raise an eyebrow at Adam. "Is this true?"

The look of guilt on his face says it all.

I pin him with a glare, letting him know exactly how much he's fucked up and scan the crowd again, until I spot the man I need. Warren Manners — the eldest son of Heath Manners, and a complete wanker.

"I'll cover whatever he owes you... with interest," I tell him, as I hold out my hands as a gesture of peace.

Warren shrugs his shoulders and smiles brightly. "Thank you, Noah, that's very kind and I heartily accept. However..." My gut starts to churn. "That little cunt stabbed me in the back, and he needs to be taught a lesson!"

Is he serious, right now?

I laugh incredulously, in an attempt to keep the demons at bay. I need to keep it together. I can't go dark right now, but Warren tries my patience at the best of times.

"You are all well aware that Adam is under my protection and part of the deal—"

"The deal you made to keep your precious bit of skirt, has nothing to do with me," Warren replies with a smugness that almost has me marching over and slapping him.

I grip my hands tightly against my sides and take in a few deep breaths, holding the air in for a moment before exhaling. People often try to cheapen what I have with Eve in order to bait me, but I will not give him the satisfaction.

"Let me make myself very clear," I seethe, as I walk closer to him. "Not only am I not going to lay a finger on Adam, but none of you will either."

"You're half right there." I turn, as Scott chimes in. "None of us will lay a finger on him — but you will, because that's your punishment."

This time I burst out laughing. "My punishment?"

"Yes!" my father barks, as he starts to walk over to me.

My laughter suddenly dies as I watch him approach, because a new feeling has taken hold; the feeling of being well and truly fucked. At first, I look him in the eye, but then my eyes drop to the black case that he's carrying, and my heart plummets to the floor.

He stops in front of me and holds out the case that I've been unable to take my eyes off.

"Open it," he orders.

I say nothing. I just stare at the case. I don't need to open it because I know exactly what is inside. I just have no idea how they found it.

"Open it!" he barks, shoving it into my hands.

There's no escaping this now. I slowly unzip it and then look at the clear bottle and syringes inside, and then I start to panic.

Dennis steps forward. "You little bastard!"

Obviously, Jane's father is going to have something to say about this.

"FERTAIN!" he shouts in my face, and his foul-smelling spit lands on my cheek. "My daughter has been going out of her mind, blaming herself for not getting pregnant, and all this time you've been injecting this shit!"

David's laugh is a little over the top. "I've got to hand it to you Noah, that takes some serious balls!" A few of the men laugh at his attempt at a joke. "That is some serious dedication to the cause."

"Why would you do this?" my father asks furiously. "Have you not brought enough shame onto the Joyson name, already?"

"You know why he did it, Dad," David replies. "If Eve can't have a baby, then Jane can't have a baby. Is that right, Noah?"

"Almost…" I reply quietly. Then I finally peel my eyes from the contents in my hands and look at them both in disgust. "That's part of it, but not all of it."

"Then enlighten us," my father commands.

"Yes, it's about Eve. I could never put her through the pain of watching me have children with someone else, but that's not all. I couldn't risk Eve getting pregnant because I know what you'd do if she did."

David swallows hard and looks down a little. He knows.

"And I cannot bring a child into this fucked up family." My father scoffs. "I cannot bring a child into this world, knowing that you have already decided what their future will be. I cannot stand by and be powerless to protect my own child from misery!"

"Right, so you're being noble?" Dennis asks sarcastically. "Torturing my daughter is noble?"

"She never should have agreed to marry me."

Everyone is quiet for a moment and I watch as they take it all in. Although, I know it won't make the slightest bit of difference. They've already calculated their next move, and there's nothing I can do to change it.

Commander Legion confirms my worst fears. "It doesn't matter. Judgement has been cast. Adam Matthews is getting a beating, and you're going to be the one to give it to him," he says as he folds his arms across his chest.

That's what he does to let you know that there's no point in arguing, but he seems to have forgotten that all I've ever done is fight them.

"And how exactly do you plan on making me do that?"

"Scott," Commander Legion orders, and his faithful grandson steps forward with his phone in his hand.

I think I dislike Scott the most. He's a snake, always has been and always will be and I hate that my sister has to spend so much time with him. I also hate the dark smile that he's giving me, because nothing good comes from that smile.

"Right now, Eve is in a club, dancing," he says, with a coldness that sends painful shivers down my spine and has me rising to a fighting stance. "She looks very sexy, by the way." He glances at the screen on his phone and it's all I can do not to rip it from his hands. "That top looks quite flimsy though… shouldn't take too much effort for them to rip it off."

I dart forward, growling, ready to rip him to shreds, but I'm immediately blocked by a wall of men.

"Stay away from her!" Adam pleads, speaking for the first time. "This is nothing to do with her!"

Scott steps around the men in front of him. "Unfortunately, for your sister, she bears the burden of being the only thing in this world that Noah actually gives a fuck about."

"You. Stay. Away. From. Her." I force out. I'm grinding my teeth so hard it feels like one might break.

"Nobody here wants to hurt Eve," David says, stepping back into the mix. "But Scott is right, Eve is the only leverage we have over you. And… if we have to… we'll use her."

Look at him, he actually looks remorseful.

"You have your teams on the club floor tonight, but we have ours too, and all we need to do is make one call, and Eve will find herself as the special guest at a party of five."

"You'd do that to her?" I spit in his face.

He shakes his head at me. "I wouldn't... and I hope that we don't have to make that call. Because I imagine what they will do to her, will make what you do to her feel like foreplay."

"I WILL END YOU!" I lunge at him, ready to beat him to a pulp again.

"Noah!" Adam calls out, stopping me in my tracks. "This is on us!"

Struggling to breathe, or even see straight, I turn around to face the boy that I think more of than I do my own brothers. Although, looking at him now, he seems more like a man than he did before.

"We. Fucked. Up. You and me... not Eve," he says with tears in his eyes. "We pay. Not her."

I walk over to Adam, put my hands on his shoulders and lean into his ear. "They are not going to let me go easy on you. You're not leaving here without serious injuries."

He needs to know what he's agreeing to.

"Better me than Eve. I won't let her be hurt because of me, and neither will you... so just do it," he says bravely, through his fear.

I pull him close. "I'll try to make it quick," I whisper. "But this is going to hurt."

"I won't hold it against you," he replies with a little laugh. "Just watch the face... I'm hoping to win Meredith back."

He flashes me his endearing smile, and in spite of this dire fucking situation that we have got ourselves into, I can't help but smile back at him. Adam... always the joker, even now.

I step back, hold my hand out and then seconds later the gloves are passed to me.

I can't believe I'm doing this, but I'm doing it, I acknowledge, as I slip them on.

Breathing hard; I try to use the dread rising in me to stop the darkness from taking hold. I can't let the darkness in. I need to keep control or there is no telling what damage I'll do. Even to Adam.

The first punch is to the gut and Adam folds in on himself, winded by the impact.

"Don't be shy Noah, my finger is getting a little twitchy," Scott sneers, shaking the phone in his hand at me.

Fuck, he is going to get it next!

I turn back to Adam who has righted himself and he nods for me to continue, and I do. I land punches swiftly, to the chest, the stomach, his whole torso. Then when Adam raises his head, I land a punch on his cheek, sending him flying to the ground. He's bleeding, moaning in pain, and he's down.

I've done enough.

I walk over to the lit barrel, looking at nobody as I pass them, but preparing myself for breaking Scott's bones, and then throw the gloves into the flames.

BANG!

I instinctively dive to the ground when I hear the gun go off! Once down, I turn towards the crowd and see five men standing around Adam, all of them have an arm stretched out in front of them, and they all have a gun in their hands.

"*H*e was only shot once," I say as I finally leave the bathroom where I've been crying on the floor for the last twenty minutes.

Noah pulls himself up from the spot on the floor by the door where he remained the entire time, trying to comfort me through the locked door. "Only one gun was loaded…" he tells me as he wipes his tears away. "It was so that I wouldn't know who did it."

I walk over to the sofa and sit down, only to jump up again and pace the room. Hearing what happened has made it all the more painful and raw. My stupid, reckless, selfish little brother couldn't help taking chances, couldn't help putting his life on the line.

Always wanting more. Didn't he realise that he was the most important thing in my life?

Didn't he know how much I needed him?

Did I not make it clear how much I loved him?

"He was so brave, Eve," Noah says as he starts to choke up again. "He loved you so much, he wouldn't let you—"

"THOSE FUCKING BASTARDS!" I scream as I grab the nearest thing within reach and throw it across the room.

The candle smashes against the wall sending glass and wax all over everything. Noah rushes to me but I move away from him.

"They take the things in your life that are good, the things that you love and just use them against you! Adam against me. Me against both of you... Gang rape! That's what they were going to do to me?" I seethe, as burning tears stream down my face again. "Of course, he would offer himself up."

I slide down the wall to the floor, wrap myself around my knees and try to breathe. Noah sits next to me and pulls me close and I curl into him and rest my head on his lap.

"I didn't want to hurt him."

"I know." I let out another shaky breath.

"Do you hate me?" he asks, and the fear is clear in his voice.

"No." I choke out. "I hate them," I add with more resolve.

"Eve... you have every right to, but you can't retaliate. Let me handle it. I'll find a way—"

"That is what you have told me since the day we met," I snap at him. "There is no way, there's only their way and there's nothing anyone can do about it!"

I get up and pace the room again, then I turn to look at Noah. "Fertain?"

He nods at me.

"How long?"

He pushes away from the wall so that he's standing. "As soon as it became available, which happened to coincide with when the pressure to get pregnant started," he replies, with an unapologetic shrug.

"And now?"

"They've cut off my supply," he says, as he looks down and clenches his jaw.

"So, they have everyone exactly where they want them now," I say bitterly. "And you'll play ball because you now know what they're willing to do and how far they'll go."

I stand staring out of the window, putting all the pieces together in my mind. The situation, the risks… and the options.

"I have some things that I need to take care of," I say, as I turn to Noah. "We need to go and fetch Adam in three days… I need to plan his funeral. I need to see John and Meredith and sort all of his stuff."

He steps forward. "Let me help you."

"No… I'm sorry but I just need to do this alone… I need some space for a few—"

"You are mad with me!"

"I'm not." I walk towards him and fall into his arms. "I just need some space to think and I need you to keep control, because I don't have it in me to help you, right now."

"I will… I promise," he tells me as he kisses my head.

I tilt my head towards him and brush a gentle kiss over his lips and even now a warmth spreads through me.

"You will call me if you need me, won't you?" he asks with concern, and I just nod at him in reply. He lowers his head and kisses me again. "I love you."

"I love you too," I tell him and then I step away from him so that he can leave.

He starts to walk away.

"Noah, before you go…" He turns to look at me. "Do you remember who was standing where?" He looks at me questioningly. "The men holding the guns," I clarify. "Do you remember who they were and where they were standing?"

"Yes… I'm not sure I'll ever forget that."

I fetch a pen and paper from the drawer and thrust them at him. "Show me."

I put the paper into the envelope that Ethan gave me without even looking at it. I can't look just yet. I need to get my head straight first. I do however, spot the business card that is nestled at the bottom and I reach in and pull it out — it's Ethan's business card. I go to my bag and pull out the envelope that Henry left for me, trying to avoid catching a glimpse of my mother, and then pull out his card too.

I sit on the sofa, place them both on the coffee table in front of me, and just stare at the names of my father and half-brother. I continue to stare at them for another five minutes before reaching for my phone.

I dial the number. A few rings later and he answers.

"It's Eve…" I say shakily.

"Eve! Are you OK?" he asks with genuine concern.

"Do you still want to help me?"

"Of course! I meant every word I said, I'll always—"

"I need you to do something for me, and it needs to be done by the time I come to bring Adam back," I instruct him, keeping my voice calm, even though my insides are twisting.

He listens to my request without saying a word and repeats it back to me to make sure that nothing has been missed.

"Are you sure that you want to do this?" he asks me.

"Can you do it?"

"Yes."

"Then I'll see you in three days… thank you." I end the call and scoop up the cards and put them back into my bag with all the other paperwork.

$\mathcal{I}$ spend the rest of the afternoon with John and Meredith lying to their faces. Making them believe that Adam had been lying to us all and had continued running goods through the gates.

I excuse myself, and go to the bathroom and quietly plead out loud for Adam to forgive me. He's dead, and I'm lying to the people that love him most and putting the blame for his death squarely on his own shoulders. Which in some way it was… still, they're going to be angry with him, they're going to feel betrayed and I can't help feeling like I'm destroying their memories of him.

Yet, I know he'd understand, because he loved them, and he would do the same thing in my position. He would lie to them in order to keep them safe. The blame and the hate needs to be directed at the other side of the wall. They cannot know that those from within are responsible because it would put them in danger. They are two of the people Adam loved the most, and my brave little brother would want to keep them safe, no matter the cost.

I let myself into John's flat with the key he gave me yesterday and I go to the room that was once Adam's. I open the door and chuckle at the mess. "You really were a shit housemate, weren't you?" I say out loud.

His stuff is all over the place. I pick up a t-shirt and hold it to my nose, it still smells like him and that has me breathing hard again and fighting back the tears.

You've got two days to sort this, I remind myself, so I get it together and start to pull open the roll of black bin liners. Anything of sentiment will be saved and shared amongst his friends, the clothes are going to the orphanage, and I need to find something for him to wear for the burial.

I focus on the task, ignoring the pain, and four hours later, I have everything bagged up. I have no car so I carry what I can to St Martins and find my way to Sister Theresa's office. Her door is open, and she jumps up when she sees me and pulls me into her warm embrace. She holds me close and I take deep breaths, trying to keep the tears at bay. I don't have much time and I need to focus, but I'm unable to stop the tears when I hear Rose speak behind me.

Sister Theresa releases me, I turn to be embraced by Rose and we cry together.

"What's all this?" she asks, releasing me and looking at the bags by my feet.

"Adam's things… there's more at the flat."

"You don't need to do this now, I can help."

"I do, Rose…" I really do. "Can we talk about the funeral?"

An hour later, I leave the office feeling drained and over-whelmed. "Rose, I'm going to get everyone together tonight. I thought we could light the old pit by the park and just… I don't know, really… talk… remember." I shrug a little. "Can you come?"

"I wouldn't miss it."

I go back to my flat and sit staring at my reflection in the mirror of the vanity unit in my bedroom. I brush my hair then select a section of it from underneath the thick dark waves, I tie a hairband near the top, plait it, tie it off at the bottom and then cut it off at the root. I then place it in the envelope that contains my note, seal it, and then write, **For Adam x** on the envelope.

I sit and stare at the other two envelopes and the pad of paper. Eventually, I start to write. After half an hour, I examine the two letters in my hand, and then place them in separate envelopes. I then put all three under my mattress, along with the envelope from Ethan, and get ready to go out.

When I arrive at the pit, John and Luke have just managed to set it aflame. There's a cooler containing beer and I add the ones I've brought with me, along with a bag of food. Everyone is here, all of my sisters, all of Adam's best friends and Meredith. I don't need to tell them why I gathered them here because they know. This is going to be Adam's official goodbye from those that knew and loved him best. The church will be full of mourners in four days' time and Father Thurleigh will talk about God's plan, but tonight is about Adam and about giving him the send-off that he would want.

Vic and Rose sit on either side of me and I rest my head on Rose's shoulder. It's getting dark, but the fire is providing light and heat and the beers are now flowing.

Luke stands up. "My first real memory of Adam, was from when we were about six… I think it was six?" he asks, looking at Paul for confirmation.

"How do I know? It's your fucking memory!" Paul replies, and we all laugh along with him.

"All right, smart arse!" Luke quips back. "Let's go with six," he says as he continues his story. "Adam was having a standoff with Sister Theresa in the dining room, over a plate full of Brussels sprouts. He was adamant that he wasn't bloody eating it, and she was adamant that he was. Naturally, she wasn't going to budge, so Adam eventually ate all of them, and then just like that..." he starts to laugh, "he puked it all back up, splattering this green shit all over her perfect white robe!" We all burst out laughing. "I don't know how, but I swear he did it on purpose!"

"Oh, he did, and she knew it too," I confirm before bursting out laughing.

He was forced to clean all of the Sisters' robes as punishment.

"I don't know about my first memory... but this is something I'll never forget," Hannah starts to say, "and I'm really sorry Eve, but I've never told you this," she adds, cringing a little.

"I'm not sure I want to hear this," I grimace, in a sing-song voice.

"Well, he must have been twelve... and you know what a little bugger he was when he was twelve?"

"Yes!" we all laugh in unison.

"Well, I went to my room alone one evening, while you were all in the mess room, I think I was trying to work on a project, or something and there was a knock at the door."

"Oh, no...." I groan, already sensing where this story is going.

Hannah flushes a little and then continues, "So, I open the door and there's Adam, with that bloody charming grin all over his face, asking if he can come in. I was confused, but let him, thinking he was after borrowing something of yours," she says, pointing at me. "Anyway, I carried on doing what I

was doing, but then I felt him next to me, and I kid you not…
I turned around to look at him and he just planted a kiss right
on my lips!"

"Good lad!" Luke calls out, and the boys all start
laughing.

"I was stunned. I could barely speak and then he did it
again!" she says, as she bursts out laughing. "I asked him
what he was doing, and he just said, 'I wanted my first kiss to
be with the most beautiful girl I know.'" She puts her hand on
her heart and gushes a little. "Then he smiled at me and
walked away, and nothing was ever said about it again."

She sits down and takes a big drink of her beer. "Sorry,
Eve…" she says, and then bursts out laughing and I laugh
right along with her.

Adam was always so confident, always so cocky and
always so charming. God, he could have done anything.

Everyone took their turn, sharing their favourite, most
prominent or most embarrassing story about Adam, and we
laugh and cry at them all. Then all eyes fall on John.

"I remember when I came out to him," John says thought-
fully. "I was more scared to tell him than anyone else."

"Yeah, yeah, we always knew he was your favourite,"
Luke interrupts with a smile.

"Well, he was just so pretty," John replies in his best,
mock-camp voice, and I almost spit my beer out. "Anyway…
I didn't know what he'd say, so I got a pizza and some beers
in and halfway through the pizza, I just said, 'Adam. I'm
gay,' and he almost choked! When he regained himself, he
said, 'Fuck me, John!' and I asked if he was offering, and
then he just burst out laughing," John says, as his tears start to
fall. "He reached over to me and put his hand on my shoulder
and told me, 'You're the best human being I know… next to
Eve, but don't tell her that. I'm sure you and your massive

cock will make some man very happy one day,' and then he went straight back to eating his pizza."

We all laugh some more, with Luke and the other boys going on to debate the size of John's penis. Then all eyes turn to me, and I let out a shaky breath.

"I have no idea…" I say, as I shrug at them all. "My first memory is easy, because I remember the day that they took me to see him like it was yesterday… but the best? There are just so many…" I put my hands over my face as the tears fall, full force and my heart rips open again. "I know how lucky I was to have him… I just hope he knew how much I loved him."

"He did," they all confirm, and then one by one we all pull in for a group hug.

Later, John watches me as we pack everything away and put out the fire, and once most of the others have left, he pulls me aside. "This felt like goodbye."

"It was goodbye… I think we did him proud," I reply, smiling.

"No… this felt like goodbye to you," he says, looking at me intently.

43

$\mathcal{O}$ ne more day. That's all I have to get things sorted before we go to bring Adam back. John dropped the rest of the bags that I left at his over this morning for me to take to the church, but there's still things to do.

I head to my wardrobe and pull out my large duffel bag and start to go through my things, but then I hear the floorboards creak and I jump out of my skin, as I turn to see Ruth standing in the doorway watching me with a cautious smile on her face.

"Hello, Eve," she says with politeness. "Welcome home."

"What do you want?" I ask, with aggression as I instantly go on the defensive.

"I just wanted to see how you were. Noah said you asked for space—"

"Then give it to me!"

She clears her throat. "He's more or less locked himself at the fight club… he can't trust himself not to come to you and he doesn't want to hurt anyone."

"Again, Ruth… why are you here when you know I don't want to see people?"

"Eve… I am part of your life and this is your home, and you can't blame us forever. Adam made his own decisions," she says calmly.

Who is this woman?

How can she lie to my face like this?

It takes all of my strength not to walk into the kitchen, grab a knife and plunge it into her chest, although if I did, I'm not sure that I'd find a beating heart in there. I turn away and take a few deep breaths, before turning to face her.

"I've lost my brother, Ruth… I just need some time."

She nods a little and starts to turn away, but then she notices the open bag on my bed. "What are you doing?"

Shit.

"I've been clearing Adam's things out… I'm taking them to the orphanage, and it inspired me to pass on some of the things that I don't need," I say, holding her gaze convincingly.

She nods, appeased by my answer and walks out of the door.

Two hours later and I'm back in Sister Theresa's office with two more bin liners and my duffel bag.

"This is the last of Adam's things," I say, gesturing to the black bags. Then I take my own bag off my shoulder and lower it to the ground.

"And what's that?" she asks, looking first at my bag before fixing me with her all-knowing gaze.

"I need to ask a favour," I say, before turning to close her door.

I can't stop fidgeting as I sit in my flat. I've done everything that I can do, that I need to do before I go to collect Adam with Rose tomorrow, but my gut is churning at the idea of going back through those gates. I don't know if I can do this.

My mind goes to Noah, locked in the old warehouse, keeping away and keeping control, just like I asked him to. God, I miss him, and I want him. I want him here with me, so I pick up my phone and call him.

"Are you OK?" he asks, as he answers immediately.

"Can you come home?"

"I'll be right there."

Fifteen minutes later, he walks through the door and into the living room, but he stands back from me a little, still giving me the space that I asked for. I'm done with space. Contact is what I want now.

I stand up and start to slowly undress, until I'm completely naked. He hasn't moved from the spot, but I've seen him swallow hard and bite his bottom lip. Holding his gaze, I walk towards him, take his hand and lead him to our bedroom, without saying a word. I stand him by the bed, and he moves his hands in order to start undressing himself, but I shake my head, move his hands back to his sides, and take over the task.

I lift off his shirt and lay kisses on his bare chest as my hands undo his belt and buttons. Then I lower myself down, as I guide his trousers down to the floor, giving his erect penis a gentle kiss as I pass it on my way down.

Once his clothes are off, I stand back up, place my hand on his chest and lower him onto the bed until he's lying down. Then I straddle him, keeping my body above his, not touching him. I lean in and place a gentle kiss on his lips, but he immediately wraps his hand around the back of my neck, grabs hold of a handful of hair and pulls me in to deepen it. He runs a hand down my side, sending pulses through me, and when his hand gets to my bottom, he grabs a cheek firmly, pulls me into him and I immediately start grinding against him.

We both gasp and he bites at my lip and sucks my tongue as I continue to rub against him. It feels so good and it's been so long, I could easily orgasm like this. I'm getting so wet and when he feels it spreading over him, he rolls us over so that I'm on my back.

"You are everything to me… promise you'll be mine forever?" he pleads, as he looks deeply into my eyes.

"I will love you forever." That I can promise.

He smiles and then he starts to trail kisses along my collar bone, making his way down to my breasts. I know he's not going to make me wait, it's been too long for us both and he knows how desperately I want him because he wants me just as badly.

He massages one breast, while he sucks at the nipple of the other, and his other hand trails down my side. I let out a deep groan because this man knows exactly how to pleasure me. He brushes his thumb over my centre and pushes his fingers inside and I arch my back and grind against them.

"Noah!" I gasp as I get close and then he lowers himself down and uses his mouth and tongue to finish the job, and he sucks at me greedily as I explode around him.

Seconds later, and he is finally inside me. He holds my legs down and spreads them further apart, watching as he pushes deeply inside. He pulls out and does it again, it's an agonisingly slow movement, and he's just watching as he enters me. I groan in complaint and he looks up at me darkly, his jaw clenching. A slow smile starts to rise from his lips; I know what's coming and I bite my bottom lip in anticipation.

"Agh!" I cry out as he suddenly goes from zero to one hundred, thrusting into me quick and hard as he continues to slowly push my thighs deeper into the mattress, and I reach out to grab hold of anything I can. Noah can go like this for a long time, and usually I'm the one who climaxes first, but not now, he's too desperate. He releases my legs, and as he presses his body against mine, our mouths collide and seconds later he cries out, "Eve!" as I feel him cum.

His moans of pleasure continue as I feel his penis continue to pulse, then eventually, he rests on top of me, his heart beating against mine. I wrap my arms around him and hold him in place, never wanting to let him go, and we both lay soundless, except for our laboured breathing.

"You may have been raised by nuns, but I swear you were made by angels," he tells me as he nuzzles into my neck.

I let out a little laugh. "What about you?"

He moves so that his head is on the pillow and his lips are resting against my shoulder. "I was raised by the Devil…" he says sadly.

"And her husband," I add, and we both smile in agreement.

We stay like this for a while, with our fingers entwined, him occasionally playing with my hair, as it slowly dawns on me that for the first time since he came to me on that Friday night; I feel at ease.

"What was it like over there?" he asks in a lazy tone.

"Posh. I was in one of Henry Southwold's hotels."

"That old man has always had a thing for you," he says as he nibbles my shoulder. "Did he try it on?" he adds with a grin.

"No!" I elbow him in his side.

"And Ethan…?" he asks with more caution.

My heart starts to beat harder and my stomach starts to churn.

"Eve?"

I sit up and look at him, not quite knowing how to answer,

but then I get out of bed and head to the drawer where I placed the photograph. I pull it out of the envelope and then walk back to the bed.

Handing him the photo, I tell him, "I wasn't made by angels, Noah… this is my mother and Henry Southwold is my father."

He stares at Louisa for a while, looking between her face and mine, taking in all of the similarities. "Fucking hell!" he eventually says.

Then he puts the photo down on the side and rests his hand on my cheek. "How are you with this?" he asks, the passion and concern clear on his face.

"I don't think I've actually started to process it yet," I tell him honestly, "and I haven't got the ability to at the moment."

"I'm going to help you through this," he tells me, whilst continuing to caress my cheek. "You'll never be alone while you have me."

"Forever?"

"Forever," he agrees, then he leans in and we start to kiss again.

I push him back down and, after teasing him for a few minutes, I take his penis in my hands, lick my lips and then take him all the way into my mouth. Once we became sexual, all those years ago, Noah told me what it was that he wanted to do with my mouth while he was watching me eat pizza, the day we first met. In fact, he showed me.

"Those fucking lips!" he'd gasped as he held my head and guided me.

He didn't need to do that anymore, I'd long since perfected it, as Noah is confirming with moans of appreciation. Moments later, I swallow him down and then slowly lick my way back to his tip as if he is the most delicious thing I've ever tasted.

He flips me over and repays me in kind, and then I climb on top and make love to him like it's the last time.

Noah kisses me goodbye as he leaves for work in the morning and I quickly get ready. I retrieve the envelopes from under the mattress and put them into my bag, before going to St Martins.

Rose is standing by the ambulance waiting for me, with Sister Theresa by her side. She takes a deep breath as she gets into the driver's seat and then I stand and face Sister Theresa. She gives me a small nod and then reaches out for me.

"You can do this," she whispers into my ear and I give her a gentle kiss on the cheek in return.

We drive through the groaning gates and follow their police escort, then after ten minutes that car speeds away with sirens blaring, and a black limousine pulls in front of us, forcing Rose to slow down.

"What are they doing?" Rose asks in confusion.

"Rose… pull over," I tell her with my voice shaking.

She turns to me, questions all over her face, and I look at her more firmly, as I say, "Rose… you need to pull over."

44

THE DAY BEFORE THE FUNERAL

NOAH

*C*limbing the walls. I have literally been climbing these four walls since Eve sent me away. Why did she have to send me away? She doesn't need to do this alone. I can help her. I know she's staying with Rose until the funeral and the Sisters will be with her, but I want to help her. I'm just petrified that she looks at me and sees me hurting Adam. How can she not be angry at me for that? Even if it was under duress.

The thought of what she is going to do next has my stomach churning and I constantly feel like I'm on the verge of throwing up. She is a fighter. She couldn't be with me and not have a warrior in her, even if she's had to suppress it for all of these years. There's no way she'll just let this go and I'm petrified of what she'll do and who I'll have to hurt to keep her safe.

I will keep her safe.

No matter what.

No matter who I need to take down in the process.

I wish I could just go up to the top of the warehouse and get some fresh air, but I've given my keys to Jimmy, with strict instructions to not let me have them back, which he won't even if I were to threaten him. Jimmy is one of the few people I can stand to be around when I feel like this, and he knows I'll never lay a finger on him.

He also knows that it's not just Eve that I want to run to. He's well aware after I trashed the locker room yesterday that I want to rip Scott limb from limb. I cannot get the look in his eyes out of my mind. The way he looked at Eve's photo on his phone, as if he'd happily be the one to hurt her.

Fucking hell, I need some air.

I open the office door and go to the locker rooms, where Jimmy is still repairing some of the sinks. "Jimmy, please let me—"

"No," he says firmly, as he turns to face me head on. "Go back to your office and sit it out."

I glare at him, but he just raises his eyebrows and cocks his half smile.

"Remember who you're doing this for."

Why the fuck does he always have to be right?

Defeated; I walk back to my office, close the door and lean against it, drawing in as much air as I can. I am doing this for Eve. For once in my life, I am going to be utterly unselfish. Unfortunately, it's a hard habit to break, hence the locked doors.

The only comfort I have is the memory of her touch from two nights ago, when she called me over. I didn't know what to expect, but I walked in, she started to undress, and I just froze to the spot.

She wanted me.

I couldn't believe she wanted me, and I didn't waste the opportunity. I felt alive for the first time since seeing Adam thrown to the ground. My angel wanted me, and I basked in her light and her warmth, and I made sure that she remembered how good we are together.

Why we should always be together.

I manage to busy myself with the books, but then a gentle knock at the door has my heart jumping up to my throat, thinking that Eve has come to me. However, it quickly, and painfully sinks back down to my stomach when Jane lets herself in. I don't even know when I last saw her, but it's good that she's here, because we do need to talk.

Jane steps in, looking as uncomfortable as I feel and I see that's she's holding a black suit in her hands, and it's all I can do to hold back the tears. Adam's funeral is tomorrow.

"So…" she says awkwardly. "It's the funeral tomorrow, and as I'm not sure if you'll ever be returning to our home, I brought this here."

I give her a slight nod. "Thanks."

"You realise that you have to go there with me… your wife?"

I stand up and walk around the desk, and lean against it, facing her, but then suddenly feeling defensive; I fold my arms around my chest. Her eyes are red and bloodshot because she's been crying, and I already know it's because of me, it always is.

"Do you know?"

She glares at me and I have my answer.

"About the Fertain injections that you've been giving yourself?"

I start to clear my throat, but Jane just shakes her head at me.

"You don't need to explain, Noah, because I get it. You never wanted me, you never wanted this. I just wish you didn't feel the need to put me through that…" she pauses as she chokes back her sobs.

"I'm sorry."

"You always are!" she snaps. "You are always sorry and yet you still do these shitty things." She takes a step towards me. "It's probably a good thing to be fair, because you're not fit to be a father."

Fuck me, that hurts! She has the right to be angry, but that hurts. No matter what I've done and who I've hurt… of all of the things that I hate about myself, being a father is the one thing I planned to get right. I would always do right by my own child.

As if seeing what I'm thinking, Jane barks out a laugh. "You don't believe that do you?" she scoffs. "You think you'd make a good Dad?"

"I—"

"You hurt the things you love, Noah! You'd do anything for Eve, I know that, but you still hurt her."

I turn away from her as the shame starts to take hold. How can I argue with that?

I take in a few deep breaths, trying to push the image of Eve's strappy top being ripped in half, by my hands and try to take the conversation back in the direction that I had planned.

"Jane… we don't work," I tell her calmly, but firmly, "and we never will. You will always be miserable while you remain my wife." She lets out a huff and a laugh, and nods bitterly in agreement. "Divorce me."

"What?"

"Divorce me," I repeat.

She throws her hands in the air. "How would we do that? Even if it was possible here our parents would block us all the way."

"I have contacts. I can make it happen and nobody needs to know about it until the paperwork is finalised."

She shakes her head doubtfully.

"I'll do right by you, Jane. You'll be a wealthy woman, free to move on."

Her eyes widen. "They will retaliate."

"Your parents aren't about to hurt you."

"Eve," she says, with such assurance, and that single word sends chills through my entire body; because she's right.

I lean forward and speak quietly in an attempt to push the venom that is rising deep down. "I will protect her with my life and so will the nuns."

She shakes her head again. "It's a big risk."

"That's the price of freedom."

She turns away from me. She's thinking, at least she's thinking about it instead of just walking away. She turns back to me and shrugs her shoulders a little.

"I'll think about it… you should come to the house in the morning so that we can drive to the church together. Got to keep up appearances," she adds with a bitter smile.

We can do this. She doesn't believe it yet, but we can.

Nothing I did before our forced marriage was enough to scare her away, but since then I've more than made up for it. She knows we cannot continue the way we are. I just need for her to step up and fight for her life.

I need her to fight with me.

I move towards her, place a hand on her shoulder and gently kiss on top of her head. "I meant what I said all those years ago… you deserve better."

She nods again and gives me a small smile before slowly walking away.

∼

I sit in the car with Jane trying to swallow down my nerves and my anger. I'm going to have to sit in the church on the same row as my family; among the murderers of the man that we're about to bury and I can't stand it. They know it and that's why they've stayed away from me since they killed Adam – except for my mother, who I've seen twice.

The first time was when she arrived back from The Other Side, to tell me that Eve was staying there. In my fear, I almost missed the angry, red handprint on her face, but when I did finally see it, I stopped in my tracks and laughed in her face, resulting in me receiving a slap of my own.

The second time was after I spoke to Eve when she came home, and my mother came to the fight club to try to find out what Eve knew.

I threw a chair at the wall and she made a quick exit.

None of my family, or any other of the families have tried to talk to me since. Unfortunately, my father made up for that this morning when he lectured me on how I was expected to behave today.

I have no idea how they expect me to just sit and watch Eve in pain, and not be able to go to her. Everybody knows about our relationship, so what the fuck does it matter if I go to her when she needs me? However, my father has been very clear on what my role is today; I'm simply there as a member of the Founding Families paying my respects. As much as it is going to kill me, I need to do as he asks, because today is about Adam, not my personal battles.

I'll just go to Eve, later. I'll hold her and do whatever she needs me to do to take the pain away. Even if it means promising to kill every last one of them.

Everyone takes their seats and I crane my head to try to catch a glimpse of Eve at the front. I can make out Rose and some of her friends, but my view is being blocked, and I can't see Eve. Then the music starts and the whole of the congregation stands, and we watch in silence, bowing our heads in respect, as Adam's closest friends walk in, carrying the coffin on each of their shoulders. They look sad, but they look proud. Proud to have known him and proud to have been loved by him; just as they should be.

The coffin is placed at the back of the church and as Father Thurleigh takes to the stage, everyone else sits down, and I once again try and fail to spot Eve.

The service is the same as all the services that take place in St Martins; religious and formal, but then Father Thurleigh softens a little, and says, "And now we have a few words that Eve would like to share with you."

My heart leaps to my throat, but then my brow furrows as confusion replaces hope, when I see Rose take to the stage with a piece of paper in hand… and something else.

Hair?

She walks to the coffin, it's opened for her at the head, and she gently places the hair into the coffin, before turning to take Father Thurleigh's place at the stand. She places the paper in front of her and clears her throat a few times.

"Eve couldn't be here with us today…"

The whole congregation starts to mumble a question at the same time, and my heart starts to beat rapidly. I need to get to Eve. If she's hurting so much that she can't come to Adam's funeral, then I need to find her. Sensing what I'm thinking, my father grabs hold of my arm and when I turn to look at him, he slowly shakes his head, whilst continuing to stare straight ahead.

Rose continues, "Eve has asked me to read a poem that she has written, on her behalf…"

She pauses. She's choking up and I can see that her tears are starting to spill over. She clears her throat again, quickly glancing at her friends, before taking a deep breath in.

> When we're brought through those gates,
> Abandoned and alone.
> Our families we create,
> In this place we call home.
>
> There are few choices,
> That we can make.
> So, we leave it to God,
> And to the hands of fate.
>
> Yet, I was given a gift,
> Shining and bright.
> Being a sister to my brother.
> Both my light and my plight.
>
> He's been called away,
> From this world he is gone.
> Yet he's safe in our hearts,
> And there he'll always stay.

Rose pauses, she's clearly uncomfortable, but she pushes on.

> The guilty are known,

My father stiffens.

Yet their sins go unshown.
But one day,
Down the line,
They'll pay for their crime.

The quiet murmuring begins again, and I turn to see that people are starting to look over at where I, and the other Founding Families are sitting.

From this world,
Adam has gone away...

Rose pauses, her tears fall and it's clear to see that she's struggling to contain the sobs that are desperate to break free. Rose is always calm, always composed, which is why Eve would have chosen her to speak for her, but right now, Rose's heart is breaking.

Adam has gone away...

She repeats, but once again she can't continue. Sarah steps up and gives her a hug, before taking the piece of paper from her hands. She looks down at it, reading the words to herself, and then her eyebrows spring up in alarm and she looks at Rose first, and then to the others in the front row. The row that is filled with Eve's sisters.

"What's going on?" Jane asks shakily, as she leans into me.

I can't even manage to shake my head, because I have no clue either, but something isn't right. This isn't right. Why are both Rose and Sarah freaking out?

Starting to panic, I glance around the rest of the congregation, as if they may have the answers, but they clearly don't. Everyone is looking at each other, some asking silently and some voicing the question.

"What's going on? Where's Eve?"

My panic turns to pure fear and I can barely breathe as Sister Theresa slowly walks to the stage. She's taking charge, she's intervening, because something is going on here. Something is fucking going on.

She takes the paper from Sarah, then gently urges her and Rose to go back to their seats. She clears her throat and stands before us all, with her resolute, and unwavering calm and begins to read.

From this world,
Adam has gone away.
And so, I bid you farewell,
For now, I too,
Must be on my way.

I jump up, pushing my father and anyone else who tries to grab me aside. The audible gasp from the entire congregation is almost deafening, and I don't miss the cries coming from Eve's sisters. I run straight to my car and speed to the flat, taking the stairs three at a time, before barging through the door.

"Eve?" I call desperately, as I run from room to room.

She's not here. Eve is not here.

I run back to the bedroom and start to pull out her drawers and go through the wardrobe. Most of her clothes are here but things are missing, small things, things that mean something to her. The flat is still full of things, and yet right now, it feels completely empty.

I feel completely empty.

Ten minutes later David comes crashing into the flat and runs straight to the bathroom. On finding it empty he runs into the bedroom where I'm sitting on the bed, holding Eve's pillow, staring at the wall, with tears streaming down my face.

So, this is how it feels to be utterly hopeless.

This is how it feels when part of your soul is gone.

"What did you tell her?" David screams in my expressionless face.

"She already knew."

"Noah… you don't understand. She once told me that if we killed Adam, then she would kill herself!"

"She hasn't killed herself," I say, completely void of any emotion.

I know she's not done that. She wouldn't take anything with her if she'd done that.

I sit staring at the wall, for a few more minutes, as David stands in front of me, practically tearing clumps of his hair out. Then I turn to him, and say, "She's just holding up her end of the deal."

I'm not sure how long I've been sitting here, holding her pillow and breathing in her scent. She's always worn the same perfume, soft, musky, with a slight floral hint — nothing too sweet, but completely perfect for her.

I'm not sure when David left, but nobody else followed him and it's starting to get dark. Darkness is fitting because that's all there will be of me now. They wanted to push me, and they wanted to see what it would take to break me, and now they've done it. The fucking fools! Haven't they learned that the darkness doesn't break me? It just makes me break anything and anyone around me.

A sudden a burst of light fills the room, startling me, and as my eyes adjust, I turn to see Rose standing in the doorway. She looks at me for a moment, quietly assessing me. Then she pulls an envelope out of the bag that she's carrying and walks over to me.

Holding it out, she says, "I don't know what's in there, but knowing Eve, and knowing you, it is probably more than you deserve."

45

THE DAY ADAM IS COLLECTED

Eve

"*R*ose… you need to pull over..."

I get out of the car and go to the back of the ambulance and take out the duffel bag that Sister Theresa put in there for me. Henry steps out of the limousine and opens the boot and takes the bag from me and places it in, then he hands me an envelope and I get back into the ambulance with Rose.

She is gripping onto the steering wheel so tightly that her knuckles are white, and she is visibly shaking. "What are you doing?"

"What I have to," I tell her as I open the envelope.

I examine the contents; everything I asked for, everything I need is there. I open up my bag and take out the three envelopes. I pass the first marked, **For Adam x** to Rose and tell her, "Keep this with him… I want a piece of me always with him."

Then I take my St Martins ID card and place it in one of the other envelopes and pass that to her too. She looks at it questioningly but says nothing. I take half of the contents of the envelope that Henry gave me and put it in my bag, and the rest I put into my third and final envelope, then I hand that to her too.

She looks at the name on it, and I tell her, "You'll need to do that secretly."

She nods her head in understanding as her tears fall, then she reaches forward and holds me in her warm embrace, and neither of us can contain our sobs. Henry knocks on the window, and I turn to him as he signals to his watch. I give him a nod, and then I turn back to Rose and take her in.

"You are the best person in the world, Rose Milligan, and I love you so very much," I tell her as my heart breaks again.

She bursts into tears and takes my hand in hers. "I love you too, Eve Matthews... now go and live your life."

I quickly get into the limousine next to Henry and we speed off away from the ambulance. I am crying my eyes out as Henry takes my bag and places a large and heavy wallet into it. He has things he needs to do, things I need to do, but right now all I want to do is turn back to Rose and run home.

He gestures to the to the wallet. "This is more than enough to keep you going until you get sorted."

I take a deep breath and try to focus on the task. I need to do this. I am doing this.

I look at the wallet, and tell him, "You didn't need to."

"Yes, I did. You are my daughter, and I am finally taking responsibility for you," he tells me, as he smiles sadly. "I know you're hurting, but you need to hold it together. I will get you through the first border into Castlepoint, from there you'll take the train to The New Order," he tells me urgently. "Eve... you need to listen. The train will stop at each state border and your ID will be checked each time. It's fool proof, but they often spot runaways by how they act and if they suspect anything, they will pull you off that train."

I nod my head at him.

"It's a six-hour train journey," he continues. "You cannot cry. At all, Eve. You need to drink. You need to eat, you need to get up and go to the toilet, but you keep this bag with you," he says as he taps my bag. "You need to play on your phone..." He puts one in my bag. "You pretend to talk to people, you pretend to send messages, you take selfies, you blend in."

"I understand."

"When you get to The New Order there will be a final border check and once through, you'll see a welcome centre. You can fall apart when you get in there if you need to, but not until you get through the doors… OK?"

I nod at him.

"We've got twenty minutes until we reach the first border… you have some time to calm down," he adds more gently, as he pats my leg.

Calm down. I need to calm down. I need to do what I've done for the past few days and just fake my way through life. Just for another six hours.

I can do this.

I think about my breathing and try my best to focus on the back of the seat in front of me, as opposed to the memory of Rose, crying in my arms. Then suddenly, I feel a hand on mine and I turn to see Henry smiling at me encouragingly.

"You're doing the right thing."

He retrieves his hand, and we sit silently for a few minutes, until I can no longer ignore the question that has been plaguing me since I saw her face. "What was she like?" I croak out.

He turns to look at me and smiles a sad smile. "Louisa was the love of my life." He looks down a little and swallows hard before facing me again. "I'm afraid you'll think badly of me... or worse perhaps, than you already do. You see, Eve, your father is a walking cliché." He gives me another sad smile. "Louisa was my secretary and Gwen was pregnant with Ethan when I started sleeping with her... but in truth... I loved her the moment I laid eyes on her."

I can't help but smile a little at him.

"Louisa was kind, strong, compassionate, but fearsome too when she needed to be... just like you. I could see that in you the first time I met you."

Tears are glistening in his eyes and I have to look away before mine fall too.

"Why did you get pregnant... twice?" I ask, without even looking at him.

He lets out a deep sigh. "You were an accident... we were careful, for years, and then there was one night of thoughtless, drunken passion," he says with an apology. "Then a few weeks later she was sick one morning at work, someone reported her, and she was tested that day."

He rubs his face a little, before continuing. "What you said was right... it broke her heart when they pulled you out of her arms. I wasn't allowed in the room, but I heard her," he says, as his tears fall, "and then they wheeled you past me in a cot and you were screaming too, and I have never felt so small... or so helpless in my entire life."

He pauses to compose himself a little, before continuing, "And I have never felt more ashamed of myself... because I did nothing to stop them."

I take a deep breath in as I push all thoughts of baby Holly, and how it felt to hold her in my arms away, and ask, "And Adam?"

"That's a bit more complicated…" he replies, shaking his head. "Louisa didn't speak to me for a long time, and when she did, I could see that she was different. Some of her spark was gone… but eventually, she started to come back to me, and I thought she was herself again," he says with a sad smile. "We were careful — always, and then one day she told me that she'd started taking the contraceptive injections which had become popular then… and I believed her… until she fell pregnant."

He rubs this hands down his face again, before shaking his head and letting out an uncomfortable laugh. "She didn't tell me, and she tried to leave Havensmere to get to The New Order, but she was standing in a queue, on a hot day and she fainted. They tested her, and since they believed that she was trying to abscond, they put her in the clinic for the entirety of the pregnancy."

I let out a deep breath as a tear falls down my cheek… that poor woman. What was she thinking?

"She only ever agreed to see me once and I asked her why she lied…" he pauses again and looks right at me. "She was trying to replace you."

I burst into tears at his words, as the realisation that my mother had loved me, had wanted me and had been broken by the loss of me, hits me full force. For the first time in my life, I understand my mother, and I can relate to her too, because the person I loved most in this world has been ripped away from me.

"I kept going through those gates, trying to get a glimpse, and then one day, I was told about an absolutely amazing new singer at The Dome." He smiles at me. "Just turned eighteen and so beautiful. Then I was told your name and I wondered, 'could it be my Eve?' and I kept going back, and then one day

God showed me mercy… because I got to see both of my lost children."

"We're almost there, sir," the driver interrupts and Henry quickly looks out of his window.

He turns to me and smiles a hopeful smile. "Now wipe those tears away, we're coming up to the first border."

Henry winds his window down and hands over both our passports to the guard.

"Good morning Mr Southwold, where are you travelling to today?"

"I'm going to Castlepoint on business and my assistant is going to visit relatives in Falcon View."

Falcon View; two states before The New Order.

The guard opens up my passport and looks at the details in front of him, and then back to my face, and it's all I can do not to throw up. My heart is beating uncontrollably, and I feel like my face must be bright red, but I feel Henry's smile on me, and I manage to force out one of my own, looking the guard in the eyes the entire time.

"Enjoy your visit Miss Adams," he says, giving me a slight nod and handing the passports back to us.

We pass through the border, pull into the train station, and then Henry opens my door for me and takes my hand in his.

"Thank you for letting me do this for you," he tells me, as his tears once again fall.

I nod at him, because I don't know the right words for this situation, and turn to walk away.

"What happened to her?" I ask, looking back at him.

He puts his hands out in apology.

"I honestly don't know. She wrote to me a month after Adam was born, telling me that she needed to be away from me," he tells me, and I can see it still pains him. "I did as she asked… I stayed away and I never even tried to find her, but I hope she found some happiness."

It was my first time on a train, and it made me feel a little sick, but I did everything that Henry told me to. I smiled, applied lipstick, everything I needed to do to convince people that I was just like them, that I belonged there. I held my breath through each border check, dying on the inside, whilst appearing normal on the outside, and I passed through each one without so much as a raised eyebrow.

I got into The New Order in the early evening and walked straight to the Welcome Centre. A smiling lady called Rebecca, asked me how she could be of service, and then her face melted into concern as she saw mine start to quiver. She immediately ushered me into a back room where I proceeded to break down in front of her.

I was expecting them to call a guard and send me back, but they couldn't have been more welcoming. This is what they did. They broke down their own wall and took in those that had escaped theirs. After a while, we ascertained that I had enough money to stay in a hotel and so they booked it all for me.

I felt bewildered, but I didn't feel lost. I was on a new track, but it was the right track. As hard as it felt, and as much as it hurt, I knew it was the right thing to do. It was also time to do what I hadn't dare to do until that point. It was time to know the truth.

I sat in that hotel and for the first time I dared to open the envelope that Ethan had given me. It was full of charts and things I didn't understand, but then I saw what I needed. The diagram of a body on the ground and the projected path that the bullet had taken. I pulled out Noah's drawing and took a deep breath in as I looked at the names he'd written; Rory Joyson, Scott Legion, Pete Green, Phillip Learner and Rupert Manners. Each name was written by a cross that had been marked against the circle, which had been drawn around a line — a line that represented Adam.

I placed the two pieces in front of me, one above the other, followed the line that the diagram took and then saw the name it landed on, repeating the process a few times, just to be certain.

"You…" I breathed out as my heart started to rage again. "Of course, it was you."

The next day, I was visited by an Official who told me that they were there to help me start my new life. We talked about finances, where I might like to live, what job I could do, all of it. I stayed in the hotel for a week, and my official 'welcome rep' came by every day and showed me around The New Order — my new home.

Henry had given me enough money to last well over a year without needing to work, and I used the financial freedom to rent a one bedroom flat. I didn't want to share, because I didn't want anyone asking me why I cried myself to sleep every night.

Because that's what I did. Every night, I would sit on the end of my bed, trailing my finger over the paper, landing on the same name each time. Each time the rage would hit me as hard as it did the first time and hot angry tears would cascade down my face, as I became overwhelmed with the burning need for revenge.

Then I would hear Rose's voice, telling me about forgiveness, and see Noah, lost in the darkness, followed by Adam telling me he loved me when I saw him that last time. Then my heart broke, all over again.

Each, and every night.

After two weeks, I got a job at a salon called, 'Stylz,' it's far more upmarket than Della's and being there made me miss home even more, but I had to work and that is what I had been trained to do. After a week, I was handed my pay slip and I think that was when it truly hit me that my old life was over — when I looked down at the name, 'Sophia Adams' instead of 'Eve Matthews.'

Two months later and it almost feels like Eve Matthews no longer exists.

Blossoms. It would be blossoms, wouldn't it? Just to make me miss what I'm already missing all the more. Lucy, a fellow stylist and according to her, my new BFF, suggested that I go for a walk today during my lunch break. I do socialise, but I often get lost in my thoughts and hide away in the staff room, but we're getting the last of the autumn sun now, and she told me that I need to experience the blossom trees before their leaves fall.

The park in The Beneath was full of big oak trees. Tall and oppressive, blocking out the light, just like the buildings that surrounded them. Like the place that they were set in. The place that I used to call home.

The last time that I was by a blossom tree was when I was sitting with baby Holly, outside St Martins, but there was only one such tree in The Beneath. One such place of peace and colour. Here there's an entire grove. That's what it's called, apparently... a grove of trees. I don't think I'd ever even used that word before I came here.

Grove... It's a bit too close to 'grieve' for my liking. Now, that's a word I'm all too familiar with.

New words, new name, new life... same me.

I don't think I ever really felt like The Beneath was oppressive when I was there, which is strange, given that the first eighteen years of my life were spent under the rule of the church and the Sisters, and the last five have been spent living by the rules of The Council. Yet here, standing amongst this mass of pink trees, each one different and unique in their shade. Each with their own history and their own story to tell. Now, I finally know what it means to be free.

Here, I can finally make my own rules, but I'm not entirely sure that the price I paid is worth it. It's peaceful, it's colourful, it's the most beautiful thing I've ever seen, but as the wind blows through the trees and the pink and white petals gently rain down on me, I remember how utterly alone I am. I've left behind everything I know and everyone I love, giving only one other the chance to find me, to join me. It's been months and he still hasn't come. I'm not sure he will come. I'm not sure he'll take his chance, or worse... whether he still wants to.

Lucy and I sit in the bar after having a Pilates session at the gym. It's become our Friday night routine; go to a Pilates session after a busy week at work, shower at the gym and then head to a bar. Lucy is bubbly and adorable, and I think I like her so much because I see a bit of each of my sisters in her. She was born here, but like most people here, she doesn't ask questions.

It was easy for her to tell that I was a runaway, because apparently, we stick out "like a sore thumb". Try as we might, we seem to appear a bit shell-shocked to begin with. Still, she doesn't ask questions, even when she has to say my name five times, because I either don't recognise it or I'm lost in my past.

"Soph..." she says, a little cautiously. "I know you say you're not interested, but—"

"But...?" I challenge her with a smile, as I take another sip of my mojito.

"But…" she replies, grinning wildly. "The most gorgeous man I've ever laid eyes on is sitting along the bar and he hasn't stopped staring at you for the past ten minutes."

She discreetly puts an elbow on the bar and tilts her head a little so that she can look behind me. "Yep. Still looking!" she says excitedly.

"Lucy…" I sigh.

"Just casually flick your hair over your shoulder and take a look," she says, as she demonstrates the action.

Sod it. Looking won't hurt and she isn't going to stop bugging me until I do, and so, mimicking her action, I discreetly turn so that I can see who is behind me, but then my head snaps uncontrollably when I take him in.

"Told you!" Lucy says triumphantly.

I sit here, speechless and utterly in awe of the man sitting along the bar, because he truly is the most gorgeous man I've ever seen.

"Go say hello," Lucy urges as she prods me a little, and it seems to take a few minutes for my legs to work, but eventually I stand and slowly walk over to him.

He stands up when I do and walks towards me, meeting me halfway and then we just stand, smiling at each other, both appearing to be unable to speak. Eventually, he clears his throat and reaches out his right hand. He's wearing a ring and I quickly glance to his left hand and see that there's no ring there. As our hands meet, he rubs a thumb over the diamonds I am wearing and smiles a smile that has me melting.

"Hello. My name is Matthew Evans," he says as he shakes my hand.

"Hi… I'm Sophia Adams," I beam back at him.

"Can I get you a drink?"

"I'd love one, thanks."

I need a drink because my mouth is now bone dry.

"Can I just ask you something first?" he asks, with a playful smile.

"Yes," I reply shakily.

This man is taking my breath away.

"Will you be mine forever?"

46

THE DAY ADAM IS COLLECTED

ETHAN

I sit alone in the morgue, with Adam's body now zipped inside a body bag. I thought about opening it, but it's been too long, and he no longer looks like himself. All this time I've been obsessing about Eve, and feeling a fucked-up mix of pain, guilt, and loss; I forgot about Adam. I forgot that the little brother that I never knew I had is dead, and I wanted to have some time alone with him before she comes to take him home.

The butterflies churn as I hear footsteps outside the door and I start to panic, knowing that I'm going to see her again. We didn't leave things well when I last saw her, and I hope I get the chance to apologise, but given what she's here to do, I'm not sure if she'll want to. She needs to hear me though because this could be the last chance I get. The last chance to say my piece, and the last opportunity to give her a chance.

The documents are in my pocket. All I need to do is slip them to her and then she can do whatever she wants.

I take a deep breath and brace myself as the door opens, but then my heart plummets as Sister Rose steps in alone. I smile at her, trying to hide the overwhelming sense of disappointment, and although she smiles back, it's clear from her red eyes, that she's hurting too. I guess she is, after all, the brother that was a stranger to me was cherished by her too.

This is wrong though. Eve should be here. Maybe she's just waiting in the ambulance.

"Could Eve not make it?" I ask, as casually as I can.

"No," Rose replies, as fresh tears fall down her cheek.

Fuck!

We walk silently together behind the gurney, and I slip my hand into my pocket, ready to pass the documents to Rose, in the hope that there's still a chance. If Rose gives these to Eve, then there's still a chance for her.

The door to the back of the ambulance is closed and Rose immediately turns to me, with an envelope in her hands.

"This is for you," she says with a gentle smile, and then she turns to walk away.

"Wait…" She turns to face me. "Can you give these to her?"

I hold out the documents and she smiles as she looks them over, before handing them back to me.

"I'm so pleased that you would do that… but there's no need."

My mouth gapes open in disbelief at the fact that Rose would block me, and she sees the confusion in my face.

"It will make sense when you read that," she says kindly, as she gestures to the envelope in my hand, and then she turns and gets into the ambulance, driving my brother away.

Palms now sweating, I grip onto the envelope, quickly walk into an empty waiting room in the morgue and close the door. Shaking, I open the envelope, slide out the letter inside, and feel my heart breaking with which each word that I read.

Dear Ethan,

I'm so sorry for the way that we left things… and I understand.

The situation we found ourselves in was more than either of us could handle and we were both hurting. I understand that you cannot just switch feelings off. There have been times when I have wanted to — believe me.

All this time you've just dipped in and out of my life at the most crucial times. I once thought you were insignificant, when in fact, you are so important.

I've always trusted you. We had a connection, I know that. It just wasn't the connection that we thought it was.

You saved Adam — our brother — once, and I will be eternally grateful to you for that, and you gave me a safe haven when I didn't know where to turn or who to trust.

I trusted you to keep me safe then, and I trust you to keep me safe now.

Love Eve

Letting the tears fall down my face, I tip out the contents of the envelope. I hold the ID card in my hands and see the face and name of the woman that holds my heart. The woman, that I hope I can one day see only as a sister... Eve Matthews.

47

THE DAY OF THE FUNERAL

NOAH

a sudden burst of light fills the room, startling me, and as my eyes adjust, I turn to see Rose standing in the doorway. She looks at me for a moment, quietly assessing me. Then she pulls an envelope out of the bag that she's carrying and walks over to me.

Holding it out, she says, "I don't know what's in there, but knowing Eve, and knowing you, it is probably more than you deserve."

I say nothing as I take it and she leaves without saying another word. I stare at it for a moment, taking in my name in Eve's handwriting, and with hands that I've only just realised are shaking, I tear it open at the top and pull out a letter.

Dear Noah,

Where can I start with this letter? Where can I start with you?

There's so much I should say and one thing that I ought to do. Yet, with you, I've never been able to do what I ought to do, because I've only ever been able to follow my heart.

So, if you truly want forever.
If you want to try something New.
Then perhaps it's time to change the Order of things.

You have my heart forever, but I have a condition.

Only come and find me if you can leave the darkness behind.

Sophia Adams
xxx

My body starts to feel warm again, and my heart starts to rise to my throat, as I feel a shred of hope start to creep back in, and then I tip out the contents of the envelope and it almost stops beating.

There is still light.

She's still mine.

48

E<small>VE</small>

*I*t's been a week and I still can't believe he's really here. I watch him when he sleeps, when he eats, I even follow him into the shower, as if I'm afraid he's just going to disappear. We've been apart for months, and I gave up hope of him coming. I started to believe he had let me go, but it turns out he was just doing what he needed to. Staying one step ahead, just like always.

He wanted to come here as a free man. Free to be with me properly. Sneaking a divorce through the courts in Havensmere took a little longer than he hoped, even with Henry and Sister Theresa's help.

He already seems lighter, like a weight has been lifted from him now that he's finally been uncaged. I always felt like I was the light in Noah's life, and now he's back and I realise that he is the light in mine too. It was just sometimes hard to see it through the darkness. The darkness, which he has promised is gone for good.

He's wrong.

The darkness, hasn't gone, it has just found a new home in me. The part of Noah that was hell bent on destroying anything that stood in his way is now breathing strength into me. Not dark and demonic like it was with him. Not unknowing, without vision, or a specific target; but fiery red and fucking absolute. I'm not blinded by it. I'm guided by it.

I haven't cried myself to sleep at all this week, because Noah has stopped tears with his touch, his warmth, and his kisses. He stopped the tears when he came back to me, because he brought my heart back to me too. My new nightly ritual is to lay in his arms, feeling his heartbeat and his warm breath against my neck, after making love to him for hours on end.

Still, once he's asleep I go back to the envelope that I keep hidden, and I sit quietly, by the dim light of the lamp in the living room, and I take out those same two pieces of paper. I've traced that line so many times that there's now a light brown trail. Each night, I follow that line straight back to the same name.

Noah believes that The Council think that the letter I had Rose read at the funeral was my final blow. My parting gift to install a bit of chaos and unrest in my wake. God, I hope they believe that. I truly hope they believe that all I want is to be happy and move on with my life.

Because then the fuckers won't see me coming.

I AM YOUR MOTHER

I am your mother,
You're still in my heart.
Even though,
They ripped us apart.

I am your mother,
You're part of me,
Even though your face,
I'll never see.

I am your mother,
And I'm full of hate,
They stole you away,
Then locked the gate.

No...

I am not your mother,

I never got the chance,

To watch your grow,

Not even a glance.

I am not your mother,

I had a lesson to learn.

A sentence to own.

A pain that still burns.

Still...

I am your mother,

I keep hold of the dream,

That one day,

I'll no longer hear the screams.

I am your mother,

I still feel your call,

I live in hope,

That you'll break through the wall.

I am your mother,

I pray to the powers that be.

That one day,

You'll be set free,

And then come running,

Back to me.

Roxanna C Revell

A NOTE FROM THE AUTHOR

It's crazy to think about how different things are now in comparison to how they were when I wrote the author's note for *Because of Hattie*. This book wasn't written in secret and it wasn't written in isolation.

I'm a fully fledged member of the indie author community and I've met some amazing people and made some new friends. Some of whom have been a big part of this story's evolution.

Massive thank you to Angela Mack, whose constructive feedback on my first draft pushed me to be better. To pack even more feeling into this book and make it what it is.

Also, to Alicia Andrews for being amazing alpha and beta reader and just a massive source of support. Your feedback still makes me well up!

Thank you also to Megan Powell for your amazing notes during editing that added an element of finesse and corrected all of my grammatical errors.

This book… I hope you love it because I do. Once again, it started as a dream and then turned into a story, a story that will have two more books to it. I really enjoy writing something with grit, and I wanted to go darker this time, whilst still writing characters with soul. Characters that you'll fall in love with, and even some that you might love to hate. Or hate to love.

Their story has only just begun and I hope you continue with the Behind the Wall series for another two books.

THE BEHIND THE WALL SERIES
BOOK TWO

Fancy a sneak peek at book two in the Behind the Wall series?

∼

Here's chapter one and two (unedited). Welcome to the mind of David Joyson.

BOOK TWO - CHAPTER ONE
THE BENEATH: ONE WEEK AFTER NOAH LEAVES

David

My mobile rings and Cassie glares at me, reminding me of the 'no phone at the table' rule; and if that isn't enough to remind me, then my voracious six-year-old daughter is.

"Daddy. Mummy says you're not supposed to have your phone at the table," Ella says with a frown, as she swipes a dark blonde curl out of her eyes.

I give her a nod and a smile, and normally I'd end the call, but nothing is normal right now, and calls cannot be ignored. I pull my phone out of my pocket and see my father's name flash up, as I suspected that I would.

"I'm sorry," I say as I stand up and leave the table, "but I have to deal with this."

Cassie wants to be annoyed; I can tell. She always likes to have an actual reason to be pissed off with me, as opposed to just being miserable because she is. However, she's fully aware of the shit storm created by Noah's disappearing act, and that now is not the time to add to it.

"Yes, Dad," I answer, as I leave the room.

"Rory is on his way already, and you're needed too," he informs me before he hangs up the call.

This is where we're all at, right now. No pleasantries, we just get straight to the point. Everyone is drained, everyone is scared, and I know what he wants me for because I could hear my bloody mother shouting in the background. Hopefully she'll be sober. Her shit is easier to deal with when she's fucking sober.

I make my apologies and head out. It doesn't take long to walk to the next street to my parent's house, but I walk slowly, dragging it out for as long as I can; a whole six minutes.

I hear her before I open the door and my heart rate starts to quicken and the dread starts to creep in. My mother is a formidable woman, but I'm not afraid of her. It's just the fact that I'm not sure which version of her I'm about to meet. It could be the mother that's hurting over the loss of her youngest son and desperate for the love of those that remain. Or it could be the cold, somewhat nasty bitch who is blaming everyone but herself for it. Judging by her tone of voice, and the way Jill scurries up the stairs as I walk through the door, I'm going with the latter.

Brilliant.

I walk past the oak dresser and look at the picture that I've wanted to smash every time I've passed it for the last week. The apple of my mother's eye, the prince of the Joyson legacy and the bane of my existence; my shitting, fucking, cunt of a little brother.

Good fucking riddance.

Taking a deep breath in, I open the door to the sitting room and see my parents and Rory – the brother that I can tolerate, just about. It's hard to form an attachment with your male siblings when you're pitted against each other from day one. Harriet is the only sibling that I have a genuine fondness for, but that's only because she's a girl and therefore not expected to perform in the way that we boys do. As long as she produces grandchildren then she'll be doing her job. Although she doesn't want to see any of us at the moment because she's gutted. Not only has she lost her best friend, but she's lost her favourite brother too.

Rory has a glass in hand, and he gives me an eyebrow raise as he takes a sip of his drink. I already knew this wasn't going to be fun, but that basically cements it, and I don't even acknowledge my parents as I walk over to the bar and pour myself a large whiskey. I take a large gulp and then turn to face my scowling mother.

Oh, joy. She's on the white wine.

Nobody says anything for a few minutes, but the anger radiating from my mother is unmissable and her fury appears to be aimed at me.

"You called."

My mother scoffs and takes a drink from her glass. "Yes. Your father called you here, because apparently nobody thinks I'm worthy of being kept up to date about what is going on!" she spits at me.

"There's not much to tell," I reply with a shrug.

"Noah would have got answers by now." She points at me, smiling with disdain, reminding me who she's always held in the highest regard — like we'd ever forget.

Maybe Noah would have got the answers, but he's not fucking here, is he.

"The guards at the gate aren't talking."

"Then make them!"

"Ruth…" My father puts a hand on her shoulder, and she shrugs him off and turns her back to us.

Rory clears his throat. "It's not as simple as—"

My mother's scoff interrupts him, and he looks to me for back up – I'm the eldest after all, and for some reason I appear to have been given the task of figuring this mess out.

"All of the guards at the gate are on the take," I tell her. "None of them are willing to talk because they're all in it up to their necks. They're sticking together because if one goes down then they all go down."

"Scare them…"

"They work for The Other Side," I say, shaking my head at her. "We can't just drag them away from the gate and inter-rogate them one by one. All we'll do is give Morgan more ammunition — that is if they don't put a bullet in us themselves!"

She turns away and downs the rest of her glass, before refilling it again. I look at my father and he just shakes his head at me, looking helpless and a little pathetic.

Commander Legion has always joked about the fact that my mother should have been born a man because she's got bigger balls than my father, and it's fucking true. My mother is manipulative, she's clever and she will do whatever it takes to get what she wants. Not many people know, but it was her suggestion to attack Adam all those years ago. My father may have delivered the proposal to The Council, but it was my mother that planted the seed.

In our world, the man is the head of the household. We hold the power, and we reign supreme, but it's my mother that has the control in this house. Robert Joyson is a puppet, it's just that most people don't know it. He does though, and his silence in this situation speaks volumes, because he has no clue how to deal with her either.

"Was Noah the only one with contacts?" she finally asks as she turns towards us, swaying a little.

Just how many has she had? I glance at the bottle behind her and see that it's almost gone.

"Was Noah—"

"We have contacts, and we are using them," I snap at her, and she straightens up a little. "We have people watching the guards and digging into their lives. We'll find the one whose hands are the dirtiest. We'll find the one with the most to lose and we'll go from there."

"It takes time, dear," my father adds, and she just glares at him in return.

"It's been a week," she deadpans him.

Yes, it has, and no doubt it's been a very happy week for Noah. A week being free from this shit and a week being back in her arms. I swallow a large gulp of whiskey in order to wash away the unwelcome feeling that creeps up from my gut and lodges itself in my throat, whenever I think about them being back together.

The room is silent, but I can tell she's not appeased. I've no idea why it is that Noah has always been her favourite. Yes, he's got brains. He's a fucking clever bastard, I'll give him that, and he's made them more money than me and Rory combined, but he's also given them the most shit.

Noah has never done anything that he didn't want to do without a fight, and I can't remember a single occasion, when he showed her any affection. Maybe that's why she craved it from him so much. The two sons that obey her weren't a challenge because she has us where she wants us. Harriet's a good girl too, but Noah presented a challenge, and like a cat zoning in on the person the least inclined to make a fuss of them; my mother just couldn't let it go.

I guess that's why she hates Eve so much. Eve did nothing and yet Noah loved her instantly. Eve was just… Eve.

The empty bottle of wine is slammed down, because apparently while I was lost in my thoughts my mother emptied her glass and then refilled it — again.

"This is all your fault!" She glares at us all in turn. "If any of you had thought to ask me, then I would have told you that executing that boy was the most stupid thing you could think to do."

"It was a Council decision," my father interjects.

"It was a mistake!" she spits, as she takes another sip of her drink. "None of you realise how fragile things are, do you?" She raises her eyebrows at us all again, but we know better than to interrupt. "Morgan is breathing down our necks, but we have absolute power... had it, at least," she scoffs, drains her glass then turns to the table, only to huff when she remembers that the bottle is empty.

"Eve was under our control," she continues, as she turns back to face us. "Everyone knows what she agreed to do and why. She was an example. A reminder of what we can do, and through her we controlled Noah."

"Adam was—" Rory starts to say, but he's quickly interrupted with a cold glare from our mother.

"Adam was untouchable." She steps closer to Rory and I'm relieved that it's him this time and not me. "He should've been, at least," she continues, "because he was the way to control Eve. He was the only control we had over her."

She turns to face us all and laughs. She's not happy though, her laugh is cold and bitter, just like her.

"But you men did what you always do," she continues, with a slight slur. "You underestimated her. You thought that she was weak. You thought that she lay on her back and just gave Noah whatever he needed. But that's because none of you have ever carried a baby..."

My father rolls his eyes. "Neither has—"

"She didn't need to!" my mother snaps in his face. "If you knew a woman's capacity for love then you would have understood how much Eve loved her brother. You would have understood that she agreed to our deal because she was strong. Because she was strong for him."

She turns to face me and Rory again.

"You thought that she was weak, and you thought her threats were empty and so you broke the deal." She shakes her head at us as her frown deepens. "Did you all miss the looks we got at the funeral? Did you not see questions and doubt from all of those people? Control is easy to establish but hard to maintain — especially when it is gained through fear! Eve broke free and if that wasn't bad enough, Noah followed her and now people are seeing our weakness."

"We'll find them," I tell her with assurance.

I don't want to find them. Personally, I'm pleased that Noah has fucked off, but she is right. We look weak, and even if the rest of The Beneath won't have the guts to challenge us, Morgan will.

BOOK TWO - CHAPTER TWO
TWO WEEKS LATER

David

This warehouse. Always this warehouse. You'd think we'd find somewhere new since Southwold and his team tore it apart; but no. Traditions are traditions. I walk over to Scott and he nods a welcome as I get to him. The Council elders are leaving this to the first-born sons, since this could get messy and they need to keep their hands clean, now more than ever. So, there's just the five of us and the one guard. One guard, sitting in a chair and quaking in his boots.

"Who do we have here, then?" I ask, even though I already know. I know everything I need to know about this dirty little fuck.

"This is Martin," Scott replies as we both walk closer to him. "And Martin has decided that he'd like to have a chat with us."

Of course, he has. That's because Martin has had a glimpse of the photographs that we've been given, and he doesn't want his wife to see them. I didn't really want to see them either, because there's some things in life you can never unsee. They're useful, mind you. Shame is always useful.

"Martin," I say as I extend my hand and shake his, before promptly wiping it on my trousers.

Why do people sweat so much when they're afraid?

"I'm David Joyson, I believe you've met my friends?"

He nods at me.

"Good," I smile. "There's nothing for you to be concerned about. You've come to us willingly…" Warren Manners snorts and I stifle my own grin. "And I believe we can be of mutual assistance."

"Spare me the bullshit, Joyson!" Martin snaps back at me.

Oh, so Martin has big balls. I must have not looked at the photographs closely enough.

"I'm here so that you give me those photos and in return I'll do what you want… that's how this goes," he grimaces.

Scott steps forward and slaps him on his back. "I'm glad we understand each other. Now we can get to business without all of the posturing over who has the biggest cock."

Phillip Learner burst out laughing at that one, but it's Pete Green that speaks.

"Well, we know it's not you, hey Martin?"

I swallow my smile and try to give Martin a reassuring nod — someone needs to play good cop.

He in turn, swallows hard. "This is about Noah… I wasn't on duty the night he left, but I know who was."

"This isn't about blame, or retribution for Noah leaving," I tell him. "He lined your pockets and you let him walk out of those gates. We get that, and it's done."

"Then what—"

"Don't be rude, Martin," Warren retorts. "Let David speak, and all will be revealed."

I clear my throat and frown at Warren. He really is such an unnecessary person, but he likes to make his voice heard.

"Noah's gone," I continue, "that's done. What we need now is information. Not just on him, but Eve too. We find one then we find the other. We need to know their new names and we need to know who helped them."

Martin nods, clearly eager to please.

"Normally I'd assume that Noah orchestrated this, but I think this was on Eve," I tell him, hoping I'm hiding how impressed I am with her from everyone around me. "Someone got her out and she got Noah out. I know he didn't know she was leaving, because I saw how broken he was after the funeral. So... Martin. How can you help us with this predicament?"

Martin wipes the sweat from his brow and looks at the men around him, who all have their arms folded and an expectant look on their faces.

"I can access the main database used to log who passes through each border," he says with an assured nod. "It has facial recognition software, so with a photograph I'll be able to find them both. It will give you their names and the last border that they checked in through."

"Well, that sounds bloody easy," Scott remarks, with a satisfied smile.

"Too easy," Pete adds, and for once I have to concede that he has a point.

"It is!" Martin, declares, sensing our unease. "That's all I need to do."

"How long will it take?" I ask him.

"I just need to find a chance to access the database..."

Scott scoffs. "Hmmm... that sounds less convincing than before."

"I just need to time it right, start a shift early..." Martin pauses and looks down a little, before continuing, "It's just that this is my last shift for two days."

"Christ alive!" Pete snaps.

Once again, he has a point.

"Martin… do we need to remind you what will happen if you let us down?" I ask, staring at him hard.

He jumps out of his seat. "No! Please… I'm not going to fail. I can do this… I can."

"Good, we'll get you what you need, and you can go back to doing… your thing," Scott smirks.

The others erupt in laughter again and Martin flushes red with embarrassment and starts sweating even more than before, as he stands up to leave.

"One more thing, Martin," I say, as he passes me. "If Eve travelled with someone, will it tell you who?"

"Erm… yes. If she was travelling with someone else, it will be logged."

"I'll be needing that name too," I tell him, with a firm nod.

Phillip follows him, they get in his car and we all watch as it leaves, heading back to the gate.

"We done here?" Warren asks.

"Yes… you can fuck off now, Manners."

He blows me kiss as he walks past, taking Pete with him and leaving me and Scott alone.

"I can give you that name, without even looking on some fucking database," Scott smirks. "Detective Southwold, with his little infatuation… he helped her. I'll put money on it."

"Eve, perhaps… but Noah?" I ask, shaking my head. "Doesn't make sense that he'd help Noah."

"Care to make a wager?" he challenges.

"Depends on what you're offering."

"I win, and I get your whore for a week. You win, and

you get mine." He smiles, that dark smile, that sends daggers scratching down my spine.

No chance. I've seen the state he's left Samantha in before and I wouldn't put Jen through that. She hates me enough most of the time as it is.

"Thanks, but my tastes are quite particular," I tell him. "But I'll happily deprive you of the contents of your wallet."

Scott laughs. "Oh... I know what your tastes are, and perhaps if things work out then you'll get to taste the real thing. I know I plan to."

The concern over Jen being hurt is now replaced by the almost crippling image of another woman on the ground, crying out for help as Scott holds her down.

"Fuck off," I fume.

He lets out a deep sigh, and he looks at me with slight concern, as if he feels sorry for me. Which he might do, since he's the closest thing to a friend that I actually have. "She'll be punished. You know that," he says, with almost a hint of an apology. Almost.

I glare at him, hoping that he sees in my eyes that if he says one more word, I'll grab his gun and shove it up his arse. He just laughs again before shaking his head and walking away. Yes. Walk away, Scott. Walk the fuck away.

Alone, with the ghosts, I turn to look at the spot where Adam was shot and try to shake the chills away. I try to block out the devastating scream that followed that gun shot – Noah's scream. Noah's cries as we had to hold him down and stop him from running over to the men surrounding Adam, as they bundled his bleeding corpse into the back of a van.

"It had to happen," I remind myself. Adam had been taking the piss for too long. He made us look weak. Our inaction would have led to other people thinking that they could mug us off too. Whatever my mother thinks, it had to be done. It did.

I walk back to my car more quickly than I left it, since the temperature in this place has just dropped and drive in the direction of The Cell. What a fucking afternoon this has been. Productive, but shit, and going back to my miserable and disappointed wife is the last thing that I want to do.

Hopefully Jen will be feeling accommodating today.

I head into the office and see Liam sitting with Rick, who is yawning. I always think it's a bit shit of Liam to make these managers meetings happen at this time of day; knowing full well that Rick won't get any rest before he runs the club at night. Since Noah left, I've noticed a change in Liam, as if he's thinking that he's a bigger man than he is. I guess he could do with a little reminder of exactly where he is in the pecking order.

"Is Jen around?" I ask, directing my question to Liam with a frown.

"I'll send her to you," he replies, without the slightest hint of emotion.

Rick on the other hand, doesn't meet my gaze. "They're dancers, not prostitutes," he told me once.

I simply reminded him that I didn't pay her.

I head for one of the private rooms and slump into the soft pink seat that surrounds the curved wall, catching a glimpse of my face in the mirror as I do. I look rough. Cassie told me the same thing this morning, and she was clearly right, but that's what happens when nobody lets you sleep.

The door opens and in walks Jen with a smile on her face that doesn't quite speak the truth. She'll always smile for me. She'll always play nice and I try to treat her nice too. I might not pay her for her services, so to speak, but I give her what she needs, and she lives far more comfortably than the other dancers do. She's not the prettiest, but she has the right hair and eye colour, and she knows what I like. She knows what I need, and she plays her part without complaint. Most of the time anyway.

The only thing I can't give her is the love and adoration that she so desperately desires.

"I haven't seen you for a while," she pouts as she sits on the top of the headrest behind me and starts to rub my shoulders.

This feels good. I need this.

"I have been busy," I sigh. "Too fucking busy."

"All work, and no play, makes David a very grumpy boy," she teases.

"It certainly does, which is why I've come to see my best girl."

She leans in and bites my ear, too hard for it to feel pleasurable, but then she intended to hurt me. "Best girl? Or only girl?"

I rub my ear and then stroke her face. "You're my only girl, because you're the best," I say, and then I tip my neck backwards and reach up for her mouth and start to devour her.

I pull her onto my lap, and she straddles me, rubbing herself against my cock which is practically begging for some attention.

She pulls her mouth away from mine and gives me a devilish smile. "What do you need today?"

"You know what I need," I reply, as I grab her hair and pull her back into me so that I can claim her mouth again.

After a few minutes, I push her gently away and she doesn't object, because she knows the drill. She gives me a smile and I see a glint in her soft, brown eyes, as she flicks her long dark hair over her shoulders. Sometimes she tries to appear as if she's offended, but I think there's part of her that likes this game too. She's a good little actress; I'll give her that.

She steps backwards and watches me for a moment with a smile, but then suddenly a look of fear washes over her face and she drops to her knees in front of me.

"David! I need you to help me!" she declares as she grabs onto my knees as if they're her only lifeline. "Please... I want to be free from him. I need you to help me... please," she begs.

I lean in and cup her face, before stroking her hair and soothing her. "It's OK, I'm here for you. I'll help you. I won't let him hurt you anymore."

"But how?" she begs, as her eyes glisten.

"I'm not afraid of him," I reassure her, as I stroke her hair and shush her again.

"I'll do anything," she says, as her hands move along my thighs towards my belt.

She undoes it.

"I'll give you anything David," she breathes out, as she unzips my trousers and holds my erection in her hands.

I let out a groan. Her touch feels so good. For the past two weeks, with no time and people constantly breathing down my neck; I've had to take care of myself, and as Jen grips me, I start to fear that I'm not going to last long enough to see this through.

"Look at you," she says with an appreciative smile.

"You're bigger than him."

She leans in and takes me into her mouth, and as her tongue and lips go to work, I draw in a deep breath in order to stop myself from shooting my load.

She pulls back and looks at me again, a smile spreads across her face. "You taste better too."

I groan again and grip her hair as she goes back to work, but then I quickly pull her away. I don't want to cum in her mouth, and she can't say what I need to hear with a mouthful of cock.

I pull her up, turn her round and bend her over the stage as I pull down her underwear. She's already wet because she can't hide how much she likes this game too and so I grab her by the hips and thrust into her.

I fuck her hard, harder than I usually do, but it's been a shit fucking day, and this is what I need, and she gasps and reaches for the pole for support.

"Tell me that I'm better than him," I rasp out.

"You're better than him!"

"Say my name!" I demand.

"You're better than him David," she calls out, as she tries to catch her breath.

"Tell me that you love me."

"I love you."

"Say my name!" I order as thrust into with more force than is necessary.

"I love you, David!" she cries, before another gasp escapes her. "David… this is too much!"

This is not part of the game.

"She can take it. So can you," I gasp, as I picture her face.

Then I picture her body bucking underneath me as she screams my name and I make her cum harder than *he* ever has.

"Eve!" I cry, as I cum hard, finally releasing my grip on Jen's hips.

I stay inside her for a few minutes while I catch my breath, and then I feel a stab of guilt as I see the red finger marks that I've left on her pale skin. Fuck, I hope they fade before she has to go on stage.

I pull out and watch with satisfaction as my cum trickles out of her, before pulling her back so that she's sitting on my lap with her back to me. I brush gentle kisses onto her shoulder, she stiffens at my touch and I look at her face in the mirror. She's not happy, and this time she's not pretending.

"Thank you for that, baby," I say affectionately, in an attempt to appease her. It doesn't work and I see her jaw clench as she tries to hold back her tears.

"Jen…" I say soothingly. "You know what you mean to me."

I lift her from my lap and lower her onto the soft, pink leather as I gently kiss her lips. She still looks like she wants to cry, and I realise that I perhaps took things a little too far. I don't want to scare Jen away because I need what she gives me, and so, I give her a gentle smile as I lower myself down between her legs and start to kiss and stroke my tongue over her. She starts to relax, and she starts to moan, and as I pick up the pace her hand fists my hair, and she cries out as she orgasms.

I rest above her as she breathes hard, finally smiling.

"You're good at that," she smiles.

"We Joysons are all about the pleasure," I tell her, before climbing off her and pulling up my trousers.

I walk towards the door and grab hold of the handle, but before I can open it, Jen speaks. "Is it because of her, or is it because she's his?"

I let out a small laugh, because this is a question that I've asked myself many times. I'm surprised it's taken Jen this long to ask it, but then I've never pushed her this far before.

"I have no idea," I say with honesty, before turning and walking out of the door.

Printed in Great Britain
by Amazon